I0634302

Jarvisfield
&
The Wayward Son

~

Gretta Curran Browne

88
Eighty-Eight Publications

ISBN: 978-0-9927374-8-1

Cover Design: PB Designs

Eighty-Eight Publications
2 Spencer Avenue
London N13 4TR

Jarvisfield

The Wayward Son

PART ONE

Chapter One

Island of Mull,
Scotland.

Early one afternoon in July 1826 the proprietor of the
Tobermory Inn, Angus McLeod, was leaning on his wooden
"Reception" counter with his head resting on his hand and
his eyes closed in sleep.

There were no guests in residence, so no more work to be
done, and the homemade remedy he had taken for his
constant headaches, together with the humid summer heat,
had sent him drooping into a doze.

Surprisingly, to all visitors to the island, Mull often
enjoyed sub-tropical heat in the summer due to the
Caledonian Forest of trees that sheltered it from the easterly
winds.

The rickety old door to the inn was suddenly pushed open,
bringing light into the dim entrance, followed by a boy's
laughter.

Angus jerked awake, stared at the two figures in the
doorway, and the comfortable expression on his face
tightened.

Now the boy ... Angus didn't know who *he* was, nor cared
... but the man at his side, George Jarvis, always caused
Angus a feeling of consternation.

There was nothing about him to dislike, and he wore the
finely-tailored clothes and had the speech and manners of an
educated gentleman, but he was still a *foreigner,* and many of
the locals who drank at the inn in the evenings found him a
constant subject for curiosity, not only because he was
different to anyone else they had ever known, but also
because he had been brought up since boyhood by Lachlan
Macquarie, a man who had been an acquaintance of the King;
and George Jarvis too, it was said, had also spent time in the
grand houses of the English aristocracy.

Angus narrowed his bushy eyebrows together as he looked

at the tall, black-haired young man talking down to the boy at his side, noting the clean brown moulding of his face and the way his body had a strong and lithe grace.

The light from the open door illuminated his extraordinary physical attractiveness, and that alone made him very easy to like, along with his polite and agreeable manner. Only the older local men were blind to all but his race, yet none were sure what race that was exactly, except for the one thing they knew as a fact – he was definitely *'no' Scottish'* and definitely *'no' one of us!'*

But money was money and business was business. 'Good afternoon to you, Mr Jarvis,' Angus hailed cheerfully. 'Are ye in town to collect your post?'

'As always, Angus, as I do every Thursday,' George Jarvis smiled. 'Only today I have brought a helper who needs some refreshment.'

Angus looked down at the golden-haired boy beside him. 'And who might this laddie be?'

It was the first time young Lachlan had been allowed to travel up to Tobermory with George, but now that he was twelve years old, Elizabeth had finally given in to her son's pestering.

'This young man,' replied George, 'is Master Lachlan Macquarie Junior, the heir to the Jarvisfield Estate.'

George glanced down at young Lachlan to see how proud he might be of such a title, but the boy didn't look proud at all, just horrified ... his eyes staring in shock at the head of a small skull staring empty-eyed at him from the side of the wooden counter.

George Jarvis had seen the skull many times and thought it's display to be obscene, but he had never asked the reason why it was placed there.

The boy moved closer to George's side, silently letting him know that he did not like this place.

Angus half-laughed at the boy's fear. 'Ach, don't be afeared of my wee skull here, it can't harm ye.'

George decided to finally find out about the skull and asked, 'Did it belong to a relative of yours, Angus? Someone ... beloved ... that you couldn't bear to bury?'

'What? A relative o' mine?' Angus was insulted. 'I'll have you know Mr Jarvis that I'm a good Christian man and the entire Church of Scotland will back me up on that. But I suppose ye wouldn't know anything about that, our religious rules and laws ... ye not being a Christian.'

'I was married in a Christian church,' George informed Angus politely.

'Whaaa ... *were* ye now? Married in a Christian church?'

Angus looked shocked. Despite his fancy English name, everyone hereabouts knew that George Jarvis was some sort of Arab from the Orient that Lachlan Macquarie Senior had adopted as a boy over in India or Egypt or somewhere. Well, fancy that now – him being a *Christian!*

Young Lachlan was still staring at the skull, and George knew the boy would pester him with questions all the way home if he did not find out the answer now.

'Is it from a hospital on the mainland then?' George asked, pointing to the skull.

'Nay, it came from a ship that sunk out there in the waters of Tobermory itself, A *pay* ship, carrying gold. The *Florencia* its name was, and they say that this here is the skull of a young blackie girl aged about twelve or thirteen who musta died somewhere down in the bowels of the ship, one of the galley slaves.'

It was not the explanation George had expected, and it disgusted him. His dark eyes fixed seriously on Angus as he said quietly, 'A young black girl, who drowned tragically in the slave-hold of a ship ... would it not be more fitting to take her away and give her a decent burial?'

'Take her away? Och nay, Mr Jarvis, she's been sitting on this counter for years. People from all over Mull come here to Tobermory just to see her, aye, they do, and from the mainland too. Brings me plenty of visitors she does.'

'How do you know she was black?' the boy asked curiously. 'The bones are white.'

'Well now ...' Angus leaned his forearms on the counter to answer the boy in the same way he had answered the same question by many another visitor. 'Those that found her said the skin on her wee face was as black as midnight, that's how

I know.'

'And how do you know she was a girl?' the boy asked.

'Because when the sailors found her,' Angus replied, 'she still had a small ribbon knotted in her hair, tied in a girlish bow, that's how the sailors knew then, and that's how I know now. A girl with black skin, one of the slaves from the gold ship.'

'And you think that's a good enough reason to have part of her remains displayed here like an ornament?' George asked. 'Because her skin was black?'

'Aye, I do.' Angus nodded his head positively and went on. 'Even Minister Bannon said there was no wrongdoing in it, and by God – here he is now! Ask him yerself.'

The door of the inn had opened and a short barrel of a man had entered, his over-red face beaming as happily as a child's at Christmas.

'Good day to ye, Angus! Has that good woman of yours got any of that delicious grouse pie left?'

'She has, Minister, a good thick quarter of it was left the last I saw.'

'Oh, excellent, my stomach is rumbling like thunder. And how are those headaches of yours, Angus? Any improvement?'

'Nay, nay, still crushing me down,' Angus groaned. 'Betimes the pain is so bad I think one of these nights my skull will explode and that will be the end of me.'

'Pray, Angus, pray hard, and God *will* cure you.'

Minister Bannon turned to look roundly at George, his eyes widening. 'Oh, Mr Jarvis, well, indeed, it's not often we see you in here. And how is Mrs Macquarie these days?'

'She is well.'

'And the bonnie lad is here with you too? Hello young Lachlan, looking after your poor widowed mother are you?'

With a great effort the boy drew his eyes away from the small skull on the counter, his face still white from the shock of seeing such a sight.

'Minister ... ' Angus butted in apologetically, 'Mr Jarvis and the laddie seem to think there is something no' right with my wee skull sitting here, but you told me there was no wrongdoing in it, didna ye?'

'Nothing wrong in it at all, Angus. The owner of the skull was certainly a heathen and also black-skinned which means she was from the darkest part of the earth where the Devil himself abides'

'Minister Bannon,' George interposed coolly, 'such a view does not dignify your role as a pastor, and certainly not your high station.'

Bannon looked at him sharply, a sudden anger creeping into his tone. 'Such a view, you say? It is a *common* view, Mr Jarvis, so why do you oppose it?'

'I oppose anything that I consider to be ignorant, cruel and bigoted.'

Angus looked at George Jarvis with shock, then looked at Minister Bannon whose fat face had turned from its normal beetroot red to a deep purple and for a moment the Minister seemed unusually lost for words.

'She was a heathen!' Bannon burst out.

'God is the Father of *all* mankind,' George replied, 'and so respect should be given to *all,* including a small black girl who is long overdue a decent burial.'

'Respect, *respect* – you talk as if she is still with us,' Bannon expostulated, 'and not a skeleton long dead!'

George contemplated the minister with an expression of remote dislike, and then replied in the same quiet tone, 'Our bones may moulder, but our spirit issues forth and lives on high in a condition of glorious brightness ... with God who is the Father of *all* mankind.'

Bannon's temper got the better of him. He snapped sneeringly, 'Is that what your *pagan* God says, whoever *he* is!'

'No, I believe it was Saint Paul who said it.'

Bannon gaped at George like an astonished trout, sucked in his breath as if to speak, then changed his mind and abruptly turned and walked away without a word.

Angus leaned over the counter to watch him marching down the short narrow passage and then violently push open the door of the dining room.

Angus turned back to look at George reproachfully.

'You had me worried there for a minute, Mr Jarvis, fearing

ye might have destroyed his appetite for that last quarter of grouse pie, but nay, nothing ever comes between Minister Bannon and his food. And mind, be prepared now ... he won't talk to you when ye go in there for your own food, Mr Jarvis, it's a cold face he'll show you.'

I don't want to eat in there,' the boy said quickly. 'I'm not hungry.'

Food was the last thing on George's mind now. He was looking at Angus with a fixed expression of grave concern. 'Those pains in your head, Angus, when did they start?'

'Oh, a long time ago ... let me see now ... just after I bought this place. Aye, a day or two after we moved in here is when the headaches started, mild at first, and then worse and worse they get with every year that goes past. Tormented I am, tormented.'

George looked at the small skull of the girl. 'Was she here when you moved in?'

'Oh, aye, right where she is now.'

'And why did the former owner sell this place? Do you know?'

'Well, before moving here I lived on the other end of Mull, down at Carsaig, so I didna know him at all, but he said he was selling because his health wasn't good, and he believed his wife was dying of some malady or other, so that's why – '

'Dying?' George interrupted. 'Of severe pains in her head perhaps? The same as the pains in your head?'

'Ach, I dunno, all he said was ... ' Angus looked into George's dark eyes which seemed to be suddenly illuminated with a glint of suspicion.

'Ach, ye canna be thinking...?' Angus turned his own eyes to the skull.

'Who knows,' George responded in an ominous low tone. 'The girl has been done a great injustice, and maybe ... without a proper burial ... her spirit is unable to rest ... and so she has no other choice but continue to harm in some way those who continue to disrespect what is left of her earthly body.'

Angus stood looking at the skull with a frozen expression on his face.

George leaned closer across the counter and asked Angus in a conspirator's whisper:

'Does your wife get these fierce pains in her head also?'

Angus snapped out of his chilled stance. 'Nay, nay the skull canna be the cause. Ye're jesting with me, Mr Jarvis. Nay, my wife's headaches are due to those long pins she sticks in her hat ... And anyhows,' he added quickly, 'the Minister wouldn't hear of it, wouldn't do it – not a proper burial, not a Christian burial, nay – '

'But *you* could return her to the privacy of the depths of the sea, Angus, back down to the same place where the rest of her mortal remains lie. It would be a decent and respectful thing to do. Shield her from the stares of any more visitors. Do you know which part of the sea around Tobermory the ship went down?'

'Aye, I do ... ' Angus cleared his throat and pulled himself together. 'Many more lives have been lost since that ship went down ... Men diving down there searching for the lost gold, but none could go that deep, and those that did never came back up again.'

'So, will you do it?' George asked.

After another frozen silence, Angus shook his head and snapped, 'Nay! I canna do it! If you think it should be done then *you* do it, Mr Jarvis. Here ... 'Angus picked up the small skull and thrust it into George's hands.

'You do it ... you can take my wee fishing boat out there, it's moored at the very end, the one that's painted blue and white, and you do what needs to be done.'

Young Lachlan shrieked with jubilance. 'Yes, we'll do it! We're not scared of the sea, are we George?'

George Jarvis was looking down at the small skull of the girl in his hands.

'Yes, we'll do it,' he answered, and then looked at Angus. 'Do you have some kind of a cloth to cover her?'

Angus gave him a small towel, and then instructions as to which part of the sea the ship had sank, adding finally, 'I just hope this burial will be the cure for the torture of my headaches... But now, Mr Jarvis, how am I going to explain to all and everyone where and why the wee skull has gone? How am I going to spare myself from their criticism and complaints?'

George smiled, that calm and gentle smile which disarmed and charmed many an adversary and which Minister Bannon hated so much.

'You could say it was stolen, by a vagabond or a drunken sailor.'

Angus pursed his lips together nervously. 'I could say that, aye, I could ... but I reckon Minister Bannon will know the truth.'

Again George smiled, but cynically. 'Minister Bannon has never known the *truth* of anything, Angus, not even the truth of his own miserable ignorance.'

Chapter Two

As they walked along the waterfront, the crew of a small trading vessel was loading its cargo, barrel after barrel of what George suspected must be kegs of Tobermory's own malt whisky destined for the mainland. All the other boats were mainly fishing boats that ventured out every morning and night and George's eyes moved up beyond the row of shops and warehouses along the quayside to the rows of fishermen's houses on the hills beyond.

At the end of the quayside they found Angus's small boat, painted blue and white, with a few lobster pots inside it.

'Maybe we could try and catch a few lobsters,' young Lachlan said eagerly, but George shook his head.

'No. Angus gave us permission to use his boat to go out to sea to do one thing only, and that is all we will do.'

As soon as both were seated on the two small wooden planks opposite each other, George untied the rope, pushed away with an oar and began to row out towards the deeper waters of the Atlantic where the gold ship had gone down.

As the boat moved smoothly and silently further and further out, only the laughter and screeching of the sea birds broke the tranquillity of the deep waters of the ocean.

Young Lachlan Macquarie felt at home on the sea. He had been born in Sydney when his father was Governor-General of New South Wales and by the time he was five years old he had been given his own private cove next to Sydney Harbour which had been named *'Lachlan's Cove.'*

At first he had simply played down at the cove, sailing little boats which the convict-servants had made for him as birthday presents; but later, by the time he was seven, he had his own rowing boat taking him further out to sea, and always manning the oars, and ensuring his safety, was George Jarvis.

George paused in his rowing, his eyes scanning the sea that was glistening sharply under a golden sun.

'I think this it, or near enough,' George said, inserting the oars into their catches.

Lachlan sat silent as George lifted the small skull and removed the towel, pausing to look down at it in his hands. 'She was just a child,' he said softly.

'That's what everyone still calls me,' Lachlan said seriously, 'just a child.'

'Then you should say the prayers for her,' George replied. 'The prayers of one child for another.'

Lachlan nodded, and joined his palms together as he had been taught to do, and began to pray aloud, his eyes closed and directing all words to his "Father in Heaven" as he had been taught to do, by his mother.

George sat looking at the closed eyes of the golden-haired boy, his heart touched by his simple childish piety. His prayers for the young black girl were as heartfelt as any he would have said for a white child, because to young Lachlan there was no difference. Since his infancy he had played and had fun with the black Aboriginal children who had been his friends back in his homeland of Australia.

'Amen,' Lachlan said finally, and opened his eyes, waiting with a sombre expression for the next part of the ceremony, which would be done by George.

George sat motionless in thought for a long moment, then leaned over the side of the boat and gently placed the skull on the shimmering sea, watching it sliding downward under the surface of the water, while whispering his own prayer.

'*Khudaa Hafiz* ... God be with you.'

Chapter Three

Angus McLeod couldn't believe it – the constant pain in his head had suddenly disappeared!

'Vanished!' he cried in a daze of euphoria, rushing into the dining room where Minister Bannon was still eating. 'One minute it was there as ever and always, and then of a sudden it was gone! *Gone* I tell ye, clear gone! How do you explain it, Minister?'

Bannon pushed the last piece of suet-heavy pastry into his mouth and chomped irritably, 'Calm yourself, Angus. You are always losing things, are you not? So I am sure you'll find that whatever you have lost has not gone nor vanished, but has simply been misplaced somewhere.'

'Misplaced? 'How can you *misplace* a thumping great pain in the head?'

Mrs McLeod came in from the kitchen to see what all the loud talk was about. Fortyish and fat she moved like a wheel, round and rolling. 'What's to do, Angus?'

Angus looked at his wife and pointed to his head. 'It's gone. The torture of the pain in my head just stopped and vanished clean away.'

The eyes in Mrs McLeod's face shot wide in disbelief. 'Oh, bye, but how can that be? Ye've suffered that pain for nigh on ten years now, it canna have just *gone!*'

'It's a miracle!' Minister Bannon cried, his face suddenly beaming a triumphant smile. 'I told you, Angus, I told you God would cure those headaches of yours one day; and now He in His glory has done just that! This calls for a celebratory drink! Mistress McLeod, if you would be so kind as to bring some malt?'

Mrs McLeod frowned. Minister Bannon was always calling for a drink for one reason or another but always forgot to pay for it.

'Nay, it was Mr Jarvis who done it!' Angus declared in his light-headed and pain-free excitement, looking at his wife. 'True as I'm alive, Lizzie, soon as he took that skull out of here to bury it, I felt a strange easing in my head, and now it's vanished altogether. I still canna believe it!'

'Mr Jarvis?' asked Minister Bannon, his face suddenly chilled.

'Mr Jarvis?' his wife also asked, a smile creeping on her lips. 'Mr *George* Jarvis?'

'I know no other,' Angus replied. 'But blow me down he came up quick as lightning with the answer to my affliction better than any doctor. Cured I am, Lizzie, cured at last!'

Minister Bannon sat back in his chair, his face stiff as stone as he glared at Angus.

'Are you trying to tell me, a representative on earth of Christ himself, that a heathen such as Mr George Jarvis took your skull away and thereby cured your headaches when all my prayers for you in my Kirk could not?'

'Och nay, sir,' Angus shook his head positively. 'He's not a heathen at all, he's a Christian.'

'He's a brown skinned Arab who has only once set foot inside my Kirk on a Sunday and that was to accompany Mrs Macquarie at the time of her husband's death. One visit inside a Christian Kirk does not a Christian make!' Mark my words, Angus, he's one of the Devil's own.'

Lizzie McLeod had heard enough. She had a good few reasons for detesting Minister Bannon, but only one for liking George Jarvis. She rolled closer to the Minister's table, deciding to give him a reminder of his own religious teaching.

'He may be a brown-skinned Arab but so was Jesus himself, wasna he? From Palestine Jesus was, or so the Bible says. And as well that, Mr Jarvis has always seemed to us to be a nice man, a good man, and also very *handsome* in his looks. All the women hereabouts are in love with him, even old Widow Mickenchie says she'd marry him tomorrow if he'd have her and he was free. And me and Angus, well, to be honest, we don't think it's right that you should damn a man because – '

'Black magic,' Minister Bannon said thoughtfully, having stopped listening to Mrs McLeod after her first two sentences. 'So Mr Jarvis told you that if he took the skull of the blackie girl away, that would also take your headaches away?'

'Nay, he didn't say that,' Angus replied, 'but now ... aye, well ... now that I'm able to think straight and clear-headed ... well, I suppose he did *hint* at it, in a way.'

'In what way?'

Angus shook his head. 'I don't know ... I just knew he wanted the skull taken away to be buried, said it would be more respectful to the girl that had owned it, and well – '

'I knew it! Took the skull but you did not *see* him bury it, did you? He's probably going to use it to work some kind of heathen evil on us all. Something he probably learned from those black natives over in Botany Bay.'

'My Lord!' exclaimed Mrs McLeod with a laugh. 'I don't think it's a glass of malt whisky you need, Minister Bannon, I think it's something cold to calm your ravings, something like water.' I'll fetch you a glass will I?'

She turned and rolled out of the room without waiting for his answer, nudging her husband to follow her. 'You can carry it back out, Angus,' she said quietly.

'Oh, aye, aye ... '

As soon as she was back in her kitchen, Lizzie McLeod lifted the water jug and poured a good measure into a glass, then quickly added a big pinch of salt to it.

'There now, salt,' she muttered mischievously, 'they say a pinch of salt a day keeps the Devil himself away.'

When Angus appeared at the kitchen door she handed him the glass of water.

'That'll soon shift him,' she said, 'if not in one way then another.'

Chapter Four

In the Macquarie house on the Jarvisfield Estate, Elizabeth Macquarie and Mary Jarvis were aware of the late hour and wondering what was taking George and young Lachlan so long.

Mary was still not acclimatised to the fact that during the four months of summer, Mull had almost no night, just a couple of hours of darkness before the sun rose again. She looked at the clock – almost ten o'clock – and still broad daylight.

So different to Australia where the sun just disappeared in a fast drop at the same time every evening, winter and summer, around seven.

'George has never been this late before,' Mary said anxiously.

'Never this late,' Elizabeth agreed, although she was not in any way worried. She was too busy looking at the books of the estate, gratified to see that the rents from the tenants had always been paid on time, and there had been no problems or complaints from any of them.

And even more gratifying, was that they all seemed happy and satisfied with the man who had overseen and run the estate in the years they had been away in Australia, a Tobermory man named Robert Dewar.

Elizabeth looked up from the books to where Mary was sitting on the sofa.

'It will be Lachlan who has caused the delay today,' Elizabeth said with certainty. 'Before his father's death it was penny plain for all to see how much he loved George, but since that awful day Lachlan now follows George around like a puppy and he would stay out with him from dawn to dark if he could.'

'It's understandable though,' Mary said. 'From the day he was born George was always there, always near, a part of his family, and so he sees him as an older brother of sorts.'

'Yes, an older brother,' Elizabeth agreed, 'but that was

before that awful day ... now he won't agree to do anything unless George tells him to do it, as if George has now taken the very high place of his father.'

Mary smiled sympathetically. 'He feels safe with George, that's all. In his heart, I'm sure that no one could take his father's place.'

'I should hope not.'

Mary slowly moved the sleeping child from her lap, laying her gently back on the sofa and stood up to walk over to the window, realising that for quite some time now it had become Elizabeth's habit to view every event and every action from how it had been *before* that awful day of her beloved husband's death, and how it was since then, every little change was noted with a tone of regret.

Gazing through the window, Mary suddenly jerked alert as she saw the horse and trap coming over the small hill in the distance.

'Here they come,' she said happily. 'George and Lachlan – home at last.'

*

As soon as George had stepped down from the trap Mary was in his arms, hugging him as if he had been away for years.

From the doorway, Elizabeth stood watching them: the slim and beautiful blonde-haired girl who was still so in love with her husband, and George who was as equally devoted to Mary – both smiling at each other as if in the first flush of romance instead of nearly five years of marriage.

But oh ... they had all been through so much together, the three of them, Elizabeth reflected, the long eight-month voyage back from Australia in a sub-standard ship, and Mary having to give birth to her first child on that ship, and then ... so soon after their arrival back in Scotland, that awful unexpected day ...

Elizabeth pulled herself out of her gloomy thoughts, remembering how fortunate she was, because as lonely as she sometimes felt at times, without the cheerful presence and support of George and Mary, she would feel totally lost, completely abandoned, and so would her son.

Later that night in the drawing-room, after Mary and the children had gone to bed, Elizabeth said, 'I will have to snap out of these doldrums of mine, George, they are wasting me physically, and I am wasting not only my time but also my life.'

George turned his face from the bookcase and looked over at Elizabeth, at her woebegone face which looked even paler above her black dress.

'You could start by disposing of your widow's clothes,' he suggested, 'and start wearing some lively colours again.'

Elizabeth smiled faintly. 'What real difference would that make?'

'Well, people would treat you differently for a start. As soon as anyone sees you out dressed all in black, they remember you are bereaved and instantly lower their voices to a sympathetic hush.'

Elizabeth looked surprised. 'Do they?'

'They do. Have you not noticed?'

'No ... I suppose I just presumed everyone was as miserable as me.'

George put the book he had been considering back on the shelf and walked slowly across the room to sit opposite Elizabeth. Her need for a fire on a warm night like this perplexed him, but he was prepared to suffer it, suspecting her feeling of coldness was more in her mind than her body.

She was no longer the woman he knew in the past, the bright girl he had met when Lachlan had first brought him to Scotland, nor the energetic First Lady of Australia, the wife of the Viceroy Lachlan Macquarie who had helped her husband to make such needed improvements to the life and culture of that infant land.

Elizabeth had been thirty-one years old when they had arrived in Sydney, and forty-four years old when she returned, having helped to build a nation and turn a convict colony into a country. A woman who had been loved by all in New South Wales for her indomitable energy, friendliness, and most especially the fairness of her general attitude to others, especially the convicts whom she always treated with compassion, insisting they may be felons but they were still human beings and not just filth to be trampled on.

Oh yes, a great lady.

George had always liked Elizabeth, but his affection and admiration for her had never felt so strong as it did on that memorable night on the ship during the voyage back from Australia, near the port of St. Salvadore, when Elizabeth had worked so hard and stayed up for almost two nights without sleep to help Mary safely deliver their baby daughter.

No wonder Mary had chosen to name their child Elizabeth, without any protest from him.

Now Elizabeth Macquarie was forty-five years old, but she looked much older. In the past two years, since her beloved husband's death, she had aged ten years in appearance. She had always been slim, but now she was thin, very thin, and her lustrous copper-coloured hair was showing strands of grey.

Successive eruptions of crackling throbbed through the logs in the fire.

'Are you ready yet to resume contact with even your Scottish friends here on Mull?' George asked.

'No,' Elizabeth replied bleakly. 'During my years away in Australia both Murdoch and my sister Margaret over at Lochbuie have died, and as for my former friends, most of them seem to have emigrated to places like Canada or America.'

'Your sister Margaret has died? But she was younger than Murdoch, much younger, by at least twenty-five years.'

Elizabeth nodded sadly. 'What can you expect though. Poor Margaret gave birth to eleven children in less than twelve years. Enough to kill any woman.'

After a silence George said, 'Your friends in Australia have not died. Have you written to any of them yet?'

'No.' Elizabeth shook her head apologetically. 'I had nothing of cheer to write to them, so I wrote nothing at all.'

'Then they may think you are dead also.'

'What?' Elizabeth's blue eyes looked startled. 'Why would they think I am dead?'

George smiled. 'I said they *may* think it, not that they do.'

'Still ... you are right ... ' Elizabeth's expression flooded with thoughtfulness as she sat thinking back to those happy days in Sydney.

'So many letters keep coming from them all,' she said, 'and I have not answered even one.'

'Have you read them, the letters?'

'No, I have not even done that.' She looked at George, and for the first time in a long time her face did not look bleak as she smilingly said. 'I wonder how Mrs Ovens and Joseph Bigg are getting on? I always had a suspicion those two might end up married. Did you?'

George almost laughed. 'Not with Mrs Kelly around, no.'

'Mrs Kelly? Why, did *she* have her eyes on our carriage driver also?'

Now George *did* laugh, remembering Mrs Kelly, the widowed Irish cook in charge of the convict-servants in the staff-kitchen at Government House, and the best friend of Mrs Ovens; an Englishwoman who had travelled out to Australia with the Macquarie group solely to be a personal cook for the Governor's family.

But Mrs Kelly ... a woman who had served her time and then stayed in Australia after being transported from Ireland to Botany Bay for the crime of attempting to kill her lover because he had cruelly deceived her with another woman.

'Mrs Kelly hated men, all men,' George said to Elizabeth, 'but she loved gossiping and getting drunk on rum with Mrs Ovens in one of their kitchens every night, so I doubt she would allow Joseph Bigg to interfere with that friendship – not without attempting his murder first.'

Elizabeth actually laughed. ' I liked Mrs Kelly, she was so funny at times.'

She paused and looked at George curiously. 'Rum? Mrs Ovens too? Every night? Getting drunk on *rum*?'

'It was the worst kept secret in Government House. Everyone knew about the smuggled rum and the two drunken cooks night after night, everyone except you and Governor Macquarie.'

'So *you* knew, yet you did not tell us.'

George smiled. 'I think those nights made their days

bearable. Their enjoyment was more to do with the shared companionship of two widows than the shared rum.'

'Still, I'm certain Mrs Ovens had a soft spot for Joseph, and I'm sure if he – '

'No, no, no!' George insisted. 'Mrs Kelly would break his head if he tried to take away her gossip and drinking partner.'

Elizabeth's demeanour had completely changed, a new liveliness infused her voice as she stood up and walked over to the writing desk at the window. 'You are right, George, I really *should* read and answer some of these letters ...'

She opened a side-drawer of the desk and lifted out a thick pile of letters and began to quickly sift through them.'

'I think I'll start with the letters from Mrs Ovens. I know she has written a few because I recognised her very small handwriting ... '

'I'll say goodnight then,' George said, standing up and heading towards the door, but Elizabeth stopped him in his tracks.

'Don't you want to know what Mrs Ovens has to say?'

She turned the lamp up to full brightness and then began to quickly unfold a letter. 'You never know – she might have told me something about herself and Joseph Bigg, does that not interest you also?'

'Oh yes, it interests me avidly.'

Something in his tone made Elizabeth lift her eyes from the letter and look at him.

'You do understand that I am lying?' he said wryly.

'Now I do' she replied tersely. 'You have no interest whatsoever in any gossip from Mrs Ovens.'

'No interest at all,' George confirmed, lifting a candle from the sideboard to light his way upstairs.

Elizabeth could not help smiling at his typical male behaviour, so reminiscent of her husband who detested any kind of female gossip.

As soon as he had left the room her eyes returned to the letter, her interest quickening as she read every detail written by Mrs Ovens, her eyes squinting over each word of the tiny writing, no doubt a habit developed by Mrs Ovens due to the cost of postage being charged by the page, smiling as she read one particular sentence that gratified her:

... Sir Thomas Brisbane is not the fine and lovely man that your husband Governor Macquarie was, we all still miss him so badly ... '

*

George paused in the hallway, his thoughts also about Australia. He turned away from the stairs and moved towards the small study where Lachlan had spent so much time in the last few months of his life.

He sat down in the chair at the desk, the same chair Lachlan had sat in. George still missed him, and in his heart still privately mourned for him, the beloved man who had rescued him from a slave-trader in Cochin when he had been only seven years old and had brought him up like a son from then on. A man whom George had always called "Father", not in the paternal way of the West, but in the reverent tradition of the East.

George opened the bottom right drawer of the desk and lifted out two documents. The first, bearing the Governor's red seal, was a grant of two thousand acres of land in New South Wales belonging to Lachlan himself, which Elizabeth now owned.

The second document was a grant of one thousand acres of land in New South Wales, which Lachlan had given to George as a wedding present on the day he had married Mary in St Phillip's Church in Sydney.

George sat thinking about that sunny land, with its vast open acres and constant bright sky. Coming from the East the sun was like a magnet to him, he loved its warmth and cheerfulness, so good for the mind and so uplifting for the soul.

Only in summer could he bear the climate here in Scotland, although he should have been used to it, having been schooled for a time in London and then later in Edinburgh, but the dark skies and freezing cold of winter depressed him – and during the last winter, which had been full of sadness, he had often fought the impulse to leave Scotland and take Mary and his baby back to Australia, a country he had grown to love.

But always he had shunned the temptation away from him, because he had made a promise to Lachlan on the day before he had died, to take care of Elizabeth and young Lachlan, to remain a part of their family and never leave them alone without a man to care for them.

As well as that he possessed an indestructible bond of loyalty and love for Elizabeth and a deep affection for her son ... so no, despite how strong his desire could sometimes be, or how bright the sun and sky over Sydney harbour, he would continue to stay here in Scotland and devote himself to Lachlan's small family as well as his own.

Australia would just have to wait.

Leaving the study and walking back down the hall, Elizabeth heard his footsteps and called to him from the drawing-room, a smile on her face as he paused by the door.

'Mrs Ovens tells me that although Joseph Bigg is no longer the Governor's coachman. *She read – 'he is still polishing the saddles and harnesses in the sunshine of the yard and he seems quite happy.'*

'That's good,' George smiled, thinking with affection of his old friend who had sailed out to New South Wales with them.

'Although,' Elizabeth added, reading the letter, 'Mrs Ovens says that he is beginning to look *"a bit bent in his frame these days, especially across his back, but I am sure, m'lady, that he will still be bent over polishing his harnesses until he's in his dotage, because of his love for all the horses."'*

'But no mention of any love for her?' George asked.

'No, no mention of that at all,' Elizabeth chuckled, and picked up another letter. 'Oh, look, here's one from Sergeant Whalan. Do you remember that beautiful garden he had started to create around his home in Parramatta?'

George had seen Sergeant Whelan toiling in his beloved Parramatta garden many times, and as Elizabeth leaned forward and got stuck into his letter, George left her to it.

*

When he quietly entered the bedroom and placed the candle on the dresser, Mary pretended to be asleep but as he undressed she watched him with the drugged eyes of a besotted lover. Her attraction to George Jarvis had started on the first day she had laid eyes on him and every day the heat of her love for him grew stronger.

He slipped gently into the bed beside her and she lovingly extended her arms to embrace him, causing him to look at her with a surprised smile. 'I thought you would be asleep by now.'

'Hush now, hush,' Mary whispered and pulled him closer to her body, kissing his lips with an eager passion.

Chapter Five

The following morning, fully dressed, Mary woke him with a daylight smile and placed his whimpering daughter in the bed beside him.

'Last night Elizabeth M needed your company, and now it's Elizabeth J's turn. I'll be back for her in a few minutes, and Mrs Keillor says she'll be serving breakfast in half an hour.'

As soon as George took the child and sat her on his chest and held her there with his hands, all the whimpering stopped and she sat looking down at him, silent and smiling.

She was an exquisite child, his daughter. He could still remember those months at sea, after she had been born, when night after night as she lay curled up in warm sleep he had watched her for hours in a silent paean of ecstasy and gratitude. There was no way he could describe the depth of his love for her.

She was almost four now, and the time since her birth seemed to have gone by in a blink. Now she could walk and talk and ask him a lot of curious questions that he had no true answer for. Why were these flowers blue? Why were these ones red? Who coloured them?

'Papa,' she said, reaching to put her small hand on his face. 'Are we going to the loch today?'

'Do you *want* to go down to the loch today?'

She nodded her head up and down, slowly and definitely.

'We will go after breakfast.'

'Mama too?'

'Mama too, but only for a short time because I have my work to do.'

'Lachlan too?'

'Yes ... ah, no ...' George remembered that today was Friday, one of the days young Lachlan's teacher, Robert Meiklejohn, came to privately tutor the boy.

'No, Beth, Lachlan can't come to the loch today because he has to do his lessons in the study with Mr Meiklejohn.'

'Can I do lessons too?'

'Not yet,' George smiled, remembering the hated classrooms of his own education. 'Plenty of time yet before you start your schooling, Beth, and soon enough after that you will be crying and asking me *why* you have to do lessons.'

Mary returned to the bedroom and lifted Elizabeth down. 'Come on, my girl, let your papa get washed and dressed.'

George said, 'I've promised her we'll take her down to the loch – after breakfast – just for a short time.'

Mary, leading the child to the door, stopped and looked back at him. 'Just the three of us?'

'Yes.'

'Good,' Mary replied, then lowered her voice, 'because I want to have a talk with you, George, a *serious* talk with you.'

*

After breakfast, the sun outside was already radiating a strong heat, making the morning perfect for a stroll down to the waters of Loch Ba, a freshwater lake at the back of the house.

Beth, whose cotton nightgown had now been replaced by a green dimity frock over white pantaloons frilling at the ankles, skipped and played and delayed the walk many times, stopping to crouch down and look at one flower after another with a litany of questions; and then stopping to examine a yellow weed which she decided was the nicest flower of them all, pulling it out of the earth to take home with her.

Mary chose that moment to start her serious talk with George.

'How long do we have to stay, George, here on Mull? It's too remote, too lonely. I love Elizabeth M, I truly do, but after General Macquarie's funeral she shut the doors of Gruline, shut them to the world.'

'That's because she did not want any visitors to see how devastated she was. Her Scottish pride would not allow any outsider to witness her grief.'

'I know, I know, but, George, that was almost two years ago, and we are all so isolated here on this island, so cut off from the rest of the world, even cut off from the rest of Scotland.'

George could not deny it as he looked at her silently.

'And as for the local Jarvisfield tenants,' Mary said despairingly, 'many of them have no English and speak only in Gaelic. They could be saying bad things about me and I wouldn't know it.'

George smiled. 'That's only the older ones, the ones that look a hundred years old. Most of the younger tenants speak English.'

'Not to me they don't! Around me they speak only in Gaelic.' Mary shrugged. 'Probably because they know I'm English.'

'Why don't you go over to Tobermory once in a while,' George suggested. 'Meet some of the locals of the town. Most of them are fluent in English; they have to be, because of all the foreign boats that come in there. The people are friendly enough, and I've seen a few young women of around your age.'

At this Mary's face became sulky and she turned her head away as they strolled on.

Having been brought up in the city of Leicester, a place with many roads and streets and avenues, she found it hard to think of Tobermory as even a town, because it had only *one* main street – one single street along the sea front – all other paths led up to the various houses where the locals lived.

Even the town of Sydney, as young as it was, had many paved streets and beautiful buildings when she had lived there – a bank, a hospital, and many shops selling all kind of produce, including tasty spices and beautiful silks from India, colourful cotton and so many other things from Capetown, making Sydney a *real* town to visit, and all thanks to the hard work and planning of Governor Lachlan Macquarie.

She said all this to George as they strolled towards the loch, and George nodded. 'Yes, but what you must remember is that Lachlan Macquarie loved the town of Tobermory, as small as it is, probably even more than he loved Sydney.'

'How could he?' she challenged, 'A man with such vision? A man who – '

'A man who grew up here on the island of Mull, a man who posted all his letters in the town of Tobermory, so all his vision, his humanity and his compassion must have once started from here, from this Scottish island, from the place where his dreams and feelings began.'

When Mary made no answer, just continued walking in thoughtful silence, George looked at her sideways and asked somewhat cryptically, 'Tell me, Mary, what great man ever came out of Leicester?'

Mary looked at him, and smiled and then laughed as she slapped him reprovingly on the arm. 'George! Don't you dare start teasing me now!'

George was smiling. 'I'm just saying that although Mull has a sparse population, perhaps it makes up for in quality what it lacks in quantity.'

'Oh!' Mary said, exasperated, 'You are beginning to sound like a proud Scotsman who was born here.'

'Well, I *was* educated here.'

'Yes, in *Edinburgh*, a thriving city, full of people. And where is your loyalty to Australia now? How quickly it has faded.'

'My loyalty to Australia?' George stopped walking and looked at her, astounded. 'I have *no* loyalty to Australia.'

'But I thought ...'

'Then you thought wrongly,' he said seriously. 'To like a country, to love a country even, is one thing, but to feel *loyalty* to a country is something else. Australia is the place where I found my happiness, so how could I not love it?'

He turned to glance at his daughter, playing safely, running around a bush and chattering to herself.

'But as for loyalty, yes I *do* owe some loyalty to Scotland and this island of Mull, because the man who rescued me from the slave trade and brought me up from childhood like a son, was himself a *son* of Scotland, born here and now buried here. A great man.'

'And now known as the "Father of *Australia*,"

'No, the father of a boy – who died worrying about his son's care, worrying about who would look after him, look out for him, on a day to day basis, just as I would worry in the same way about the care of our daughter. Why are you so hard-hearted about this, Mary? It is not in your nature to be unfeeling or unkind, so why be so about this ... why?'

Mary bit her lip guiltily, knowing she was being very selfish, and was now showing no gratitude to Elizabeth Macquarie who had been so kind to her. She loved Elizabeth, she truly did, but she did not possess Elizabeth's gentry class to shield her against the cruelty of the world; nor did she possess George's dignity and intelligent manner that either charmed or saw off all would-be detractors because he was brown-skinned and of foreign birth.

No, she did not possess such armour against the cruel world. She was just an ordinary girl with many weaknesses and fears of her own, and only in Australia would she feel safe from castigation.

In Sydney she had lived in Government House and so was regarded as superior and a cut above all the rest. Not one of the population would dare say a word against her, especially not after she had become one of the Governor's household and then a member of his family by marrying George.

But here, in Scotland, they seemed to look down on anyone whose only offence was no more than being *English* – and she was English – worse even it seemed than being brown-skinned and a *real* foreigner like George.

'Mary?'

She looked at George, her wonderful husband who had changed her life, changed her heart and taught her that life can never be good if there is hatred in it, hatred for anyone – or fear, because fear was a poison that crippled the mind and eventually the body.

'I'm sorry, George,' she whispered, and then put her hands around his shoulders and hugged him close. 'I'm sorry for being selfish, I won't speak of this again.'

George drew back and looked at her with an uncertain smile. 'You promise?'

'I promise.'

'And will you go into Tobermory and get to know some of the people there?'

Mary nodded her agreement, but was unsure if it was a promise she would be able to keep.'

'Papa!'

Beth was walking towards them cradling something in her small hands and, from the delighted expression on her face, it was something wonderful to behold.

'Look Papa, look Mama ...'

George and Mary looked down at the small slimy green frog captured within her hands. 'Can I bring it home with me?' she asked excitedly.

'No, no,' George said gently, 'because that would be unkind to the frog.'

'Why?'

'Because he must have water ...'

Mary stood watching as George led Beth back down to the stream, her mind returning to their conversation and the promise about Tobermory.

She had only once been over to the town and had quickly left it as soon as her purchases had been completed. And now, not even to please George would she ever consider attempting to make friends there, because she was too afraid that somehow they would discover that she had once been a convict.

Not that she had ever done anything wrong, well, not *very* wrong. She had been a maid in a house in Leicester, sharing an attic bedroom with three other maids, they had no mirror in the room, and Mary, seeing the mistress had so many mirrors in her bedroom, Mary often sneaked in there and borrowed a small mirror for the maids to use, especially when one of them had a night off, and the mirror was *always* quickly returned.

Until the night she was caught coming out of the mistress's bedroom with the small mirror in her hand, and the mistress – a woman of many natures and all of them mean – became so enraged at the maids using her mirror, she had Mary immediately arrested and charged with theft at Leicester Assizes, where she was sentenced, at the age of seventeen, to be transported as a felon to serve seven years in His Majesty's prison camp in Botany Bay.

The shame, the pain, the heartbreak of that time was all forgotten now, because she had been lucky. As soon as the ship had docked at Sydney, and John Campbell, the

Governor's secretary, had come aboard to inspect the convicts, he had immediately decided that Mary looked refined enough and spoke well enough to be chosen to serve as a maid in Government House.

And it was there, in Government House, in the private apartments of Lachlan and Elizabeth Macquarie, that Mary met George Jarvis and instantly fell in love with him.

At times their romance seemed hopeless, because she was a convict and George was free, a member of the Governor's family, and in New South Wales no free person was allowed to marry a convict.

There were times, in those sunny days, when Mary thought she would die of longing, so consuming was her love for George Jarvis, and the worst heartache of all was Mrs Kelly and Mrs Ovens constantly warning her that Governor Macquarie would never allow George to have any personal relationship with a convict.

But they were proved wrong, because they did not understand the deep bond of affection that existed between Lachlan Macquarie and George Jarvis.

And later, solely due to the personal request of George – aided and supported by Elizabeth – Governor Macquarie granted Mary a pardon and her freedom, which allowed her and George to marry.

No, dear Elizabeth needed her and George now more than ever. The dream of starting a new life by returning to their own grant of land in Australia would have to wait until Elizabeth was more settled back here and young Lachlan had grown older.

Unless ... a new thought suddenly came into Mary's mind ... unless Elizabeth M also decided to return to Australia! She had many friends over there now, more than she had here in Scotland, and she owned a huge plantation of land just outside Parramatta which Major Antill was presently overseeing on her behalf.

A smile came on Mary's face as she looked over at George and Beth crouched down together by the bank of the loch, their fingers playing with the water.

No, Mary realised, it was not George she had to try and

persuade to return to Australia, it was Elizabeth Macquarie ...
all of them returning together.

Chapter Six

Although George Jarvis always seemed perfectly in control and unflappable, whenever life got too tough, or his problems with the women of the household seemed difficult to resolve, he sought solace by spending time with a special male friend who always listened calmly and silently, and never interrupted – his horse, which he had bought in Oban a year earlier, a handsome strapping horse which the owner had named Brodie.

In the stables, George smoothed his hand down the horse's sleek brown face and asked his friend, 'So what is the solution, Brodie? Where do my *true* loyalties lie? To the promise I made to my father to look after *his* wife and child, or to the desire of my own wife and the future of my own child?'

Brodie gave an upward shrug of his head, as if to say he didn't know the answer.

'No, how could you know?' George agreed. 'You're just a horse.'

George flopped down on the straw at the front of the box and continued the conversation.

'Your problem, Brodie, is because you are Scottish, born and reared here, so you don't know the difference between here and the rest of the world. Now, Elizabeth Macquarie, she is Scottish too, so her heart and soul have an affinity with this land, and especially with these intemperate Highlands.'

Brodie gave a small whinny of approval as if he too had a love of these intemperate Highlands, the place of his birth.

George turned his head and looked languidly out across the stable yard, bright with sunshine.

'Of course, in summer it's different. In summer it's warm, bright and cheerful, but how long does summer last here?' He made a *'pfffff'* sound and snapped his fingers. 'Three or four months, then gone.'

George sat for a long moment thinking, and then he continued:

'In winter though, it is hard, Brodie. If Mull was a woman I would call her fickle ... fickle and capricious. Who knows what her weather is going to do next? Without any warning she drowns you in rain, then screams through the windows in many of her gales, bites you hard with her coldness, and then blows down the chimney trying to scatter the flames of the fire into the room. But then ... in summer, she changes her ways and becomes soft and beautiful again.'

After another long silence, George sighed resignedly and stood up, his hands brushing the straw from his jacket and breeches.

On impulse, he lifted down the saddle from the wall and then slowly led the horse out to the yard.

'A good energetic gallop will get rid of our frustrations. Are you game, Brodie?'

Brodie lifted his front hoof and scraped the ground eagerly, shaking his chestnut mane with excitement.

Minutes later the two of them were trotting easily down narrow winding roads while overhead golden eagles wheeled and flew and every field and hedge displayed an array of colourful wild flowers.

George took in every aspect of the various views, the hills, the lochs, and the volcanic cliffs in the distance, all presenting scenery that was breathtaking in its beauty.

'Yet only in her summer dress,' he murmured to Brodie, but the horse had seen enough; he had been promised a gallop and showed his irritation at being reined in.

George grinned and gave him a small kick with his boot, and Brodie joyously shot forward, racing at full speed for mile after mile over the land until they finally slowed to a careful trot on the steep downward slope that led into Tobermory.

When George entered the Inn for a cooling drink, Angus McLeod greeted him with a big smile of welcome.

'Och, Mr Jarvis! I've been wanting to see you and thank ye. My bad headaches ... I'm cured of them! Not a one have I had since you took away the wee skull and buried it in the sea.'

George couldn't help laughing, certain the removal of the skull had nothing to do with the cure of Angus's headaches. It was merely the suggestion of it. Such was the power of the mind in healing the body.

Chapter Seven

Despite being married to George, Mary had never relinquished her role as Elizabeth's personal maid. She tended to Elizabeth's needs, which were not many, just the usual duties of bringing her water to bathe in the morning and later buttoning the back of her dress. Even so, they spent a lot of time together, and so Mary was pleased to observe the change in Elizabeth as the summer months went by.

A change that had began with the opening of the letters from Australia. Strangely, Elizabeth seemed more willing to connect with the people of that far country more than she did with her friends or relatives here in Scotland, and that fact gave Mary renewed hope of their eventual return.

She sat knitting and smiling to herself as Elizabeth wrote page after page to Sergeant Whalan.

'Mary, do *you* remember Sergeant Whalan's lovely garden? You must have seen it during one of our stays at the summer house in Parrammata?'

Mary nodded. 'His garden was full of the most beautiful roses I have ever seen, especially the big yellow ones

'And all grown from seedlings sent to me at Government House from India,' Elizabeth replied.

'I would love to see how his garden looks now,' Mary said quietly.

'Oh, me too,' Elizabeth agreed in a yearning tone. 'How I would *love* to see all the new shrubs and flowers he has imported from India and Capetown. He says his garden is now three times the size it was when we were there, so I'm sure it now looks absolutely wonderful.'

'Do you think you will ever go back?'

'To Australia?' Elizabeth pondered for a moment. 'Well, I do have land and stock there, and some wonderful friends –'

'Excuse me, Madam?' Cook was standing by the door, claiming Elizabeth's attention.

'Yes, Mrs Keillor?'

Mary was so delighted with Elizabeth's answer she had to

leave the room and rush out to the back garden to sing out a note of delight.

It was coming – their return to Australia was on the horizon and coming closer – just a little more patience, a little more time.

*

Elizabeth's letter-writing to Australia absorbed her. Too much at times, George decided, because young Lachlan was turning to him more and more for answers to questions and general guidance as well as companionship in his daily life.

One evening in October, when the evenings were darkening early, George waited until Mary had taken Beth upstairs to bed before broaching the subject with Elizabeth.

He found her in the drawing-room, seated at her desk as usual and immersed in her writing.

'Elizabeth.'

She looked round. 'Oh. George, I'm just replying to Reverend Cowper. Do you remember the day he married you and Mary in St Phillip's?'

'Have you given any more thought to Lachlan's education?'

Elizabeth's eyes widened. 'Well, isn't that strange – I was just writing on that very subject to Reverend Cowper.'

George sat down in one of the armchairs by the fire as Elizabeth continued:

'You see, I knew that Lachlan had planned for our son to go to Eton, but when he died in that sudden and untimely way, I couldn't bear to lose young Lachlan as well by sending him away to school in England, not so soon after his father's death, that's why I kept Mr Meiklejohn on.'

She glanced down at the letter she had been writing. 'I'm sure Reverend Cowper will tell me that my dear husband would have understood and forgiven me for not carrying out his wishes.'

'I'm sure he *will* tell you that, but at some point Lachlan should go out to school. Meiklejohn doesn't have the knowledge to teach him everything.'

'He doesn't need to know everything,' Elizabeth returned. 'He is the heir to this estate and when he's old enough he will become its laird and run it.'

'Yes, but right now Lachlan is innocent and unworldly and very shy in his manner. He needs the company of other boys.'

'Other boys? Well he has plenty of male cousins over at my sister's home at Lochbuie. Perhaps I should have taken him there sooner but I just didn't possess the fortitude to do it.'

She leaned her elbow on the desk and put a hand to her brow. 'I just couldn't face it, listening to people blabbing their sympathy and then neighbours coming in with their condolences and offers to come and visit and comfort me. And apart from that, Margaret's boys are such a *rowdy* lot.'

Which was just the kind of company young Lachlan needed now, George thought.

Elizabeth seemed uneasy about the subject and quickly ended it.

'Forgive me, George, but I really want to get on with this letter telling Reverend Cowper about Governor Macquarie's final days, which I know he will pass on to all our friends in his congregation. And I want them all to know that in his final weeks of life down there in London, all of Lachlan's final actions, all his meetings with politicians, and even his meeting with the King, were all done to help the people of Australia. I want them to *know* that his affection and thoughts to the last were of the them, the people in his favourite country, the one he ruled for so long and gave it the name of Australia.'

George nodded and stood up to leave, knowing Elizabeth's mind was too deep in memories of her husband now to be capable of giving any serious or sustained thought to the matter of her son.

Yet now that the subject had been mentioned, he knew that Elizabeth would give it thought, but not until after she had finished that letter of eulogy to Reverend Cowper about the husband she had idolised.

Ten weeks passed before the letter was completed. It totalled forty-six pages in it final form, but tens and tens of pages had been torn up and started again until Elizabeth was finally satisfied with it.

Now it was December and a freezing winter had arrived.

Young Lachlan and Beth were beginning to suffer cold after cold, both coughing continually and watery-eyed.

'I think she needs a doctor,' Mary said anxiously, her palm on Beth's forehead, 'she's burning up, I think she has a fever.'

George bent over his daughter, felt her forehead, felt the heat, saw how ill she was, and his heart began to thump. He would never forget that cold winter in Perthshire so many years ago when Lachlan and Elizabeth's baby daughter had died at three months from the bitter cold and pneumonia.

'I'd better check young Lachlan too,' he said quickly, and then headed across the landing to find Elizabeth in Lachlan's bedroom, bending over him and sponging his face.

'How is he?' George asked.

Elizabeth turned to him and George saw that her face was not anxious as Mary's face had been, it was white with terror.

'He's as hot as a furnace and yet he's shivering and saying he's cold.'

'Beth is the same. I'll go for the doctor and bring him back with me. Where does he live?'

'Dr McLean, he lives in Salen, the first house on the left as you enter the village.'

George moved to the window, looked out at the black night, then over at the clock on the dresser. 'It will be after eleven when I get there. Will he come out?'

'He'd better come out!' Elizabeth snapped. 'Salen is part of the Jarvisfield estate and he is living on Macquarie land! But George, *you* don't have to go – send one of the servants, one of stable boys.'

'No,' George said firmly. 'Beth is my daughter and too ill for me to rely on anyone else to bring a doctor as quickly as possible.'

Elizabeth sucked back a breath, relieved that George had taken charge of the matter, as he usually did these days. Always so calm, even in times of distress, George was the one person she felt she could always depend upon, no matter how bad the situation.

Young Lachlan opened his eyes, looked round the room and said croakily, 'Was that George?'

'Yes, my darling.' Elizabeth touched her son's forehead

again. 'You are still so hot. Let me sponge you again.' She rinsed out the flannel in the basin of cold water and resumed sponging Lachlan's face.

'Where has George gone?'

'To fetch you a doctor, my angel.'

The boy smiled his angelic smile and closed his eyes tiredly again. 'I love George, Mama.'

'I know you do, my darling.'

Down in the stables George was speaking quickly and firmly to the stable boy he had ordered to bring him a lantern and fix it to Brodie's saddle.

'It's going to snow, Mr Jarvis,' the boy said uneasily. 'I can feel it in the air.'

'Then I'd better move swiftly,' George replied, mounting the saddle. 'Lead me out.'

Lifting his own candle-lantern and shivering in the cold, the boy walked ahead, lighting the way out of the stable and down the narrow path that led out to the road.

'Mr Jarvis, I could ride over for ye. I know the way to the doctor's house betterer than ye.'

George looked down at the boy, twelve years old and shivering like an old man suffering with the ague.

'You get back into the warmth now, Hector, and stay there. Did you put some extra candles in the saddlebag?'

'Aye, sir.'

'Then goodnight.'

And on that George rode into the darkness.

*

'His wee daughter must be bad,' Hector said to Mrs Keillor when he returned to the warm kitchen. 'He looked like nothing would stop him from venturing out.'

'Aye, and the young master too. Those children are not hardy like us, Hector, too much pampering.'

'Aye.' Hector squatted down by the fire and was inclined to agree. 'They're no' like us, are they? The other day Master Lachlan told me he was no' Scottish at all, he was Australian.'

Mrs Keillor sat back in her chair and thought about that. 'Well, he was born there, and he lived there until he was eight years old ... so, aye, that place must be his homeland, true enough.'

Hector looked into the flames. 'They're all foreign, except Mrs Macquarie. Even Mary is English.'

'Mary is a grand lass, English or no,' Mrs Keillor said fondly. 'The Mistress's personal companion she may be, but Mary has no uppity airs about her, nay, she's just a normal lass. So let me hear no bad opinion about her from ye now.'

'I wasna going to say anything bad about her, just that she's an English *sassenach*, that's all.'

Mrs Keillor yawned and looked at the clock 'Away to your bed now, Hector. I'm staying put here by my fire until Mr Jarvis gets back, just in case I'm needed to make hot drinks for the bairns or the mothers. I'll have meself a wee nap sitting here while I'm waiting, so go on now, away with ye.'

Hector got to his feet, but his mind was still curious. 'That place, Australia ... Da says it's the place where the English send all their criminals.'

'Aye, so I've heard, to a place called Bottomless Bay. But I'm sure that's thousands of miles away from where young master Lachlan was born and lived.'

'So which place was *he* born then?'

'A place called Sidney.'

'Sidney? That be a man's name.'

'Aye, so maybe that man Sidney was the first criminal the English sent out there,' Mrs Keillor wondered. 'But anyhows,' she yawned again, 'at least there's one thing we can be sure of – with a name like Sidney, he was no' Scottish!'

Chapter Eight

The air was bitterly cold. George wrapped his cloak tighter around him and pulled his three-cornered hat down low over his brow. The night was so black, with no moon at all, he could see no further than a few paces in front of him, lit only by the dim light of the lantern.

Heading for Salen, the narrow winding road had led him into a glen, long and dark.

He had never realised that riding through the glen at night could be so eerie, so black, so silent, no sound other than the clopping of Brodie's hooves.

Something flew past his face, an owl probably, or a bat. Looking around him, seeing nothing, but feeling the enclosure of the glen, he began to wonder if the Scottish were right about these glens being filled with spirits that only came out at night.

A shiver ran through his body, but then he checked himself, realising how foolish his thoughts were. If there were anything unnatural and unseen in the glen his horse would sense it, as all animals seemed to be able to sense the unseen. Brodie's ears would prick up, and he would react with a whinny of warning; but no, Brodie was plodding along calmly, as if knowing the way in the dark was one of his natural talents.

But still the eerie feel of the glen continued to unsettle George. Who knew what strange animals might lurk here?

Again he checked himself, deciding he would risk them all, spirits or night animals or anything else that came on his path: all that mattered was his sick daughter and getting a doctor to her. For his little Beth, his precious girl, he would risk the sight of the Devil himself and fight him if he had to.

The thought of fighting anyone took his mind back to that long ago time when Lachlan's regiment had crossed the Egyptian desert from Suez to the Nile, a march of over one hundred and fifty miles.

It all seemed such a long time ago now, those days when he

46

was only sixteen, and how they had all hated the dry heat of that desert, marching under the sun for mile after mile with no shade from even an occasional cloud in the sky.

He felt the cold biting into his face and wished he could feel some of that Egyptian heat now.

At last he saw a light in the distance and knew they were approaching the end of the glen. Relief flooded through him and he leaned forward to pat the horse's long neck.

'You're a champion, Brodie. You would have made a great war horse if you had been bought by the British Army and not me.'

*

The light had come from the first house at the edge of the glen, Dr McLean's house.

The housekeeper answered George's knock in her nightcap, a thick shawl wrapped around her nightgown.

'Aye,' she said, 'the doctor must be still awake because I saw a light under the door of his bedroom.'

George realised that must have been the light he had seen when approaching the end of the glen, the light from the doctor's window.

'But bye! This is a very late hour of night to call, and Dr McLean is already in his bed.'

'Yet his light is still on,' George said, 'so he must be awake.'

'Aye, he must be,' she grunted, opening the door wider for George to enter, 'reading those books of his no doot!'

She led George into a parlour and bade him to sit down. 'And no doot ye'll be needing a hot drink yerself.'

George moved towards the heat of the banked-down fire. 'It's freezing out there,' he said. 'As cold as ice.'

'Aye, I'll stir up the fire for ye.' She moved in front of him and lifted the poker, stabbing into the base of the fire until the flames flared.

Who is it that's ailing?'

'My daughter.'

'Your dattur? A child then.'

'Yes, and a young boy, both are very sick and need the doctor.'

'Och,' the housekeeper shrugged, 'children are never as sick as they seem.'

'No, that's not always true,' George replied. 'Years ago in Perthshire when little Jane got sick, her cold turned into pneumonia and she died.'

'How old was she?'

'Three months.'

'Oh, a very *wee* bairn then.' The housekeeper pulled her shawl tightly around her. 'Aye, well that can happen when they're that young. But now, sit ye here and I'll go up to Dr McLean and then I'll heat ye up a dish of beef broth.'

'Thank you, but I don't need any refreshment.'

At the door she paused and looked back, as if suddenly remembering. 'What name will I tell him? What house is it?'

The Macquarie house at Gruline.'

'Macquarie? You mean ... the house of the young laird of Jarvisfield?'

'Yes, he is the boy that is sick, as well as my daughter.'

'And your dattur is?'

'Elizabeth Jarvis.'

'Macquarie, Jarvis ... Jarvisfield ... oh my!' She turned and quickly left the room, clumping up the wooden stairs as fast as her feet would take her.

George finally removed his cloak and sat down by the fire, holding his hands out to the flames and feeling the wonderful warmth, listening to the sound of voices in the room above and hoping the doctor was not going to be contrary about the late hour.

And as he sat there, looking into the flames, it suddenly struck him, as it must have struck the housekeeper, that there would be no doctor living here, no house standing here either, no human habitation at all – if Lachlan Macquarie had not bought the land and built the village of Salen.

This was the first village Lachlan had planned to the last detail with his architect, and then arranged for the stonemasons to come in and build it – only six years before he had re-designed Sydney and turned it from a shabby collection of shacks into a respectable city with so many new and necessary buildings, including a hospital.

George smiled as he remembered those early days when Lachlan was planning the building of Salen.

A young officer in his late thirties, he had returned from India a wealthy man, and bought nothing of any extravagance except half of the island of Mull.

He had chosen the area of Gruline to build his Scottish home, but in Salen he wanted to build some comfortable houses where his new tenants could live in comfort. By the end though, Lachlan being Lachlan, he had insisted upon a grocery store, a blacksmith's, a doctor's house, and even a Post Office to make the village complete and independent of Tobermory.

George had not witnessed the building of the village, because as soon as they had arrived in London, Lachlan had forced him to attend a private boarding school for a full year, before moving him up to a college in Edinburgh. Yet here it was, the village of Salen, built and owned by Lachlan Macquarie, and now George was depending upon its doctor to come and attend upon Lachlan's son.

Footsteps on the stairs.

Moments later Dr McLean entered the parlour still wearing his nightshirt and nightcap and carrying a black bag. A man in his late forties, he pushed his spectacles further up his nose and peered at George, then held out his hand.

'Mr Jarvis.'

George stood and shook his hand. 'Dr McLean. My apologies for calling on you at such a late hour.'

'Och, tis something I expect in winter. In the summer I rarely have a caller at all, day or night, so I can't complain.'

He peered over his spectacles at George again. 'Mr Jarvis, yes, I have heard of you, but we have never met before this, have we?'

'No, sir.'

'Now tell me the symptoms of the two sick children, but first the boy, the young laird.'

George described the symptoms of the constant coughing, the watery eyes, the constant and miserable tiredness and now the high temperature.

'And my daughter's symptoms are exactly the same.'

'So, all in all, I would say they are symptoms that should not worry you overmuch, just one of the many maladies of winter.'

George instantly felt annoyed by the doctor's complacency. 'But the symptoms *do* worry me, sir. In particular, the constant coughing and the high temperature. Could they not be symptoms of developing pneumonia?'

'In some cases, yes, but let me tell you why children cough so much in winter. Firstly, they get a small cold in their head, and this is aggravated by the fires we burn in every room in winter, even our bedrooms, emitting smoke that aggravates the children's throats and makes them cough, as well as making their eyes more watery than usual.

'Secondly, the continual coughing puts a strain on their lungs and leads to increased tiredness. Also, as our bedrooms are kept much warmer in winter, when children are confined to bed they *do* get very hot.'

George looked at Dr Mclean, wondering if he was an absolute fool, or a very good and practical doctor?

Dr McLean opened his medical bag. 'Now I will give you a bottle of linctus to soothe their coughs, and some powders to reduce their temperatures, and then let the body do the rest of its natural work in the healing process. But you must – and I do stress this point – you must ensure that their bedrooms are not kept *too* warm, otherwise they could become dehydrated which then leads to strong headaches and very unhappy children.'

Well, he didn't sound like a quack, and George began to wonder if his visit here had been too hasty.

'Dr McLean,' he said hesitantly, 'forgive me for asking, but where ... did you ... do your medical training?'

'Oh, I practised on cows and sheep, the odd goose here and there, a few old cats, the odd young dog – but now I practise on humans.'

The alarmed expression on George's face made Dr McLean throw back his head in laughter.

'I'm jesting, Mr Jarvis, something I always do when someone dares to question my qualifications. I can assure you that I received my medical training in one of the best hospitals in Edinburgh.'

'My apologies, sir.'

'Accepted.'

'But Mrs Macquarie does insist that you come to Gruline House to examine her son, and I do request the same for my daughter.'

'Certainly, I will call on the young laird of our land if it is so demanded, but not until tomorrow morning, after I have had my night's sleep. To rush out now would be an unnecessary folly.'

George struggled with his thoughts, still worrying about Beth, yet reassured by Dr McLean's medical advice.

'I'll take the linctus and powders back with me now, but I can rely upon you to visit Gruline tomorrow?'

'Most certainly you can.' Dr McLean smiled. 'If only for the purpose of presenting my bill.'

*

As George rode away from Salen he saw that Hector had been right in his prediction: a powdering of snow lay on the ground and more snow was falling.

The blackness of the silent glen was beginning to feel eerie again, wild and desolate, not a place for humans at night.

George adjusted the pole carrying the lantern and bent it forward, giving Brodie more light on the ground underfoot.

A mile and a half or so inside the glen a wind began to whip up, rustling the trees and blowing the snow into George's face, as well as unsettling Brodie.

Leaning forward and stroking the horse's neck, George started a conversation to distract him, to calm him, but Brodie was not listening, his concentration on the ground before him, snorting his irritation.

The air was so cold it was turning the falling snow into ice as soon it reached the ground and the horse began to slither slightly with every few steps he took.

Alarmed now, George wondered if they should turn back and seek refuge for the night in Salen, but he reckoned they were now deep in the middle of the glen, and it would be as long a journey to go back as it would to go forward.

The wind became even stronger. George bent forward against it, head low, continually patting the horse's neck to comfort him; but the wind, the snow, the ice, and the darkness of the glen despite the small light of the lantern, all wreaked their havoc on the man and his horse, causing Brodie to suddenly slither forward and go down on his front legs, sending George toppling over his head, one foot still caught in the stirrup.

Whinnying in pain, Brodie tried to stand, but the ice underfoot prevented him, the effort leading to both man and horse falling sideways off the road until they were crashing down over the rocks and boulders into the blackness of unconsciousness.

Chapter Nine

True to his word and his bank account, Dr McLean arrived at Gruline the following morning, just before noon.

He greeted Elizabeth with deference. 'My apologies for arriving so late in the morning, Mrs Macquarie, but the snow and ice on the road has made my journey here a slow one. How is the young laird?'

'Much the same.' Elizabeth looked past him to the closed front door. 'Is George not with you?'

'George? Oh, you mean Mr Jarvis? No, he left Salen last night. I believe he and his horse were heading for the much shorter route back through the glen.'

Elizabeth's breaths were becoming uneven. 'Did you journey here through the glen?'

'Good grief, no. I'm not up to riding a horse anymore, not with this touch of arthritis in my hip. No, these days I travel by trap, and so I took the main road from Salen to Tobermory, and then had to double halfway back again to reach you here at Gruline.'

Elizabeth's fists were irritably knocking against each other. 'But don't you understand my fear? If George left Salen last night and he has not yet arrived here, then something must have happened to him in the glen.'

'The glen?' Dr McLean finally understood and became equally as alarmed.

'Then something must be done! A search party perhaps? I am not exaggerating when I say that in this freezing weather, with all the snow and ice, it would not take very long for someone to die of exposure out in that glen.'

'You should have stopped him from returning then!' Elizabeth snapped. 'Seeing the snow falling, and knowing how cold it was, you should have offered him hospitality in your home until the light of morning. That's what we thought you had done.'

Dr McLean looked shocked. 'It never occurred to me ... He seemed determined to get back as swiftly as possible, and also ... well, he seemed so capable in every respect.'

Elizabeth had heard enough. She turned and left the doctor standing and headed for the kitchen where she alerted Mrs Keillor and then found Hector.

'Hector, I want you to wrap up as warmly as possible, and then you must ride to Robert Dewar and tell him a search party must be gathered amongst the tenants immediately. Every strong man and boy must stop what he is doing and start searching the route from here to Salen through the glen.'

Hector looked bewildered. 'For why?'

'Mr Jarvis left Salen last night and he has not yet returned. He must be injured, somewhere along the road through the glen. Tell Mr Dewar, tell any tenant you see, tell everyone – George must be found, and quickly!'

'What about his horse?' Hector asked. 'If Mr Jarvis was injured or hurt, Brodie would have come back here looking for help, aye, I know he would.'

'Or maybe Brodie is acting the dutiful sentinel and is standing guard over George until someone comes and finds him!' Elizabeth snapped. 'Now *go!*'

Hector fled, and Mrs Keillor made a small sound in her throat and gave Elizabeth a slight nod of her head to turn and look at the open door of the kitchen.

Elizabeth turned and saw Mary standing there, her hand to her throat and her face as white as a sheet.

'Mary ...' Elizabeth moved and bundled the girl inside her arms. 'Don't worry, Mary, we will find him, and all will be well. A few cuts and bruises, maybe even a broken leg, it happens all the time to riders, but George is strong and determined and he will recover quickly.'

'What if they can't find him?' Mary asked.

'Of course they will find him!' Elizabeth replied with certainty. 'Mary this is *Mull*, and these people are Scottish people, *Highland* people – they know every inch of the terrain and will not fear to battle it. And George is a soldier, you know that, all the time he spent with Lachlan and the soldiers of the British Army, marching across deserts, surviving without water. George will know what to do to keep himself safe until help arrives.'

Tears were slipping down Mary's face. She leaned closer into Elizabeth to draw in more of her comfort and reassurance, saying softly, 'Yes, George always knows what to do.'

Chapter Ten

When she was given the news, ten hours later, Elizabeth's reaction to George's death was that of a woman stunned.

It was not possible, George Jarvis dead? No, it couldn't be true!

Even when Mary screamed and screamed and then finally collapsed into a chair with heartbroken sobs, Elizabeth was unable to comfort her. She stood in the centre of the drawing-room, silent and staring wide-eyed at Mary, convinced this was all just a hideous dream.

Later, after Dr McLean had given Mary a few drops of laudanum to calm her and help her sleep, he came back into the room and said to Elizabeth in a matter-of-fact tone:

'She will sleep now, that will give her some respite. As for the two children, both are beginning to recover from their colds, just as I knew they would. They'll be up and about in no time.'

'So, there was no need for George ... '

'No need at all,' Dr McLean replied. 'And certainly not at night, in this weather.' He shrugged. 'But we must make allowances for all the parents of sick children, and Mr Jarvis did seem to be a very caring father.'

'George was very caring about everyone,' Elizabeth murmured, feeling sick with grief. 'Do you think Mary will be able to cope with this?'

'No, not for some time,' Dr McLean replied quietly, his mind recalling the face of the beautiful young girl with tears still streaming down her face, even as her eyes closed under the drugging effects of the laudanum.

'She is heartbroken.'

Elizabeth nodded, and then her composure completely changed. She began walking slowly up and down the room, wringing her hands and speaking in tones of painful regret at having allowed George to venture out so late at night and in such bitter weather.

Dr McLean was hugely relieved to be able to escape when

Mrs Keillor arrived to escort him up to his room.

'Now, I've put a hot-jar in your bed,' said Mrs Keillor, leading him up the stairs. 'And Maggie has got a good fire going in there now, so ye'll be nice and warm, Dr McLean, nice and warm."

'And I'll wake up with a blocked nose, a chesty cough and a bad headache,' the doctor retorted. 'Is there water in the room?'

'Aye, sir, a large jug of water for drinking or washing, whichever ye please.'

'Well, thank you for the hot-jar in my bed, that will do me fine.'

As soon as the door had closed behind Mrs Keillor, Dr McLean lifted the jug of water and poured some slowly over the fire, listening to it hiss and splutter and watching it darken.

'These women and their bedroom fires!' he muttered tiredly. 'What do they think blankets and bed-quilts are for?'

Mrs Keillor returned to the kitchen to find Hector still squatting by the fire's hearth, and still crying profusely.

Maggie was bent over the boy, a hand on his shoulder, endeavouring to comfort him. She looked up at the cook, a hopeless expression on her face.

'Nothing I say to him does any good, Mrs Keillor. He canna be consoled!'

'Aye, well ...' Mrs Keillor nodded at the new scullery maid who was only a year older than Hector. 'He was very fond of Mr Jarvis was Hector, as we all were, Maggie.'

'I'm crying for *Brodie*,' Hector wailed. 'Three of his legs broken and a gash down his head! Do none of ye care that Brodie died too!'

'Ah, we do care, Hector, aye we do,' Mrs Keillor muttered sympathetically. She sat down in her chair, unable to restrain a tear falling onto her cheek. 'But Mr Jarvis suffered just as badly ... '

She lifted her apron and wiped at her eyes. 'And he was such a fine man, aye, such a *fine* man ... He'll be a sore loss to the family and this house, that's for sure.'

Chapter Eleven

On the day of the funeral, Mrs Keillor's kitchen was busy and unusually crowded due to the number of young girls – the daughters of nearby tenants – who had come in to 'lend a hand' with the serving of the food and drinks.

'By! It seems like only yesterday since these same bunch of grand people came to Mull for General Macquarie's funeral,' Mrs Keillor said anxiously, stirring a wooden spoon into a cauldron of simmering chicken soup. 'Do ye think they'll ken that my menu today is the same as the last time?'

'They'll no' notice,' said Lorna McLaughlin, a fifteen-year-old who had helped out at the previous funeral. 'They've come to pay their last respects to Mr Jarvis, and won't care about the food.'

Mrs Keillor turned and looked at the girl. 'How stupid are ye? Since when did ye turn into a blathering fool, Lorna McLaughlin?'

Lorna's eyes were wide. 'But Mrs Keillor – '

'But nowt!' Mrs Keillor snapped, her anxiety turning to impatience. 'Everyone knows that the *food* to be provided is the most important thing people think about after a funeral. Same as after a wedding. And it has to be *good* food, otherwise the occasion is a disgrace. Why d'ye think I stayed up all night baking and roasting?'

George was being laid to rest with Lachlan Macquarie Senior and his baby daughter in the small private cemetery on the estate, a short distance from the front of the house.

Maggie Kennedy – who had been standing at the front door house watching for the return of the mourners – came running back into the kitchen in shock.

'There's bad trouble at the grave. Mrs Keillor! Aye, there is! Master Lachlan is kicking and punching Minister Bannon and trying to push him away! He's no' letting him say the prayers for Mr Jarvis!'

'No!' Mrs Keillor would not believe it, ripping off her apron and running through the house to the front door where she saw the commotion in yon cemetery garden. Mr Bannon was down on his back now, with two of the male mourners bending to help the hefty cleric his feet, while Mrs Macquarie was trying to restrain her son.

Lord save us!' Mrs Keillor muttered in shock. Young Lachlan's face was contorted as he screamed out his rage:

'George wouldn't want a bigoted ignorant and unholy man like you saying his last prayers! You told everyone he was a heathen! Aye, some of the tenants' lads told me what you've been saying about George! Now get away from his grave and get off my land. Get off my land!'

Mrs Keillor had her hands over her mouth, her big eyes staring.

Of course it *was* his land now, she realised; he had inherited it from his father and now his mother was just holding it in trust for him.

'Get off my land!'

Mrs Keillor turned quickly and moved back inside the house. 'I canna look nor listen any more, Maggie! It's too upsetting. Ye keep watching – and ye as well, Lorna – and then come back to the kitchen to keep me informed! By! Young master Lachlan! Always as sweet as an angel! Who would have thought it!'

Ten minutes later Maggie came running back in again to tell Mrs Keillor: 'Two of the gentlemen helped Minister Bannon into the trap. Hector is taking him away and back to his manse.'

'So what's happening now?'

Mary is going to say the last prayers. Tis a good thing they took the Minister away because Mary was looking like she wanted to hit him too, and she said something to him that I couldna hear. But now she's crying.'

'Go back out – keep me informed!'

Lorna crossed paths with Maggie as she too now ran into the kitchen.

'Mrs Macquarie called me over, and she whispered for me to tell ye that when they all get back to the house, everything is to be done as if nothing un... un – '

'Untoward?'

Lorna nodded. 'Aye, as if nothing un-to-ward has happened.'

'And young Lachlan? Now Minister Bannon has gone? Has he calmed down?'

'Och!' said Lorna. 'He's no' calm at all. He's weeping buckets! He looks even more heartbroken than Mary.'

'Oh no, that's no' possible,' Mrs Keillor said moodily. 'No one could be more heartbroken than Mary is now.'

'Will I go back out?'

'Aye.'

*

'They're coming back,' said Maggie. 'The funeral is over.'

Mrs Keillor flew into a panic, barking out orders like a drill-sergeant.

'Ye, Lorna, take that tray of drinks to the hall and greet the mourners with it.'

Lorna quickly lifted the silver tray of crystal glasses filled with sherry and rushed out of the kitchen.

'And ye, Maggie Kennedy, 'ye do the same with the tray of whisky glasses, but only offer a glass to the gentlemen, no' the ladies.'

'Why no' the ladies, Mrs Keillor?'

'Because ladies usually prefer to drink nothing stronger than sherry – least, no' in public company anyways. Now scoot!'

Mrs Keillor turned and stood ranging her eyes over the food on the large table in the centre of the kitchen, judging its quality and quantity: three roasted geese and a shank of boiled ham, a joint of beef pickled with onion gravy; six large vegetable pies – the pastry on all of the pies as golden as they should be ... aye, the food was good enough and plenty enough ... and so *she* at least, had not let Mr Jarvis down. The feast she had prepared for his guests was as good as the one she had prepared for General Macquarie. Oh, and the chicken soup!

She rushed over to the cauldron and gave it another stir. After their sherry and whisky the guests would sit down and need a warming dish of hot soup to banish the chill from their bodies after standing outdoors in such bitter weather.

Finally, she gave a short sit-down to herself in the chair by the fire, satisfied to know that all was as it should be in the house, having checked all the rooms earlier. Young Hector had got good fires burning in both the drawing-room and the dining room, a warm welcome for their guests, just as important as good food.

She sat back and sniffed with satisfaction. Mrs Macquarie would have no complaints, nor Mary, the widow – aye, both women should be very pleased with all the work she had done on their behalf.

*

In the drawing-room, her emotions still in turmoil, Mary Jarvis was finding it very difficult to converse with the other mourners, but as George's widow she knew it was her duty to do her best to be sociable, especially to those people who had taken the time and trouble to travel up to Mull, some from as far as London.

She accepted a glass of sherry and looked around at the guests … most of them she did not know, and most of them seemed more eager to speak with Elizabeth rather than her.

There was only one gentleman she recognised, a man in his sixties, and he was standing with his back to the fireplace warming himself while drinking his whisky – a very stern-looking man, Mary had always thought, although she personally had never spoken with him.

Lord Strathallan, the new executor of the Jarvisfield estate and young Lachlan's legal guardian, saw Mary's eyes on him and he smiled at her.

Hesitantly, she smiled back, and he immediately crossed the room to speak with her, very gently.

'Mrs Jarvis, my sincere condolences.'

'Thank you.'

'I remember George as a very beautiful young boy, only ten years old when I first met him, and well … it is fitting that he should now be laid to rest in the same grave as Lachlan.'

Mary's interest instantly quickened. 'You knew George … when he was a *boy*?'

Lord Strathallan nodded. 'The first time I met George was in China. Of course then and there I was not called Lord Strathallan, just plain James Drummond, a doctor attached to the East India Trading Company in Macao.'

Mary knew all about George's visit to China with Lachlan and Jane, Bappoo and Marianne, but he had never mentioned the fact that Lord Strathallan had been there too.

'Over the years, of course,' Strathallan continued, 'during my stop-off in India, and then my return to Britain, Lachlan and I became good friends, close friends, and during that time I came to know George very well too.' His face became stern and stiff again. 'It is very sad that he has died so young.'

Mary could not bear to think about that. She looked across the room at a man who seemed to be hogging Elizabeth's attention.

'Who is that gentleman speaking with Mrs Macquarie?' she asked.

Lord Strathallan turned and looked. 'Oh, that is Charles Forbes, another old friend of Lachlan's from India. He returned to England some years ago and is now a member of our Parliament. He also knew George very well.'

Mary then spent a further hour in the company of Lord Strathallan while he pointed out various people to her and told her who they were, as well as numerous little stories about them, but the only stories she fully heard were the ones that contained scenes of George in them.

When the time came to go to the dining room to eat, Mary accepted Lord Strathallan's arm and was pleased to find she would be sitting next to him at table, simply because he was the only guest she knew, and she was also eager to hear more of his stories about George.

As she moved to sit down, one of the local girls serving as maids came and whispered to her. 'Mrs Jarvis, there's a man and a woman outside the front door, asking to speak to Mrs Jarvis.'

Mary looked at the girl perplexed. 'Who are they?'

'I don't know, I didna see them. Mrs Keillor just said to ask ye if you would mind going to speak to them. She said they've travelled down from Tobermory.'

Mary excused herself to Lord Strathallan and left the dining room, crossing the hall with trepidation. She didn't know anyone in Tobermory.

At the open front door she saw a short wiry man with very bushy eyebrows and a short fat woman standing beside him, both muffled up to the nose with scarves and shivering with the cold.

'Yes?'

'Mrs Jarvis?'

'Yes.'

'Mr George Jarvis's widow?'

'Yes.'

'I'm Angus McLeod,' said the man, 'the proprietor of the Tobermory Inn. We came here on this sad day, if ye don't mind, to pay our last respects to Mr Jarvis, who we liked reet well, aye, very well indeed, and to give our sincere condolences to his widow.'

'Why ... thank you.'

'And I've brought you a gift,' said Mrs McLeod, opening up a parcel and taking out a small pillow covered in a white linen case on which the name *George* was embroidered in blue and surrounded by little blue embroidered flowers.

'It's just a little comforter,' Mrs McLeod said gently, 'something for you to hold on to in these first early nights of such sadness. I made one for myself when my wee boy was taken many years ago, and aye, it helped me through, having something with his name on to hold.'

Mary's heart was thumping and her eyes brimming with tears as she took the pillow into her hands, looked down at the name, and then held it close to her chest.

'You don't need to be told, I suppose,' Mrs McLeod added, 'that those blue flowers are called "forget-me-nots". I would have covered the whole pillowcase in them but my time to finish the embroidery by today was so short.'

Mary was breathing slowly and painfully in an effort to calm her emotions. 'Please, come in,' she opened the door wider and beckoned them inside. 'Please, come in ... you must have some refreshment to warm you after your journey.'

She turned and saw Maggie Kennedy still hovering nearby

and listening to every word.

'Maggie, will you take Mr and Mrs McLeod to the kitchen and tell Mrs Keillor to see that they are well looked after.'

'Aye, Mrs Jarvis.'

Mary turned back to the couple, too emotionally moved for any more words other than to say again, 'Thank you.'

And then turned and ran to her bedroom where she flung herself down on the bed, still hugging her new comforter and crying, 'Oh, George, George ... I miss you so much ... we *all* do!'

Chapter Twelve

Later, looking back, Elizabeth was able to pinpoint the time of George's death as the time of the sudden and disturbing change in the personality of her son.

Overnight, it seemed, Lachlan had changed from an angelic young boy into an absolute devil, vicious and violent in his tempers.

He had reacted to the death of his father with tears, but he had reacted to the loss of George with *rage* – fighting with everyone in the household and even managing to give Hector a bloody nose.

'You damn swine! Don't you *dare* say George was to blame for the horse's death!'

'He was! He shouldna have taken him out in the dark when I told him snow was acoming!'

At the sound of the raised voices Elizabeth had stepped into the yard only seconds after Lachlan had lunged at Hector, knocking the surprised stable boy to the ground and punching him hard in the face.

'Hoigh! Hoigh!' Mrs Keillor had cried in shock. 'That's no way for a young Scottish gentleman to behave!'

Lachlan had looked over his shoulder at the housekeeper with pure hate on his face.

'I'm not Scottish, I'm *Australian!* And I'm going back there! This country kills people when they come here – first my father and now George. I hate this place, I *hate* it!'

'He has always been such a *good* boy,' Elizabeth later insisted to Mrs Keillor, 'but he is still very distressed.'

'As we all are, Mrs Macquarie, as we all are, but that was a terrible lathering he gave poor Hector. And aye, it's left me dazed, because I wouldn't have thought young master Lachlan was capable of such violence in his temper.'

Two days later Elizabeth again found herself defending her son in response to complaints from his tutor, Mr Meiklejohn.

'He is distressed, as we all are, Mr Meiklejohn,' she insisted impatiently. 'You *know* Lachlan is a good boy. You have said so many times yourself?'

'He *was* a good boy,' Mr Meiklejohn replied crisply, 'but now he's behaving like a *crazy* person.'

'Crazy?' Elizabeth's expression became icy, her voice chilled. 'If that is your opinion, Mr Meiklejohn, then you may end your role as his tutor immediately.'

Meiklejohn paused for a moment, and then replied quietly, 'If that is your wish, Mrs Macquarie, but if you will pardon my temerity, may I also say, with all due respect, that Mr Jarvis was right ... it really is time that Lachlan was sent *out* to school. He's now at an age when he needs the company of other boys like himself.'

'Like himself? *Crazy* boys?'

'Bright boys, of his own age, and of his own class. Boys who will be his friends and help him to have some enjoyment in life, not cooped up in this house with bereaved adults. I'm quite sure if he *did* go out to school it would help him to recover from the loss of both his father and Mr Jarvis more easily.'

Elizabeth's expression was still cold. 'And what kind of school do you suggest for my son, Mr Meiklejohn?'

'The tutor hesitated for a moment. 'I would suggest a ... a *boarding* school, away from his home.'

'Away?' Elizabeth looked shocked at the suggestion. 'Away from his mother?'

'Away from his pain, his heartache, and his overwhelming feelings of loss.'

PART TWO

Chapter Thirteen

It was not until eight years later that Lachlan Macquarie Junior finally returned to his home on the island of Mull.

During those years he had been educated in England, at schools in Woodford and Finchley, and now, at nineteen, coming on twenty, he was a very different person in every way to the boy who had left the island all those years ago.

Disembarking from the ferry at Tobermory, he hired a horse from the local blacksmith and while it was being harnessed he decided to refresh himself with a drink and some food inside the Tobermory Inn.

Angus McLeod was at his counter, engrossed in conversation with another old local, and neither man seemed aware of Lachlan's entrance.

'And because there was such a sswell on the ssea we had trouble keeping the lobsster pots deep enough for a catch,' the local man was saying to Angus. 'Nay, tiss no' like the old days, twass much better then, there was more people on the island, more people to ssell to.'

Angus nodded. 'And these days – the high cost of everything! I dunno how I keep this place open, especially with the high price ye charge me for the lobsters.'

'Nay! I charge no more than any other fisherman, Anguss! *Everything* iss more costly these days. Now, how much were ye charged for the building of yer new boat? More than ye were charged for the building of the old boat I'll wager.'

'Aye, a lot more! And I'm thinking I was mebbe robbed on that, aye, robbed.'

'Good morning, gentlemen.'

The heads of the two men turned around to look at the tall golden-haired young man who appeared at first glance to have stepped in from a life of luxury, judging by the fine navy corduroy of the riding jacket and breeches he was wearing and the white silk at his neck.

'Good day to ye, sir,' Angus said, instantly recognising the young man to be of the Quality and jerking alert. 'Is it a room or a meal I can provide ye with?'

'Some breakfast please.'

'I have a nice quarter of grouse pie left,' Angus offered.

Lachlan raised a cynical eyebrow, a half smile on his face. 'That wouldn't be the same last quarter of grouse pie you offered to Minister Bannon eight years ago?'

'What? Eight years ago?' Angus looked utterly perplexed.

'When I was last here, in the company of Mr George Jarvis.'

'Mr Jarvis?' After a moment, Angus's eyes opened wide. '*Ye* were the young laddie with Mr Jarvis that day? The day he cured my headaches! Och, now I remember ye, aye, ye were with him when he took away my wee skull.'

The fisherman who clearly had a problem with his s's was now looking eagerly at Lachlan, eager to get a word in.

'If ye'll pardon me, ssir, but ye'll no' get a finer breakfasst than a good lobsster, sstraight from my own ssea potss and fressh ass the dawn.'

The thought of the ignorant and bigoted Minister Bannon chomping on that last quarter of grouse pie all those years ago made Lachlan smile at the fisherman. 'Lobster it is then. I'm sure it will taste delicious.'

The fisherman beamed. 'Thank ye, ssir, ye're a sshentleman.'

'As I recall, the dining room is that way?' Lachlan said to Angus, pointing down the small corridor.

'Aye, sir, aye,' Angus said, continually nodding his head towards the dining room door until Lachlan disappeared through it.

'Ye see, Anguss,' the fisherman gloated, 'sshentlemen will always prefer the lobsster to any old pie. Ye sshould take more of them off me.'

Angus's eyes were still staring at the dining room door, musing to himself. 'Well, now ... wait'll I tell Lizzie. And he's grown to be handsome looking too. When he was younger he was as bonnie as a lass, but all that's gone now. Aye, he's a man now, as true as men come and as fine as they go.'

Angus looked at the fisherman. 'D'ye know who that is, Donald? That's young Mr Macquarie. Home to the west after being schooled for years in the south.'

'I knew he wass a sshentleman.'

'Och, he's more than that,' Angus replied. 'He's the new Laird of Jarvisfield. Least he soon will be, when he reaches the age of one and twenty.'

Angus jerked alert and waved a hand of dismissal. 'Now let me see to him and his breakfast, Donald, or he'll up and go. I'll need to heft in a bucket of water and get Lizzie to start boiling the lobster.'

Chapter Fourteen

The hired horse he was given was almost blind, plodding along dolefully no matter how many times Lachlan urged him on with his boot. The journey to Gruline seemed endless.

He took another deep breath of the air that was heavy with the fresh scents of summer and the clean smell of the sea. Only now, after such a long absence, and riding at such a slow pace, was he able to take in the true splendour and beauty of Mull's scenery, tranquil and sublime.

A world away from the noisy streets of London.

He thought back to those early days when his mother had decided he should be sent away to school; remembering how much he had wanted to go, and not wanted to go, finally deciding if he had to go anywhere his choice would be back to Australia, back to the sunshine and away from the deathly cold and ice of Mull's winters.

His mother had been horrified at the very suggestion of returning to Australia. 'There are no good schools there yet! And the schools your father opened are still in their infancy.'

He had then sought support for a return to Sydney from Mary, knowing how much she longed to go back, and wondering if she could take him there, telling her he didn't really need to be schooled anymore – he had learned enough from Mr Meiklejohn.

But Mary had changed since she had lost George, looking almost as horrified at the suggestion as his mother had done, but for a different reason.

'George is here,' Mary had said, 'and I will never leave him. I'm content to stay here in Mull now, and no doubt I'll end my days here. Go to England, Lachlan. You may want to get away from your memories of your father and George, but I don't.'

He remembered being very surprised when Mary said 'England' because he had believed that if he was going to be sent out to school, it would be to Musselburgh in Edinburgh, the same school his father had attended.

But no, his mother had other ideas. England was her choice because only in England could she kill two birds with one stone – install him in school, and then rent a house in London from where she could carry on his father's fight for the people of Australia.

And fight she did, with the only weapons she possessed. She informed the parliamentary representatives of the Colonial Office that she would not accept a penny of her husband's pension until his reports on that country were published and presented to Parliament for debate.

The Colonial Office decided they might publish some of the papers, but thought it politic if other papers were suppressed.

It took three years for her to win the battle, helped and aided by friends of his father who now lived in London. And when the *Macquarie Papers* were at last printed as a parliamentary paper and submitted to the House of Commons, his mother finally agreed to accept the pension.

But it was not the end, just the beginning. By the time he had moved up to school in Finchley she had enrolled the help of Sir James Mackintosh in her determination to lobby Parliament for the right of the Australian people to trial by jury.

Meanwhile Lachlan just got on with his own life, enjoying the company of his own friends, although as his tutor once wrote to his mother – *"Lachlan is good-natured and good-humoured but shows no inclination to study."*

Which was unfair, because he did study as much as any of the others, the only difference being that he did not seem to need to keep his head down for so long in order to show the tutors what a hard-working swot he was.

Lord Strathallan's son, William Drummond, also attended the same school in Finchley, and in him Lachlan had found his greatest friend and ally. By the time they were seventeen both were weary of being educated, truly bored with the whole tedious business of learning Greek and Latin and so many other useless subjects, preferring to sneak out at night to go into London and have as much fun as they could.

Of course they were found out in the end, much to the dismay of the other students who took great pleasure in hearing about their exploits, especially with the young girls from the music halls.

'Actresses, my darlings,' Drummond would tell them in his smooth intoxicated voice. 'All are actresses with no strait laces to untie.'

Neither had been successful enough to find out if the actresses had any hidden laces to untie or not, but Drummond's bragging and lying tales were always amusing to Lachlan, and excitingly shocking to the others.

All in the past now, all learning and schoolboy misbehaving was over. The time to grow up and behave like a man had come.

*

After he had been riding for some time he recognised a few of the tenants' cottages spread here and there and realised he was on his own land and nearing home.

Wearily the horse began to slowly pick his way down the narrow track to the road that led to the house at Gruline.

Lachlan was now certain that the horse was not only half blind, but also half dead.

'I've been ordered to get a stable boy and send you back straight away,' he said despairingly to the horse, 'but after all this plodding I don't believe you will make it back before next week.'

The horse pricked his ears at the sound of his voice.

'Truth to tell, I don't believe you will make it back at all, not unless you are watered and fed and given a good rest in the stables overnight.'

The horse seemed to wake up, pricking his ears again and shaking his mane.

'Ah, you like the sound of that, do you? A good rest, eh?'

As the horse reached the steep bend onto the road a sudden fierce barking erupted into the air and a dog charged at the horse, making it stumble with fright and almost fall.

'Judas!'

Lachlan quickly dismounted and caught the horse's reins.

'Bugger off!' he ordered the dog, but the sharp-nosed collie began to move even closer to the terrified horse who was whinnying and trying to back away.

'Go on – *bugger off.*'

'Robbie! Robbie!' A girl came running around the bend. 'Here, boy, here!' she called, slapping her knees. '*Now!*'

The black-and-white collie immediately lost his ill temper and trotted over to the girl, allowing her to stroke his head and calm him into a gentle nuzzle, her long black hair falling over the dog's face.

She was about twelve or thirteen years old, and Lachlan was about to rebuke her angrily for the dog's wild behaviour; but then she lifted her head and looked at him with an apologetic smile ... and although his mouth opened, his breath stuck in his throat and no words came.

'I'm sorry,' she said. 'Robbie thinks he's a Celtic warrior protecting our animals and land.'

Lachlan stood looking at her, like someone hypnotised and speechless. She was tall for her age, and slender, wearing black boots and a pair of boy's breeches under a loose shirt, but of all the girls he had ever seen in his young life, he had never yet seen one with a face of such heart-stopping beauty.

'We've been waiting for you,' she said, and then tilted her head sideways and looked at him curiously.

'You *are* Lachlan Macquarie aren't you? I could barely remember you, and we both must look very different now, so you probably don't remember me at all. I'm –'

'I know who you are,' he said quickly, because he had known as soon as she had lifted her face and smiled at him. 'You're George's daughter.'

*

Mrs Keillor had prepared a feast fit for a king. 'If he caught the morning ferry he should have been here long before now,' she said to Mary. 'Is Mrs Macquarie getting impatient?'

Mary nodded. 'Beth has gone with Robbie to watch out for him on the road.'

'What I canna understand is why he didna come back with his mother a week ago?'

Mary sighed with impatience. 'Because he's no longer a child! He's a young *man* now and he probably wanted the freedom to come back in his own time and in his own way.'

'And how d'*ye* know what he wanted or didna want to do in his own way?' Mrs Keillor asked curtly.

Mary sighed again. 'All I know is what Mrs Macquarie told me. Lachlan chose not to return with her because he had been invited to spend a week at Strathallan Castle with his friend William Drummond. And as Lord Strathallan is still his legal guardian, Lachlan did not think he could refuse the invitation.'

'Didna *think* he could refuse ...' Mrs Keillor chuckled. 'Didna *want* to refuse I'm thinking. From what I've heard that Lord Strathallan is always having parties on that estate of his, *lavish* parties where there's always plenty of whisky and foreign wine.'

'That is not our concern nor our business, Mrs Keillor.'

'So what young man would not want to go there for a week, eh? I know I'd go meself in a flash if I was asked.'

'Exactly,' Mary said.

*

The old horse, still nervous of the energetic young dog, kept backing-stepping and rearing his head as if wanting to turn back. Lachlan held tightly onto his rein and walked beside him. He apologised to Beth for being so late and bringing her out to look for him.

'Oh,' she replied, carelessly dismissing his apology, 'what does time matter?'

And that was true, here on Mull, Lachlan remembered. Keeping in time with Time held less importance here than it did down in London.

'That dog of yours – '

'Is a *working* dog,' she said quickly, unwilling to hear any criticism. 'But he's still very young and he was probably trying to round up the horse in the same way he rounds up the sheep.'

Lachlan smiled. 'Young and stupid then.'

'Robbie's not stupid, no, not at all!' she insisted. 'He can round up sheep and cattle and even the hens better than any other dog on Mull. Robbie has "the eye".'

'The eye?'

'Aye,' she said, 'a dog with "the eye" seems able to mesmerise animals, especially the sheep.'

He was feeling a bit mesmerised himself, but not by the dog.

'And when you want the lambs up and out and dogged up to the hills,' she added, 'Robbie's the dog to do it.'

She was looking at him seriously with eyes of the lightest brown under black lashes, and the pale tan of her face made her look sun-kissed after a hot long summer. God, those eyes of hers reminded him so much of George, and she had also inherited much of Mary's pale loveliness.

He looked away, out over the fields, and couldn't stop himself thinking that – despite her boyish clothes – if she looked so beautiful now, at the age of twelve or so – how in God's name would she look at the age of sixteen?

Curiously he asked her, 'Why are you wearing boys clothes?'

'Why? Look at my boots!'

He looked at her boots; the soles and heels were very muddy.

'How so?'

'I took Robbie for a walk and a play in the stream. He doesn't like being washed so I have to pretend we are just going for a walk along the bank, but he always charges in, trying to round up the ducks, and by the time he comes back to the bank he's shaking himself so hard to get all the hated water off that he ends up nice and clean.'

Robbie raised a whiskered eye to Beth, knowing she was talking about him again.

'I often plough about in the mud of the vegetable garden too,' she said, 'and it would be silly to do that wearing petticoats and skirts.'

There was something about the breeches and loose shirt that clicked on a memory. 'Where did you get those clothes?'

She smiled guiltily. 'From the wardrobe in your room. I found them a few months ago. You left quite a few clothes behind when you went down to London. Do you mind?'

'Not at all,' he said smiling. 'Do they look like they would fit me now?'

Yet the fact that she was wearing his clothes caused Beth a sudden and strange feeling of embarrassment.

Robbie seemed to sense it, and rubbed his head against her leg. Beth bent to stroke his head and then returned to her former topic.

'Without the mesmerising eye, a sheepdog is fairly useless. Did you know that?'

'No.'

'And Robbie has the magic in *both* of his eyes.'

'Which is more than my horse has,' Lachlan said. 'Not even one good eye. The poor thing is almost blind. And Robbie there nearly frightened the life out of him.'

Hearing the tone of disapproval in the young man's voice, and sensing that the young man did not like him as much as his mistress did, Robbie sauntered over to Lachlan and began to sheepishly lick the back of his hand.

'He wants you to like him,' Beth said.

Lachlan laughed and bent to stroke the dog's head. 'I don't *dislike* him, I just feel very sorry for my horse. A number of times I had to dismount and walk part of the way just to give him a rest. He really should be put out to pasture and not hired out to anyone.'

Beth stopped the horse, turning to stand directly in front him, putting her hands on each side of his face and staring into his eyes.

'Aye, his sight is very bad. It's terrible that he should be still made to work in his old age. Why don't you buy him and put him out to pasture in one of the fields near the house?'

'Buy him?' It was an idea that would never have occurred to Lachlan, and it appealed to him.

'How much would you say he is worth?'

'Oh goodness, nothing at all,' Beth replied. 'But if you sent the blacksmith a few shillings more than he would expect for the horse, then I believe he will probably be over the moon and very relieved to get rid of him.'

Lachlan smiled, a perfect solution. 'The pasture field it is then,' he said.

She looked away from him, towards the entrance to the

leafy lane that led up to the house, and from where Elizabeth had just emerged, a cloak slung loosely over her shoulders, her hands held out in greeting and her face smiling as she walked towards her son.

'My dear ...'

He bent and kissed his mother's cheek, and then suddenly remembered. 'I picked up a letter for you at Tobermory – it looks very serious, from a firm of solicitors.' He took the letter from his jacket pocket and handed it to her.

'They're not suing you for being a nuisance to the grand members of parliament are they?'

Elizabeth laughed. 'Let them dare!' She scrutinised the envelope and the name and address stamped on the back. 'Now this *does* look interesting.'

Mary!' Lachlan could hardly believe his eyes as Mary also strolled out of the lane. Mary had not changed one bit – still as lovely as ever. She walked towards him with the same expression of surprise, because *he* had changed so much.

'Oh my!' Mary laughed with pleasure. 'I was not expecting you to be so tall and ... and *grown-up!* I've been reminding myself that you're a man now, but I keep seeing you in my mind as the boy you used to be!'

'Oh, he's long gone,' Lachlan grinned, and seconds later he was pulled inside Mary's arms. 'Oh, my handsome! Come here and give me a hug like in the old days.'

Mrs Keillor then arrived on the scene, panting and puffing towards him as she hailed, 'Welcome the prodigal son! Home at last and I have a fine feast ready for ye!'

When Lachlan eventually looked around, Beth was walking away towards the lane in a long-legged young stride with Robbie following at her heels. Behind him the horse was hungrily tearing at the grass on the bank and munching ravenously.

'Let's all go inside now,' Elizabeth suggested, clearly eager to open her letter. 'Lachlan – were did you get such an old horse?'

Lachlan sighed. 'From a hard-hearted rogue in Tobermory.' He caught the reins and pulled the horse away from the grass, leading him forward. 'He badly needs to be watered and fed.'

In the stables, Hector – who was now also older and taller – had been feeling nervous and very uneasy about the young master's return, remembering how viciously Lachlan had once felled and punched him.

Yet when it came to discussing the state and pity of the horse, he and Lachlan were of one mind and in one accord.

'That blacksmith should be put in a box for working a horse this old and blind,' Hector said angrily. 'If twere up to me I'd guide him straight to the gallows for it.'

Lachlan nodded agreeably. 'He deserves no less.'

'He does, aye. Will ye be taking him back?'

'No. He's on Macquarie land now, and on Macquarie land he'll stay.'

'That blacksmith though,' Hector added, 'won't take it kindly. He's a tough old bastard and no' a man of peace.'

'And I'll no' be caring how tough he is,' Lachlan shrugged. 'The horse is here and here it stays and I'll send him due financial recompense, which is *more* than he deserves to get.'

'Aye, aye,' said Hector, nodding his head in concurrence. 'He deserves the gallows and no less.'

By the time the old horse was brushed down and blissfully lapping up water from a bucket, the two young men were almost friends.

*

Elizabeth waited until they were all seated at dinner before she revealed the details of her letter; although it was to Mary she gave the details and not Lachlan.

'Do you remember some months ago, Mary, I wrote and told you that my Aunt Henrietta had died in London?'

'Yes. She was very old though, wasn't she?'

'Oh, very old indeed.' Elizabeth placed her napkin on her lap as Mrs Keillor walked around the table serving ladles of hot chicken broth into the soup bowls.

'When I was at school in Hammersmith I used to stay with her at her house in Wigmore Street,' Elizabeth continued, 'but later, much later, when her son Lord Breadlebane married and started a family of his own, Henrietta removed herself to a smaller house in Upper Charlotte Street, just off Portland Place.'

Elizabeth then directed the rest of the information to her son, as it affected him the most.

'That letter, Lachlan, was from Henrietta's solicitors, informing me that in her will Henrietta has not only left to me her town house in Upper Charlotte Street, but also the sum of two thousand pounds.'

Mrs Keillor almost dropped the bowl of broth. '*Two thousand* pounds! Grief! – that's a fortune in money, ma'am!'

'A *small* fortune, yes,' Elizabeth replied, giving Mrs Keillor a look that said it was not her place to comment on it.

'So, now that we will have our very own London residence, Lachlan, I think I may return there shortly to carry on my work.'

'Your work?'

'Yes, for Australia – trial by jury.'

'Oh, Mother ...' Lachlan shook his head. 'Do you honesty think that one woman on her own –'

'But it won't be one woman on her own,' Elizabeth cut him short. 'In a few months time D'Arcy Wentworth will be arriving in London from Sydney, *also* to lobby parliament with me on behalf of the emancipists – and William Redfern should be arriving any day for the same purpose. Do you remember him, Lachlan, young Dr Redfern? He delivered you.'

Lachlan smiled. 'Yes, I do remember Dr Redfern, but not as far back to the day of my birth.'

'And also supporting us will be Sir Thomas and Lady Brisbane.'

'Brisbane? I thought you *hated* Brisbane?'

'I did.' Elizabeth shrugged. 'But that was before I had personally met him. However, one must be fair, and I must admit I was very surprised when he and Lady Brisbane called on me in London, and despite some initial tension between us, I found them to be nice people. Brisbane's whole attitude to Australia has changed. He had been Governor-General in Sydney for only a year before the Exclusives turned on him because he wouldn't do their bidding in their continued opposition to any rights for the emancipists. That's why he resigned and came back so swiftly. And Lachlan – these are the sort of people we need on our side – people who *know* New South Wales and *know* how unfair it all is there.'

Mary was nodding in agreement; but Beth, now wearing a blue dress, and knowing absolutely nothing about New South Wales – not even the fact that her mother had once been a convict there – was feeling utterly perplexed by it all.

'How is it unfair?' she asked Elizabeth. 'In what way?'

'Because of the *Exclusives*,' Elizabeth replied, and Lachlan turned up his eyes knowing Beth had opened the subject of his mother's deepest-held annoyance.

'"The "Exclusives" are a bunch of penny-farthing nobodys who emigrated as free-settlers to New South Wales,' Elizabeth informed Beth. 'And the word *free*-settlers suited them well, oh yes, because without a penny in their pockets they had arrived in Sydney seeking to build their fortune on the *free* government land grants and the *free* labour of the convicts. Ignorant upstarts who then set themselves up as the mock "gentry" of the country, or as they preferred to term themselves, the *Exclusives*.'

Lachlan could see that Mary's face was flushing a deep red, but his mother was so impassioned she didn't seem to notice.

'Mother ...' he said, attempting to change the subject

'My husband despised them,' Elizabeth continued, looking at Beth. 'He rejected outright their demand that all emancipated convicts should be forced to continue in a life of servitude to them – even though they had served their sentence - and he also rejected their demand that any man who had once worn leg-irons should *never* be accepted into any of the places frequented by free-settlers.'

Beth could not understand her indignation. 'If I was a free settler I would not wish to mix with murderers and villains.'

'Murderers and villains?' Elizabeth almost laughed. 'My dear, that is why the politicians here in England needs to *know* about New South Wales, the truth of it. The real villains are the magistrates and judges that send people out there for no good reason under law – other than to get rid of as many of England's poor as they can.'

'But murderers?' Beth protested, 'Someone who has actually *killed* another human being?'

'Murder,' replied Elizabeth patiently, 'is a capital offence, Beth, and it carries only one sentence – death. Anyone who commits murder is disposed of on the gallows. A very different type of felon to the ones unjustly transported to New South Wales. My husband was severely criticised by the Exclusives for what they called his "light-handed" treatment of felons, but that was because he knew that many of those felons were mere youngsters sentenced to seven years in Botany Bay for what he considered to be trifling misdemeanours ... such as a young servant couple getting married without their master's permission, or an eleven-year-old boy sentenced for stealing a pie, or a twelve-year-old girl sentenced for filching a strip of lace from her mistress's sewing basket.'

'A twelve-year-old girl – *my* age,' said Beth, blanching with horror at the very thought of it. 'And did *she* have to wear leg-irons?'

'No, never, at least not while my husband ruled. All young girls were usually employed as servants or sent to work in the government wool factory.'

Lachlan was watching Mary who had not touched a morsel of her food while his mother and Beth continued their conversation. As he remembered, this topic of the convicts was the only aspect of Australia that Mary had always preferred not to talk about – and especially with Mrs Keillor or any of the Scottish servants lurking nearby.

'Yes, the wool factory, I remember that,' Lachlan said quickly, looking at Beth, 'because Australia has such fine grazing land for sheep, but alas, no good sheep *dogs* – not like your Scottish collie with his magic eye.'

'No sheep dogs?' Beth looked disbelieving. 'So how do they round up the sheep?'

'The men do it. The only dogs in Australia are dingoes. Wild dogs who hide out in the bush and the forests, and the only thing a dingo would do for a sheep is eat it.'

'Tell Beth about my tame wallabies,' Elizabeth suggested. 'Oh, I was so fond of my wallabies, even if all they did throughout the day was sleep.'

And now the subject had been diverted to Australia's animals, Mary glanced at Lachlan and smiled, appreciatively.

Chapter Fifteen

The following morning, Hector brought out one of the Macquarie horses for Lachlan to ride.

'This is more like it,' Lachlan said admiringly, looking over the strong young horse.

'Aye, yon Mr Dewar got this one for Mrs Macquarie from a good trader over in Oban,' Hector said. 'And Mr Dewar was careful in his choice, seeing as the mistress is such a fine horsewoman. Three years old he is, and a nice nature, though sometimes he do get a bit frisky if he's made go too long without a gallop.'

Lachlan raised an amused eyebrow. 'I can't believe my mother does much galloping.'

'Nay, she takes it steady most of the time, that's why Wentworth will be happier with a young man on his back.'

'Wentworth?'

'That's what she named him. After some man who crossed a mountain.'

Hector glanced up at Beth who was already mounted on her grey mare, patiently waiting; dressed in a brown riding jacket and brown skirt and wearing a black three-cornered hat.

'Miss Jarvis likes to gallop though,' Hector grinned. 'You should see her go – fasterer than the wind sometimes.'

Beth pulled slightly on the reins and gave her horse's head a tug. 'And we are eager to be off.'

Lachlan mounted, back-stepping his horse to allow Beth to lead the way down the lane. She knew all the tenants and had offered to take him round to meet some of them and introduce them to their future laird.

She set the pace of the horses to a trot, but once they were free on open land she sped up to a race until Wentworth was getting the fast gallop he so badly needed.

At times, to Lachlan, it felt as if he and Beth were moving together, racing pace for pace through the warm wind, and after his years in London the freedom and the speed felt exhilarating and joyful.

By the time they reached Robert Dewar's house they were both laughing at the fun of it.

Robert Dewar had come out to greet them. 'I saw ye both coming from yon distance. I thought the devil himself was chasing ye.'

Beth was still laughing as she jumped down. 'Mr Dewar, this is Mrs Macquarie's son, Lachlan. Home from England.'

When Lachlan dismounted she told him, 'This is Mr Dewar, our farm manager, he takes care of everything for us.'

As the two men shook hands, Dewar smiled amiably and said to Lachlan. 'I remember ye well. Ye came here once with your father, and a then a few more times with Mr Jarvis.'

'Did I?' Lachlan had no memory of it, but then he had blocked off a lot of memories when he had left Scotland all those thousands of moons ago.

After leaving Robert Dewar they rode over the land, stopping here and there to meet cottagers and their wives, declining all invitations to come inside for a drink or a bite to eat; pausing to talk with farm labourers while dogs barked and chased their horses as they rode off again.

One thing Lachlan noted remarkably was that every single cottager and farm labourer appeared to love the young girl on the horse. All appeared to know her very well, so she obviously did not spend much time cloistered up in the house.

'How do they all know you so well?' he asked her. 'Tenants are not usually so familiar with anyone from "the House".'

Beth sat on her horse silently for a long moment, allowing the mare to chomp at the grass.

'I'm a working girl, just like Robbie is a working dog,' she said quietly. 'And all the people you have met today are my friends. It's not my choice to sit around a house all day, so I like to be out and about working with the people.'

'What about your education – schooling?'

'Oh,' she smiled, 'Mr Meiklejohn says I am a fine attentive pupil, and much easier to teach than you.'

'What?' Lachlan laughed. 'Meiklejohn is teaching *you* now?'

'Aye, he's been schooling me since I was five. He says I have my father's intelligence.'

'Oh, if you have *that,*' Lachlan told her, turning his horse around, 'then you already possess far more intelligence than I do.'

She laughed at his self-deprecation, and moments later they were racing again, towards Gruline and home.

*

And so it continued, all through the summer. To the cottagers and farm labourers the sight of young Mr Macquarie with Miss Jarvis at his side had become a regular occurrence. Like brother and sister they were in their manner, but not so in their looks. One older and one much younger, one handsome and one pretty, one with fair hair to his collar and the other with long flowing hair that was as black as coal.

Hector didn't like it, didn't think it was right.

'And why not?' asked Mrs Keillor.

'Well, he is what he is, a gentleman of land and property, and she is what she is, the daughter of his mother's maid.'

'Och, Mary is more than that to the mistress. She's one of the family, and well ye know it.'

'No matter how the mistress puts Mary in charge of the house an' all, and allows her to eat with them an' all,' Hector insisted, 'Mary's still one of us, one of the servants. But the way *he's* treating Beth now, like she's his own equal. He's spoiling her, and so now she's started showing me airs and graces that she never had before – airs and graces above her station.'

'Doona be daft.' Mrs Keillor chuckled. 'Beth has never shown any airs and graces, no to me and no to ye, so doona be making things up.'

In her chair by the fire, Mrs Keillor sat back and folded her arms, her eyes narrowing in thought.

'He's changed, he has.'

'Aye,' Hector agreed. 'He's grown to be fair enough in his ways.'

'Highly-strung he could be as a lad' Mrs Keillor continued,

'with a temper in him, but only for some of the time. Mostly he was full of fun and chatter and light-hearted. Now ... well now he just seems to be light-hearted all the time with no temper left in him at all.'

'She's too young to be alus going everywheres with him, and he's too old to be alus going everywheres with her.'

'Mebbe he's biding his time until she gets a wee bit older.' Mrs Keillor shot Hector a shrewd look. 'Same as ye are.'

'Me?' Hector's expression of annoyance gave way to one of surprise. 'I'm no biding for anyone.'

'Ye like her though, young as she is. Ye've seen the way the future beauty is beginning to show in her now.'

'I like her, aye, but I'm no biding for her!' Hector protested. 'Why would I do that? My family is pure Heiland and pure Scottish, and God' blood! – my father would no' allow our Scottish bloodline to be tainted by a foreigner.'

Mrs Keillor gawped at him in astonishment. 'Beth's no foreigner. She was reared in this house since she was a bairn in arms.'

'Aye, but she was still sired by an Arab from India or wherever it was Mr Jarvis came from. Her bloodline and stock is inferior. If she was a horse, a mare, she would no' fetch as high a price as a Scottish mare. A lot less would be her price, and that's only if anyone would be willing to take her at all.'

Mrs Keillor blinked, not sure if she fully comprehended what Hector had just said to her; but as unsure as she was, she shot him a look of fierce warning.

'Ye'd better be careful, me laddie, and make sure ye no' let the young master or Mary or Mrs Macquarie hear ye talking in that way about young Beth. Because if they *do* hear ye talking that way, ye'll be kicked out on your backside by the mistress, and likely Mr Lachlan will find his temper again and spill that pure Scottish blood of yours all over that lane outside.'

'But ye ken I'm right in what I said?'

Mrs Keillor shut her eyes tight and put a finger to her lips, shaking her head as she hissed, 'I don't want to hear it, and I don't want anyone to find me listening to ye. Go now, Hector, leave my kitchen, I'll no' be a conspirator with ye in this. I'll no' let ye talk about Beth like this. So go, *go* – before I stop being civil and take my big iron ladle to ye!'

Chapter Sixteen

At the end of autumn, worried about the chilling effect of Mull's cold winters on her health, Elizabeth decided to spend Christmas in London at her new home in Upper Charlotte Street.

Once again she failed in her attempts to persuade Mary to accompany her, but Mary would not leave Mull, and Beth would not leave Mary.

'You don't need me down there with you,' Mary said. 'You'll have plenty of company with all your visitors, and you said most of your aunt's servants are all still in residence.'

'Oh yes, the servants ... a fine enough bunch.' Elizabeth pouted. 'But I can't chat away with *them* the way I do with *you*. Mary. Oh, my dear, I *will* miss you.'

Mary smiled. 'I know, love, but you'll not miss me as much as you think you will. After a week or so you'll be so busy and the time will just fly past until it's time for you to come back again. Is Lachlan not going down with you?'

'I haven't asked him yet, but I see no reason why *he* would refuse.'

Elizabeth successfully persuaded Lachlan to accompany her, insisting she needed his help in entertaining the Australian emancipists who were now in London and who would be calling on her regularly.

'And Lachlan,' she reminded him, '*you* are an Australian by birth, so *you* should also be playing your part in all this.'

Lachlan was happy to agree, deciding he would also invite his friend William Drummond to spend some time with them down in London, and this time their visits to the music halls would be less of a rushed and hushed event.

On the day before their departure, Lachlan and Beth rode over to Robert Dewar's house and received the usual friendly greeting from the farm manager.

'I see the cold wind has stung some red colour into your faces,' he said, smiling.

'Yes, it was a cold run today,' Lachlan nodded. 'And the

wind from the sea is fierce.'

'Well, seeing as it's the season, will you sit in and take some food and a wee dram with us, Mr Macquarie? We can leave business aside for an hour or so.'

'No food, thank you all the same, but a wee dram will warm the blood,' Lachlan replied, looking at Beth who nodded at him in agreement.

'A wee dram for myself also, Mr Dewar, she said, shivering.

Dewar looked surprised at her request. 'Are ye not too young for something so potent?'

'Not if it's just a wee one and you don't tell my mother.'

Inside the large parlour room of the Dewar's farmhouse, Lachlan was introduced to a few strangers – locals who appeared very pleased to meet the young laird – telling him they were just "looking in" on the Dewar family, seeing as it was near the time of Christmas and good will and cheer to all men.

'And is it young Miss Jarvis ye have with ye?' one asked, and once again Lachlan found himself thinking that everybody on the island seemed to know Beth.

One of the locals tried to stand up to shake Lachlan's hand, but half way up he collapsed back down in his chair again.

'Are you all right, Mr MacLaren?' Beth asked anxiously. 'You don't look so well.'

'I'm fine, lass, fine, I've just got a load on.'

'A load of what, Mr MacLaren?'

'A load of wee drams.'

Robert Dewar laughed and made Lachlan and Beth sit in seats close to the huge fire where they both quickly drank their drams of the warming whisky.

Lachlan's glass was instantly refilled, but when Beth held up her glass again with hopeful eyes, Robert Dewar shook his head in silent refusal.

'Now your father, General Macquarie,' said Jamie MacLaren, leaning towards Lachlan, 'I knew your father verra well. I could aye tell ye many a story about him.'

'Ye couldna have known him verra well,' his wife intervened, 'because he was never here! He was alus away somewhere with the Army.'

'In his red tunic, and as fair as yourself,' Kennedy continued as if his wife had not spoken, 'but that was a long while ago, when he came back from India and before he bought the land of Jarvisfield.'

Lachlan was interested, asking questions, and while his attention was diverted Beth slyly lifted his glass and quickly sipped from it.

More neighbours "looked in" as the afternoon went on and all hailed the young laird with great welcome. Mrs Dewar and her daughter handed round plates of thick slices of bread and cheese with slices of boiled ham on top, followed by plates of raisin and rum cake.

Some of MacLaren's stories were very funny to Lachlan, constantly making him laugh, because he knew they were all made up without a word of truth in them.

Beth leaned over and whispered to him curiously. '1817? Wasn't your father in Australia then?'

Lachlan nodded and spluttered more laughter while MacLaren continued in a proud tone, '"In my house" says he on that occasion, says General Macquarie – course he was only a captain then – "in my house, ye Jamie MacLaren, will alus be welcome!'

'But ye see, what I'm wondering now,' said MacLaren's wife, who had been watching Beth intently and not listening to a word her husband had said, 'what I'm wondering is ... where exactly were ye born, Miss Jarvis?'

'In the port of Saint Salvadore,' Beth answered happily, her cheeks flushed with too many wee drams.

'Saint who? So what place would that be?'

'Brazil.'

'Oh, Brazil ... so you're from a place called Brazil?'

'No, I was born on the ship coming from Australia to Britain, but at the actual time of my birth the ship had docked in the port of Saint Salvadore, which is at Brazil.'

Knowing that Mrs MacLaren had too much curiosity for her own or anyone else's good, Robert Dewar changed the subject to fishing. 'The next night we go out night fishing you should come with us, Mr Macquarie.'

'And the next time we go out,' Jamie MacLaren put in,

'we're going to try for a good catch in the waters off Calgary.'

Lachlan looked at MacLaren with some surprise. The man looked as if having "a load on" was a regular occurrence – surely not safe in a boat at night. 'Do *you* go night fishing too?'

'Aye, any fish on our table is alus a fish I've caught meself. Isn't that so, Peggy?'

He looked round for confirmation from his wife, but she had gone into the kitchen where she was whispering to Mrs Dewar and her daughter and two other women.

'She was born in a place called Brazil.'

'Oh, I ken where that is,' said Dewar's daughter haughtily. 'It's in Spain.'

'Is it?' Mrs MacLaren narrowed her eyes. 'Now that makes some sense of it all. I alus thought Mr Jarvis looked a bit Spainey ... those dark eyes and that black hair.'

'I alus thought Mr Jarvis was the handsomest man,' said Dewar's daughter, a plain girl of no remarkable looks. 'And such a *nice* man ... it was so sad what happened ... I cried when he died.'

In the parlour Robert Dewar interrupted another long story from Jamie MacLaren about General Macquarie, saying: 'It will soon be dark, Mr Macquarie, and the ride home will be even colder.'

'Yes,' Lachlan stood up, 'time to make a move.' Thank you for your hospitality Mr Dewar.'

His words were slightly slurred and his walk a bit unsteady.

Outside Robert Dewar was looking somewhat anxious. 'The local brew is very potent ... maybe ye've had a few too many drams, sir.'

'Don't be ridiculous,' Lachlan replied cheerfully. 'It would take a lot more than that to get *me* intoxicated.'

He quickly mounted his horse and almost fell off again down the other side, pulling himself back up in the nick of time. 'Boot missed the stirrup,' he said with a grin. 'Nothing to worry about, Mr Dewar. I'm as sober as Saint Salvadore.'

Beth laughed, not quite sober herself.

They rode off at a trot, and contrary to what Mr Dewar has

said, the air was not colder but much milder, the sky blanketed by a warming layer of thick clouds and the wind from the sea had dropped.

Neither seemed willing to go any faster than a steady jog. 'Did you enjoy your afternoon at the Dewar's?' Beth asked.

'I did, yes,' Lachlan nodded, and his tricorn hat fell over his face.

He pushed it back on his head and laughed. 'With the exception of that damn MacLaren woman asking you impertinent questions. If she'd asked *me* where *I* was born I would not have said Australia, I'd ha' said I was born in Timbuktu – and then see what gossip she made of *that!*'

Beth chuckled. 'Isn't it always more simple to just tell the truth?'

'Stone me! Tell the *truth* to a nosy old gossip when it's none of her business to ask? I'd be poxed if I would!'

Beth felt a wet drop on her face and looked up at the black sky. 'It's starting to rain.'

Chapter Seventeen

'Twenty is too young to settle down to the running of your Scottish estate, my boy. Your *mother* may want you to do that, but your father would want you to get some more experience of the ups and downs of life first.'

Lord Strathallan had also decided to spend Christmas in London, and during an evening at the Macquarie house in Charlotte Street, decided it was time to give his young charge a few words of manly advice.

'Plenty of time for you to settle in the future, plenty of time. I was thirty-seven before I left the rest of the world to get along without me. And it was only a year or two before I left the wider world that I met your father in Macao. Now, how difficult would it have been for me to meet your father in Macao, in China, if I had stayed in Scotland, eh?'

'Very difficult,' Lachlan agreed. 'Even, dare I say it, physically impossible.'

'And remember, the Jarvisfield estate is not yours yet, not until you are twenty-one.'

William Drummond looked at his father with bleary eyes, having imbibed too much wine during dinner.

'And you are still his legal guardian for another year.' Drummond knocked back the last of his wine. 'So tell him, father, tell him what you want him to do.'

Lachlan laughed. 'I know what *you* want me to do, Drummond. You want me to hold your hand while you march bravely into battle.'

'Your father spent his life soldiering in the Army,' said Lord Strathallan. 'Made a career of it.'

'And what was good enough for your father should be good enough for you,' William Drummond advised. 'At least for two or three years anyway. I've no intention of serving for longer than that – just enough time to get me the title of "captain". An officer and a gentleman and all that. Women love it!'

Lachlan sat musing: a few years in the Army may be

interesting ... especially with a sociable crackpot like Drummond at his side. And it would also serve as a sort of tribute to his father; following in his footsteps, like a good son, if only for a few years.

'I think he's actually considering it, Father, I honestly do.'

And after a few years away in the Army, when he returned to Mull, Beth would be older, nearer to womanhood ... the time would go quicker, the years would move faster ...

'Well, Macquarie?' William Drummond asked. 'Are you seriously considering it, or are you just having a short nap?'

Lachlan looked up with an amiable shrug. 'The Army it is then, for two or three years, why not.'

*

When Lachlan returned to Mull in early February, Mary was shocked to learn that he and William Drummond had signed up as ensigns in the 42nd Regiment.

'Had you both been drinking too much when you signed up?' Mary asked

'Well, we didn't just *sign up*,' Lachlan replied. 'It was a process that required much thought – and much money!'

Mary frowned, perplexed. 'What does money have to do with it?'

'A man can't just walk into the Army, sign a paper, become an officer, and then climb up on horseback and get on with it. We had to *buy* our commissions.' Lachlan shrugged testily. 'Money opens every door.'

'What's wrong with you?' Mary asked.

Taken aback by the question, Lachlan stared at her. 'Nothing is wrong with me.'

'Why are you so irritable then?'

'I'm not irritable. You're imagining things.'

Mary made no answer, but she kept looking at him. Maybe she was imagining things, and maybe she wasn't.

Lachlan glanced at Beth, annoyed that she was showing no reaction whatsoever to the news of his imminent departure overseas, sitting by the fire doing her sewing silently as if the conversation was none of her concern.

Or was it that she was even more like her father than he

had realised. George was always calm, even in distress, and never one for a rushed or a thoughtless response to anything.

'What say you, Beth?'

Beth paused in her sewing, but she did not speak, not until a few moments later when she asked, 'Where do you think they will send you?'

'I've no idea. I'm waiting for my orders to report. Probably first down to Portsmouth or Southampton to embark, then out to India or Egypt or somewhere in the East where the British have a presence. It definitely won't be anywhere as near to Britain as the European continent, Drummond assures me of that. No point, not since the defeat of Napoleon.'

Mary said, 'And your mother – '

'Will join me at whatever seaport it is and see me off. As will Lord Strathallan.'

'Did she approve of you joining the Army?'

'Well, she could hardly show any *disapproval*, could she? Not when she has spent all her married life as a soldier's wife.'

'Yes, but I know she was very anxious for you to settle down here on Jarvisfield and learn how to manage the estate. And there's also the – '

'We will miss you, Lachlan,' Beth said suddenly. 'India is so far away.'

'I will write, every week,' Lachlan assured her. 'Long letters filled with my news about every thing and every person I meet, be they sadhus, beggars, or bejewelled maharajas.'

Next morning, to everyone's surprise, the military dispatch containing his order to report was delivered by a horseman.

'Came in on the morning ferry,' he said. 'Military seals on it, so I rode out fast as I could.'

Lachlan rewarded him with some money, and then carried the dispatch into the drawing-room.

'Oh no, so soon,' Mary exclaimed in dismay. 'I was hoping it would not come for a few weeks at least.'

The sound of the horse had not escaped Hector's sharp ears, and when the horseman was brought around the back of the house and into the kitchen to have some refreshment before making his return journey, as was the Highland custom, Mrs Keillor was all ears.

'Military seals,' said the horseman, 'that's all I know.'

'His orders,' said Mrs Keillor to Hector. 'Must be.'

Panting and puffing with excitement, Mrs Keillor found Beth in the vegetable garden, kneeling and digging and wearing her male breeches again.

'Tis no' right for ye to be wearing breeches, m'lassie!' she said in disgust, then remembered why she had come out. 'He's got his marching orders – a horseman just brought them.'

Beth jumped to her feet and quickly brushed down her knees and then ran past Mrs Keillor who eventually caught up with her and followed her into the drawing-room.

'I'll kill Drummond!' Lachlan was saying angrily to Mary, his eyes aflame. 'He gave me no warning that *this* might happen!'

Mary held a hand over her mouth, and Beth wondered if she was trying to stop herself from crying.

'Well?' Beth asked. Where are they sending you? Is it to India?'

'No,' Lachlan replied through stiff lips.

'Egypt?'

'No.'

'Where then?' asked Mrs Keillor impatiently. 'Sakes alive – where's the Army sending ye then?'

'Timbuktu,' Lachlan replied.

No!' Beth gasped in astonishment. 'And only before Christmas you were saying – '

'He's not going to Timbuktu,' Mary said, still trying to stifle her laughter. 'Not as far as there.'

'No, but I wish I *was* going to Timbuktu!' Lachlan said angrily. 'Or even to Hell and back – anywhere but *this*!' He looked once more at the dispatch then walked over to the fire and dropped it onto the flames.

Mary took a deep breath and said steadily, 'They are sending him to Birmingham.'

'Birmingham ...' Mrs Keillor frowned. 'Where's that?'

'In the midlands,' Mary said. 'About halfway between here

and London.'

Chapter Eighteen

Lachlan served only three months in training with the 42nd Regiment, before he transferred to the 2nd Dragoons.

'If I am to spend my time in the Army based solely in Britain,' he wrote home to Beth, *'then at least it will be more enjoyable if I do it on horseback.'*

William Drummond, of course, had transferred with him.

'They don't treat the horses right, them dragons,' Hector said to Mrs Keillor. 'They ride 'em too hard and too fast and they dig their spurs into 'em.'

'Nay.' Mrs Keillor shook her head, tired of Hector's sly digs and griping about the young master. 'Them horses are trained to be *war* horses, fit for battles, so the dragons canna be mooning and sopping over them all the while like ye do.'

'Aye,' said Beth, entering from the garden carrying a basket of herbs and coming in on the conversation. 'Those horses are soldiers too, serving their country along with the men.'

Beth hadn't looked at Hector as she spoke, and she heard him breathe heavily before he replied.

'Aye, but who *asked* the horses if they wanted to be soldiers, eh? Who lifted their hoof and got them to sign up? Nay, the horses wasna asked, the horses didna sign anything – they was just roped in whether they wanted to be war horses or no'. And then them dragons ride 'em like bulls.'

'Lachlan would never ride a horse too hard,' Beth insisted. 'He loves horses as much as you do, Hector.'

'Nay, nay *nay*! Don't say that to me!' Hector replied angrily. 'No one loves or cares for horses in the same way as me. But that's yer trouble, Miss Beth, ye is incapable of even *thinking* a bad thought about Master Lachlan, the golden boy of Jarvisfield. Not one bad word, not one bad thought, have ye ever had about *him*.'

Beth was looking at him now, her brown eyes gazing at him in a very direct way as she said quietly, very quietly, 'No, I have not ever had a bad thought about him, Hector, because he has never given me any reason to think anything but the best of him, the *best*.'

When Beth turned and walked out of the kitchen, Hector seemed to be having trouble forcing the saliva down his throat.

Mrs Keillor chuckled. 'There now, that's told ye.'

*

In the two years that followed, Lachlan came home to Scotland twice a year and, as always, spent most of his time riding out and about with Beth.

During the third year he came home in time to celebrate Beth's sixteenth birthday, and William Drummond came with him. Both were now lieutenants, and in Drummond's company Lachlan showed a difference in his behaviour and attitude that was not his normal way, Mary noticed.

Two weeks after their arrival, when Mary took the trap into Tobermory to collect some personal provisions, and then later dropped in to see the McLeods at the inn, she learned that the two young officers had already caused quite a stir amongst the young people of the town.

'Lord's my life!' said Lizzie McLeod. 'The two of them! And that young laird of Jarvisfield – well, whenever we see him he's as likely to be kissing as many girls passing his way as he can, or brawling with any lads who object.'

'But it usually ends in laughter amongst them all, lads and lasses alike,' Angus put in, having become quite fond of the two red-jacketed young officers who frequented his inn a few nights of the week.

'But that tall and broad one,' said Lizzie. 'The one called William. By! – He can knock back the whisky as easily as I can drink water. Isna that so, Angus?'

Angus nodded his head happily. 'Spend a fortune in here they do. I've had to up my stock of whisky just to keep up with the one called William. Mind, he wasna pleased when I said I had no wine.'

'William Drummond,' Mary said. 'He's Lord Strathallan's son.'

Angus banged his fist triumphantly on the counter and then looked at his wife. 'I told ye, Lizzie, I said that William had money to waste. And now we know where he got it – from his rich father.'

'Where does he abide?' Lizzie asked curiously. 'This Lord Strathallan?'

Mary shook her head. 'I don't rightly know, somewhere on the mainland, in Perthshire I think. I heard William say one day that Strathallan Castle was about four hours ride to both Glasgow or Edinburgh, depending on which way you go.'

'And who made his father a lord?' Lizzie demanded to know.

Mary smiled. 'I don't know that either. All I know is that he is the 8th Viscount of Strathallan.'

'*Viscount?*' Angus was beside himself with excitement. 'And his son drinking in my inn, and even sleeping up in one of my rooms upstairs! Wait'll I tell the fishermen and my other neighbours.'

'Sleeping in one of your rooms?' Mary frowned. 'When was that?'

'Och, pay no heed to Angus,' Lizzie said quickly, catching Mary's arm and urging her down the passage towards the dining room. 'Come in to ma kitchen and have a drink and a bite before ye head back.'

Once inside, Lizzie McLeod rolled around her kitchen quickly making Mary some refreshment, but once she got her sat down and eating, Lizzie sat opposite her and began to tell Mary all the gossip she had collected since the last time she had seen her.

It was all tittle-tattle, mildly interesting, until Lizzie could not stop herself from telling Mary about William Drummond.

'I wouldna say anything,' Lizzie insisted, 'if Angus hadna let it slip out there. But the one called William, he's taken a room here on a few nights, and Angus is no' the only one who's been doing some slipping – because twice now, twice, I'm certain that one called William slipped a lass up there. I didna see her, mind, so I don't know which lass it was, but I know the giggling of a lass when I hear it.'

Mary's eyes were wide. 'And Lachlan? Did he take a room too?'

'Nay, he alus rode away on his horse, but I'd say he's as

102

familiar with women as that William is. He's no angel, no saint, that I can tell ye, he knows what's what, that's for certain – but that William,' Lizzie rolled her eyes and then whispered, 'he's a *devil* for the lasses.'

An hour later, as Mary drove the trap back to Gruline, she thought over everything Lizzie had told her, every little bit of conversation between the two men that Lizzie had heard from deliberately eavesdropping or had accidentally overheard.

Finally, Mary thought she had the picture, and it dismayed her, concluding that Lachlan was no longer the refined and innocent young gentleman he had been when he had left Mull to go to the Army.

No, with no battles to fight and no war to fear, and under the influence of that rapscallion William Drummond, he had now learned to drink hard and had become one of the "fast set" of his regiment, and – from what Lizzie had overheard – many of their escapades had not only been dicey and disorderly, but had also been wickedly debauched.

At Gruline, as the trap rolled along the road towards the house, she saw the two figures on horseback coming along the road. They were not galloping or even jogging along, but keeping their horses walking at a slow but steady pace, their heads turned to each other as if in deep conversation.

At sixteen, Beth was no longer the girl she had been either; her body had curved out and she was showing all the signs of the beautiful woman she was going to be. She wore a long navy riding habit with cream lace at the neck and cuffs, and a black three-cornered hat which brimmed the fall of her lustrous long black hair.

A soft passion of love came into Mary's heart and eyes as she thought, 'Oh George, my darling, I wish you could see her as she looks now, your beautiful daughter.'

Normally Mary would have turned the trap into the lane and left Beth and Lachlan follow her in at their own pace, but today she sat waiting for them, and watching them.

Lachlan looked as happy in Beth's company as he always did, and Beth was laughing at him in the same happy way. They were close those two, very close, and always had been.

When the trap had been emptied and Lachlan and Beth had stabled their horses, they came into the drawing-room where Mary was sitting stiffly.

She glanced at Lachlan coldly but he didn't seem to notice, coming over to her and kissing her cheek in the same affectionate and respectful way as always.

'Where is your friend William?' Mary asked.

Lachlan shrugged carelessly. 'God knows. He declined to come riding with us, so he has probably taken himself off to Tobermory. He seems to prefer the business of that town much more than our country life here in Gruline.'

'He told me he likes going to Tobermory because he enjoys watching the fishermen,' Beth said.

Mary now understood the small smile of amusement that Lachlan gave to Beth when she said this.

Yet at dinner, Lachlan was so much his natural self, his old self, as refined and as good mannered as he had always been, declining to drink any wine and showing nothing more than fond companionship to Beth as he had always done; so much so that Mary found herself wondering if much of what Lizzie McLeod had told her about him had been mere gossipy exaggeration.

*

On the day they were due to leave and return to their regiment, William Drummond sat in the drawing-room still attempting to charm Mary; and even though she could not stop herself from laughing at his funny wit, Mary was still convinced that he was a rake of the first order.

Lachlan was busily walking from room to room, searching for Beth, eager to have a last half hour or so with her, when perhaps they could take a walk along the bank of Loch Ba and talk in private; and maybe he could even give her some hints about his hopes for their future.

Out in the stables, he asked Hector, 'Have you seen Beth?'

Hector was busily harnessing the two horses in readiness for their departure. 'Aye, I know where she be.'

'Where?'

Hector pointed. 'Over in yon bluebell field talking and

laughing with the two fat cows.'

Lachlan grimaced. Beth's love of animals had no limits ... but to go off like this on the morning he was leaving for perhaps another year was rather remiss of her ... or maybe she had a very good reason.

'Is there something wrong with the cows?' he asked.

'Oh, aye, there's a lot wrong with those two fat cows,' Hector nodded positively. 'They could thin down for a start. Ye never see a horse lolloping around with flesh bouncing in all directions like that. No' a *good* horse anyways – nay, no' *any* horse as I've seen.'

Lachlan was getting confused, and somewhat irritated by Hector's habit of seeing every aspect of life from an equestrian viewpoint.

'It's bad enough,' Hector continued, 'when Mrs Macquarie is residing here and those two cows come to help Mrs Keillor and do the cleaning work, but now they're over here all the time when none of the Macquaries are here, including ye – over here telling Miss Beth stories and leading her along by heir reins, leading her *astray* I say.'

'Hector, what the pox are you talking about?'

'She's over in yon first field,' Hector replied, tightening one of the girths. 'They alus sit propping up one of the trees down there.'

Lachlan walked towards the bluebell field. There was a slight breeze stirring, but the morning sun had a soft warmth.

He walked down towards the loch until he finally saw the three of them ... lounging back against the thick trunk of the tree in the sunshine, and so wrapped up in their chattering that none were aware of his presence.

Beth was in the middle, between Maggie Kennedy and Lorna McLaughlin, lying back and smiling as she listened, while the two older females were sat upright, talking to each other over her head and laughing.

For one long moment he stood staring at Beth, at the seductive way she was lying back, without a care in the world. She looked like a beautiful dreaming princess in the company of her two older ugly sisters.

'Beth.'

Her brown eyes turned and looked at him; full of surprise, while the two others quickly pulled themselves to their feet and bobbed a slight curtsy.

'What are you doing?' he asked Beth curtly.

Beth moved to her feet and brushed bits of grass from the back of her dress. 'I'm enjoying the sun with my friends.'

'Your *friends*?'

'Aye, my friends, and you know them well, Maggie Kennedy and Lorna – '

'I know who they are,' Lachlan cut her off. 'I'm leaving shortly and I need to speak with you.'

Beth's brown eyes were wide again. 'Oh, is it *today* you are leaving? I thought it was tomorrow.'

Maggie and Lorna bobbed another curtsy and bustled away as quickly as they could.

Lachlan watched them go, and then eyed Beth reproachfully. 'You shouldn't be so familiar with the servants, nor should you be lying back like that, like ... like a farm girl.'

Beth half laughed. 'But I *am* a farm girl, Lachlan, what else could I be, living on a farm as I do.'

'You do *not* live on a farm, you live in the laird's house.'

'But I do *work* on the farm.'

'Nobody makes you work on the farm. Nobody makes you go out helping Robbie to dog the sheep or work in the vegetable garden. Nobody makes you do *anything,* Beth. So why can't you do as other young ladies do and sew or paint or read books?'

'I *do* read books, and I also do plenty of sewing, but those are things I do in the evenings, when there is little else to do. Why are you suddenly taking on so?'

Indignation flashed darkly in her eyes. 'And to tell me not to become too familiar with servants when my own mother is a servant in your house!'

'Mary is *not* a servant – not on that level at all. She is much more than that to our family, much more.'

'She is now your mother's housekeeper, and before that she was *your* nursemaid in Australia. Was she not a servant then?'

'Oh, enough,' Lachlan shrugged. 'I just wanted a short walk

and a talk with you.'

But it was too late for that now and both of them knew it. The mood was all wrong, and looking back he could see that Hector was already leading the horses out, saddled and bridled.

Lachlan's tone softened. 'I'm sorry, Beth, it's just that ... well, never mind that now, but next year I'll be back in time for your seventeenth birthday, even if I have to sell my commission in the Army I will, I promise.'

'Why?' She looked at him curiously. 'What's so special about my seventeenth birthday?'

'You are, Beth' he said softly. 'You are very special on any day or any birthday, but it's your seventeenth that I have long been waiting for.'

PART THREE

Chapter Nineteen

Elizabeth (Beth) Jarvis was a young girl of intelligence, but few complications. She had inherited not only her father's appealing good looks, but also his calm manner and dispassionate acceptance of life as it was, dealing with every day as it came, and rejecting most excuses to complain. Her nature was happy and gentle and considerate of others, and she considered herself very fortunate.

Her greatest love in life was the place in which she lived. Unlike others, she did not stand on the coastline of the island of Mull gazing out towards the wider world pining for more than she had, because she believed here on Mull she had it all.

Her home in the leafy countryside of Gruline was a secluded haven of peace, where the view of the green hills was stunning in the soft glow of a red sunset, and the silent serenity of Ben More and the smaller mountains calmed her spirit and then her eyes into a tranquil gaze, allowing her to dream.

And only here, in Mull, could she dream her favourite dreams.

As young as she had been when she had last seen him, she still had vivid memories of her father. Misty memories as if seen through a veil of thin white gauze; his wonderful smile when she looked up at him as he held her hand and walked her down to the stream, his calm voice as soothing as a summer breeze.

She had loved him then, and she loved him still, and the older she got the stronger she held onto her memories of him. As scant as they were, they were still enough to keep him alive in her heart and in her mind, and were added to over the years by the many little stories her mother told her about him.

And he was, very different, very special, and everybody had loved him.

And he was here, in the island of Mull, a fact that bound

her mother to this island and one of the reasons Beth had such a great love for it.

But she also loved Mull for itself, a natural paradise where golden eagles cruised in the sky and red deer paraded harmlessly amongst the hills. And down on the shore she loved watching the otters languishing on the rocks, their nature as happy and as playful as her own, making her laugh when they used the wet sand on the beach in summer or the snow or mud on the rocks in winter to make a waterslide and then sliding on it into the water for no other purpose than fun.

And she also loved the *people* of Mull, oh, the people were the best of all; wary of strangers but possessing kind hearts and easy smiles, she had grown up in the bosom of their friendship and caring community and loved them all, even though some were quite loony in their ways, especially Kirsty Dewar who never got any of her facts right, yet could never be persuaded that she might be wrong.

'Halooo Miss Jarvis!'

Checking her horse, Beth looked round to see who the caller was – and waved to an old man who many years ago had emigrated to Mull from the nearby island of Ulva, accompanied only by his pet goose.

'*Iolaire-suile-na-grein!*' he shouted, pointing upwards at a huge White-tailed eagle flying above her, and Beth nodded, knowing that was Gaelic for '*the eagle with the sunlit eye.*'

She paused to watch the White-tailed eagle as it cruised towards the coastline and the sea to catch a fish to take back to the mountains for its dinner.

She rode on, thinking that although The White-tailed were the biggest of all the seabirds, they were also the *meanest* in her opinion, because they were always swooping down to steal the fish caught by the otters and swooping away again.

Reaching Gruline, she slowed and turned her horse into the lane leading to the house, her slim young body relaxing on the horse as it plodded unhurriedly towards the stables at the back.

Before she had even dismounted Mrs Keillor came running out of the kitchen into the yard to greet her, all abustle and apuff and excitedly holding up a letter.

'A letter – for ye – from Master Lachlan! It says he'll be home in a week or two, for your seventeenth birthday in May, and with him he'll be bringing ye a very special present.'

Beth curiously turned the letter over, front and back, and saw that it was still sealed with red wax.

'It's unopened, as it should be, a private letter to me – so how do *you* know what he says in it?'

'Oh I don't *know* what he says in it,' Mrs Keillor said with a grin, her eyes all-knowing, 'but I think ye will find, my Bethey, that my guessing is correct.'

*

Sitting in the drawing-room reading the letter, Beth learned that Lachlan would not now be able to return to Mull in time for her seventeenth birthday.

His letter explained why.

With very short notice, his regiment had been posted over to Ireland, to a place called Limerick, and the first remarkable sight he had seen there, remarkable enough to write home about, was some of the most stunning horses in the world. Magnificent thoroughbreds that raced so lightly over the grass with a natural grace and speed it took your breath away. He was determined to buy one, and bring it back with him.

Until then he wished her all the best, and reiterated his wish that in the meantime she would not, *please do not*, become too friendly and familiar with the common servants such as Maggie Kennedy and Lorna McLaughlin, and also *to please stop* wearing breeches.

'Well?' asked Mrs Keillor, hovering curiously by the open door. 'Well?'

'Well, men are so *unobservant*,' Beth said indignantly, folding the letter. 'I stopped wearing breeches almost a year ago.'

Chapter Twenty

Elizabeth returned to Mull, as she always did in the summer, but this year she looked worn out, complaining of a constant cough brought on by the infernal smog in London.

'Why they insist on having their fires burning night and day down there is beyond me,' she complained. 'Chimneys chuffing out smoke and polluting the air all the time, especially at night. I never allowed a fire to be lit in my bedroom. I remember only too well what Dr McLean said about that. Have you seen him of late?' she asked Mary.

'No, no need,' Mary replied. 'We have all been well.'

'He will have to come and see to my chest, but first I will wait and see if a few weeks of our clean Highland air will cure it. Where's Beth?'

'Oh, she's gone up to the hills with Maggie and Lorna and a few more of the locals. There's a bonfire up there today.'

'A bonfire! On a warm day like this?'

Mary smiled. 'Yes, but in a few hours time it will be Midsummer's Eve.'

'Is it? Oh yes, of course it is. And the young must be allowed to celebrate and have their fun.'

Elizabeth sat back in her chair and smiled fondly at Mary. 'Now, my dear, it's time for us to share all our news. You first.'

*

The young people of Mull always celebrated Midsummer's Eve, as did many of the older ones, gathering to welcome in the Summer Solstice.

Everyone brought delicacies of food and drink of some sort to share around, and huge baskets of trout brought by the young fishermen were grilled over the fire. Musical instruments were also brought to the gathering by those who had them, and the sound of tinkling fiddles echoed through the air.

Holding hands with Maggie Kennedy and Lorna

McLaughlin, Beth was dancing in a circle around the bonfire and loving every minute of it. For years these two older girls had been her very best friends and she did not care if Lachlan approved of them or not.

Maggie Kennedy was singing happily and loudly as she danced, which sent Beth into fits of giggles, because the fisherman always complained that when Maggie Kennedy sang you could hear her far out at sea and it frightened the fish so much they dived straight down to the seabed and hid there until she stopped squawking.

Lorna McLaughlin had dressed herself up fine for the occasion, pinning a bunch of wildflowers into her hair and now they were falling one by one onto the ground as she danced.

Beth wore a simple green cotton dress with a wide black ribbon around the waist, as simple in style as her long black hair that had been tied back with a green ribbon.

'Ah, your fine Celtic headdress,' she said to Lorna when the dance was over, bending to pick up some of the fallen flowers.

'Aw!' said Lorna. 'Aw ... it took me hours to pick them flowers.' She looked at Beth's green ribbon. 'I tell ye what – you lend me your green ribbon, Beth, and ye can pin these nice flowers in *your* hair, the ones that are not crushed... look here's three that look as good as new, and a nice mixture of colours.'

'But with only one hairpin they'll fall out of *my* hair too when we dance again.'

'Aye,' Lorna whispered in a pleading voice, moving her face close to Beth's, 'but I need to look my best if I'm going to catch me a marrying man tonight, but ye've got one. You don't *need* the ribbon.'

'Me? What marrying man have I got?'

'Master Lachlan 'course. He's just been biding his time till yer old enough to be wedded and bedded. Ask Hector, that's what he do say. That's what *all* do say.'

Beth looked earnestly at Lorna and whispered back. 'And why do they *all* say that.'

'Cause of what they see – you and he alus everywhere together when he's here, and the way he *looks* at ye, Beth, even a fool like Hector kens what Master Lachlan has in his head. And lookit how he didna like seeing ye be so free with me and Maggie – that's 'cause he wants to make ye the *lady* of his house some day. But me, I'll be happy if I catch me a gleg fisherman, so give me the ribbon.'

Beth was a girl who rarely spent her time looking too seriously into the future, but now Lorna's words made her think about Lachlan's determination to come back in time for her seventeenth birthday ... and yes, the only reason for it's unusual importance was that he had probably intended to ask her to marry him.

The thought did not make her unhappy, it filled her with a pleasant warmth because she enjoyed being in Lachlan's company, and if their lives together were to continue more closely through a marriage then she would live on Mull forever and die happy.

She untied the green ribbon in her hair and gave it to Lorna. 'No, I don't want the flowers,' she said, shaking her hair loose, 'they will just fall off when I dance again.'

While Lorna fussed with her hair and the ribbon, Beth strolled over to where Maggie Kennedy was taking to a fisherman in a blue jersey, but to Beth's surprise Maggie's voice in response to the man's questions was no longer loud and normal, but doll-like and simpering.

Smiling, Beth strolled on. Thank goodness she did not have to spend *her* time looking for a suitable marrying man.

At the edge of the hill she stopped and looked up at the sky ... the golden globe of the sun appeared to be standing still, as it always did on Midsummer's eve. It was going to be a night that some of the fishermen would not bother to go out, because the sun stayed too high above the horizon and the time of darkness was short.

She stood looking out over Mull filled with contentment, loving its volcanic cliffs, it hills and forests and lochs. How, she wondered, could anyone wish to live anywhere else in the world?

As she strolled back to the bonfire she thought about Lachlan, and wondered if he was still enjoying his life in Ireland with all of its stunning horses.

In Limerick, Lachlan and William Drummond had just finished testing two of the finest horses in the county.

'Look at the legs, the sleek haunches,' Drummond said admiringly as his horse was led away across the stable yard. 'Thoroughbred, pure thoroughbreds, both of them.'

Lachlan grinned, filled with the same admiration and still exhilarated from the speed of the smooth ride. 'I think I might like to keep racehorses one day, breed them, train them, race them.'

Drummond cocked an eye. 'Not in Mull. The ground's not flat enough.'

'No, not in Mull, but maybe somewhere else in Scotland, somewhere flatter, on the mainland.'

'Not anywhere in Scotland, old chum, you would have to go further south, somewhere in England. Should be easy enough to get the land and some good stables down there. Get the staff to train them too.'

'Well, it's a long time off, something to think about in years to come. How long do you think we'll be based here?'

'Not long I'm told; no more than six months.' Drummond gazed around him. 'It's a peaceable enough place though. I've encountered no dangerous rebels, not one ... apart from you, that is.'

Lachlan's cheerful expression gave way to one of surprise. 'Me?'

'Yes, you.' Drummond bit his lip thoughtfully for a moment, and then explained. 'You see, those horses now, they're a very good example – would you be as full of admiration and want to possess one if they were not thoroughbreds? Can you not *rely* on thoroughbreds to be good value for money and give a better performance than any other breed?'

Lachlan frowned, confused. 'William, what the pox are you talking about?'

Drummond gazed around him again. 'Well, one has to use the same judgement with women as with horses. And well ... what you told me in confidence last night, about ... wanting to marry Beth Jarvis, well, it's just not on, old chum, in fact it's sheer madness.'

Lachlan's anger was rising. '*Why* is it madness?'

Drummond scoffed. 'Well if you have to ask *why* then you are obviously still more Australian than Scottish. The years in London and in the Army have not polished you well enough. And does Miss Jarvis want to marry you? Know you that?'

'No I don't know that,' Lachlan replied through gritted teeth. 'As yet I know only my own choice. But now I want to know *why* you think my choice is madness?'

Exasperated, Drummond looked at him as if thinking he must be the biggest fool ever born.

'Because she's a *half-caste* that's *why!* Mixed blood, and not even good blood at that. As fine a man as I'm told her father was, nevertheless my own father tells me that *her* father was an Arab of uncertain lineage, and her white mother is nothing better than a glorified Macquarie *servant*. Now look, do you honestly believe that any respectable doors of Scottish society would be open to you if you married someone like that? All doors would be shut to you. And as *for English* society – '

The smash of Lachlan's fist into his face sent Drummond toppling backwards. Shocked and dazed he half lay on the ground and then put a hand to his lips and felt the blood.

'Good God! It was only in your best interests – '

'You're lucky I don't kill you right here!' Lachlan said, enraged. 'I intend to marry her! And a pox on your Scottish and English society – and a worse pox on anyone else who disapproves or tries to stop me!'

*

Midsummer's Eve came in with mellow warmth, the glow of the sun still bright. A few new stragglers arrived on the scene laughing as they watched the dancers and then joined in the songs.

Across from the fire, Beth and Maggie and Lorna were propped up against a tree. Beth was chewing one of Mrs Keillor's pastries while Maggie and Lorna tucked in to grilled trout.

Maggie finished her trout and looked up and around the

crowd of gatherers. 'Oh, there's Mr Dewar, he found time to come after all.

Beth looked over at Robert Dewar and saw a young man standing with him, his body half turned from the crowd and his conversation with Robert Dewar appeared serious.

She kept watching them, especially the young man whom she did not recognise at all, concluding he must be a stranger to these parts. He was tall and slender and wore a brown corduroy riding jacket and black knee breeches, grey wool stockings and black leather shoes. His jacket was of the finest cut, as finely cut as all of Lachlan's clothes. His hair was dark brown and the sun glinting on it showed it was washed clean as clean can be. He looked like a gentleman, but no gentlemen came to these Midsummer gatherings to welcome the Solstice which was usually only celebrated by the locals and farmers of the island.

Beth saw Robert Dewar starting to smile, and so did the young man, both of them smiling, followed by each shaking the other's hand as if coming to some form of agreement.

Finally the young man turned and looked towards the bonfire and Beth saw his face full on. The blue of his eyes showed up vividly against his sunburned face and oh ... oh ... so handsome.

Beth's attention was claimed back by Maggie who was chattering to her about something Beth could not now quite take in.

Oh by!' Maggie said suddenly, 'I think ye have an admirer, Beth ... over there.'

Beth looked 'over there' and saw the young man looking at her in the same wondering way she had been looking at him earlier.

'Do ye know him?' Maggie asked.

Beth shook her head. She was certain she did not know him. How could she know him when she had never known anyone so ... so *attractive*. For a long moment they looked at each other, and then, as if realising he had been staring – he turned away and slowly walked over to where Robert Dewar and his wife had settled themselves.

Minutes later Robert Dewar's daughter came running over

to the three girls, breathless and excited.

'Miss Jarvis, my cousin John has just asked father who ye are. So *I* told him ye are from Brazil in Spain.'

'I am *not* from Brazil,' Beth objected. 'I was only born at a seaport there. And I do not believe that Brazil is in Spain either.'

'Since when did ye have a cousin hereabouts, Kirsty Dewar,' Lorna demanded to know. 'Since when?'

'And if he truly *is* yer cousin,' Maggie said dubiously, 'and ye're not making up more fancies in yer head, then why have we not seen him before now?'

'Oh! Maggie Kennedy! I *never* make up fancies, and he *is* my cousin, though only a third or fourth cousin, and no' one of us has seen him for years because he has been away in the Navy.'

All four looked over at the young man who was once again in conversation with Robert Dewar.

'Aye, a handsome lover he'd be,' Maggie said with narrowed, interested eyes. She cocked one eye at Kirsty. 'How old or young d'ye know him to be?'

'I think he's two and twenty, but he could be three and twenty.'

'The torch-fires! The torch-fires! Come aroon an' light yer torch-fires!' a voice cried.

Maggie and Lorna and even Kirsty jumped to their feet in excitement and rushed closer to the bonfire where Mrs MacLaren was handing out small wood and straw torches from a basket. One after the other each held their torch to the flames and then proceeded to form a ring around the bonfire, although it was only the females who participated in this ritual, believing as they did that any wish they made on this Midsummer's Eve would come true.

Beth stood watching as the ring of females began to sing an old Norse song as they danced in a circle around the bonfire, wishing she could join in, but both her mother and Elizabeth had always forbid her to do so because this was one part of the Solstice celebrations they did not approve of.

'It all looks a bit pagan to me,' said a quiet voice close to her ear.

Beth turned her head and looked up at the young man who had been with Robert Dewar.

'Like the ancient days of sun worship,' he said smiling at her.

She stood speechless, looking at him, at his brown hair, curling slightly at the edges above his collar, and those blue eyes, still so vividly blue even in this strange light of shadows and sun and fire.

'Yes ...' she finally answered, 'that's what my mother says ... this part of the ceremony is not Christian.'

'No, but then most of the people on Mull descend from either the Celts or the Vikings ... mostly the Vikings. They may be Christian now, but the old ways still remain.'

'Are *you* from Mull?'

'No, I'm from Edinburgh, but my father descends from Mull, and now he is planning to return here.'

And then, as if suddenly recollecting himself, he said quickly, 'Your pardon, Miss Jarvis, allow me to introduce myself. I am John Dewar, a distant relative of Mr Robert Dewar and his family.'

'And Mr Robert Dewar told you my name?'

He smiled again. 'Only because I asked.'

Beth felt herself flushing, and wondered if he could hear her heart pounding? And *why* was it pounding? She didn't know what else to say, so she spoke the truth.

'This is the time I usually slip away, once the torch-fires have been lit. My mother is very strict about my leaving ... because of all the drinking and carousing afterwards.'

'Drinking and carousing ... even the young women?'

Beth nodded, flushing again at some of the tales she had heard from Maggie and Lorna who always insisted that *they* had never caroused ... well maybe a *wee* bit, a kiss here, a hug there, but nothing more than that, not until a proposal was on the table.

'If you are leaving, then may I escort you home, Miss Jarvis?'

A hint of an unsure smile passed her lips. 'I'm quite safe on my own. It's barely half a mile, less than that.'

'Then allow me to escort you for my own pleasure,' he said.

'My uncle is watching us, so he will know who is responsible if you come to any harm.'

Beth looked over and saw that Robert Dewar *was* watching them, and seeing her looking at him the farm manager smiled and nodded, giving his approval.

They walked for a time in silence. Beth looked up at the sky. 'It always confuses me ... if summer begins in June, then why is *mid*-summer also in June?'

'Because here in the northern hemisphere, this is the time when the sun is at its farthest point from the equator, and it's highest point in the sky, and when it appears to stand still.'

'And does it stand still?'

'According to the sundials it does, but only fractionally, for a very brief time. The description comes from two Latin words, "*sol*" which means sun, and "*sistere*" which means to cause to "stand still". Hence, the Summer *Solstice.*'

'Oh, I see ...' Beth smiled at him, admiring his knowledge. 'Kirsty says you are in the Navy.'

'Yes, a midshipman.'

'A midshipman? What is that?'

'A rank below a third lieutenant.'

'So, you are an officer?'

'A very *junior* officer.'

They had reached a stile between fields. He climbed over first, and when she then climbed onto the step he offered his hand to help her down.

Too shy to take his hand, she jumped down, which made him laugh.

'Miss Jarvis, you look very feminine and very young but you jump like a boy.'

Beth nodded. 'I have always suffered the disadvantage of being young, from as far back as I can remember.'

He laughed again, and she quickly added. 'I mean, always being the *youngest* of the household, too young for this, too young for that. And I have *always* preferred breeches to skirts.'

His tone was surprised. 'But surely you don't go abroad *wearing* breeches, do you?'

'Yes, but only when I'm ploughing about in the vegetable

garden, or helping Robbie to dog the sheep back down to their pens.'

'Do you not have a farm boy to do that, pen the sheep?'

'Oh yes, but Robbie prefers me at his side to anyone else.'

'Now that I can understand.'

She looked up at his smiling face, the orange rays of the night sun gleaming behind his hair, and for a moment she felt as if the world was spinning.

'If ...' she said on a breath, 'if you are in the Navy, why are you not at sea?'

'I'm on leave.'

*

At ten o'clock, although it was still light, Mary took a lantern, left the house and walked down the lane.

The older Beth grew the more she worried about her, especially on a night like this when the young ones got carried away with all their excited talk of this night being magical, as well as all the drams that would be secretly drank, even by the lasses.

She looked up at the sky, knowing the sun would set tonight around half past ten, so it would be darker on the return journey if she had to go all the way up to the bonfire to bring Beth home.

She paused, checked that the candle inside the lantern was still alight, and moved on.

She had only been walking for five minutes or so when Robbie came barking after her, galloping past her at speed, and Mary laughed. 'So she's near, Robbie, is she? Near to home?'

Moments later the barking became furious, echoing through the air, and Mary knew instantly that a stranger was also near, near to Beth, else why was Robbie so angry and making enough fuss to wake the dead?

Seconds later she heard Beth's voice issuing commands to the dog, and after a few short growling complaints Robbie calmed down ... All was well, nothing amiss.

She waited, and then saw two figures coming into view from around the trees and walking down.

Beth ... and a young man who appeared to be in his early

twenties walking beside her ... He was not a local, and he was not dressed like a local either, so who was he?

Moments later Beth was upon her – her eyes sparkling radiance, her face illumined with smiles. 'Mama, this is John Dewar. He very kindly escorted me home.'

John bowed slightly. 'Ma'am.'

'Dewar?' Mary said. 'Are you related to – '

'Mr Robert Dewar? Yes. He is my father's cousin.'

'Oh well, then,' Mary smiled, feeling relief as well as surprise, 'you must come inside and have some refreshment, and also meet Mrs Macquarie, the owner of Jarvisfield.'

Beth was disappointed when John politely declined. 'Thank you, but the hour is late, and I have to be in Tobermory very early in the morning.'

He glanced quickly at Beth, and then back to Mary. 'But, perhaps I could meet Mrs Macquarie tomorrow ... in the late afternoon? Would she be in?'

'Oh yes, and she loves to meet new people, we see so few strangers here. You would be very welcome.'

Again he glanced at Beth. 'Until tomorrow then.'

He bent and patted Robbie's head, and then said his farewells and took his leave, pausing at the bank to look back and give a smile and a brief salute.

Beth returned his wave. Robbie began to bark again, but in a more friendly tone.

Chapter Twenty-One

The following afternoon, Elizabeth's welcome was warm and gracious. She instantly liked the young man on sight.

'A midshipman?' She seated herself back in her armchair and accepted a glass of port from the tray Mrs Keillor was offering around.

'Well, officially, I am now a mate.'

'A mate?'

'A midshipman who has taken his lieutenant's exams and passed. A sort of sub-lieutenant.'

'And how long in the Navy?'

'Five years, ma'am.'

'And have you seen much action?'

'Not as such. Since Napoleon's defeat at Waterloo and the peace with France, the Navy has been involved with other duties.' John smiled apologetically. 'And the war with France, of course, was before my time.'

'Yes, of course, so it was. Goodness, how time flies!' Elizabeth sipped her port. 'So what are these other duties our Navy is involved in? Your last voyage, where did it take you?'

Beth sat crumbling the cake on her plate with her fingers, anxiously fearing that John Dewar might perceive Elizabeth to be giving him the third degree, which she really had no *right* to do.

Mary felt no such apprehensions, knowing that Elizabeth was genuinely interested in all news from the wider world.

'Our last voyage took us down to the South Atlantic,' John replied, 'patrolling the waters off Africa.'

'*Africa!*' all three said together.

Elizabeth sat upright. 'What on earth is our Navy doing in Africa?'

'On earth, I couldn't say, ma'am, but on the sea our Navy is maintaining a blockade off Africa to counter the illegal slave trade.'

Now all three were *very* interested. 'But,' said Elizabeth, confused, 'there are *still* slaves right here in Britain! Why, down in London, in every gentleman's household there are black men and women who may be dressed very well in their master's livery, but they are most certainly *slaves*.'

'Not according to the law,' John said. 'Under the law they are now free men and women since the Slavery Abolition Act was passed in eighteen-thirty-three.'

'So why are they still there?' Mary asked with some perplexity. 'If they are free under the law why do they stay in those houses?'

John shrugged, he did not know. 'Probably because their conditions have changed. Under the law they must now be paid a wage for their employment and be free to leave at any time.'

'And our Navy?' Elizabeth asked. 'What is their role in all this, what exactly do they do?'

'Well, clandestine slavery still goes on,' John said. 'So our role is to stop and search all British trading ships to ensure they have no captured slaves hidden below in their holds.'

'And if they have?' Mary asked.

'We return the slaves to land and set them free, and the captain of the ship is fined one hundred pounds for each and every slave found on his ship, which can often rise to a colossal amount, dissolving any profit he hoped to make from his illegal trade.'

'And if he doesn't pay?'

'His ship is commandeered, but whether he pays or not, his licence to master a British trading ship is revoked permanently.'

'I see ...' Elizabeth nodded.

'Although ...' John added, 'I believe a new law will soon be coming into force, whereby the captain of any ship found to be carrying slaves will be regarded as a pirate and his punishment will be death.'

Elizabeth's face showed her disgust. 'In London, in the past, whenever I was invited by any lady or gentlemen to visit their home for a musical evening or supper or whatever the occasion may be, if I entered and saw they were using black slaves I immediately turned around and walked out.'

She looked intently at John. 'This new law ranking

captains of slave ships down to criminals – when does it come into force, do you know?'

'No, all I have learned since coming ashore is that the Bill has been passed in Parliament, but still has to be passed by the House of Lords.'

'The House of Lords – that lot! A feasting pig will be eaten in Jerusalem before that lot pass anything sensible!'

'With all due respect, ma'am,' John said hesitantly, 'The House of Lords *did* pass the Abolition Act.'

'And all thanks to the late Mr Wilberforce.' Elizabeth sat back. 'My husband was an ardent admirer of William Wilberforce. He was a *great* man indeed.' She looked at John. 'Do you agree?'

John set down his glass of port on the side-table, hesitant to answer, or perhaps hesitant to answer in a way that might displease his hostess.

'Yes ... I do agree that William Wilberforce was a great man ... but a major battle, such as the war on slavery, can never be won by just one man, and all credit should not unfairly be given to just *one* man. There was an army of campaigners throughout the Kingdom helping Wilberforce, all doing arduous and important work. And the hardest campaigner of all was Thomas Clarkson, have you heard of him?'

Elizabeth said 'No.' Mary said 'No.' While Beth sat silently leaning forward in her armchair, listening and gazing at John Dewar, as if entranced.

'No, few people outside of London and the Abolition Movement have heard of Thomas Clarkson,' John continued. 'But you know, although Wilberforce was the man who carried on the fight in Parliament, he could not have done it half so well without the constant gathering of information and public mobilisation against slavery organised by Clarkson.'

Elizabeth was gazing with soft eyes at the young man sitting in her drawing-room. He reminded her in ways of young D'Arcy Wentworth, one of the leading revolutionaries so passionate in his fight for the rights of emancipists in Australia.

'Your ship?' she asked. 'Which part of Africa?'

'Our watch is between West Africa and South Africa, but in the main we were stood off the port of Cape Town.'

'And your next voyage?'

'The West Indies, I believe. Jamaica.'

'Goodness,' Elizabeth said, her mood animated, 'my husband served in the West Indies – in *Jamaica*. He told me all about the awful slave markets there at that time, in quiet a lot of detail too. He found it all quite sickening. Perhaps I could pass some of those details on to you.'

'And we know Cape Town,' Mary added. 'Our ship docked there on our journey back from Australia.'

Elizabeth clasped her hands together in eager anticipation. 'Mr Dewar, it's been such a pleasure, but we have so much *more* to talk about – will you *please* stay for dinner?'

*

While Elizabeth went to refresh and change for dinner, and Mary went to the kitchen to give instructions to Mrs Keillor to set an extra place, Beth took the opportunity to ask their visitor:

'Do you know where the seaport of Saint Salvadore is? I mean – *exactly* where?'

'Yes, if you have an Atlas I can show you?'

Beth stood up and began to search along the bookshelves. 'I'm sure we do have an Atlas somewhere, but I believe all such books are kept in General Macquarie's study ... and no one is allowed to go in there, apart from my mother and Mrs Macquarie.'

She turned and met John's eyes.

He said, 'Why do you want to know where it is ... *exactly*?'

'Because ... ' she shrugged, 'well, I was born at sea, on the way back from Australia, but the next port of land the ship stopped at was Saint Salvadore, and so General Macquarie has my place of birth registered as Saint Salvadore. So I would like to know ... *exactly* where that is.'

'Oh, I see ... ' John glanced towards the desk near the window. 'If you have some paper I could sketch it for you in a line-map ... the *exact* location.'

'Oh yes, paper, we have plenty of *that*!' Beth said

jubilantly. 'Elizabeth spends most of her time here writing letter after letter to people in London and Australia.'

She opened a drawer of the desk and took out a few sheets of vellum. 'Will a pencil do?'

'A pencil will do it better than a pen.' John joined her at the desk and the two stood together as he began to draw.

'The ship would have left New South Wales *here*,' he wrote the name, and then continued his pencil line, 'and then continued on through the Indian Ocean to *here* at Cape Town ...' He frowned. 'And then for some strange reason ... the ship must have veered way off its course to over *here* ... to put in at the port of Saint Salvadore in Brazil.'

'Why strange?' Beth asked.

'Well, unless it was in dire need of fresh water or some other supplies, or somebody needed the care of a hospital or some other emergency, the ship should have gone straight up the Atlantic on course for Britain.'

They were standing close together, looking at the drawing as he marked out the correct line from Cape Town straight up the Atlantic Ocean towards ... 'North Africa and then Europe ...'

Beth's eyes were fixed on the clean lines of his fingers and his tanned hand as he drew ... aware again of that strange stirring in her body that she had felt for the first time last night ... It unsettled her, his *closeness* now unsettled her in way she had never felt unsettled before. She had lived long enough on a farm to know the stirrings of the animals in their seasons, but her own sexual feelings had always been undeveloped or dormant, due to her age she had thought, so it had never concerned her. Until last night she had always thought that a woman's sexual feelings did not stir or come alive until she wed, part and parcel of the marriage contract, and certainly not until *after* she had been bedded.

'... past Portugal and Spain, and then France, across the Channel – '

'So Brazil is *not* in Spain then?'

'Not even near,' John said, smiling at her. 'Spain is *here* and Brazil is –' she watched his pencil skim back down and across the paper to '*here* – thousands of miles away.'

'I knew Kirsty was wrong,' Beth said, 'but she won't be told. So will *you* tell her how wrong she is about Brazil being in Spain. She's *your* cousin.'

'A third or fourth removed cousin,' he said, 'but I *will* tell her if you wish me to.'

'I do.'

Mary and Mrs Keillor passed the door of the drawing-room together heading for the dining room, with Mrs Keillor talking at the top of her voice about some complaint regarding the tablecloth.

John and Beth's heads were bent close together, still looking at the drawing on the desk when he murmured quickly, 'Miss Jarvis, would it be possible to see you tomorrow *alone*? If only to give me a chance to speak with you directly. Would that ... be at all possible?'

Beth glanced briefly into his candid blue eyes, and then returned her gaze to the drawing. 'I think,' she said on a quick breath, 'that might be possible, Mr Dewar.'

'You do?' he answered in surprised relief. 'Where?'

Beth stared fixedly at the drawing on the desk and then ran her finger along the line of the Atlantic Ocean. 'We could meet by the trees along the side of the stream.'

'What stream?'

She picked up the pencil, turned over the paper on which he drawn his line-map, and drew her directions in the same way.

'This is the front of the house *here,* and if you go across the field to *here,* you see a line of trees *here,* and just a few yards down you will see a stone boulder *here,* and if you go through the trees by the boulder there is a long bubbling stream behind it.'

'What time?' he asked.

'Sometime in the forenoon would be best ... say ten o'clock?'

'Ten o'clock,' John said.

'Can you ride?'

'Of course I can ride. How do you think I get between here and Tobermory?'

'Well, I thought that perhaps with you ...being a sailor ...'

'You thought that perhaps I went down to the sea each morning and *swam* to Tobermory?'

They were both laughing when Mrs Keillor came in and said dinner was ready to be served.

Chapter Twenty-Two

Upstairs, Elizabeth was far from ready. Not only was her chest still troubling her, but also the stabbing pain from her arthritic right knee was spoiling her enjoyment.

'Such a nice young man, and so interesting,' she said to Mary who was buttoning the back of her dress. 'And very different from the usual conversation we get up here. Am I done?'

'All done up,' Mary said, patting the last button into place. 'But really, Elizabeth, you can't expect the people up here to have the same conversations with you as those down in London. Down there it's all politics and parties and more politics. The people here are too hard working and too busy for all that talking. Farmers are more concerned with the animals and the weather and the fishermen are always having to watch the moods of the sea.'

'I know, my dear, I know, but the *mind* must also be kept working, kept engaged. I think I will take just a small spoon of laudanum to ease the pain in my knee.'

'Laudanum?' Mary stared at Elizabeth as she moved to her dresser and lifted a small bottle from the top drawer, followed by a slim wooden box that contained a small silver spoon. 'Where did you get that – in London?'

'Yes, from my doctor in Harley Street, Dr Chisholm. A good man, and very understanding of the ills that befall us as we get older. When the pain in my knee gets too strong, he says a small amount will help.'

'I don't think ...' Elizabeth had knocked back a spoonful of the laudanum before Mary could finish her sentence.

'I've read in the newspapers about laudanum,' Mary said, 'and I know all the ladies in London think it's a miracle remedy for all ailments, but I don't think ... I really don't think it should be mixed with wine or port, Elizabeth, and you've had quite a few glasses of port already today.'

'That's because my knee was hurting so badly, but don't worry, I shall be very circumspect about how much port I drink after dinner ... probably none at all.'

'Still,' Mary said, as they descended the stairs, 'I don't think Dr McLean would approve.'

'Dr McLean!' Elizabeth laughed. 'What does he know about anything outside Salen? I don't think that man has ever ventured further than Edinburgh.'

'And if he has not, what's wrong with that?'

Elizabeth paused and looked patiently at Mary. 'In medicine, as in all things, Mary, one must keep on learning about what cures, what does not cure, and any new advancements that may help a patient and ease their pain. And Dr McLean will never learn anything new if he never ventures away from Mull.'

*

Over dinner Elizabeth did much of the talking again, which pleased Beth, as it allowed her to listen while Elizabeth asked all the questions she would never have dared to ask, nor was it her place to ask.

Watching John Dewar's occasional, easy smile, and the way he pushed back a lock of brown hair that kept falling over his brow, she learned that he was in Mull for one reason only – to find and buy a house for his bereaved father to live in. Anywhere on the island would do, his father had told him, as long as it was in Tobermory.

'Why Tobermory?' Mary asked.

'Because he wants to be able to watch the sea from his front door, he says, so he can keep an eye on me.'

'All the way over in Jamaica?' Mary smiled. 'Well they do say that some of the Scots have second sight?'

'Ah yes, but it is my father's *first* sight that is beginning to weaken. His eyes are not as sharp as they once were, so now he is making plans for his eventual retirement. Not yet, not for a few years, but he wants to make some occasional visits to Mull beforehand so he is used to the quiet life when he does finally settle here.'

'Understandable,' Elizabeth agreed. 'Mull is like an entirely different world to the busy city of Edinburgh. What does your father do?'

'He is a tailor, at Mortimer's.'

Elizabeth almost spilled her wine. 'There you go again! My husband *always* used Mortimer's in Edinburgh. He insisted it was *the* finest gentleman's outfitters in the entire Kingdom, not just Edinburgh.'

'And they make all the uniforms for the Army,' John said, pushing back a lock of brown hair from his brow, 'I expect they made your husband's uniforms too?'

Elizabeth nodded. 'The last uniforms they made for him, before we left for Australia, four sets I think it was, or maybe five, but they looked just as good coming back as they did going out all those years before.'

'And are you residing on Mull with your relatives?' Mary asked. 'At the Dewars?'

'Yes, and if I fail to find a suitable house, Robert Dewar has agreed to keep on looking while I am away. He and my father were very close when they were lads. Both will enjoy being neighbours again.'

Elizabeth was looking perplexed. 'Forgive me for asking, Mr Dewar, but how on earth did the son of a tailor manage to enter the Navy as an officer? Did your father buy your commission?'

'No, ma'am, the Royal Navy has never allowed the sale of commissions. Advancement in officer ranks is solely by merit.'

'Why is that? Purchase of commissions are allowed in the Army.'

John answered with a faint cynical smile. 'I suppose the reason is that an officer in the Army can get away with incompetence on the field, but a captain of a ship on the seas must have the best crew possible if he wants his ship to stay afloat and prevent death by drowning of all his men.'

'Quite.' Elizabeth hesitated for a moment. 'But still, are there not certain requirements for entering at officer level?'

'The requirements are prohibitive, yes' John admitted. 'You must have a sound education and a fair knowledge of mathematics, which I do, having attended the Royal High School in Edinburgh. But I would have had no chance at all of getting a commission in the Navy without the patronage and letters of recommendation from Lord Donaldson.'

'The patronage of Lord Donaldson?' Elizabeth was impressed. 'And how did you manage that?'

'I managed nothing,' John confessed. 'My father has been Lord Donaldson's personal tailor for years at Mortimer's, and over time they have become very fond of each other. So when my father told Lord Donaldson of my desire to go into the Navy, he offered to provide all the documentation that was required.'

'But what of the cost?' Elizabeth frowned. 'It cost my son Lachlan a *fortune* to enter the Army. He had to buy everything – his commission, his sword, compass, spyglass – even his horse! But the most expensive of all was his uniforms – a fortune! Did you also have to buy everything you needed for the Navy?'

'I did, yes, compass, spyglass, everything – except of course the cost of my uniforms which were made for me by my father.'

'At Mortimer's?'

'No, in his time off at home. He is excellent at his craft, and whether it be in Mortimer's workroom or in his own home, his finished garments are always superb.'

Mary detected that John Dewar was not at all comfortable answering all these personal questions about himself and his father, but Elizabeth was so taken with him – *and* she was drinking far more than she should after that laudanum. Under normal circumstances Elizabeth was too much of a lady, had too much discretion, to question any newcomer in such a way, but today – and now tonight – she was acting like an impertinent old dowager.

On impulse, Mary felt the need to say something kindly to the tensed-up young man, something to make him relax again.

'I'm sure you look very handsome in your Naval uniform, Mr Dewar,' she said sincerely. 'I have always liked Navy blue on a man.'

'Mary!' Elizabeth turned to stare at her, slightly miffed and somewhat bleary-eyed. 'You said precisely the same to Lachlan when you first saw him in his red Army jacket. So which is it – your favourite colour on a man? Army red or Navy blue?'

'Both,' Mary replied. 'Army red *and* Navy blue.' She lowered her eyes and fingered the stem of her untouched wineglass. 'And, if you remember,' she said softly, 'George often wore navy blue.'

'George ... oh, yes ... dear George ...' Elizabeth's eyes became wide and watery as she stared off into the distance, lost in her own personal thoughts.

'George?' John said to Mary, but it was Beth who answered him with a small, proud smile. 'My father,' she said. 'Everyone loved him.'

'Loved? He is ...'

'Yes, in accident, when I was small.'

'You see,' Elizabeth said sadly, looking at John, 'that is why your Mr Clarkson and the Abolition Movement *must* keep up the fight to abolish slavery in all its forms and in *every* country. I believe it's still rampant in India, especially Ceylon. And the terrible suffering caused by this human trafficking is nothing less than *evil*.'

She took another drink of port and then continued: 'Take George Jarvis for example – his mother was just a young girl of fourteen when she was snatched on a Tangier street in Morocco – a young Arab girl taken without warning from her family and shipped to India, sold to an Indian prince as a concubine, and then when her son was born he too was captured by more slave-traders and sold to someone in Cochin – a beautiful young boy of seven forced to walk naked around a slave-market with a rope tied around his waist and the slave-trader lashing a whip at him. How cruel! How inhuman! God knows what would have happened to that boy if my husband had not come upon the scene and rescued him.'

Mary was speechless for a moment, her blue eyes wide with horror as she moved to her feet and finally blurted out, '*Elizabeth* – how *could* you!'

In the silence that followed, it took Elizabeth a few seconds to come back to herself and look around her and realise what a monumental blunder she had made, what an *awful* mistake.

Her hands went to her mouth. 'Oh, Beth, my dear, I am so, so sorry ...'

Beth's face, in that moment, stayed with John Dewar for a long time afterwards – the pale skin of her face as if all the blood had drained away; the speechlessness of her shock; and then the pain that glistened in her dark eyes as she looked up at Mary. 'My father ... was a slave?'

'Your father ... ' Mary got out, her eyes brimming, 'was the most wonderful man in the world.'

'Naked ... and *whipped*?' Tears were now spilling down Beth's face.

'Oh, please, Beth, please don't cry,' Mary pleaded, 'I know how hurt you must feel but – '

Beth knocked her hand away and stood up. 'I'm not crying for *me* – I'm crying for *him!*'

And then in a fast dash Beth was gone, out of the room and out of the house into the night.

John Dewar was also on his feet, and also shocked by what had just happened. He looked questioningly at Mary. 'Until tonight – she didn't know?'

'No.' Mary shook her head and wiped at her eyes. 'It was something George never wanted anyone to know, especially Beth, and we ...' she glanced briefly at Elizabeth, 'we have always protected Beth from knowing anything she does not *need* to know.'

Elizabeth was sitting with her elbows on the table and her hands covering her face, deeply distressed 'I'm sorry, so very sorry, I don't know why or how –'

'*Laudanum!*' Mary cried. 'From your fancy doctor down in London! That's why! That's how! And I *did* warn you about taking that stuff and drinking wine as well.'

John Dewar made a move to leave. 'I think I must go after her. She is still in deep shock, so she should not be out there alone.'

'Oh, thank you, thank you,' Mary nodded appreciatively. 'I was about to go myself but you will catch up with her more quickly than I. Please bring her back and tell her ... tell her it was all a drunken mistake! Tell her that Elizabeth was talking about some other man called George Jarvis and *not* her father!'

John hesitated only for a moment at the door, looking back disbelievingly at Mary. 'You know she will not believe that.'

Seconds later Mary heard the door of the house shutting behind him.

Chapter Twenty-Three

It was after ten and the sun was beginning its slow descent when John Dewar set out on his journey, convinced that Beth had run for the hills, running blindly, desperate to get away from the truth she had just learned.

He could still feel his own shock at the sudden and calamitous turn of events, but as he walked – his eyes searching around him every few steps – it now all began to make sense to him – the puzzle of why a blonde-haired and blue-eyed woman like Mary Jarvis had given birth to such a dark-haired, dark-eyed girl.

And Mary Jarvis – how old was she? No more than thirty-seven or thirty-eight. An attractive woman, still comely; but it must have been from her father that Beth had inherited her striking exotic beauty. No wonder so many of the islanders thought she came from a place called Brazil, which they thought was in Spain.

The only puzzlement was that none of the islanders appeared to treat Beth as *'an outsider'* which was a real puzzlement indeed, because in his own short time on Mull many of the locals had eyed him with narrow suspicion, some referring to him as 'a foreigner' because they knew him to have come from as far away as Edinburgh.

When he reached the hill where the bonfire had been lit on Midsummer Eve it was deserted. He cupped his hands to his mouth and called *'Beth! Beth...!'* But only the seagulls answered him.

Some time later, having satisfied himself that she was not hiding behind any tree or bush or rock, he stood looking around him, wondering where to search next. He did not know Mull that well, but she did ... so where would she go?'

Darkness had fallen as he returned down the hillside, missing his footing occasionally, slipping and sliding in the dark.

Back at the lane leading down to the Macquarie house, he could see the glow of candlelight in one of the windows. Was there any point in going inside and saying he had not found her, when that would only cause greater distress for the women.

He turned in the opposite direction and began to walk again. Sleep would be impossible, knowing there was a heartbroken young girl out here in the dark somewhere on her own.

He walked for miles, constantly cupping his hands to his mouth and calling out "*Beth...! Beth...!*" but unlike on the sea, his voice brought back no echo, and no answer.

He walked on, down leafy lanes, over fields and up hills, not knowing where he was going in the darkness, but at least the orb of the moon was nearly full in its glow and the sky was bright with stars so he did less tripping and slipping.

His voice was hoarse from calling her name, and when he eventually arrived back at the house at Gruline the dawn-light was beginning to brighten the sky and it was after five in the morning.

It was not until he was walking down the lane to the house that it suddenly occurred to him that Beth might have returned home from another direction after he had left, and was now sound asleep in bed.

But when Mary opened the door, and she saw him alone, her tears began to spill again. 'I'll make you some tea,' she said.

In the dining room Mrs Macquarie was also still up, still sitting at the dining table, her face weary and looking much older. And she, too, when she saw him alone, seemed to shrivel in her chair with dismay.

'No sign?'

He shook his head.

'Where did you look?'

'I don't rightly know. I just kept walking and calling her name, but I must have covered a fair few miles.'

'Poor Beth ... the young find it so hard to cope in matters like this, and Beth has always been so ... so *innocent* about the world beyond Mull.'

'Mrs Macquarie, I think you should go to bed now,' he said. 'You look in want of some rest.'

Elizabeth put her hands to her watering eyes and said quietly, 'All I want is to die.'

Exhausted himself, he sat down on a chair by the window and remained silent, knowing no words of his would console her.

Mary arrived carrying a tray of cups and saucers and a silver teapot.

'Not for me,' Elizabeth said, rising to stand and walking slowly and wearily towards the door.

Mary quickly set down the tray and moved to block her path, putting her hands on the older woman's shoulders and looking into her swollen eyes.

'Oh Elizabeth,' she said softly, 'you did not intend this, and we all make mistakes, and please believe me when I say I forgive you.'

'I don't deserve to be forgiven,' Elizabeth replied. 'And I know I will never forgive myself.'

For a moment the two women stood looking at each other, and John looked on as they both suddenly hugged each other, and remained hugging each other for a very long time.

'Let me help you up to bed,' Mary said. 'Nothing can be gained by you staying up any longer.' As they reached the door Mary glanced over her shoulder at John. 'Help yourself to some tea, I won't be long.'

John eventually moved over to the table and poured himself a cup of black tea, drinking only half of it, then turned and stood looking down the room, his hand to the top of his head in thought.

Where could she be? Out all night in the darkness?

Hell's flames! He wished Mrs Macquarie had not questioned him so much. If she had only stuck to polite niceties and not had such an enquiring mind the subject of the slave trade would not have arisen. And Beth would be out this morning, none the wiser, her usual innocent self, meeting him at the stream, and no doubt that dog of hers would be jealously circling them again.

His hand came down from his head, his eyes widening as a realisation came to him.

He turned as Mary came back into the room and he said

quickly, 'Can you give me something that Beth wears regularly? A glove, a hat, anything.'

'Why?

'Her dog – Robbie!'

Mary stared. 'Oh my goodness – yes! Robbie always knows when Beth is near or on her way home.'

She rushed into the hall and came back holding Beth's black tricorn hat. 'She often wears this, especially when she's out riding.'

John took the hat. 'Do you have a horse I can use?'

'No, we will take the trap, because I'm coming with you.'

John frowned. 'A horse would be much swifter.'

'It would,' Mary agreed, 'but if we saddle up a horse in the stables for you to ride without Hector's permission he will be wanting to know why – and *why* you are still here when you only came for dinner. And knowing Hector, he won't stop lurking and listening until he finds out *why*. And what happened here last night must never be learned outside the four of us – you, me, Elizabeth and Beth.'

'Yes, I understand.'

'I often set off in the trap for Tobermory this early, and I'm quite capable of harnessing the mare myself.'

'I'll help you.'

'No, we cannot risk Hector being up and about and seeing you, although he's never usually up and around as early as this, not until after seven when Mrs Keillor cooks the breakfast. Her room is above the kitchen but she never wakes before half past six.'

'So what shall I do now?'

'You go down the lane and wait for me by the trees. Have you had some tea?'

'Yes, thank you.'

'Have some more. I won't be too long.'

*

John was standing by the trees with Beth's hat in his hand when Mary turned the trap onto the road, Robbie wagging along beside it.

John bent and patted his head and then held the hat under

his nose. 'Where is she, boy, where is she?'

As soon as he got the scent of the hat Robbie barked and started running around in circles of excitement.

John and Mary looked at each other.

'Don't be stupid, Robbie,' said Mary impatiently, 'we want you to – ' her sentence remained unfinished as Robbie darted forward in the direction of Salen and minutes later was gone from sight.

'At least we know which direction he is heading,' John said, jumping up on the trap as Mary chucked the reins and urged the mare to go faster than usual. 'Go girl, *go!*'

'They had travelled two miles in the direction of Salen and still no sign of Robbie.

'What do we do now?' Mary asked miserably. 'There's two turnings ahead and I don't know which one to take. A fat lot of use that dog has turned out to be. He probably saw a rabbit and went chasing it. What do we do now?'

John was still holding the hat, still convinced that it was no rabbit that had sent Robbie off in a mad run.

'We do what we would do with humans,' he said, standing up in the cart and cupping his hands around his mouth and calling '*Robbie! Robbie!*'

Minutes later Robbie came tearing back towards them, barking and circling the trap and dashing off again.

'He's heading into the glen,' Mary said. 'Parts of the track there are so narrow I won't get the trap through.'

'Then I'll walk.' John jumped down and began running after the dog. Seconds later Mary threw down the reins, abandoned the trap, and ran after him.

Hurtling back again, and seeing John coming into sight, Robbie turned and led the way – running forward round a bend, and coming back – running forward out of sight, and coming back.

Half a mile on, Mary was losing her breath and her patience. 'How do we know he's not playing a game with us?'

'We don't know, so we'll just have to trust that he's not as crazy as he seems.'

They came to a part of the track that was narrow enough for only a single horse to pass through and shaded by thick overhanging trees.

John led the way and Mary followed close behind, both emerging to see Robbie standing at the side of the track in utter silence, gazing down into a gulley.

Mary felt her heart stop for a moment and put a hand to her chest. 'Oh, God, she whispered. 'Oh, God.'

Both moved to look down the side of the gulley and saw why Robbie was remaining so silent ... Beth was lying curled up in a ball, fast asleep.

'Oh God,' Mary said again, tears spilling down her face, 'I should have known this is where she would come ... but how could I have known ... it's years since I brought her here and showed her ... and she was only about ten years old then.'

'Showed her what?'

Mary gulped in her throat. 'She's lying in the same place where George was found ... when he died ... her father.'

John exhaled his breath. 'Then one can only deduce that she has probably come here many times since then. You stay here.'

He moved down the gulley, through stones and rocks, until he reached the sleeping girl and bent to touch her shoulder.

She did not respond.

He shook her shoulder more roughly this time, and she stirred, turning on her back and slowly opening her dark eyes, her face as waxen pale as someone who has been through a long illness.

'Come, Beth, come ... time to go home.'

She closed her eyes and turned away, back into the same position.

Mary could watch no longer, making her way down the gulley, snagging her skirt on rocks here and there, until she reached her daughter.

And then John stood watching as Mary did the strangest thing ... she stretched out the ground and lay at her daughter's back, putting her arms around her and cupping herself close into Beth's body, whispering tenderly into her ear, words about her father, loving, comforting words ...

'It wasn't as bad as it sounded, the whip never touched him, General Macquarie saw to that ... He was only seven, and from that day forward he knew only love, everyone loved him, and his life was wonderful, travelling all over the world, to the farthest parts of it, to China and Egypt and England and Sydney ... educated at the finest schools in London and Edinburgh ... One day he said to me, "Why does it hurt you so much, when it does not hurt me. I have no memory of that time, it was all so long ago and I was so young. It was like a dream that is forgotten as soon as the eyes open after sleep. You know the dream was a bad dream, but hard as you try you cannot remember any of it...'

After a short silence, Beth stirred and turned inside Mary's arms, her eyes confused, her voice weak. 'If he could not remember, then how did you know about it?'

'I never knew the details, not until Elizabeth told me. I made her tell me, I forced her.'

'How did she know?'

'General Macquarie told her. Don't forget, he was an adult at the time, capable of remembering everything, but George was just a child. And Elizabeth had to have an explanation as to why George had the name of Jarvis ... the same name as General Macquarie's first wife.'

'And why did he?'

'Because Jane Jarvis *loved* him so much she legally gave him her own name of Jarvis. She was only twenty-three when she died.'

'And how old was General Macquarie then?'

'Thirty-one, I think. He was only a captain then, and years later, when he married Elizabeth, over time she and George became very close, very fond of each other. In fact, it was only because of Elizabeth's goodness and kindness that George and I were able to get married.'

'Why?'

'Well, because ...' Mary bit her lip as she thought of some lie to tell her daughter. One shock was enough.

'Well, because ...'

John heard no more, walking away up the gulley and away from a conversation that was none of his business, a conversation that under less traumatic circumstances would not have taken place in his hearing.

He looked around for Robbie who had disappeared again, and then later found him stretched out on the bench of the trap, asleep. What a dog – what a mad, crazy, harum-scarum loveable dog.

Without looking back, John continued walking in the direction he had come, out of the glen and onwards under the brightening sky, until at the end of two miles he had reached the Dewar's house.

'By!' said Robert Dewar when John entered. 'That was a long afternoon cup of tea over at Gruline.'

John blinked his eyes tiredly. 'We drank port.'

'It was a long drink of port then. Were ye asked to stay for supper?'

'I was.'

Robert's curiosity was burning. 'So what kept ye there all night? They musta liked ye to keep ye there so long. Did her ladyship ask ye to stay and play some cards? She likes a game of cards, Mrs Macquarie, just so long as there's no money gambling in it.'

'Yes,' John said tiredly, pushing his hair back from his brow. 'We played cards.'

'What game? Twenty-one or Twenty-five?'

John was tired of people questioning him. He sighed. 'No, we played whist.'

'Whist? Never heard of it. What kind of card game is that?'

'A game of intellectual exercise using both caution and mathematical calculations to work out the chances of winning the rubber.'

'Stone me, I think I'd prefer to spread manure over the crops than play a dreary game like that. And ye played this game all night, did ye?'

John nodded. 'It's a hard game to play. It can take all night.'

Robert Dewar could not believe it, would not believe it.

'In God's truth, are ye telling me that Mrs Macquarie and Mrs Jarvis stayed up all night and did not go to bed?'

'In God's truth, Mrs Macquarie and Mrs Jarvis stayed up all night and did not go to bed.'

Looking at him, Robert knew that John had spoken the

truth.

'And Miss Beth?'

'She did not go to her bed either.'

'The three of them – staying up all night – why?'

'You need four to play whist.'

Robert Dewar chuckled. '*Whist* – exercise and caution and all to win nothing more than a piece of rubber! God's breeches! That must be a card game for women then, because what kind of *men* would want to play a dull card game like that!'

'A lot of young men on Her Majesty's ships,' John said, turning to leave the kitchen and heading for the stairs and his bed – bumping into Kirsty at the open door.

'Oh, yes, Kirsty, good morning, and Brazil is *not* in Spain. Brazil is in Brazil.'

'No it's not.'

'Yes it is.'

'Who says?

'I do.'

'Then ye are a liar, John Dewar,' she said haughtily and pushed past him into the kitchen.

*

John did not even attempt to keep his arranged appointment at ten o'clock with Beth later that morning. He saw no point in waiting down by the stream when he knew she would not appear.

Nor was he surprised that she did not appear later that afternoon when he called at Gruline. Only Mary appeared to be home, and she seemed happy to see him.

She led him into the drawing-room and then looked at him with some surprise. 'The sleepless night seems to have had no tiring effect on you.'

'I'm used to sleeping in four-hour shifts. And you? How are you?'

Mary shrugged. 'I had a few hours sleep this morning. Tonight I'll go to my bed early.'

'And Beth? How is she?'

Mary gestured for him to sit down, and then sat down

herself, looking very tired.

'She is in her room, but whether she is now sleeping or not, I don't know. Whenever I go in she pretends to be asleep, keeping her eyes closed, but I always know when she is awake. So ...' Mary sighed, 'I've decided to leave her alone until she feels ready for some company.'

John sat thoughtful. 'And Mrs Macquarie?' he asked.

'Oh, the late night did not go well with Elizabeth. She's tired out. I made her go back to bed for a rest. Although she will not get *into* the bed, the most she will do is lie on top of it, insisting it's against the Scottish way of living to lie in bed in daylight.'

John stood to leave. The only reason for his visit today was to express his wish that all was well with the family, and after the cataclysmic night of events of which he had been a party, it was no less than Mrs Jarvis would expect him to do.

'Thank you for coming today, Mr Dewar,' Mary said sincerely. 'Thank you for ... everything.'

He smiled. 'You may call me John.'

'Oh no, too personal,' Mary said with a small smile in return. 'Elizabeth would be horrified.'

'Oh well, the choice is yours.'

Mary accompanied him to the door, and as he stepped out, he suddenly turned and looked at her, his eyes thoughtful.

'Mrs Jarvis ... back in the glen ... I'm sorry for what happened there, the accident, and the sad loss of your husband.'

'Oh,' Mary said quietly, a soft expression coming into her blue eyes, 'George has never been lost to me. He lives on in Beth, more and more he lives on in her. Every day, every year as she gets older, when she smiles, the occasional look in her eyes, I see George all over again, as clear as day, and that has always been a great comfort to me.'

'And now Beth will need a great deal of comfort from you.'

Mary nodded. 'We will comfort each other, we usually do.'

*

For a number of days Beth did not want to see anyone, talk to anyone, preferring instead to ride off alone and spend her time on the hills with only Robbie and the sheep for company.

Sitting alone she wondered and thought about the events of life, which seemed to come and go and change in tune and mood as swiftly as the seasons.

At least the only seasons she knew, the ones she saw on Mull. In spring the land came alive in colour, red and yellow and purple wild flowers growing along every roadside and hedge, followed by the long and warm days of summer when the sky was a light blue and you could clearly see all the neighbouring islands, and even the White-tailed eagles seemed less predatory in their mood.

And then autumn, a quietening down into subdued greens and browns, followed by the darkness of winter ... the season her heart was in now, winter.

Perhaps if she had been told ... bit by small bit, at an earlier time, the shock would have been less, the pain would have been less. It was not good enough for people to excuse it all by saying her father had been a child at the time, as if such brutality was felt less by a small child than a big adult.

Now she understood why the main thing she remembered about her father was his gentleness, in touch and tone, always gentle and always calm, and now she knew why. No problem, no turmoil, must have seemed beyond his coping, not when in his childhood he had suffered the worst – captured and forced into slavery – so everything else since then must have seemed easy and painless in comparison.

She dashed the tears from her eyes - *captured and forced into slavery* – what kind of a cruel world was out there? Well, she would not be a part of that world, no, never. She would stay here on Mull where life was safe and the people were decent and the animals were less cruel than humans.

In the days following at Gruline, Mary saw the change in her daughter, the difference. Oh, she was not petulant or sulky and carried on her conversations with Elizabeth and Mrs Keillor and the cleaning girls in the same old friendly way, but Mary knew that her daughter *had* changed. She saw it clearly, even though the others didn't seem to have noticed or be aware of it.

All the happy innocence had gone from Beth's eyes. She

had learned that the world could be a hateful place at times, as Mary herself had long ago learned also. But then George had come along and helped her to recover from the misery and depression of it all. But who, now – apart from herself – would or could help Beth to recover?

'Does Lachlan know?' Beth asked Mary one night as they sat sewing in the drawing-room. 'About Papa?'

'No,' Mary replied honestly. 'Lachlan knows no more than you did.'

'Do you think it would matter much to him, if he knew?'

'Lachlan doesn't need to know anything,' Mary replied tersely. 'Elizabeth will not make the same mistake again.'

'It mattered to John Dewar.'

'What?' Mary looked up from her sewing. 'Why do you say that?'

'Well, because ...' Beth kept on sewing, 'the last time I saw him he appeared like an apparition bending over me in the glen, and then he disappeared in a blink, obviously having decided not to travel part of the way back with us in the trap, choosing a long walk instead.'

'I believe he felt – '

'And it's been more than a week since then and he has not sought to visit us here again and enjoy our alarming company.'

'He did call here, Beth, that same afternoon, but both you and Elizabeth were in your bedrooms. He wished you both well.'

After a long silence, Mary said, 'John Dewar gave me the impression of liking you very much, Beth.'

'He gave me that impression too.'

'So don't you think that you are now being very unfair to him? He spent most of the night out searching for you, when most other men would have bid a polite goodnight and hastily returned their bed. And it was his idea to use Robbie to try and find you.'

Beth sat silent, no longer sewing.

'Perhaps,' said Mary, *you* should ride over and call on *him*, if only to thank him for being so kind and helpful to your mother.'

The following morning, Beth endeavoured to do just that. She rode over to the Dewars' house and was immediately forced by Kirsty to taste one of her freshly baked oatcakes.

'Oh, still hot!' Beth smiled, swallowed, and then asked, 'Is your cousin at home, or has he gone to Tobermory?'

'He's gone to Edinburgh first, and then to Portsmouth.'

'Portsmouth?' Beth frowned. 'Where is that?'

'In London. All the big ships dock in London's docks, especially the *Royal* Navy ships, because that's where the Royal Family and King George lives.'

With an air of preoccupation Beth looked around her, her eyes fixing on the open kitchen window through which she could see Mrs Dewar pegging a white sheet on the line to dry ... a white sheet that made her think despondently of the sails on a ship.

'So he's gone then, back to the Navy?'

'Aye, and he won't be back here awhile, no' for a long while, probably no' for five years, that's how long it was before we seen him again the last time.'

Beth looked at her. 'But was that not because he lived away in Edinburgh, and not because he was away at sea for all that time?'

'Och no!' Kirsty laughed. 'Ye're thinking of the trading vessels that come in and go out, Beth, like they do at Tobermory. But that's no' how the *Navy* ships do it – they go out and stay out for years.'

Riding back to Gruline, Beth was certain that Kirsty was *wrong*, as she was about most things. If Kirsty did not know the answer to something, she just made one up in her head, and then believed it to be so, no matter how many times she was corrected.

Elizabeth was in the drawing-room at her desk writing letters when Beth walked in.

'Elizabeth, is Portsmouth in London?'

'Goodness, no,' Elizabeth replied. 'Portsmouth is much farther south, in the county of Hampshire.'

'Are you sure?'

'Of course I'm sure. It was at Portsmouth that my husband

and I boarded our ship *The Dromedary* for our voyage to New South Wales.'

Beth flopped down into an armchair. 'I think the next time I go into Tobermory I should buy an Atlas and give it to Kirsty. She believes she knows where every place in the world is, but *all* her locations are wrong.'

'Kirsty Dewar?' Elizabeth laid down her pen. 'Surely, dear, that would be a waste of money? That poor girl can neither read nor write, so how could she read an Atlas?'

Beth had forgotten that.

'But *you* could read an Atlas, Beth, then you would not have to ask Kirsty the location of anywhere. There's one in the study, why don't you go and get it.'

Beth was surprised. 'But I thought no one but you or Mama was allowed to go in there?'

'Oh, that was when you and Lachlan were younger, but now you are old enough to know not to go anywhere near my husband's desk, or interfere with any of his papers on the shelves.'

'When is Lachlan next home?' Beth asked.

'Soon, he keeps telling me in his letters, very soon.'

As Beth walked out the room, tall and young and graceful in her navy riding habit, Elizabeth's eyes followed her and a sad ache thumped in her heart as she remembered her awful mistake ... Beth had suffered sore because of that, and yet the girl had tried hard not to cause anyone else to suffer afterwards ... such a forgiving girl, so genuinely kind-hearted, no malice in her at all, and *so* like George.

Some words from her favourite playwright came into Elizabeth's mind, words from one of his sonnets,

*'Thou art thy father's glass, and he in thee
calls back the lovely April of his prime ...'*

Elizabeth lifted her pen and returned her gaze to her letter, quite sure that Mr Shakespeare would not have minded her mentally changing his word of 'mother' to 'father'. No, in this circumstance, Mr Shakespeare would not have minded at all.

*

Beth found the Atlas in the study, took it straight up to her bedroom, and the first place she tried to find in its pages was ... Jamaica. Wasn't that the place where John Dewar had said his next ship would be going?

A guilty flush rushed into Beth's face. Why was she looking for Jamaica, when she knew that in time she may be marrying Lachlan and *he* was in Ireland.

Chapter Twenty-Four

The long summer days of bright skies until midnight had passed into the shorter and cooler days of autumn, and now the murky cold weather of winter was making its way down the hillsides with black clouds settling into their hidden contours.

Elizabeth's health became a constant cause for concern as she suffered one cold after another and seemed unable to shake them off.

'You are getting old, m'dear,' Dr McLean told her, which led to a sharp indignant response from his patient, 'I'm younger than you!'

'Only by a year or so, and I have not polluted my lungs in the smog of London as you have done. Now keep taking your medicine, and again I prescribe rest, rest and even *more* rest, preferably in your bed.'

Elizabeth glared at him in disgust. 'You expect me to be a lazy lay-abed night *and* day!'

'Aye, if only to stop you hindering the natural work of your immune system.'

Later, as he took his leave, Dr McLean paused by the open front door and gave some final advice to Mary.

'At least *try* and make her stay abed for longer in the mornings, that would be some help.'

Elizabeth obdurately refused to stay in her bed, preferring to take her rest in the armchair by the fire, a warm shawl around her shoulders.

The arthritis in her right knee was a constant pain and, strangely, was only relieved by the soothing effect of Beth standing behind Elizabeth's armchair and gently brushing her hair.

'Oh, Beth, that's almost as good as laudanum,' Elizabeth sighed blissfully, 'and equally as relaxing.'

So whenever the pain in her knee was very bad, Beth reached for the hairbrush and began her ritual slow strokes that always sent Elizabeth into a mesmeric stare into her thoughts.

'You know, Mary used to brush my hair for me in Australia, but not as good as you, Beth, not as gentle.'

'Tell me about Australia,' Beth murmured, 'from the day you arrived there.'

'Oh, we were *all* so young then, back in those days in Sydney ... Lachlan, George, Mary ... and even *me,* all so young ...'

'I thought General Macquarie was older than you.'

'He was older than me ...' Elizabeth blinked. 'I suppose I must be remembering our earlier days, when I first met him, here in Scotland. He was thirty something ... and I was twenty-five. Goodness, it all seems such a long time ago.'

'Tell me about Australia,' Beth asked again. 'Tell me about the land and the people and the animals.'

So Elizabeth told Beth, day after day, so many things, but without any laudanum in the house there were no further slip-ups for Mary to worry about. Sick in body she may be, but Elizabeth's mind was as sharp as always.

'And now,' Elizabeth said, 'Reverend Cowper has told me in his last letter that John McArthur has been officially pronounced insane, which does *not* surprise me. All that scheming against my husband and the emancipists ... I knew no good would come of it.'

'But ...' Beth ventured, 'I read in the newspapers that John McArthur has done wonders with the growth of the wool trade in Australia.'

'Oh yes, that cannot be denied. He owned the best merino rams in New South Wales and he used them. But all that plotting and scheming ... no wonder his mind gave up under the strain.'

As always, Elizabeth's eyes finally closed, and Beth left her in silence to sleep.

'Even an hour or two asleep in the chair is good for her,' Mary said to Mrs Keillor.

Yet a short while later, as always, Elizabeth's coughing erupted and broke the sleepy silence of the drawing-room.

'Now ye *must* stay in bed!' Dr McLean warned Elizabeth on his next visit, and eventually she did so, getting weaker and weaker as the days passed, her face as white as the sheet under her hands, until Dr McLean sadly informed Mary, 'I think the time has come for ye to send for her son.'

Hector rode as fast as he could to Craignure to deliver Mary's letter in time for the packet boat over to the mainland.

Mrs Keillor made pot after pot of nutritious hot brose for Mary to feed to Elizabeth, in the hope that it would 'help to bring some of Mrs Macquarie's strength back.'

During the night, Mary and Beth took it in turns to sit in the chair by Elizabeth's bed and keep a watch on her, in case she awoke in need of anything to aid her comfort.

And then the night came when Elizabeth awoke, needing only the comfort of her Bible.

Mary remained sitting silently, watching her as she read, fearing to disturb her in such a religious moment.

Elizabeth finally let the book fall open onto the eiderdown, turned her head slowly and, looking at Mary in a very peaceful way, she held out her hand.

'Mary ...'

Mary leaned forward and clasped Elizabeth's hand in her own. 'What is it, love?'

'When my dear Lachlan died,' Elizabeth said croakily, 'it was my belief that his death was simply an interruption in our relationship, and that one day we would be reunited again. That's not a foolish belief, is it?'

'No, not foolish at all,' Mary answered, kissing Elizabeth's hand. 'Love is a strong chain. I feel the same about George, that his death is just a short suspension of space and time until he and I are together again forever.'

'Please God,' Elizabeth whispered, her free hand moving to rest on her Bible as she gazed so fondly at Mary, and then her eyes closed in sleep.

Mary sat back in her chair and kept up her vigil, unaware that Elizabeth's time in life had already passed.

*

Lachlan arrived on the morning of his mother's funeral in the company of Lord Strathallan. The weather had been bitterly cold for some weeks, and although Lord Strathallan was draped in a full-flowing elegant cloak, Lachlan wore a plain grey Army greatcoat over his uniform.

He appeared to be very shocked by the unexpected death of his mother, and deeply grieved.

Although afterwards, during refreshments at the house, Lachlan became resentful and defensive when Mary asked him why he had not been to visit his mother more often – especially as Lord Strathallan had just told her that Lachlan's regiment had been back in England for almost four months – and he had not even informed his mother of that.

'It's not as if I *knew* she was going to die, or even expected it,' he protested. 'I thought she would live to be at least eighty.'

The following morning, when Lachlan made the decision to accompany his former guardian in his return to Strathallan Castle, Mary knew there had to be a very good reason for his eager departure.

'Is your friend William Drummond at Strathallan now?'

'Yes.'

'And you prefer his company to ours?'

'At this time, yes, with everyone so sad and sorrowful here, what help can that be to me? It will serve me no good to stay up here in the back of beyond. I need cheering up. I need my friends in the regiment. And Mary – William Drummond has always been my very *best* friend!'

After he had left, Mary was fuming – not only because Lachlan had completely ignored all the tenants who had come out in the cold and rain to attend his mother's funeral – but also because he had not once looked in Beth's direction nor attempted to speak a word to her.

PART FOUR

Chapter Twenty-Five

For Beth, the rest of the winter seemed endless. There was no work to be done in the vegetable garden, and the land all around was bleak and dormant.

Not until late February was she able to make herself busy and feel useful again, staying up through the night helping the ewes to birth their lambs, and loving every moment of it.

'This one I'm going to keep,' she said to Robert Dewar, sitting on the straw in the barn with a small lamb in her lap.

The farm manager shook his head in refusal and laughed, 'Nay, I dinna think Robbie would like *that*. Now away home to your bed, lass, and get some sleep.'

By mid-March most of the lambs were up on the hills with their dams; and with the coming of spring the land became alive with colour again, pink and yellow wild flowers peeping out from under hedges; and then in April moving out in stronger and fuller groups along the verges and woodland banks.

The woodland around the Jarvisfield estate had its own population of fallow deer that were usually content to roam within their trees, but now a young stag was daring to venture down to the lane of the house and into the garden, chewing the heads off the daffodils.

Hector was getting annoyed. 'Another one!' he said to Beth. 'Them deer have no right coming down here, an' if they come near my stables I'll get me knife and we'll be eating deer till summer.'

'Don't you dare!' Beth cried. 'The fallow deers have been here since Norman times, so they have more right to be here than *you*, Hector Allen from *Oban!*'

'Ah-haha,' Hector attempted a laugh. 'It's been many a long year since my ain people emigrated from the mainland over to Mull, as many as eighty years or more.'

Beth was not listening. She had walked in a creeping fashion around the back corner of the house to halfway down the lane, and now she was stroking the young stag's head in a gentle motion with her palm.

Mary opened the front door quietly and stood watching Beth, with Mrs Keillor creeping up behind her.

'By!' whispered Mrs Keillor. 'I've never seen a stag let a human get so close.'

'It's Beth's strange way with animals,' Mary whispered back. 'She seems to have a way of not frightening them away.'

Beth turned her head, saw them at the door and smiled. 'It's the same one,' she said quietly, 'the same one that's been coming down these past few days.'

'How do you know that?' Mary asked in a soft hush. 'How do you know it's the same one?'

'He's only got one antler growing ...' Beth moved her body back so they could see the one, small stump of an antler growing on the left side of the young stag's head.

The stag bent his head and continued chewing as Beth stroked his fawn-grey body. 'Oh, my beauty, your coat will be a lovely rich brown colour come the summer.' She turned her head to the women at the front door and smiled again. 'He's adorable, I want to keep him.'

Mary and Mrs Keillor exchanged a weary look. Of late they had heard this from Beth so many times about so many animals – always wanting to keep one as her own and take care of it.

'She's looking for something to love,' Mrs Keillor whispered.

Mary nodded. 'Or someone.'

'She's at that age now,' Mrs Keillor observed. 'Only a few weeks shy of eighteen.'

They watched as Beth slowly escorted the stag back up towards the woods.

'Reckon she'll be happier to see Master Lachlan when he gets home again,' said Mrs Keillor thoughtfully. 'Last time his visit was so short and they were both too upset about Mrs Macquarie going down the road of no return to have any idle talk to spare for each other. D'ye think aye, hen?'

'Aye,' agreed Mary, turning back into the house and cutting off any further talk on that particular matter.

*

The warm Atlantic currents brought a thick flowering to the island in May, primroses, harebells and bluebells abounded everywhere.

Beth took Robbie down to the flowing waters of the stream to give him his usual wash. Robbie objected in his usual way, growling in complaint. Yet as soon as he saw two ducks cruising near the opposite bank he dashed carelessly into the water to round them up, sending an unseen baby duckling fleeing in fright.

'Robbie!'

The flapping of wings and din of quacks made Beth take off her shoes, pull up her skirt and run into the stream to get the dog away and save the duckling from harm.

Robbie was now barking fiercely in response to all the flapping and quackery.

'Robbie! Robbie! *Robbie!*'

Hearing the angry tone in her voice, Robbie swam to the bank, darted swiftly into the trees and disappeared from sight.

Beth looked closely and saw the baby duckling was now safely tucked under its mother's wings and both ducks skimmed swiftly past her, still loudly quacking their complaints.

Beth sighed. 'Oh, that mad bad dog!'

She stood in the stream, the water around her knees, and then began a slow wade back to the bank, stopping in shock when she saw a young man leaning against a tree on the bank, watching her tranquilly.

He smiled. 'Good afternoon, Miss Jarvis.'

She instantly dropped her skirt to cover her bare legs, her face flushing a deep pink as she stepped onto the bank.

'How l-long have you been standing there?' she stuttered.

'Not long.' He took a fob watch out of his white waistcoat pocket. 'By my calculation, I am only eleven months, three weeks, five days and fourteen hours late for our appointment.'

'What appointment?'

'To meet by the stream at ten o'clock.'

He was still smiling, and Beth's heart was pounding again.

He was dressed in his Navy uniform and looked even more handsome than she remembered.

'I have no memory of any appointment.' She bent down to squeeze the water from her skirt, hiding her face as she waited for her heart to stop racing.

'May I help you?'

'No, no.' She slipped her feet into her shoes and then bent again to tie the laces. 'How did you know I was here?'

'I didn't know. I was on my way to your house and then I heard Robbie at war with some ducks followed by your voice in reprimand, so down I came, and what I saw ... was a sight worth waiting for.'

'Please stop smiling.'

'Why? It's a beautiful day and, unlike yours, *my* clothes are not wet.'

Beth was still flushing, gazing around her with an air of preoccupation and feeling that unsettled reaction again, *unsettled.*

He stopped smiling. 'Come on, I'll escort you back to the house and some dry clothes.'

'Why were you going to the house in the first place?' she asked as they walked.

'To pay my respects. I have just learned about the death of Mrs Macquarie.'

'Oh yes,' Beth said softly. 'We all still miss her.' And then she realised, a frown coming to her face. 'But ... for a man who was on his way to pay his respects to a bereaved household ... I hope you do not intend to give your condolences about Elizabeth's death to my mother with that happy smile on your face?'

John Dewar laughed. 'No, of course not. I'm just happy to see *you* again.'

'And yet, almost a year ago, you did not think to call on us at Jarvisfield and say your farewells.'

His laughter faded, and now it was he who gazed around him in hesitation before he answered.

'No, almost a year ago I felt no wish to go near the house at Jarvisfield again. Although, I should have done, I realise that now, if only to say farewell to your mother and Mrs

Macquarie.'

Beth looked at him, perplexed. 'But not to me?'

'No, certainly not to you.' He hesitated again. 'At that time I had been told by Kirsty that everyone knew you would soon be marrying the young laird of Jarvisfield.'

'Oh, that's not true! There was a time … but no, I believe Lachlan and I have both learned that our affection for each other was more like that of a brother and sister. A marriage is out of the question.'

'So I have been informed.'

She did not have a chance to ask who had informed him because they were now walking down the lane to the house and her mother was standing in the garden – staring at John Dewar as if seeing a ghost.

'Mr Dewar!' Mary called, coming out of the garden to meet them, a smile widening on her face. 'Oh, I *am* happy to see you again!'

Beth left them to go and get changed out of her wet clothes.

When she rejoined them, in the drawing-room, Mrs Keillor was placing a tray of tea and buttered scones on the small table in front of the fireplace, looking as delighted to have new company in the house as her mother did.

Beth moved to a chair nearer to the back window, but before she sat down she caught a glimpse of Hector lurking outside the window and listening. He quickly bent down, but too late, she had seen him.

'Where are you going, Beth?' Mary called after her as she swiftly walked out of the room again.

Outside in the yard she found Hector pretending to be bent over a wooden tub of washing that Mrs Keillor had left soaking.

'What are you looking for?' she asked him.

'Well,' said Hector, scratching his head with one hand while still searching with the other hand through the washing. 'There's a pair of me breeches I canna find, so I'm seeing if she's been washing 'em.'

'And is that why you were listening at the window?'

'What window?' Hector straightened and stared at her. 'I

was by no window. I was here looking for my stolen breeches.'

'Stolen?'

'Aye, someone musta stole 'em if I canna find 'em.'

'Hector, it is very rude to stand and listen at windows when we have a guest.'

'A *guest?*' Hector replied indignantly. 'Well *he's* no guest that the laird would approve being in his house. No, I'm telling ye *no.*'

Beth was baffled. 'Why not?'

'He'll no' like *him*, the laird,' Hector insisted, 'He'll no' like *him* at all.'

Again Beth asked, 'Why not?'

'Because ye don't pit two bulls agin each other, do ye? And if one's red and the other's blue, then the red one won't like the blue one, no, I tell ye, *no.*'

Beth was wondering if Hector had been secretly drinking drams of the house whisky in order to spout such nonsense, but Hector was deadly serious.

'Tis like all that argumenting and quarrelling I hears in Tobermory. Who is the greater man – the Duke of Wellington or that Horatio Nelson? And I says it has to be Wellington, 'cos he's head of the *Army.*'

Beth was beginning to think she understood why Hector objected with such animosity to John Dewar in his Navy uniform.

'And you prefer the men of the Army?' she asked.

'Course I do!'

'Why though? They both serve the same country and are on the same side. So why do you prefer the men of the Army? Is it because your employer and laird is now in the Army?'

Hector stared at her incredulously as if thinking she must be a fool.

'Nay, tis 'cos the men in the Army serve alongside *horses.* Aye, tis the *horses* that pull their cannons and carry their officers into battle and lead the charge, and tis the *horses* that win their wars for them, aye! No' like those navy blues who just sail around in ships. Now Wellington – he alus rode a horse, didna he? But that Horatio Nelson – he couldna ride a

166

horse could he? *He* could only ride in ships and that's why *he*'s dead and the duke isna.'

Beth turned up her eyes, turned around and walked back into the house, thinking she must truly be feeling *unsettled* to think she could even *attempt* to have a sensible conversation with Hector.

When she returned to the drawing-room, John Dewar was preparing to leave.

'So soon?' her mother said. 'Could you not stay for dinner?'

'Sadly, no. The new lady in my life is preparing a very special dinner for me tonight, and I promised her I would definitely *not* be late.'

'Your ... new lady?' Mary said, glancing quickly at Beth who looked equally as surprised.

'Yes, my new landlady. I am staying at the Tobermory Inn.'

'With Lizzie – Mrs McLoud!' Mary laughed in relief. 'Oh, if Lizzie made you promise that then she must be planning something very special for you.'

'Her cooking's not as good as mine though,' said Mrs Keillor with a sniff.

'So you are not staying at the Dewar's house?' Beth asked. 'Like last time?'

John met her eyes. 'No, last time I came to Mull to look for a house for my father and gave it very scant attention, spending too much time elsewhere. So this time I must stay in Tobermory until I find one, because he is getting impatient and also nearer to his planned retirement.'

'Do you think you will find one?' Mary asked dubiously. 'Tobermory is not a big place.'

'I think I might. The agent in Tobermory sent a letter to my father saying he might now have the type of house he is looking for. The front door and windows look directly onto the sea.'

He turned to Beth. 'Would you like to come and view it with me, Miss Jarvis. I share a berth with three other men when I'm aboard ship so my taste is not the best when looking for a land dwelling.'

'By! – You have to share a bed with three others?' Mrs Keillor was shocked. 'I'd've thought the Royal Navy treated its men betterer than that!'

'No, no,' John grinned. 'A berth aboard ship is a cabin – a room – containing sleeping berths. It is neither large nor small and is quite adequate for our needs.'

He again looked at Beth. 'So would you like to accompany me tomorrow, to view the house? If you're free to do so, that is?'

'I would love to,' Beth said eagerly. 'Yes, I would be truly happy to accompany you to view the house.'

When John smiled back at her, Beth realised she would probably be happy to accompany him to the ends of the earth if he wished it.

Chapter Twenty-Six

Beth left early the following morning, wearing her new brown riding habit and black tricorn hat. She had arranged to meet John inside the Tobermory Inn at nine, in time to meet the agent of the house at half past.

When she reached the inn's stables and handed over her horse to the stable boy, she wondered if she would need the horse again to reach the house. The town of Tobermory itself was small, but its population and houses were spread widely all over the hills.

John was standing in the morning sunshine outside the inn, waiting for her. He was no longer wearing his uniform, and nor was he wearing breeches, she immediately noticed. He was wearing straight-legged trousers down to the ankles.

'I saw you and your horse approaching through the window,' he said, taking her arm, 'I have already collected the keys from the agent. It's just a short walk up to the house.'

As they walked up the first hilly street she kept looking at his trousers. 'Are they a new fashion?'

'No, they have been the style for a number of years now, in the cities anyway.'

'In cities like Edinburgh?'

'Most cities, especially London, but yes, Edinburgh too. Although they have long been in fashion in the Navy.'

She smiled cheekily. 'Did your father make them for you?'

'He did indeed. He is after all my own personal tailor.' He looked over her brown riding outfit. 'Who cuts your clothes?'

'A tailor and his wife in Salen make all our clothes. Do you approve?'

'The cut is good, but the stitching is ...' he glanced at her apprehensive face, 'perfect!'

She smiled as they turned up another hill. 'There's the house,' John said, pointing. 'Just there on the left.'

Beth glanced up and saw a lovely white house basking in the sunshine on the side of a green hill. 'It looks bonnie and ... charming,' she admitted. 'And its windows are *gleaming!*

Who owned it before? Do you know?'

'I've no idea of the name, other than that the gentleman who lived there liked to paint pictures of the sea and the harbour, hence the wide gleaming widows for light – which is exactly what my father is looking for, a house with a lot of light.'

When they reached the house it had a wooden gate and a short gravel path to the blue front door, and inside it was... 'Beautiful,' said Beth as they walked from room to room. 'And yes – so bright!'

The house had four rooms downstairs, one a kitchen, and four rooms upstairs; bright square rooms with a good fireplace in every one.

'And *here*.' John said, standing by the window of the downstairs front room, 'is where my father will spend a lot of his time, either hand-stitching a garment, or looking out to sea.'

Beth joined him at the window and both stood for a silent time gazing out to sea.

'Even the harbour looks enchanting from here,' Beth murmured.

'Yes.'

Her eyes fixed on the distant horizon of the sea. 'Why did you choose to go to sea with the Navy?'

John shrugged. 'Even as a lad, whenever I looked out to sea I always longed to be ... *out there* ... mastering the waves and the ocean, seeing what lay beyond.'

'I've never wanted to be anywhere but Mull. Does that make me dull?'

'Oh, sweet girl, no. It makes you ... stable.'

'So you think I'm horse-like then? I'm sure I'm not.'

They were still laughing and teasing each other as they left and locked the house.

'My father is coming to Mull on the evening ferry on Saturday, to see the house on Sunday,' John said as they walked back. 'Would you like to meet him?'

'Well, yes ... but why would he want to meet *me*? He sounds very possessive of his only son.'

'No, not possessive. My father is now very *dependent* upon

his only son.'

'Dependent? In what way?'

'Emotionally. I'm all he has left now. I think that's why he wants to renew his relationship with the Dewar family here, and a few others he knows from Mull.'

'Yes, I would like to meet him.'

John smiled. 'And when you do, you can bring him up to date on how Mull has changed since he last lived here as a boy.'

Beth laughed. 'Mull *never* changes. Not even Tobermory.'

*

They spent the day in the town, walking along the harbour watching the activity on the various trade vessels and fishermen's boats, taking a late breakfast, and then an early dinner at the inn, where Lizzie McLoud joined them and gave Beth all the latest gossip to take home to Mary.

For Beth it had been a wonderful day, so different to her usual day, and as she mounted her horse in the stables she felt sad at parting from John, until he mounted a horse also.

'What are you doing?'

'I'm escorting you home.'

Delighted, yet maintaining a straight face, 'There is no need. I would know my way home blindfolded.'

'I'm sure you do, but it will soon be dark and you are a young lady who should not be out alone at night. There are sailors in the town, Beth, sailors from the trading ships, and not all of them are gentlemen.'

Beth thought she detected a hint of Navy snobbery in his tone.

'So, in your view, a sailor from a trading ship is not so much a gentleman as sailor from a Navy ship?'

'No, that's not my view. When I say not *all* of them are gentlemen, I'm referring to men in general, no matter their status.'

He turned his horse around and led the way out of the stables and she followed until they were on the road out of town.

'In Edinburgh,' he continued as their horses ambled along,

'Mortimers is truly renowned as the finest outfitters for "Gentlemen" in the whole of Scotland. And indeed, so renowned is the quality of their designs and tailoring, the demand has now led to Mortimers opening a second establishment in London.'

'London?' Beth was impressed.

'Yes, but my point is ... in all the years that my father has spent measuring and dressing and speaking with all those "gentlemen" who frequent Mortimers, he says he has learned there are *two* types of men of the gentry: one type he would certainly regard as true gentlemen, but the other type he merely refers to as "gents".

He looked at her. 'And the same is true on ships, Navy or Merchant. Some officers have worse manners and baser instincts than the ordinary sailors who climb up the mizzen-mast.'

Beth nodded. 'I understand now.' She turned away to look towards the sea, a smile on her face as the gentle breeze lightly rippled against her hair.

'Apart from that,' John added, 'Angus told me there was a lot of trouble last night when a sailor tried to molest a Tobermory woman which led to some fighting between the local men and sailors down on the waterfront.'

Beth's dark eyes rounded as she stared at him. 'Here? In Tobermory? That's unusual.'

'Not when a foreign ship is in, apparently.'

After a silence as they rode along, Beth asked, 'Do you think your father will like the house?'

'I'm sure he will love it. Anyone would love that beautiful house.'

'But ... is it not on the big side for one man on his own?'

'Hardly, he will need a live-in housekeeper to do his cooking and cleaning for a start. Since my mother died he has been taking all his meals at a nearby hotel.'

'Tell me about your mother,' Beth asked gently. 'Not about when or how she died, but about her life.'

Darkness was looming by the time they reached Gruline. And by that time also, Beth had learned a lot more about John Dewar.

Mary was still up when Beth came in, sitting in the drawing-room waiting for her daughter's safe return from her day in town.

And so was Mrs Keillor, who seemed to be spending less time in her kitchen and spreading herself more widely around the house since Elizabeth's demise, Beth noticed; but her mother did not seem to mind.

'Did you have a good day?' Mary asked.

'Very good,' Beth answered, her face illumined again. 'It was the most perfect day.'

'And Mr Dewar?'

'Oh, Mama, he's *wonderful*!' Beth exclaimed with passion. 'He rode with me all the way home, and now he's on his way back to Tobermory in the dark.'

Mrs Keillor sat forward. 'Did he try to kiss ye when he said goodnight outside?'

'No!' Beth said hotly. 'He's a gentleman!'

'A gentleman, eh? An officer and a gentlemen, eh?' Mrs Keillor winked an eye. 'They can be the worst of all.'

'Oh, what do *you* know about men?' Beth challenged. 'And that mysterious husband of yours – I notice you have said very little over the years about *him*.'

'Oh, now, *my* husband,' said Mrs Keillor, sitting back and folding her arms, 'was the worst man of all. So the least said about *him*, the soonest forgotten.'

'So why did you marry him?' Beth queried.

Mary waved her hand impatiently. She knew all about Mrs Keillor's vanished husband, but tonight she wanted to know about Beth.

'When are you seeing him again, Mr Dewar?'

'Tomorrow. He's coming to Jarvisfield to see his Uncle Robert and the Dewar family, and then he and I are meeting to go for a walk together.'

Mary smiled her approval. 'Did you dine at the Tobermory Inn?'

'Yes, we did. And, oh … Mrs McLeod asked me to tell you that those two gentlemen you and she were talking about some time ago – she said you would remember if I told you that one of them could down whisky easier than water.'

Mary searched her mind and then her eyes widened as she remembered the conversation – about William Drummond and Lachlan.

'Oh, yes, two gentlemen from Perthshire, I think. Although I cannot remember their names or who they were.'

'Mrs McLeod said to tell you that a gentlemen over from the mainland and staying at the inn, said he knew that young man well – the one who drinks whisky like water – and it seems him and his friend are in bad trouble.'

Mary sat upright. 'What kind of bad trouble?'

'Too much drinking and gambling with cards in the gaming houses in England, and now both are in very bad debt.'

After a silence, Mary managed a careless shrug. 'What matter is that to us?'

'Debt is a terrible worrying thing though,' remarked Mrs Keillor. 'It's something I mercifully have no' had to fret about since the day I arrived at Jarvisfield.'

'Off to bed now, Beth,' Mary urged, and Beth was glad to say goodnight and run up the stairs to the privacy of her bedroom where, she was certain, she would *not* be able to sleep.

She was asleep as soon as her head hit the pillow.

Not so Mary, who paced up and down her bedroom endeavouring to make sense of the message that Lizzie McLeod had sent to her.

If William Drummond was in bad debt, then she could not see that problem being too difficult to resolve. His father, Lord Strathallan, was rich enough to buy his son out of any hole.

But if Lachlan was in bad debt ... she wanted to know by how much?

Oh yes, Lachlan had changed drastically since he had entered the Army. From his letters to Elizabeth, Mary had deduced that he had become one of the 'fast set' in his regiment, but Elizabeth had not shown any real concern, seeming to be certain that *'time will give him wisdom.'*

Yet at the funeral, Mary had studied his face and known

that Lachlan had been taught to drink hard and to play hard, and now this possibility of bad gambling debts.

She finally went to bed, but was unable to sleep, her mind churning over the amount that the bad debt might be?

She fervently hoped to God that it was not large enough a debt to put the Gruline house and the Jarvisfield estate at risk.

Chapter Twenty-Seven

There were no clouds in the sky, no wind, the afternoon sun streamed down the hills like a golden flood.

Standing near a tree by a small lochlin brook, shaded by overhanging branches, there was no talking between John and Beth. They were bending down, mutely watching a brown and yellow Willow Warbler sitting on a nest of eggs and calling to her mate.

'Hoo-eet! Hoo-eet!'

The nest was very close to the ground, set back in some scrub under the tree. The bird's calls to her mate continued repetitively until she suddenly gave a long *'Hweeeeeeeeeeeeeeeet!'*

'Oh, she's getting impatient,' John whispered, and Beth put a hand over her mouth to stop herself giggling.

'I think we should move away,' he whispered, taking a quiet step back. 'I don't want to be a witness to any domestic bird quarrel when her mate gets back.'

'Hoo-eet! Hoo-eet! *Hweeeeeeeeeeeeeeeet!*'

The last long impatient call sent Beth back-stepping down the bank in muffled laughter.

'I don't know why you're laughing, it's not funny,' John said seriously as they walked on. 'I know what it's like to feel so impatient. It's a half sister to agony.'

She stopped and looked at him. 'Do you mean, when you are confined on your ship?'

'No, Beth, I mean *now*. Here under these shady trees with a bubbling brook and birdsong, it's the perfect place.'

'For what?'

'For finally relinquishing my impatience.' He pulled her into his arms and kissed her. Her soft lips were like half open petals.

When he drew his lips away, she looked at him in silence with her dark eyes, much darker than they had looked only moments ago, and then she put her hands to his face, her lips moving up to meet his, and she kissed him back.

*

Mary sat down at Elizabeth's desk and began writing a stern letter to Lachlan.

She had, she told him, got wind of a rumour that he had incurred some serious financial difficulties and so would be very relieved if he could inform her that this was not true.

She also sought to remind him that she had been his nursemaid in his infancy, and had continued to play a large role in his care and upbringing ever since then.

'And now that your mother has passed on,' she wrote, *'and although you are now a grown man, I still consider it my duty to be concerned about your welfare, as your mother would expect me to be. The maintenance of the house has also been left to my care in your absence, so I would be grateful if you could write and assure me that this rumour of you being in financial debt is wrong.*

Yours, as always, and with good wishes.

Mary Jarvis

She sealed the letter, and then went outside to the stables to instruct Hector to get the trap ready.

'Is it to Tobermory ye be going?'

'No, Hector, to Craignure.'

'Craignure? Why so?'

'Is it your business to ask?' Mary relented and sighed, too fond of Hector to remain stern. 'I need to get an urgent letter onto the evening packet boat for delivery to the mainland.'

'I could ride it there for ye,' Hector offered. 'I'd be much faster riding a horse than ye would be in the trap.'

'No, Hector, thank you, but I'm in need some air and the journey will do me good.'

Mary's true need was seeing her letter delivered to the packet service with her own eyes, so that her mind could be certain that it was on its way to Lachlan.

'Reet then,' Hector said, turning away, 'I'll get the trap ready for ye.'

A short time later, as Mary turned the trap onto the road,

she saw the two figures of Beth and John Dewar coming over the field, walking hand in hand under the slanting shadows of the late afternoon sun.

She looked away, her eyes on the road before her, about to chuck the reins when she suddenly stopped and looked at the two figures again ... walking *hand in hand!*

'Oh my,' she breathed. 'Well thank goodness *some* things around here are going the right way.'

She chucked the reins. 'And let's hope they continue to do so.'

Chapter Twenty-Eight

On Sunday morning, Mr John Dewar Senior was not at all happy with the white house on the hill in Tobermory.

'What were you thinking, son, what were you *thinking* when ye chose this house? You could not have been thinking about *me.*'

He looked at Beth, as if deciding she must be the reason for his son's lack of due thought and consideration. Oh, not that he could blame him. She was a beauty that would turn any man's mind away from necessary concentration.

But this house now! It was a bad choice. He looked at his son. 'And you say you've already paid a deposit on it?'

'What is *wrong* with the house?' John asked in bafflement. 'It has everything you need – plenty of light, good-sized rooms – and the view of the harbour and the sea is perfect.'

'Perfect,' Beth supported. 'It's a lovely house, Mr Dewar. One of the finest in Tobermory.'

The older man looked at Beth, and then at his son, and then he shook his head wearily. 'You young people, you see the world with young eyes and expect everyone else to see it the same.'

'But you haven't even *seen* the other rooms with young eyes or not,' John said in frustration. 'Not the rooms at the back, nor the bedrooms upstairs, and not the garden either. Only *this* room have you seen, and yet you pass judgement. Is that fair?'

'I've seen enough,' his father responded wearily. 'I would have told you back down there on the path that this house was not suitable, not for me anyway, but I didn't have enough puff left in my chest to get a word out.'

'Oh,' Beth said, finally understanding the problem, but John was still baffled.

'It's too *high*, son,' his father explained. 'Up two steep hills. Sakes alive, for a while there I thought I was climbing Ben Nevis.'

'But ...' John looked at Beth and then at his father. 'Beth

and I had no problem walking up here a few days ago, no problem at all.'

'That's because she's a Highland lassie, so she is used to it. And you're young and strong and active. But *me,* I've spent most of my life sitting on a chair in front of a sewing machine or standing at a table cutting cloth. So what makes you think my knees or my lungs would now become as strong as those belonging to a mountain climber? *Retirement,* did you say? *Rest,* did you say?'

John finally realised his mistake. 'I'll find you somewhere else.'

'Will you get the deposit back?'

'I don't know.'

'Why did you pay it in the first place?'

'Well, because...' John fluffed, 'I was, foolishly, certain that you would like it as much as I did, and because ...' he shrugged, 'my time here is short and I just wanted to get the whole business out of the way.'

'Out of the way?' His father gave him a slow smile of understanding. He turned to Beth. 'Come on, Miss, let's get back down to the Tobermory Inn for a seat and some refreshment. At least the descent will be a lot easier.'

*

'Oh, now, this is *my* kind of level,' said John's father, easing himself blissfully into a chair in the inn's dining room. 'And in fact, so is this entire street. So next time you go looking for a house for me, John, see if you can get one here on Main Street, or, preferably, one street above it. Just so long as I can sit in my own house viewing the sea without having a mountain to climb to do it.'

The descent down had been as easy as the walk up, to Beth's mind, and she could see John was thinking the same.

'But Edinburgh is a very hilly city,' John said to his father. 'That's why it never occurred to me – '

'Edinburgh is that all right, and its hilly streets were no problem for me in my young days. But now, with all my years of sitting and standing, even the hills in Edinburgh are a strain on my legs. At least the road between our house and

Mortimers is a fairly flat walk.'

Angus McLeod arrived on the scene, followed by Lizzie, both eager to hear the result. 'Well, what did ye think of it?' Angus asked.

John's father smiled. 'It near killed me, Mr McLeod. The trek up there.'

Angus and Lizzie exchanged a satisfied glance. 'We thought that would be the case,' said Angus.

Lizzie agreed. 'I could no more climb those hills once in a day, never mind go up and down more than once for anything I might need. What if you wanted fresh fish in the morning, and then again fresh fish for your supper? What would ye do?'

'Starve,' said John's father.

'And what if ye wanted to pop down here for a glass or two of an evening,' Angus added. 'Or even a nice supper. How would ye get down?'

'Oh, getting down would be easy,' said John's father. 'It's getting back up that concerns me.'

'Now what will you have to eat?' Angus asked. 'But first of all, what will ye have to drink?'

'Oh, a brandy will heal all wounds,' John's father laughed. 'The smoothest and best you can provide.' He looked at Beth. 'And you Miss ...'

'Jarvis. Elizabeth Jarvis. But you may call me Beth.'

'As my son does.'

'Yes.'

So what will you have to drink, Mi – Beth?

Beth would have loved a tot of brandy to calm her nerves, but not wishing to make a bad first impression she requested only water.

John agreed to a brandy.

The conversation after that became natural and friendly and Beth decided she liked John's father, despite all the fuss he had made about a few small hills.

Lizzie had prepared them a light lunch of roast duck and vegetables, followed by apple tart and cream.

Beth found it difficult to eat the tart, because throughout the meal she had noticed John's father occasionally looking at her with a strange expression in his eyes. It discomfited her, made her nervous and killed her appetite as she kept wondering what he was thinking.

Maybe he was now noticing that her skin was not as pale as other Scottish girls, or maybe it was because he knew she could not be Scottish at all – not with an English name like Jarvis.

Lunch over, Angus brought him another glass of brandy and while the two older men exchanged more pleasantries, John touched her hand. He could see she was no longer relaxed, and lifted a questioning eyebrow.

'Jarvis?' said John's father when Angus had left the room. 'That is your surname, Beth?'

'Yes.'

'Well, I have been looking at you, and although it may seem strange after all this time ...' He paused for a moment, and then smiled. 'Y'know, my dear, I believe I have already met your father.'

'What?

John and Beth both stared at him. 'But how could you have met him?' John asked. 'He was in Australia for years, and then – '

'As I indicated, it was a long time ago.' Again Mr Dewar looked wonderingly at Beth. 'Is your father Mr *George* Jarvis?'

Beth nodded, speechless.

'And as a young man, was he a student at the college in Edinburgh?'

Beth nodded again.

'And was he ... a *brown* man, of foreign looks?'

Beth nodded yet again, too speechless with shock to say a word.

'I thought so.' John's father smiled in satisfaction and sat back.

'It's not often you meet a man like him in Scotland,' he went on. 'And I remember him well because on the day I met him, it was the blue jacket he wore that caught my attention. Oh, a handsome young man, we all noticed that. But while others were looking at his face, I was more interested in his coat.'

'But *where* did you meet him?' John asked curiously.

'Oh, didn't I say?' Mr Dewar sipped some brandy. 'We shared a coach from Edinburgh to Perthshire. The rest of the passengers were a rum looking lot. A woman eating a fried sausage, and a man in a red plaid cape who kept telling funny stories that were not funny at all. And then there was this striking young man who sat with his eyes turned to the window as if he wished to remain distant from it all.'

He took another sip of brandy.

'There was something about his bearing, a dignity and graciousness that was very lacking in the other passengers. But best of all – he was wearing one of *my* jackets from Mortimers. A mixture of wool and cashmere, a very fine yarn, in dark blue.'

He looked at Beth and explained. 'I knew it was one of mine because of the cut of the lapels, you see. Every artist knows his own work, and I was a master of my craft, even back then.'

Beth was looking at him as if mesmerised.

'So, as he was clearly a customer of Mortimers, I asked for his surname. I was young and vain and thought it would be nice to know, seeing as he was wearing one of my own creations. And he told me his name was Jarvis – George Jarvis – just like Beth answered her name in the same way when I asked her – Jarvis. Elizabeth Jarvis. It's been digging away at my memory of all through the lunch. And the same dark looks as he ... and now John is saying he went off to Australia? Well that explains why I never saw his name on the fitting or order books after that.'

He smiled warmly at Beth, very warmly. 'Will you give my regards to your father, Beth, tell him I remember him well. Tell him I was the young man in the coach who vowed to him that one day I would become the head tailor in Mortimers, and I have been that for a long time.'

After a quick breath John quickly explained that Beth's father was no longer alive, due to a riding accident.

The response from his father was one of mortification. 'Oh, my dear, I *am* sorry ... but it's not every day or every year that you meet a man like your father, that is why I recall – '

Beth had risen to her feet and moved to his side of the table, tears glistening in her dark eyes.

She bent and kissed him on the cheek. 'Thank you,' she said softly, 'thank you. I will treasure that story of your encounter with my papa.'

'Beth?'

She glanced briefly at John as she pointed to the door. 'A little air. A few minutes. I won't be long.' And then she walked quickly out of the inn.

'Is she all right?'

'Your encounter with her father was ... very unexpected,' John said, 'even to me. Why have you not told me about this meeting with George Jarvis?'

'Why would I? It happened years ago. Before you were even born. And how was I to know that one day in the future you were going to start courting his daughter. And damn me, when I started telling her about it – I didn't know her dear father was dead.'

After a silence, John pushed back his chair and stood. 'I think we both need another brandy.'

'May I shrivel and waste if I have offended that lass. It was not my intention.'

'You have not offended her,' John said. 'She told you she'd treasure the story of your encounter with her father, didn't she?'

'She did.'

'So then?'

'So all is well and no harm done. That's a relief. But I still need that brandy. I'm aching sore after that hike up those hills today.'

'I'll fetch Angus.'

Later that night, in the privacy of her bedroom, Beth wrote in her diary:

'The fact that our two father's met each other so very long ago, and now their two children have also met, although living in two different parts of Scotland and one often away

184

at sea, surely that is a sign of Heaven at work and Fate at its best.'

Chapter Twenty-Nine

Mary was surprised by how speedily Lachlan responded to her letter. Less than two weeks had passed and here was his reply.

My Dear Mary,

I can assure you that you have been disgracefully misinformed. I know not where this rumour of my being in financial difficulties has come from, and can only conclude that it must have come from the dregs of some beggar's bottle.

My situation has indeed changed, but only insofar as that I am now thoroughly fed up with the Army and seeking to sell my commission and return home.

I believe I have spread my wings far and wide until they can reach no farther, and now I think it is time for me to marry and settle down as laird of my estate. Because of this I send you my deep appreciation for your care of the Macquarie house at Jarvisfield, and I look forward to seeing you all again soon.

Yours fondly,
Lachlan

Mary did not know what to make of it. Return home? Marry? Settle down? She sincerely hoped that these three things did not also include Beth – not after the way he had ignored her at Elizabeth's funeral – and not after the way he had stopped writing to her after only six months or so in the Army.

And hadn't he also, after Elizabeth's funeral, referred to his home here as 'the back of beyond'. He seemed to have changed his mind and attitude about everything. So what had changed it?

And no financial difficulties'? The 'dregs of a beggar's bottle'? Well, there was only one way to find out about that.

Once again she instructed Hector to get ready the trap.

'Is it to Craignure ye be going again? To send another letter?'

'Yes, Hector, to Craignure.' She was too alarmed and too confused to bother with any conversation with Hector other than to agree with whatever he asked. 'Yes. Yes. Yes.'

Hector stood and watched her as she reached the end of the lane and turned the horse and trap to the north – not to the south as she should have done if she was going to Craignure.

He lolloped into a sprint down the lane after her, calling out, 'Ye be going the wrong way, Mrs Mary!'

She ignored him, and continued on in the direction of Tobermory.

Hector returned to the yard at the back of the house, and then sauntered into the kitchen to complain to Mrs Keillor.

'I'm the only one around here that's no' gone mad,' he said bleakly. 'There be Miss Beth, walking around all the time like she be in cuckoo land and still dreaming, and now Mrs Mary has gone round the bend in the wrong direction.'

Mrs Keillor made no answer as she placed a chicken pie in the black iron oven above the fire and then closed its two doors 'Mary never goes in the wrong direction to anywhere,' she said, reaching for a broom to sweep inside the fender.

'It could be the mare,' Hector said thoughtfully. 'Aye, it could be the mare. She's losing her nose.'

'Who's losing their nose?' Mrs Keillor said, sweeping.

'And ye must be losing your *ears!*' Hector replied huffily. 'I said the mare – *the mare.* She be getting old now and her nose scent is weakening so bad that she'd get lost if someone didna guide her all the way home.'

'So what's to worry? She's got Mary to guide her hasna she?'

'But I just *told* ye!' Hector exclaimed irritably. 'Mrs Mary has gone round the bend in the *wrong* direction. So *her* nose must be getting as poor as the mare's now.'

*

Mary knew exactly where she was going. As soon as she reached Tobermory and parked the trap, she headed straight

187

for the Inn and sought out Lizzie McLeod.

'He says he's in no financial difficulties, Lizzie, so who was this man who told you he was in bad debt? Perhaps it's not true.'

'Aye, it's true enough,' Lizzie responded. She had taken Mary into her kitchen where they could sit down and talk in private.

'The man who told me is a footman over at Strathallan Castle. He was over here on a visit to some of his people who live down near Loch Frisna. I know him and his people well. He said young Mr Macquarie is there most times he is on leave – at Strathallan Castle – that's when he and the one called William are not frolicking in Glasgow or Edinburgh or card-gambling down in England.'

'But how did he know about any debts?' Mary asked. 'Surely a footman would not know anything as personal as that?'

'No, but one particular night he was on his way to Lord Strathallan's library-room with a tray of drinks, and when he approached the door, his lordship was roaring fury at his son – at both of them – saying they had seen their way through a fortune and *he* had no intention of bailing them out this time.'

'And when was that, Lizzie?'

'A day or two before I gave young Beth the message to give ye, so the night of his lordship's fury musta been just a few weeks before that.'

So Lachlan had *lied* in his letter, Mary realised. And the reason he was now trying to sell his commission in the Army was probably to try and raise some money.

'I'm worried about the house and estate, Lizzie. The main reason General Macquarie bought the estate and built Salen was so that his children would have a good living and a good future to inherit. And now his son has inherited and – '

'Och, his debts couldna be *that* much, Mary. The Jarvisfield farm and lands must be worth a fortune.'

'And there's something else, Lizzie – Lachlan wrote in his letter about coming home and settling down to marry.'

Lizzie frowned. 'But that's a good thing, isna it?'

'Not if he's thinking of Beth.'

'Oh, nonsense!' Lizzie sat back and laughed at the very idea. 'Ye've no need to worry there, Mary, not now she's keeping company with young Mr Dewar. By! I could *eat* that young man I could. And a delicious bite he would make too!' She laughed saucily. 'But don't tell Angus, will ye?'

'I don't know though,' said Mary, her eyes thoughtful. 'There has always been a special bond between Beth and Lachlan, ever since they were children. How do we know she's keeping company with John Dewar only because Lachlan seems to have turned his back on her.'

'Nay, *nay!*' insisted Lizzie, her face straightening with seriousness. 'Ye only have to *see* those two together to know that whatever bond Beth had with Lachlan is gone.'

Mary hoped so; and driving the trap back to Jarvisfield she allowed her mind to dwell on Beth and John Dewar and how over the past few weeks they had spent so much time together. Every minute that could be spared was spent in each other's company.

She remembered Beth's sparkling eyes and radiant face on that first night John had escorted her home from the bonfire on Midsummer's Eve a year ago.

Oh yes, she realised, Lizzie was right. Any bond Beth had with Lachlan was gone now. Broken from the first day she had set eyes on John Dewar.

*

The following afternoon Mrs Keillor was grumpy with frustration.

'I don't know what I'm supposed to be doing, hen,' she complained to Mary. 'First ye tell me I have to be thrifty now with simple dishes and no waste of food, and now ye are telling me to make all the best delicacies I can for Beth to take on a picnic!'

'Yes, but tomorrow is their last full day together. He leaves the day after to return to his ship. But no, you are right, a fresh buttered loaf and some cold pork and cheese will be enough.'

Now that she had been let off the hook, Mrs Keillor

relented.

'I suppose I *could* make a fruitcake, and mebbe some jam tarts – plenty enough for all of us. Hector loves his cakes and jam tarts. Although when I give him some extra tarts to take over yon to the farmboys, he never does – he feeds them to the *horses* instead. Now I willna give him any extra, no matter how much he pleads with me.'

Mary smiled.

'Aye,' Mrs Keillor decided, whipping on her apron. 'I'll get on with the food for Beth's picnic now, before I start preparing the dinner.'

Chapter Thirty

Beth thought it sad that John had never seen Calgary Bay.

'That's why I chose it,' she said smiling, 'as a special treat for you. Although maybe as you have seen a lot of the world and a lot of beaches, Calgary may not seem so special.'

'Well, it's been a hell of a journey, so I'll let you know when we get there,' John replied. 'If it is a disappointment I'm turning around and heading straight back.'

She checked her horse and looked back at him, and saw that he was not serious.

There was not much talk between them as they rode on, due to the single file tracks that made it necessary for one to ride behind the other.

He let her lead the way and let his mind wander as he looked around at the scenery and the sheep peacefully grazing on the green high hills, and then outwards to look at a rim of the blue sea in the distance. Just one more day here – and then back out there – sailing away from this peaceful paradise.

Well, maybe to others it would not seem like paradise, but for him, she made it so. What other time, and where else in the world had he ever stopped to watch a plump little Willow Warbler and listen to her calling to her mate?

Where else in the world had he taken the time to watch otters at play, and enjoyed it?

She had opened his eyes to a whole other world of the natural life all around them.

Heaven had blessed them. During his time here the weather had been sunny and warm, and at times very hot. Not even one day of cold winds or rain, just sun, sun, sun every day.

'Look!' she said as they came out from the trees into a clearing and sat looking down on the low rippling waves of the blue sea onto a long beach of pure white sand, surrounded by rugged green hills.

'This is Calgary Bay,' she said, 'and it's always empty,

always deserted, apart from the wildlife of course.'

Later, when they had dismounted and led their horses down through the sloping dunes covered in green carpets of tender grass, and reached the white beach, he could not believe that such a stunning place could be found anywhere in Scotland.

The seawater was sky blue and so transparently clear and sparkling that he said with amazement, 'We could be on a beach by the Indian Ocean!'

And the sand, so white and as soft as powder. 'We could be in the Caribbean!'

'So you like it?'

'It's stunning! Beth, you could not have chosen a better place for ...'

'Your last day here,' she said quietly.

'Yes.' He met her eyes, and the mood changed.

She looked out to sea for a long silent moment, and when she turned back to him she was trying very hard to smile. 'Let's pretend it is your first day here, not your last.'

'No,' he said. 'Let's just make it the best day of all.'

*

Mrs Keillor would not have been pleased to know that the food she prepared was hardly touched, just a bite or two of cheese, a small cut of the bread.

Somehow, to John, the food in the bag seemed all wrong for a place of such natural beauty as this.

After a long afternoon walking hand in hand on the beach exploring the small inlets and pools, they eventually moved through the grassy dunes and collected enough pieces of light wood and twigs for him to make a fire and bring it to light with the help of his tinderbox.

Then John cut and cleaned and cooked the mackerel he had caught on the fire.

It was, Beth agreed, a more fitting meal for a place like Calgary Bay, and delicious.

'These fish must have been swept onto the shore on a wave this morning,' John said in wonderment. 'No wonder the fishermen of Mull do so well.'

'Fishing and farming are the only livelihoods on Mull,' said Beth, staring at the edge of the sea that was slowly retreating backwards. 'The sea is leaving us, the tide is going back out.'

Washing their hands in a small pool, they stood under the weakening rays of the sun watching the sea retreating farther and farther away, leaving only a few narrow slicks of water behind on the darkening sand.

'I wish this day could last forever,' Beth said.

John looked out to sea. 'I was thinking the same thing.'

They walked towards the back of the bay and the base of the green dunes, reluctant to leave but knowing they must, until he looked back and saw a majestic purple and orange sunset colouring the sky above the sea.

It was so spectacular they stopped and sat on the soft grass of one the dunes to watch it, the colours magnificent in a sky of flame reds and pinks and purple and dark blues.

'Red sky at night, sailor's delight,' he murmured.

She reached for her bag and took out two glasses and a flask of wine.

'Do you like wine?'

John looked at the sky and said, 'The sun is well over the foreyardarm so, yes, it is late enough for me to drink wine.'

'Late enough?' Beth queried.

John smiled as he explained. 'A direction from the Admiralty – no officer to partake of any liquor until the sun is over the foreyardarm.'

'And what time is that?'

'Usually – just before noon,' he grinned.

She half filled the two glasses, gave him one, and then reached to clink her glass with his. 'To –'

'Ahhhh!' He swiftly moved his glass away from her glass. 'Naval officers and crew never clink glasses when drinking.'

'Why?'

'Because life at sea is full of superstitions,' he told her. 'And it's long been believed that the ring of a glass tolls the death of one of the sailors.'

She momentarily shivered at the thought.

'Raising the glass is enough.' He smiled and raised his glass. 'To you, Beth.'

She sipped her wine and sat looking at the far-off sea. 'Are you looking forward to being ... out there ... again?'

'No, and once I'm on ship and out there, I know I'll be wishing I was ... back there ... with Miss Elizabeth Jarvis.'

'How long will it take for you to reach Portsmouth?'

'From Oban by coach, seven days, or near enough.'

'That long – seven days!' She sighed dismally. 'So even Portsmouth is a long way from here.'

'Very long, especially when you're confined inside a coach with people who don't bathe.'

'How long will you be away?'

'About a year. Another eight months on watch at Kingston.'

'Is that in Jamaica?'

'Yes, we're stood off just outside Kingston's harbour, or patrolling between there and Hunt's Bay.'

'Last time ... did the Navy find any ships with captured slaves hidden in them?'

'Yes, but ... Beth, let's not talk about it. Let's just enjoy our time together today, and forget about tomorrow or any other time.'

'Just tell me – were the captured slaves freed?'

'Of course they were. They were brought up on deck and returned to shore in a cutter.'

'And the captain?'

'The captains were dealt with. No more questions. Soon enough I'll be back there, but now I'm here with you and that's all I want to think about.'

They sat for a time in silent harmony in the full colour of a warm Hebridean evening.

John gazed around Calgary Bay, at the emptiness and the serene peacefulness of it all, and then lay back on the dune with a sigh and watched the magnificence of the sunset, his eyes moving up to the last seagulls flying overhead. It was an evening for fantasising, for dreaming ... even the hills seemed greener and higher with a kind of dusky magic in the air. He gazed at the sunset again, at all the amazing colours shading and shaping together like an artist's painting of an explosion in the sky.

'I've no wish to leave here.'

'Nor I,' she murmured.

'This is bliss, this Mull of yours.'

'So it's Mull you love, not me?'

'Yes, it's Mull.'

He glanced at her sideways and smiled, and then pulled her down beside him and kissed her.

'No, it's you, Beth, you ...'

He kissed her again, and even the kiss felt different to all the other times he had kissed her.

'Would you ...' she asked him softly, 'would you ever wish to *live* on Mull?'

'Yes,' he said honestly, 'if it meant I would be coming *home* to you.'

The lowering sun was now like a blazing fireball suspended over the darkening horizon surrounded by pink and purple rays of light, but they were no longer aware of the sky or the sea or the land; oblivious to all but each other as they kissed and let their hands move over each other, unmindful that the darkness was coming.

Time passed, a cool night breeze came in off the sea.

'We should have left here hours ago,' John said, sitting up and looking at the night sky.

Beth also looked at the sky, only now becoming aware of how late it was.

'It will be difficult and dangerous riding on the narrow tracks in this darkness,' she said.

She slowly sat up to join him and he looked at her. Her lustrous black hair had come loose from its ribbon and was now tumbled down over her shoulders.

'Even in the dark you look beautiful,' he murmured.

She smiled and touched her lips to his. 'So do you.'

'And in the dark you *feel* beautiful too.'

Her lips were moving on his. 'So do you.'

Seconds later he asked smiling. 'So are we forced to stay here all night? Just the two of us alone?'

'At least until first light. It would be cruel and dangerous to make the horses trek those tracks in the dark.'

'It would,' John agreed, and then moved down to where the two horses were tethered and removed the two blankets, as well as the two saddles to allow the horses more comfort also.

Then he led both horses down the beach to one of the many freshwater pools between the rocks and waited while the horses drank their fill before he led them back again to their tethering spot.

Returning to the dune, he found a secluded spot out of the breeze between two rocks and spread one blanket on the ground. When Beth lay on it, he sat down beside her and pulled the second blanket over her.

'John.'

'Are you warmer here?' he asked.

'I have not been cold.'

He had taken off his jacket earlier and now folded it to make a pillow for her head. Beth was gazing up at the half moon.

'John.'

He paused and looked down at her.

'Did you mean it when you said it was me you loved?'

Even in the darkness she could see his smile. 'I love everything about you ... most of all those beautiful dark eyes of yours.'

'It does not trouble you ... that my eyes are dark because I was made by two people who were not of the same race? When you first saw me, did you not see that?'

He looked at her silently for a long moment. 'Do you want to know the truth?'

'Yes.'

'When I first saw you, I did not see a girl made by two people of two races, all I saw was a girl that I thought must have been made in Heaven.'

He slid down beside her and she moved inside his arms, smiling, relieved of her anxiety, putting her hands around his neck and half strangling him with love.

He pulled one of her hands away and kissed her fingers. 'Or maybe ...' he said, 'I am still in some wonderful dream and you are not in fact truly *real*.'

She smiled. 'Then it must be my wonderful dream too, and maybe *you* are not real.'

He grinned, his eyes moving over her face. 'I think we should investigate further and try to find out for certain once and for all.'

His hands began to move down her body, lightly touching her breasts, her waist and her thighs like someone who needed to be reassured. 'Yes, you feel real ... you feel ...' He turned up his eyes and let out his breath.

She kissed his mouth and both lost their smiles as the grip of her hands on his shoulders became more urgent, their bodies quickening, moving closer.

In their hastening passion John suddenly became conscious of his obligations as a gentleman, but she was more in tune with the ways and freedoms of the natural world all around them and she hushed him, touching his face softly and whispering her love for him. She wanted him as much as he wanted her and she told him so.

'I *love* you.'

And then, to Beth, it all became so wonderful as he kissed her and turned her onto her back and her bodice became unbuttoned and the world began to spin again as she lost herself in the blissful spinning of it.

She had once thought that she would be happy to accompany him to the ends of the earth if he wished it, and now he was using his hands and his lips to take her there, to the ends of the earth ... until finally he took her there, on the blanket, on a dune in Calgary Bay.

An owl in a tree somewhere above began to complain about her soft cries into the night, which interfered with his own night calls.

And when, a short time later, they made love again, lost in their own tender love-dream, and her broken and heightening love cries again rose into the night, the owl complained louder and swooped down past them, returning to his tree ignored.

Beth knew she would never forget one single moment of this beautiful night of looking up at a navy sky and the crystal clear star fields sparkling across it, hearing only the occasional hoots of a passing owl and the waves breaking gently on the beach.

A magical and beautiful night of sweet worship and tender passion, and the night of her first sexual experience, the most blissful of all.

'*The night*,' she later wrote in her diary, '*when I knew that all I wanted was to be his wife, or die unwed.*'

PART FIVE

Chapter Thirty-One

At the end of October, Mary received another letter from Lachlan.

My Dear Mary,

This is the briefest of notes to inform you that I am betrothed to marry Isabella Hamilton Dundas Campbell, a daughter of the Laird of Jura and Craignish. The marriage is to take place after Christmas, following which Isabella and I will be returning to my Jarvisfield Estate.

I am sure you will be happy to have a full house again, and I am also sure that Isabella and Beth will become good friends.

Yours fondly,
Lachlan

PS: I am also happy to tell you that I now own a number of fine racehorses that I keep at a very good stable in Bunbury in Lancashire.

Mary was so delighted she showed the letter to Beth, who was equally as delighted. 'Oh, that's *wonderful* news. And yes, I am sure Isabella and I *will* become good friends.'

Mrs Keillor was not so pleased. She sat back with a sigh. 'A new mistress, eh? Y'know what this means, Mary? It means I'm going to be kept cooking night and day with all the fancy dishes they'll be wanting every night.'

'Oh, I don't think Lachlan ever had much of a taste for fancy dishes,' Mary replied.

'No, but what about his future lady wife, eh? He says she's a daughter of the Laird of Jura and Craignish, so she must be used to good food and fancy living. And they'll be entertaining their friends, 'course they will – inviting them over to Mull to stay. By! For this to come at my time of life, just when I was getting comfortable with having little to do.'

She unfolded her arms, frowned, sat back and folded them again. 'There's only one thing forrit – ye'll have to get Maggie and Lorna in here working full-time once the laird is back with a wife. Will ye do that?'

Mary nodded, not really listening – too happy in the knowledge that Lachlan was now truly preparing to settle down, and with a wife that was not her precious Beth, especially in view of the difficulties that would now present due to Beth's relationship with John Dewar.

Oh yes, she had known, as soon as Beth had come back that day in July after staying out all night with John Dewar, she knew their relationship had become more intimate, but Beth had refused to answer all questions, so Mary had eventually stopped asking them.

She had tried very hard to be angry with John Dewar, but somehow she could not blame him. If she was to blame anyone it would be Beth, but knowing how much Beth loved that young man, it was hard to blame her either. Two young people in love, just like she and George were in Sydney. And they had also been unable to wait.

Oh, George, my dearest wonderful darling George...

'Racehorses, eh?' said Mrs Keillor curiously. 'If he's bought racehorses, why is he keeping them down in England if he's going to be living here?'

Hector, who had been lurking ands listening by the kitchen door, stepped in quickly and answered her. 'If they be racehorses, *real* racehorses, then he'll need somewhere to train 'em, won't he?'

'So why canna he train them here in Mull?'

'Too rugged, not flat enough. Only place flat enough here for him to give racehorses a good run, is on one of the long beaches.'

'So why canna he do that then?'

Hector shook his head as if thinking Mrs Keillor was now as mad as the rest of them. 'If the horses are going to *race* on grass, then they must be *trained* on grass. He won't get much good out of 'em on race courses if they've been trained on *sand*. Any fool would know that.'

'Aye, and that explains why *ye* know it,' Mrs Keillor

answered with a decorous sniff. 'Mary, he's been lurking and listening again.'

Mary was lost in thought, their voices merely mundane sounds in the background.

And obviously, she was thinking, any financial difficulties Lachlan may have had in the past were now behind him, otherwise he would not have been able to afford to buy a number of racehorses to stable in Lancashire.

She couldn't help wondering what this Isabella Hamilton Dundas Campbell would be like?

Well, she finally decided, it didn't really matter *what* she was like, because as Lachlan's wife, and a young lady new to Mull, she was determined to make her feel very welcome.

*

A late winter afternoon in February brought the latest Mrs Macquarie to the Isle of Mull, and her new home in Jarvisfield.

Wrapped in a heavy seal-skin cloak against the bitter cold, she looked small in height, but when the cloak was removed, Mary could see she was indeed a petite girl, with light brown hair and large blue eyes, and a face and manner that seemed nervous, but very sweet.

By the glowing light of the candles Mary could clearly see Lachlan's face ... and the change the years had brought to his looks. His face was leaner, harder, and looking slightly older than his twenty-seven years. Still handsome though, yes, but the years of fast living had taken their toll.

But his manner was light and happy and young and in this respect he was Lachlan again, back to his old self.

'Mary, this is Isabella, my wife of almost two weeks.'

'Welcome,' Mary said, taking the girl's hands in her own. 'I hope you will be happy here in Jarvisfield.'

The girl still looked nervous. 'I'm sure I will,' she answered. 'My husband has promised to take very good care of me.'

'That I have. And Isabella ... there is Beth ...'

Both seemed to pause and hesitate as Beth came out of the shadows into full light with a warm and welcoming smile on her face.

'Hello, Isabella, I'm sure you are going to *love* Mull when you get to know it, but you will not see it at it's best until spring arrives.' She gave the girl a light kiss on the cheek, and then turned to Lachlan, unable to hide her delight at seeing him again. 'Welcome home, stranger. We have missed you.'

'Beth ...' It was he who moved to give her a light kiss on the cheek but his manner was stiffer, and he quickly drew away.

'So,' he said cheerfully to Mary. 'A good fire and a light meal is what we need now. Are our rooms ready?'

'Everything is ready,' Mary agreed. 'And it is more than a light meal that Mrs Keillor has prepared for you.' Mary looked over her shoulder. 'Where is she?'

Mrs Keillor came rushing into the hall wiping her hands on her apron. As soon as she saw Lachlan she was startled – he looked taller and older and more authoritative in his bearing – He looked like what he was – a young Army officer.

She immediately dipped a slight curtsy. 'Welcome home, sir.' And then, finally noticing the girl. 'Welcome, ma'am.'

Isabella gave a small laugh. 'It's so strange to be called "ma'am", but now I am married I will have to get used to it.' She looked up at her new husband adoringly. 'Won't I, dear?'

'How old are you?' Mrs Keillor asked audaciously, certain the girl was no more than seventeen.

'Isabella is the same age as Beth,' Lachlan said, glancing briefly at Beth. 'Almost nineteen.'

Beth laughed. 'Lachlan – how easily you remember! You always had a strange way of remembering my age, even when I myself forgot it.'

'Come into the fire now,' Mary urged, leading them into the drawing-room. 'Isabella, would you like some tea to warm you up?'

Isabella nodded with her sweet smile. 'Yes, please.

'No tea for me, Mary,' Lachlan said quickly. 'Just wine.'

When Mary entered the kitchen, Mrs Keillor had a grim look on her face.

'She seems nice enough,' Mary said. 'So why the face?'

'I don't like the look of him,' Mrs Keillor brought a knife down hard to split a turnip in half. 'I think he's pretending to be very happy when he's not. And that wife of his is too thin. I hope she's not been starving him as well.'

'Don't be ridiculous,' Mary laughed. 'She is not responsible for what he eats. And I would not say she is thin. Her figure is very neat and slim.'

'Leastaways, officers always get good food in the Army, so I reckon he'll be glad to get back there.'

Mrs Keillor could not have been more wrong, because when Mary returned with the tea and a decanter of wine, she learned that Lachlan had resigned from the Army four months previously.

'There's no fun or excitement in peacetime soldiering,' he told her. 'I was hoping for battles and charges and the camaraderie of men spilling blood on the battlefield together, like the Army was in my father's time. Now that was a *great* time to be a soldier, defending one's king and country. But now...' he shrugged dismissively. 'Now we have a girl on the throne, supported by her German consort who always appears wearing a magnificent uniform, but I don't believe he has ever seen any *real* service either.'

'I think it's wonderful to have a *queen* on the throne now,' Isabella said excitedly. 'And they say Queen Victoria is very fond of Scotland.'

'She can stay fond of it, as long as she stays away from it!' Lachlan said. 'As I remember the last female on the English throne spitefully ordered the death of our Mary Queen of Scots.'

'Husband!' Isabella said, offended. 'Mary Stuart was a *Catholic!*'

Mary Jarvis quickly excused herself from the conversation, after an apology about needing to instruct Mrs Keillor about dinner. She did not care for discussions about any kind of politics, nor indeed did she care who was on the throne in London, because it mattered little to life here on Mull.

Beth remained, interested. She asked Lachlan. 'What do you think of our Navy?'

'Our Navy?' Lachlan drank some wine. 'The Royal Navy is the greatest navy in the World. Britain's naval power dominates the seas. But what are our great ships doing now –

in peacetime? They are chasing after trading vessels that might have a few slaves in their holds.'

Beth also excused herself, leaving the room and standing in the hall for a moment, bitterly disappointed and hurt that Lachlan had obviously forgotten that her father had once been a captured slave.

But then ... she remembered, Lachlan did not know that, just as she herself had not known. And knowing how much Lachlan had always loved her father, and over the years hearing from Mrs Keillor and Hector how crazy with grief he had become after her father's death, she could not blame him, only forgive him.

She returned to the drawing-room and sat down with a smile on her face. 'Only another couple of months and then the bluebells will be out,' she said cheerfully to Isabella. 'They grow everywhere around here. But I can also take you to some other lovely parts of Mull. Do you ride'

Isabella grimaced. 'Only when I have to.'

Lachlan smiled. 'No, Beth, unlike you, Isabella is not a good horsewoman. She much prefers lying in bed all day, and loves it even moreso since her wedding, don't you my darling?'

The blush that coloured Isabella's face sent Beth out of the room with another excuse.

Something was wrong with those two, Beth decided. Something was *very* wrong. She could only judge from her own experience, but she was certain that John would be incapable of embarrassing her like that in the company of others, or even in private.

Yes, newly-weds those two may be, but something was just *not right*.

Mary realised the same when she approached the dining room later that evening.

As she approached the door carrying a tray, she heard Lachlan and Isabella, who were already seated, arguing in hushed tones.

'But it's just not *normal*, having housekeepers and servants dining at the same table,' Isabella was saying. 'Father and Mother would never allow it at home.'

'And this is *my* home, not your father or mother's home,' Lachlan replied in low anger. 'And Mary and Beth are part of *my* family, always have been, because they are *George's* family, his wife and daughter. Even my father would be shocked at your suggestion, not to mention my dear mother. Listen, Isabella, you *must* understand – Jarvisfield is *their* home too, and legally so. My father's trust decrees that all and every one of the family of George Jarvis and his descendants shall have a home on Jarvisfield *for ever.*'

'Yes, I understand that, a home on the estate, and I don't at all mind them living here in this house with us as staff, but not to dine at the *same* table.'

Mary quickly turned about and headed back to the kitchen where she lay down the tray and stood with head bent, one hand on her hip and the other on her brow, taking a number of deep breaths.

'What's up?' Mrs Keillor asked, frowning at the tray and tureen of hot vegetable broth. 'Don't they want the broth?'

After a long silence, Mary pulled herself together, and said firmly, 'Mrs Keillor, I want you to go into the dining room and remove two of the four place settings. Apologise and pretend you have set them their by mistake.'

'I did no such thing!'

'I said *pretend* that you did.'

'Why?'

'Just do it. I'll explain later.'

Mrs Keillor looked keenly at Mary with her sharp eyes, and then nodded and left the kitchen.

Mary followed her out, and quickly went upstairs to pop her head inside the door of Beth's bedroom.

Beth looked up from her diary.

'We are eating in the kitchen tonight. Don't go near the dining room.'

'What?' Beth laid down her pen. 'Why?'

'I'll explain later.'

*

Later, as they ate their dinner at the kitchen table, and after Mary had revealed the conversation she had overhead, their

207

was utter silence for some minutes.

'Oh well, ho-hum,' Beth said with a shrug. 'Food is food and one table is not much different to any other table, so why fret about it. Allowances must be made for newly-weds I suppose.'

'It's not that they are newly-weds,' Mary explained, attempting to be fair in her thinking. 'It's just that ... well, life in the Macquarie household has always been different to others, more relaxed in the way it has been run, with little regard to convention and customs.'

'That's true,' Mrs Keillor agreed.

'I mean, it was the same back in Sydney. Governor Macquarie brought the wrath of the Exclusives to his door because he occasionally had emancipists dining with him at his table in Government House.

'That doesn't surprise me,' said Mrs Keillor, chomping on a mouthful of beef. 'A prince of a man he was, but no pomp in him, none at all. And a *fair* man in all his ways.'

'But for Isabella,' Mary continued, 'that's not the way things have been done in *her* home, which obviously adheres to all the conventions, and that's what she is used to. And Lachlan ... well, his duty and loyalties now belong to his wife, and not to his former nursemaid or her daughter.'

'Aye, and so ye are both banished to the kitchen now,' Mrs Keillor said. 'By! Who would ever have thought it? Not Mrs Macquarie, that's for sure. The *old* Mrs Mrs Macquarie I mean.'

'She wasn't that old,' Mary responded. 'She was only fifty-six.'

'And sorely missed,' said Mrs Keillor, looking at the glowing fire and its red flames.

'Still,' she added cheerfully, 'ye are both better off eating in here with me in my kitchen and kept warm by my big fire. Aye, it's much warmer in here than sitting in that draughty old dining room, isna it now?'

Mary made no answer, still despondent about it all, but Beth smiled in response, 'It is, Mrs Keillor, much, *much* warmer than the draughty dining room.'

'That's my lass!' Mrs Keillor said with satisfaction. 'And

yer mother will get used to eating in the kitchen soon enough.'

Mary half laughed to herself, thinking back to all those nights she had sat eating in the kitchen at Government House in Sydney with the two cooks Mrs Ovens and Mrs Kelly. But then ... that was before George, and before she became Mrs Jarvis and part of the Macquarie family.

Chapter Thirty-Two

Apart from the dining arrangements, life at Gruline carried on as it had always done, and Mary could find no big fault with the new Mrs Macquarie, just minor things that often irritated her and sent her into a mood of frustration.

Isabella's manner was always mild and polite, as a young lady usually is with her servants, yet at other times she could be very friendly and was always seeking out Beth's company.

Beth was happy to oblige, occasionally going on long walks with Isabella, showing her the Mull countryside, and then both girls would return talking cheerfully together, and always holding bunches of the earliest spring wildflowers.

Yes, apart from the changed dining arrangements, Mary decided that Lachlan's wife was nice enough – until the night Isabella stepped into the kitchen after dinner and looked around in a searching way. 'Where is Beth?'

'We've just carried the tub up to her room,' Mary said, drying her hands with a towel. 'She's about to have her bath.'

Isabella bit her lip for a moment, disappointed. She turned to walk away, then quickly turned back.

'Mrs Jarvis, do you think Beth would agree to be my maid? My *personal* maid? To help *me* at my bath time? I nearly slipped and fell the last time.'

Mary stared at her, her blue eyes flaming. 'Now let's get one thing clear. *I* may be a servant here, but Beth is not! She is here, legally, under the Macquarie Trust, because she is the daughter of George Jarvis, and she is *not* here as a servant!'

Isabella looked shocked and flummoxed. 'But I ... I need help with my dress and ... and my hair.'

'If you cannot manage without a personal maid, then you must send for the one you had at Craignish,' Mary replied. 'I trust you *did* have a personal maid at Craignish if you're looking for one now? So I suggest you send for her as soon as possible, but in the meantime, *I* will assist you with your dress and hair.'

'What's wrong?' Lachlan appeared behind Isabella, his face

concerned. 'What's all the fuss? You sound angry, Mary.'

Isabella said quickly, "No, no, it's nothing, we were just talking about matters to do with the household.' She forced a fake smile onto her face. 'Thank you, Mrs Jarvis, goodnight.'

Lachlan did not look entirely convinced, and his concern seemed to be all for Mary. 'Is all well, Mary?'

'All is well,' Mary nodded. 'I'm off to bed shortly. Goodnight, Lachlan.'

'Goodnight, Mary.' He nodded and walked away, following his wife.

'By!' said Mrs Keillor, when they had gone, 'I thought ye were going to punch m'lady then, I did!'

'I don't do such things,' Mary said dismissively. 'But I did *feel* like taking her by her bustle and throwing her out the kitchen door there. *Where* does she think she is – in a hotel in London? This is the back and beyond of Scotland, for heaven's sake! And she must have *known* that before she came, because he has said it often enough.'

'He has, true.'

'Why, even Mrs Macquarie, older as she was, and even when she was a younger woman in Sydney, never expected nor asked me to attend on her when she was naked in her bath!'

Mary was still so angry she had to sit down. 'She's entitled to a personal maid, if she needs one – but not my Beth!'

'And y'know,' Mrs Keillor put in, 'I don't think Master Lachlan would be happy to see Beth reduced to being his wife's personal maid either.'

*

Lachlan was not happy about many things these days. He had accepted his limits, and had returned to Mull to settle down, but at a price – a high price!

So a few days later, after seeing his accountant in Tobermory, he rode back in a fury to the Macquarie house in Jarvisfield, dismounting and throwing the reins to Hector in the yard before marching into the house through the kitchen door, and then looking searchingly into the drawing-room and then the dining room.

'What is wrong?' Mary asked him, coming down the stairs.

'Where is she?' he demanded through gritted teeth. 'That wife of mine, *where is she?*'

Mary did not know. 'If she's not down here, then she must be up in her room, I presume.'

'Still in her bed again – and it now almost noon!'

Mary watched him charge up the stairs and then all she could do was remain at the bottom of the stairs and listen, and what she heard was not pleasant.

'*Ten thousand!*' she heard him rage. 'That's the dowry your father promised me for marrying you, *ten* thousand – not *two* thousand. How in hell can I pay off all my debts with a shortfall of eight thousand? I was promised *ten* thousand!'

After a silence – no doubt a *shocked* silence – Isabella sounded just as outraged.

'*Ten thousand pounds?* My father does not have that kind of money. He has other daughters who will need dowries, and he has always said the dowry for each would be *two* thousand.'

'Drummond assured me that your father had agreed *ten* thousand!'

'Who? William Drummond? That man is a liar and a braggart and you should not believe a word he says.'

'*You* told me ten thousand! *You* boasted it to me! You said whichever man was lucky enough to get you would receive your dowry of *ten* thousand pounds. So it's *you* that is the liar – not William Drummond!'

'And is that the only reason you married me – for money?'

'*Yes!*'

The desperation in his voice was clear, but what came next was vicious.

'Isabella, forgive me, I *did* intend that one day I would settle down here peacefully on my family estate with the woman I love – but sadly that woman is not *you!* And although I agreed to the ten thousand pounds, I would certainly not have married you for *two!* My racehorses cost almost that!'

Mary had to move quickly down the hall as he came running furiously down the stairs and out through the kitchen to the yard. Minutes later he was back up on his horse again – leaving Hector staring after him.

'I havna tightened the girths!' Hector shouted, but Lachlan recklessly rode on, eager to get away from the house as fast as he could.

Mrs Keillor had also been listening and had ducked into the dining room when she heard Lachlan coming down the stairs.

Now she returned to the kitchen and she and Mary stared at each other in consternation.

'So now we know,' Mary said sadly. 'The marriage was nothing to do with love, just a bargain to clear off his debts.'

'A bad bargain then, if he was promised a dowry of ten and only got two.'

'But even *two* thousand pounds is an almighty sum of money,' Mary said. 'When you think that our farm manager Robert Dewar earns only eighty pounds a year, and that's *good* pay.'

'Does he? I only get thirty.'

'Yes, you get twelve shilling a week – and that also is *good* pay!'

'Along with my bed and room and all the food I can eat, so I'm not complaining. How much do ye get, Mary?

'I get nothing from this estate,' Mary answered honestly. 'My money comes from a trust that General Macquarie left to George. And Beth's money comes from a separate trust that George left to her.'

They moved to sit down at the table where Mary slumped for a moment, her hands to her head as she said sympathetically. 'That poor girl.'

'Why? She hoodwinked him. Boasting about her big dowry.'

Mary suddenly jolted upright. 'Now don't you *dare* say a word about what we heard from upstairs today to Hector or anyone else on Jarvisfield.'

'Me?' Mrs Keillor looked at her wryly. 'I heard nothing at all. I was in the dining room tending to my own business.'

'And in particular – not a word about this to Beth. I don't want her to get dragged into it or become involved in any way. And what she doesn't know, can't trouble her.'

*

Throughout the rest of the day Mary kept venturing upstairs to knock on Isabella's door and see if she needed anything. She felt sorry for the poor girl, to be so disillusioned so early in her marriage, and in such a cruel way.

Unsure whether Mary and the staff had heard the quarrel, Isabella said she was feeling unwell, and so would stay in bed. And no, no, she did not want anything to drink. And when Mary knocked again later, no, no, she did not want anything to eat.

'Just to sleep,' she said tiredly, stretching out on her side and pumping the pillow under her head and then moving one leg over the other into what Mary concluded must be her favourite sleeping position. 'I have a weak constitution.'

'She eats like a bird at the best of times,' Mrs Keillor observed when Mary returned with the dinner tray. 'A pick here, a pick there, no wonder she's so thin and tired all the time.'

'God help her though, she's away from her home, in a strange place, so it must be difficult for her.'

'Difficult for who – Isabella?' asked Beth, walking into the kitchen, her hair soaking wet.

'Yes, she is feeling ill,' Mary said. 'And so will you be if you don't get that wet cloak off you.'

Beth removed her cloak and draped it over a wooden chair near the fire to dry.

'Oh, the rain! Only a short way riding back from the Dewars' place when I looked up and saw the low black clouds and knew I was in for a heavy soaking.'

She bent over the fire, squeezing the rain out of her long black hair. 'Poor Isabella. As soon as I change I'll go in to see her.'

'No don't – leave her be,' Mary said quickly. 'She's asleep and ... Lachlan is out.'

'Out? So where has he gone, do you know?'

Mary didn't know, but she could make a very good guess, and if she was right then Lachlan would not be back for days.

'Strathallan Castle, I think.'

Chapter Thirty-Three

When Lachlan rode up to the front door of Strathallan Castle, William Drummond came down the steps to greet him with an eyebrow raised in surprise.

'On your own? Is the honeymoon over? So soon? When I married I did not see the light of day for over a month!'

'Damn you, Drummond!'

Drummond caught the reins of the horse. 'Hang on and I'll call you a groom, but oh, I forgot –' he said with a laugh, '*you* are a groom!'

'I'm a fool,' Lachlan snapped, dismounting. 'And why did you *lie* to me?'

'I have never *lied* to you.' Drummond's laughter faded. 'Who says I did?'

'Isabella.'

'Oh good grief, I knew it! That's what women always do y'know. As soon as they get a husband they immediately try to turn him against all his friends.'

'Yes and *she* lied to me also! Am I now a laughing stock?'

'Not in this house you're not,' Drummond said, leading the way up the steps. 'This is beginning to sound serious, let's talk in the library.'

*

'Taste this,' Drummond suggested, pouring out two glasses of dark amber wine. 'It's a new Madeira I had shipped in a few days ago, and in my view, it's quite fair.'

Lachlan tasted the wine and then looked darkly at his friend, envying the difference between them. Upon his father's death William would become the 9th Viscount of Strathallan, and would receive all the property and money that went with that title. And even now he had plenty of money of his own – a yearly allowance that most men could only dream of.

'Why did you tell me that Isabella's father had agreed a dowry for her of ten thousand pounds?'

'Yes,' Drummond nodded. 'That was the amount, I'm sure of it.'

'How sure? Did he actually *say* that amount? Did he actually *say* ten thousand pounds?'

'Well ...' William thought back. 'I approached him on the matter, on your behalf, telling him that Isabella had made it very clear to me that she wished to marry you, and he was not only agreeable but keen, oh yes, very keen.'

'I know that. But what did he say then?'

'Thank you, Lord Strathallan.'

'William!'

'Ah.' Drummond knocked back his wine. 'Well, after I had told him that I was not Lord Strathallan *yet*, and that my father still appeared quite hale and hearty, he said he was very agreeable to an engagement between you and Isabella, even a short one, very agreeable indeed.'

'And the dowry?'

'Yes, I told him that as my father had been your former guardian since boyhood, I asked if Isabella was correct in saying her dowry would be ten thousand pounds? And he ...' William frowned as he thought back, 'he ...'

'Dammit!' Lachlan was losing his patience. 'Did he *agree* to that amount of ten thousand pounds? Did he verbally *agree* that amount with you?'

'Well, now that I think about it, he did not exactly agree it, in words – but then he did not *deny* it either. He just raised his glass and suggested we toast the happiness of the young couple's future.'

'So he did not agree ten thousand, but he did not deny ten thousand either – so you were taken by Craignish but it is *me* who now looks the fool!'

'Why, what happened? Did he pay you only five?'

'Two. And it was not paid into my bank until *after* the marriage.'

'Lord save us; I don't believe it. *Two* thousand. The canny rogue.'

Lachlan refilled their glasses. 'We've both known for some time now, William, that marriage for me could not be a matter of preference.'

William nodded.

'And that if I wanted to get free of my debts then I would have to marry for land or money. So I married for money – a girl that is likeable enough, but only in small doses. Now I find that the money I married is only a pittance of the amount I need.'

'So what are you going to do?'

Lachlan looked at him, a forlorn expression in his eyes. 'I don't know. Your circumstances are so superior to mine, so as a last resort, I was hoping you could help.'

Drummond did not answer, his eyes on his finger as he ran it around the rim of his wineglass on the desk.

'I could end up in a debtor's prison,' Lachlan said bleakly. 'Would you enjoy seeing me in there – in a debtor's prison?'

'It would be an entertaining sight, I must admit,' Drummond said smiling, 'but only for a few minutes, then it would pall.' His face straightened. 'No, we can't allow that to happen.'

'So you will help?'

Drummond nodded. 'I'm sure we can come to some sort of business arrangement.'

Lachlan's brow puckered. 'What sort of business arrangement?'

'Jarvisfield. If I was to lend you all the money you needed –'

'Ten thousand pounds.'

Drummond nodded. 'Say ten thousand pounds. Then I would need you to put up a section of the Jarvisfield land as security.'

'Agreed.'

'Also, no more gambling, that is the cause of your damnation.'

'You started me, you led me into it – *you* were the one who insisted on us going to the card games every night.'

'Ah yes, but I could afford to play, and so could you, until you started trying to recoup your losses. First rule of gambling – wager only as much as you can afford to lose.'

'And I lost everything.'

'You lost more than that, old chum. You lost your senses

when you recklessly bought four racehorses before you had even received the dowry, whatever the amount. That was a big mistake.'

Lachlan closed his eyes and put his head back on the cool green leather of the armchair. . 'I know, I know, I know ...'

'And there is just one other thing,' Drummond said thoughtfully. 'If I send a messenger with a note for my solicitor to call tomorrow, to draw up our business agreement, I will expect you to return to your wife and make the best of it. If you throw her aside I will not be able to support you. In a few years or so I will be the next Viscount Strathallan, eligible to take my father's seat in the House of Lords. I now have a reputation to protect.'

Lachlan sat with his head back, gazing at the ceiling ... wishing he was dead, a sweet release from it all ... If only, if only, if only he had stayed on Mull and never joined the Army, his life might have turned out so different ...

He sat up and looked at William Drummond. 'Agreed,' he said wearily. 'I'll go back and try and make the best of it.'

'It's the only way,' Drummond said, refilling the glasses and regaining his humour.

'Now Lachlan, I implore you, no more of this tedious talk about money and debtor's prisons. It's as foul as being forced to eat pig's kidneys. Stay a few days and regain your spirits, and by the time you return to Mull your financial difficulties will all have been sorted.'

'Yes,' Lachlan said, realising that he was indebted to William Drummond in more ways than just financially. William had come to his aide, as he had always done. He had always been a friend when a friend was needed, and always a very good friend indeed.

He said, 'Thank you, William. You have my sincere gratitude and appreciation.'

'Oh *uffff,*' Drummond laughed. 'We have been friends for too long to need that kind of talk. I propose a toast. He raised his glass. 'To hell with the creditors!'

'I'll drink to that,' Lachlan laughed, his spirits brightening. 'But *you* are my main creditor now.'

'Then to hell with me!' Drummond knocked his wine and

looked for a refill.

'And now, my favourite toast of all, which is quite fitting in the circumstances.'

'Which is?'

'To our wives and sweethearts – may they never meet!'

Lachlan laughed. 'Oh yes, I will *definitely* drink to that!'

Chapter Thirty-Four

Upon his return, life at Gruline House went on as much as usual with Lachlan doing his utmost to make the best of his marriage, and Isabella regaining her health and spending less time in bed.

With the onset of spring, Beth was back in her breeches, ploughing about in the vegetable garden, while Hector looked on disapprovingly.

'He willna like it,' Hector warned her. 'The master. He willna like ye wearing those breeches again.'

'These breeches,' Beth replied, 'are *his* riding breeches; old ones he had no further use of.'

'So ye stole 'em?'

'No, I asked if I could use them and he didn't seem to care.'

'Then *he's* changed hasna he? He used to hate ye dressing up in breeches and ...' Hector scratched the back of his head in an angry motion, 'and tis *no* right and *no* fair I tell ye!'

Beth straightened up and turned to look at him, her dark eyes puzzled. 'What's not fair, Hector?'

'Those *breeches,*' Hector exclaimed pointing. 'He alus gave his old breeches to *me* – so what am I going to do if ye keep stealing 'em from me?'

'Hector, I'm sorry, I didn't realise – '

'And them's *good* breeches,' Hector pointed out. 'Made in Edinburgh to last for years. Made o' the best codroy!'

Beth looked down at her corduroy breeches, tucked at the knee into black boots. 'So I'll clean them and give them to you,' Beth said. 'It was simply because of the heavy rain –'

'Ye got mud on 'em – look, wet mud. My horses don't like wet mud.'

'And are the horses going to be *wearing* the breeches?' Beth asked dryly.

'Don't be doltish! Tis *me* who'll be wearing 'em!'

'Then when I'm finished I will clean the breeches and give them to you,' Beth said wearily.

'And no mud on 'em?'

'And no mud on 'em,' Beth repeated, walking back to the house.

'And ye willna steal any more of my breeches, will ye, Miss Bethy?' Hector called after her.

Beth refused to answer, feeling in a rare gloomy mood. Summer seemed to be taking so long to come, and all the excessive politeness in the household was making her anxious. Lachlan's constant politeness to his wife seemed forced and shallow. Isabella's meek politeness in response to him was stiff and tense. Her mother and Mrs Keillor were always whispering. Even Maggie and Lorna were always whispering about something or other. But nobody was whispering to *her* about anything.

Up in her bedroom she peeled down the breeches and stepped out of them.

She was being kept in the dark about something, as if she was some delicate child that needed protecting.

She slipped on her petticoat and then a warm grey tweed dress and fastened the buttons down the front, buckled the belt around her waist.

In the mirror she looked at herself and saw a healthy young woman of almost nineteen, an age to be respected.

Discontented, she stood thinking for a few minutes, looking out across the water of Loch Ba, and then she quickly turned and left the room to run down the stairs, lifting her cloak from the hallstand, throwing it around her shoulders and tying the cords.

Minutes later she was back in the yard, saddling her horse without needing any help from Hector, mutely refusing to be hindered by his protestations or babble.

And then she was riding away from the house, doing what she always did these days when she felt discontented, riding towards the sea.

Finally she drew rein on the cliff; sitting very still on her horse, staring out over the ocean while her dark hair blew about her face in the wind.

She sat there for a long time, staring out far and wondering, as she always wondered, in which direction lay Jamaica.

She was about to turn her horse around and ride back when she heard another horse behind her. She looked over her shoulder and saw the rider was Lachlan.

He hailed her with a smile and she turned her horse about and took a few paces down to meet him.

'Lachlan?'

'Beth.'

'What are you doing here?' she asked with some surprise.

'Like you – out riding to nowhere.'

She smiled. 'I rarely go riding to nowhere. I fancied a closer look at the sea.'

'Why?'

'It's calming. Don't you find it so?'

He gazed out to sea. 'There are not many things I find calming these days. Anyway, the sea looks quite rough, as if there's a storm brewing.'

'Rough or smooth, the sea always has a comforting effect on me,' Beth said as she rode on.

'You never seemed to care so much about the sea before. It was always the land you loved.'

'I love both,' Beth said. 'I love everything in and around my island. I love life.'

He looked at her strangely. 'Yes, and you always have done, haven't you?'

She drew rein and looked at him with concern. 'Lachlan, is anything wrong?'

He seemed about to answer, then paused. 'No, nothing.'

They continued at a walking pace. 'I miss the old days, you know, when I was young.'

'You are still young, Lachlan, still in your twenties.'

'Yes, but sometimes I feel as if I've seen it all and done it all and none of it was worth a spit. And while I was doing all that, I missed out on all the best parts, all the *good* things of life.'

She felt a pang in her heart. He was unhappy, very unhappy, and it hurt her to know that.

He smiled at her as the horses walked on. 'It was good in the old days, wasn't it? When we were both so young and would ride everywhere together; over to the farm manager's house all the time, sitting with the locals and listening to all their talk of the day. And Mr MacLaren, do you remember him?'

'I still see him regularly.'

'And is he still telling all those proud and fabricated stories about himself and my father?'

'No, not as I have heard. He still loves his fishing though. And still often has "a load on" but usually only at the end of his day's work.'

Lachlan nodded. 'It was all so simple then, simple but *good*. Every morning was a new day to get out of bed and enjoy.'

'Lachlan ...'

'And then I joined the Army and a whole new world and it all seemed so exciting then.'

He looked heartbrokenly at the girl he still loved, the *only* girl he had ever loved, the girl whom Drummond had referred to as a *half-caste* and the daughter of a servant of low blood – '*Yes, beautiful and perfect for a regular and delightful tumble in the hay, but never to be thought of seriously as a wife.*'

And then, when he had made so many friends amongst the other young officers, he knew they would be of the same opinion.

Weak-minded and easily led, not much of a man really, and certainly not a good and strong-minded man like his father.

His disgust with himself became so potent he angrily kicked the sides of the horse and abruptly rode off at a gallop, leaving Beth far behind him.

He did not return to the house at Gruline for two weeks.

Upon his return, after only three days and another enraged quarrel with Isabella, he left again. And this time Isabella left also, in tears, to return home and spend some time with her family at Craignish.

Chapter Thirty-Five

Beth was tired out waiting for the summer. Every day of May had seemed so long, and June was almost through to its end and still no sign of John returning.

Every moment of every day she expected to look up, or turn around, and see him standing there, smiling at her; but at the end of every day she went to bed disappointed. To wait for a year had been hard enough, but to wait even longer was almost impossible to endure.

Her waiting finally came to an end in the second week of July when a letter arrived, addressed to:

Miss Elizabeth Jarvis
Macquarie House
Jarvisfield
Isle of Mull

The postmark was Portsmouth, which made her give a little cry of delight.

'He's back in England!'

The sender's name was written on the back of the cream square of vellum sealed with red wax.

Lt. John Dewar RN,
The Fountains Inn,
Portsmouth.

Mary was relieved to hear that John Dewar would soon be on his way back to Scotland. Another day of watching Beth looking so discontented and impatient she simply could not tolerate.

'And he's written to tell you he is on his way?' she asked.

'But, Mama, it takes seven days to get here by coach! *Seven* more long days to wait!'

'No,' Mary said, thinking about it. 'The mail coach is faster than the stagecoach because it doesn't stop to pick up passengers and it travels through the night – what's the date?' Mary looked at the date of the postmark. 'There you go

– five days ago, so he must be following close behind. Well, are you going to open it?'

'What?'

'The letter.'

'Oh *yes!*' Beth was so excited her fingers had trouble unsealing the letter carefully so as not to tear any of the paper, unfolding it carefully, surprised to find it contained *two* sheets of paper.

She sat down on the edge of an armchair and read:

My Dearest Beth,

Arriving back in Portsmouth I find that my leave ashore is for only two weeks, which does not provide me with enough time to get up to Scotland to see you and back again to Portsmouth in time for our next voyage.

This has vexed me greatly as I have spent so many months looking forward to seeing you again.

The reason for such a short leave ashore is due to all officers and crew of our ship being immediately commissioned to join the Royal Navy's "West Africa Squadron." The British Government has now established a settlement in a place called Sierra Leone, and the duty of the West Africa Squadron is not only to run down and capture slave ships but also to transport in our ships as many former slaves who are too frightened of recapture or reluctant to return to their own country, and so they are being brought to settle in this new land of Sierra Leone – or which those former slaves who have already arrived there have named it – "Freetown."

I have not yet learned how long our time out there will be, but I'm told it could be for almost two years from sailing out to return. So once again that half sister of agony will accompany me daily in my impatience to return home and see you again.

But, Beth, although I hate to say it, in all decency I must say it. I cannot allow MY duty to the service to put any kind of hold on your life, especially as you are yet only nineteen.

So despite the "understanding" we made with each other

in Calgary Bay, I feel bound to release you from it, as you must be free to keep company with any man who may come along and capture your interest during the coming two years while I am away at sea. (If that should be the outcome, then the sorrow will be mine)

So all I can do now is send to you my apologies, my regrets, and my love.

John

Beth must have read the letter four or five times before she finally looked up, and then silently handed it over to her mother. Although by then, judging from the fleeting expressions moving on Beth's face while she had read each page, Mary knew it was bad news.

Reading the letter, Mary did not understand the second last paragraph. 'What "understanding" is he releasing you from?'

Beth did not answer, because she had already left the room, throwing on her cloak to go walking towards the hills.

Robbie saw her go and leaped into a mad dash after her, barking with excitement.

In the weeks that followed Beth spent most of her time up in the hills with only Robbie and the sheep for company.

Mary grieved for her, knowing it was the release from the 'understanding', which was hurting Beth so much, even more than the wait of another two years.

He should not have written that, Mary decided. She understood *why* he had felt duty-bound to write it, but still, he should *not* have written it, a big mistake.

In so many ways Beth was every bit as proud and as dignified as her father had been, and if she once thought for a moment that the word 'released' had been politely used in place of 'dismissed' then John Dewar had no chance of ever being allowed into Beth's company again, no chance whatsoever.

And Mary hoped that would not be the outcome, because she liked John Dewar very much. She had secretly held high hopes for him and Beth, and she knew that George, also, would have approved.

Like herself, George would have seen that although John Dewar was not the laird of his own land and estate, he was the laird of his own mind and his own life; strong enough to fulfil his duty to his Navy and the freedom of the world's slaves when he would most probably have preferred to resign his commission and return to his sweetheart in Mull.

If only Lachlan could be that strong-minded, Mary wished. If only Lachlan could get a grip of the reins and start working to become a *real* laird of Jarvisfield, keeping it safe and protected from all harm and making it a good inheritance to pass on to his children.

'*Time will give him wisdom,*' Elizabeth had said, but with each week that passed, Mary was beginning to doubt that.

Chapter Thirty-Six

Having sold his racehorses, Lachlan put most of the proceeds into the Jarvisfield estate, keeping enough back to join William Drummond in another revelry down in London.

For all of Drummond's insistence that Lachlan should remain faithful and supportive to his wife, he had no hesitation in encouraging his friend to leave her for weeks on end while they endeavoured to have fun in the big bad city, on the excuse that they were 'attending to matters of business.'

Once again Mary was fretting about Lachlan's spendthrift ways, and she was now beginning to wonder if those ways were all due to his upbringing?

Treasured by his father and worshipped by his mother, Lachlan had been born into a life of great privilege in New South Wales. In the first eight years of his life he had wanted for nothing, and everywhere in Government House the servants were ready to attend to his every need. He was, after all, the son and namesake of His Majesty's Viceroy, Lachlan Macquarie.

Spoiled by his father and mother, spoiled by the servants, and even George and she, also, had spoiled him with affection, so likeable the boy had been.

And then as a young man William Drummond had come along to spoil him with his friendship, and was *still* spoiling him with handfuls of money to splash around and waste, taking him on revelries to London and allowing him to stay at Strathallan Castle for as long as he liked, despite the fact that he had a wife at home and an estate to run.

*

Isabella returned to Jarvisfield a few weeks later, and within a matter of days Lachlan also arrived back.

Once again Lachlan endeavoured to be a good husband, polite and attentive, and since his return he and Isabella seemed to be getting along quite nicely.

'Let's hope it lasts this time,' Mrs Keillor said, but Hector

229

did not think so.

'Why?

'Well, the way she do walk round the garden,' Hector said, 'like a mettlesome filly who alus walks like she's got flies attacking her flanks.'

'There's nowt wrong with the way she walks!' Mrs Keillor defended. 'She walks like a lady as she should do. It's only when she sees *ye* lurking about that she gets all twitchy and jumpy.'

Mary put down her sewing and said, 'Well I think Lachlan is doing his best and trying very hard to make things right now. He has even assured me that he is going to spend more time on the estate and not leave Mull for weeks on end like he has done in the past. He assures me that he is ready at last to shoulder his responsibilities as both a husband and a laird.'

'Amen to that,' Mrs Keillor said with a sigh. 'And about time too.'

*

It was like the years had never passed and they were both very young again.

In resuming his duties as a laird, Lachlan and Beth had also resumed their old friendship and both of them had never needed that friendship more.

Beth, because she was trying very hard to forget John Dewar and the easy way he had released her from their pledge in Calgary Bay to marry as soon as he had returned from Jamaica – or as she viewed it in her own heartbroken way – releasing *himself* from that pledge.

Lachlan, because he was trying very hard to spend as little time as possible with his wife. That way calmness at least would reign, if not happy contentment.

Once again the tenants and farmhands saw the fair young laird and the dark-haired girl riding everywhere together as they used to do in the old days, stopping to talk with the cottagers and farmhands and – once again – when the Christmas season arrived 'looking in' at the farm manager's house for a dram of seasonal cheer with some of the locals.

Robert Dewar was happy to welcome them, and old Jamie

MacLaren the happiest of all; here today without his wife, and not yet with 'a load on.'

'By! If tis not young Captain Macquarie! Welcome sir, welcome!'

Beth gave Lachlan an enquiring look. 'Captain?'

Lachlan nodded, telling her he had left the 2nd Dragoons for a captaincy in the Scots Greys based in Lancashire, serving for only a few months before he had sold his commission. He had told Robert Dewar about it long ago. Had he not told her?

'No.' Beth shook her head, and then wondered if he had in fact told her, but her mind was too preoccupied at the time with thoughts of John to listen.

Kirsty Dewar was handing around a tray of her scones and not at all pleased to see the young laird and Beth sitting so friendly together, and he with a wife at home.

'How is John?' she asked Beth loudly. 'Ye remember, John Dewar? My cousin from Edinburgh?'

Beth stared at Kirsty, wondering why she had asked, and why she sounded so angry.

'John is away at sea,' Robert Dewar put in, 'and well ye know that Kirsty.'

'Aye, and Beth knows it too!' Kirsty replied sarcastically before flouncing with her tray out of the room.

'John?' asked Lachlan, frowning, looking from Robert Dewar to Beth, and asking again, 'John?'

'My cousin's son,' Robert Dewar answered. 'In the Navy and away at sea.'

'So how do *you* know him?' Lachlan asked Beth, still frowning.

'Och, he's been over here to Mull a few times in the last two years,' Robert Dewar answered. 'His father is looking to retire here one day, looking for a house in Tobermory?'

'So how well did you get to know him?' Lachlan asked Beth inquisitively.

Beth finally spoke. 'We ... became friends.'

'Friends?'

'Yes, good friends?'

'How good?' Lachlan demanded. 'Should I not have been

told about this?'

Beth blinked at him. 'Why should you have been told?'

'Because I am your *laird.*'

Robert Dewar again intervened. 'Aye, John and Beth became good friends,' he said quickly, 'because they both enjoyed playing whist.'

'*Whist?*' Lachlan and Beth said together, both staring at the farm manager who shrugged.

'Tis not a card game I would bother with, and not many a man from around here would bother either, playing for a piece of rubber, but John says the lads on the ships play it a lot.'

Beth had not a clue what Robert Dewar was talking about, and she also wondered why he kept answering on her behalf.

'Of course they always played it in the company of your mother. The late and dear Mrs Macquarie, didn't ye, Beth?'

Beth nodded, not knowing why she was nodding or joining in this deception. It was nothing to do with Lachlan who she was friends with, laird or not.

'And this son of your cousin, Mr Dewar,' Lachlan asked politely, his mood returning to amiable. 'Where is he now? Where at sea?'

'Well, last I heard,' said Robert Dewar, walking around the room refilling the glasses, 'was that he was going out with the West Africa Squadron, chasing slave-traders.'

'Now, isna that a strange subject for ye to be talking,' said Jamie MacLaren, sitting forward in his chair with more interest, 'because just there a while back, I was talking to a Navy man about the same squadron in West Africa.'

Jamie made a grim face. 'Och, ye wouldna want to be going out there if ye were a Navy man, Captain Macquarie.'

Robert Dewar frowned. 'Why is that?'

'I had gone over to Craignure with the trap,' said Jamie, 'and my youngest son Aulay in it, and he was for catching the ferry over to Oban. So while we stood waiting, a man was sat down on the bench waiting for the ferry to come in also.'

Jamie sipped his drink. 'He was in the Navy uniform and soon as he saw me standing, and me so much older than him, he straights away gets up and offers for me to sit down.'

Robert Dewar nodded. 'An officer was he?'

'He was,' Jamie confirmed

'I thought so,' Robert answered. 'Politeness is one of the strict codes for officers of the Royal Navy. Even when they capture an enemy they have to question the enemy with politeness at all times. A strict code.'

'Oh, aye, he was polite enough. He was a man about thirty I'd say, but to me he looked as pale and sickly as a man waiting more for his coffin than a ferry. So I said to him, "I thank ye kindly for the offer, sir, but I'm thinking ye need the seat more than I."'

Lachlan opened his mouth to speak but Beth quickly touched his arm to silence him, her face intent. 'What was wrong with him?'

'Well,' continued Jamie, holding his glass up to Robert Dewar for another refill. 'He stood up and insisted I take the seat, and when I did so, the three of us got to talking – my son Aulay asking him most of the questions, mind, not me. He told us he was not long back from two years out with the West Africa Squadron, and now he had been over in Mull, at a place near Fishnish, staying with a relative in an effort to get some rest and restoration before returning to the Navy.'

Jamie sat back, sipping his whisky and looking as if he had come to the end of his story.

'So what did he say about the West Africa Squadron?' Beth asked impatiently. 'Is that all he said, that he'd been out there with them? Nothing else?'

Jamie blinked at her, the whisky beginning to have an effect, and then he sat forward again, remembering the point of his story.

'Aye, he said it was one of the *worst* postings in the service, and most of the men hated it because so many fell ill with the diseases passed around by a flying insect called the *moskita,* and there was alus a large loss of lives of the white sailors. A ship going out with a full crew alus came back with only half a crew. And tis hard work sailing a Navy ship without the full complement of officers and sailors aboard.'

Robert Dewar's face was also looking pale now, his eyes filled with grave concern. 'And would my cousin's son John have known that? Before he went out?'

Jamie guzzled back the last of his whisky before answering.

'He woulda known it, and known it well, because the officer told Aulay it was a posting that every officer and sailor prayed no' to be given – the West Africa Squadron – and to keep that in mind if Aulay ever got a notion of joining the Navy. And aye, it made Aulay think, cos he's alus had a fancy to join the Navy and go fighting under sail – but not to get killed by a flying *insect*. Nay! Where's the honour in that?'

Lachlan had been silent with interest. 'I'm glad I chose the Army then,' he said. 'All I had to do was ride a horse and attend parades, and the only insects we had to contend with were flies, so not much danger in all that.'

Beth's mind was in a daze, realising now why John had released her from their pledge and set her free from any understanding of marriage they might have had.

She began to feel sick. 'I think I should not have drank so much whisky,' she said, rising to stand unsteadily, even though she had drunk only one small dram. 'I think I should go home.'

The ride back was done at a fairly slow and easy jogging pace, and with some relief Beth saw Lachlan blinking his eyelids to fend off a spell of sleepiness from drinking too many drams of the whisky.

Lachlan's sleepy ride home was done by instinct, and not by sight, with the help of a path known well to his horse.

Beth was silent throughout, and glad when she was finally able to dismount in the yard, rush into the house and whisper to her mother to come up to her bedroom.

Mary followed her up, concerned; and once inside the bedroom she asked, 'What is it? Did something happen out there today?'

Beth nodded, and told her about Mr MacLaren and the Navy man and all that he had said about the West Africa Squadron.

Mary dismissed all fears with a shrug. 'Are you forgetting, Beth, that John Dewar knows all about the hazards of Africa. On the first day he came here, did he not tell us that he had just returned from serving near Cape Town? And that is

South Africa, just down the coastline.'

'Is it?'

'Yes, and your father and General Macquarie suffered no harm when they went out about in Cape Town, although I stayed in my cabin being pregnant with you and was within weeks of giving birth. And as well as that,' Mary continued encouragingly, 'there were mosquitoes galore in Australia and none of us suffered any harm.'

'No?'

'No. I think you will find that Navy man was a weakly type of man in the first place, probably not used to serving any further than the English Channel, but John is young and strong and the young and strong are always the hardest to knock down.'

'So ...' Beth asked, her mind now full of confusion, 'why did he release me from our ... understanding?'

'Oh, I think that was more to do with the length of time he knew he would be away, two years, maybe longer. Time on the sea is not as definite as on land.'

'What do you mean?'

'Well, for example, when we were due to leave Portugal we were held back in port and unable to sail for over two weeks due to adverse winds. And before that, at St Salvadore, we were delayed there too, due to the amount of time it took to get fresh supplies on board. It was supposed to take no more than three days but in the end it took *nine* days.'

Beth was smiling, feeling so much better about it all. Impulsively she hugged her mother and gave her a kiss on the cheek.

'So you think he truly intends to come back to Mull – to me?'

Mary smiled. 'Of course he does. He struck me as being an honest young man who follows his own mind and only says what he wants when he *knows* what he wants. So when you two made this ... understanding ... did he *say* he wanted you?'

'Yes.' Beth was still smiling.

'Do you love him?'

'Oh, Mama, I would *die* for him!'

Mary laughed. 'Oh, I don't think he would want you to do

that! I think all he is hoping is that you will *wait* for him.'

When the two of them descended the stairs together, they could hear Lachlan and Isabella quarrelling in the drawing-room.

'Poor Lachlan,' Beth whispered, 'I feel so sorry for him at times, being so unhappy, and trapped in a loveless marriage.'

Mary nodded. 'To be honest though, I feel more sorry for Isabella, because I believe she truly *does* love Lachlan, despite all his faults.'

'So there's hope?'

'Oh yes,' Mary said. 'In any situation there is always at least *hope* for better times to come. But for them, I believe the marriage will only settle down and become happier when Isabella gets pregnant and gives birth to Lachlan's child.'

The drawing-room door was half open, and Beth caught a glimpse of Isabella sitting in an armchair delicately dabbing her eyes with a handkerchief.

'As you say, Mama, there is always *hope,*' Beth said with a sigh, knowing that she too would be spending the next eighteen months doing a lot of *hoping* for the time ahead to fly past quickly, hoping for happier times to come.

Chapter Thirty-Seven

The time could not have moved slower, Christmas came and went. William Drummond and two of his friends arrived in Mull to spend the first few days of the new year at Jarvisfield with Lachlan and the house was full of merriment and laughter, but Beth avoided them, keeping to herself and spending much of her time over at the Dewar's house in Salen with Kirsty.

The winter months were full of frosts and the air was sharp. At the end of February Beth helped Robert Dewar with the birthing of the lambs and as always she beamed with joy at the delight of it, fussing over the tiny newborn lambs as if they were her pets.

Within weeks the lambs were up on the hills with their dams and Beth was elated when spring finally arrived and the frosts began to melt away.

One day in early April, Beth arrived at the Dewar's house to be greeted in the kitchen by Kirsty who had news she was eager to tell.

'We've had a letter from John,' said Kirsty. 'Father says I can write a letter back to him – but dinna worry, Beth, I'll no' be telling John that ye are back to spending so much of yer time now with the laird, always riding around in his company again.'

Beth stared at her friend. 'But, Kirsty, you don't know how to write, so how can you write a letter to John?'

'Ma father says *he* will write it for me. If I tell him the words I want to say, he will do the writing of it. And as I said – I'll *no'* be telling John about ye and yer bad ways, Beth, but only because ye are *my* friend as well as his.'

Beth digested this for a moment. 'I have no bad ways, Kirsty. I've done nothing bad.'

'Aye, ye have,' Kirsty said with a knowing glint. 'Ye've let the laird think he owns ye again, let him think ye are still *his* Beth, even though he's now wed and married to a wife. Least, that's what ma father says.'

Beth had no time to waste on such nonsense: all she wanted to know was – 'What did John say in his letter?'

'He said he didna know why ma father should be so worried about him. He said they all knew how to avoid the deadly mosquitoes and that was by not going ashore at night time, which he never does, and anyways, he said he spends all his time aboard his ship at sea, and rarely gets a chance to go ashore, day or night.'

'Was the letter from Africa?'

'Aye.' Kirsty frowned. 'Where else would it be from?'

Beth's heart was pounding. The last letter *she* had received from John was months ago, from Casablanca, so there was also undoubtedly a letter from Africa waiting for her at home too.

Kirsty was full of indignation when Beth ran out of the kitchen, out to her horse, jumping up on it as quickly and as lightly as a dancer and grabbing the reins to turn the horse around.

Kirsty ran out after her. 'Where are ye going? I *told* ye I wouldna tell John about ye and the laird!'

Beth was not listening so gave no answer, kneeing the horse into a fast gallop to get home as soon as possible.

Her excitement had built up to its height during the ride and her face was flushed with the thrill of anticipation as she ran into the house and bumped into her mother.

'Beth! Goodness – what is it?'

'A letter?' Beth gasped. 'Has a letter come for me?'

'No,' Mary said. 'No letters at all have come here today.'

'No?' Beth could scarcely believe it. 'Are you sure?'

'Of course I'm sure.'

'The Dewars at Salen received a letter from John today?'

'Ah ...' Mary said with understanding. 'Well, maybe your letter was put in a different batch and it will come tomorrow or in the next few days.'

'Yes,' Beth said despondently, knowing now that it would feel like an age before tomorrow came.

After a silence and a long deep breath, she said finally: 'At least ... at least I don't have to worry any longer about the African mosquitoes hurting him or even killing him. He told

238

the Dewars in their letter that the mosquitoes were only a problem on shore and at night, and he never goes ashore at night.'

'There now,' Mary said, putting a comforting hand on Beth's arm. 'Didn't I tell you that John Dewar knew all about the hazards of Africa and how to avoid them.'

Beth nodded, yet she could think of nothing else throughout the day but her coming letter, wondering what it would say, and *certain* it would be written in a different tone and in a different way to the letter he had written to the Dewars.

Because he *loved* her, and he didn't love them; they were just relatives. And when her own letter came she would stop feeling jealous about it all.

No letter came for her the following day, nor in the days and weeks or months that followed it. No letter from John at all. No words or love for her from Africa, only silence.

Beth was so hurt, so heartbroken, she stopped going to the Dewars for a time, and when she did, she was always in the company of Lachlan, so Kirsty had no chance of telling her about any other letters.

Whether any more letters from Africa had come or not, Beth did not want to know, not as long as no letter came from Africa addressed to her. And no letter came.

Towards the end of summer, Mary became so concerned about Beth, that on one of her regular visits to Tobermory, and her usual hour spent with Lizzie McLeod in the kitchen of the inn, she confided to Lizzie her worries about Beth.

'She's cheerful enough with me and Mrs Keillor, and even when she is with Lachlan, but Lizzie ...' Mary shook her head, 'most of the time she seems so *separate* from us all, so lonely within her own world. At least John Dewar helped her with that, helped to bring her out of herself during the time he was here, but now that he seems no longer interested in her, not even to write her a letter now and then, she's gone back to the way she was before.'

'Aye,' Lizzie agreed. 'I've noticed how she's gone back to her quiet ways and her shy manner. But I did *warn* her. I've warned her many times in the past, from as far back in her youth when she started developing breasts I have warned her.'

Mary frowned. 'About what?'

'About men!' Lizzie said. 'And most of all I've warned her about having nothing to do with any man that's also a *sailor*.'

'Why?'

Lizzie sighed and shook her head at the innocence and inexperience of these Jarvisfield females.

'Because, Mary, when it comes to *sailors,* who alus have a ship to jump back on, a female canna believe a word they do say.'

'No, no,' Mary insisted. 'John Dewar was not like that. He was a good and decent young man, a very *nice* young man.'

'Aye, he was,' Lizzie said, and then gave one of her saucy grins, 'verra *nice* indeed.'

'Lizzie!'

'Nay, to be serious though,' Lizzie said seriously. 'The best way to make a young woman forget about a man, is to settle her down with another young man.'

Mary could see some sense in that. 'But I doubt if Beth would even *look* at any other young man. It's John Dewar she wants, so I can't see her showing any interest elsewhere.'

'Aye,' Lizzie agreed. 'But there's many a young man who would give up an eye to have a beautiful girl like our Beth. Aye, some might even give up a leg along with it if twould make a difference to sealing the match.'

Mary laughed. 'No, none of your matchmaking now, Lizzie, not for Beth, because she won't have it, and neither will I.'

'I know that young Ewan Macpherson is already mad about her.'

'And who is he?'

'He's the postmaster here in Tobermory. A very respectable young man if I may say so. Always reading books. He has a fine and cosy cottage up on one of the hills here, overlooking the harbour. And he has a good and well-paid job, and he's *alus* talking to me about Beth he is.'

'No!' Mary said again. 'I want you to have nothing to do with this Ewan Macpherson, not in any way that my Beth is concerned.'

'I canna stop him from being in love with her,' Lizzie insisted. 'I have no power to do that.'

'Just don't encourage him,' Mary said. 'Do you hear me, Lizzie, do *not* encourage him to pursue Beth, because all he will be doing is wasting his time.'

Chapter Thirty-Eight

At the same time that her mother was in Tobermory with Lizzie McLeod, Beth was sitting on a hill overlooking the sea. Her legs were drawn up and she sat with her hands around her knees. It was still summer and the afternoon sun was red and gleaming.

All around the land was quiet and peaceful, a tranquil haze from the hot sun misted over the horizon of the sea. White seagulls flapped their wings in the blue sky high above, but all else was calm, sleepily calm.

A time for dreaming ...

She dropped her head onto her knees and closed her eyes and allowed herself to dream ... the only escape from reality she had now ... to dream, to remember ... that long, long time of two summers ago ...

And it was all ... so beautiful ... that long ago summer ... from the long walks hand in hand, the laughter and the fun, the serious conversations, the silent kisses within the shade of the trees by the bubbling stream ... all ending on that dark night of stars on the dune in Calgary Bay ... experiencing what she had never before known, and all those wonderful feelings in her body, sending her mind reeling and spinning ... and then afterwards, lying in his arms, tranquil and blissful, she could still remember every word they had said afterwards ...

'*We are lovers now,*' she had said. '*When you are away at sea, I will always think of you in that way now, as my lover.*'

He did not answer, his eyes closed, but she knew he was not asleep.

'*Will you think of me in that way too, as your lover?*'

'*No,*' he said, opening his eyes. '*When I'm away at sea, Beth, from now on, I will always think of you as ... my ecstasy.*'

And he had been so *loving,* right up to the moment he had kissed her goodbye, a mist of sorrow in his eyes, and he had promised, faithfully *promised* that he would keep in touch with her by letter, and he would come back as soon as he could and ...

She lifted her head and stared out to sea. No, no, she would *not* believe he had lied to her. She would *not* believe she had been a fool to believe him.

It was Lizzie McLeod who was the lying fool! It was Lizzie McLeod who thought that all sailors were alike. No difference betwixt one and another, all the same.

She jumped to her feet and began to walk in the direction of home, fast-paced and angry. No! She would *not* believe that he had taken her, just to break her, and then move on to another virgin. No, he was *not* like that!

By the time she neared home she had calmed down, her mind rational again. Any day now, a letter would come addressed to her, she was sure of it, and then sometime after that *he* would come back ... and then it would be Lizzie McLeod who would be seen as the foolish one.

As soon as she got indoors, she went straight up to her bedroom and then spent hours in solitude writing in her diary.

*

The evenings were drawing to a close, Mary noticed. Soon they would be gone altogether, and the afternoons would be followed immediately by the onset of night. Still, it was mid-October, so nothing unusual in that.

'The nights will soon be drawing in,' she said to Mrs Keillor, returning to her seat by the fire and lifting her sewing.

'Aye, and I need yer help with this list of provisions for the Christmas cooking,' Mrs Keillor said, looking at the list in her hand.

'Christmas cooking ... is it not a bit early to be thinking of that?' Mary asked.

'Early?' Mrs Keillor's eyes widened. 'How many Christmases have ye and me been together in this kitchen?'

'Quite a few.'

'*More* than a few. And have ye not learned yet, Mary, that I like to have the Christmas cake baked a good month or two before Christmas. And then the pudding done at least six weeks before so the flavours can blend. And then after that I have *Hogmanay* to think of, and ye know Master Lachlan will want a good table for the New Year that's coming along.'

Mary nodded. 'Yes, *Hogmanay* is an even bigger event for Lachlan than Christmas.'

'As it is for all Scots, ' said Mrs Keillor, looking at her list. 'Now will ye take a look at this list, Mary, and tell me if I've left anything out.'

Mary put down her sewing and took the list, the business of running the household always foremost in her priorities, apart from Beth of course.

*

Beth was riding back from Salen with Lachlan. He had deliberately slowed their pace to a walk so he and Beth could do some personal talking together, his face friendly and smiling.

'Next year, you will be twenty-one, Beth. Mistress of your own life and able to do what you want.'

When Beth did not answer, he asked: 'Do you even *know* what you want?'

She looked at him, deflecting the question. 'Do you?'

'Do I what? Know what *you* want? Or know what *I* want?'

'Know what *you* want?'

He thought about it for some time, and then sighed. 'To be honest, I think I made a big mistake in getting married. If I hadn't of done that, I think all our lives would have been happier.'

'In what way?'

'Well, in the way it used to be before I went into the Army, in the days my mother was alive. It was all so happy and peaceful then. If I had one wish, it would be ... to go *back* to that time. Coming home every day to you instead of Isabella, not needing to drink so much, and all of us dining together like the family we truly are, and –'

'No!' Beth said, checking her horse and staring at him. 'You never came home to *me*. You just came home to the family *house*.'

'Yes, yes, that's what I mean,' he said quickly. 'And when I said coming home to *you,* I meant, as a member of the family, like a ... a sister, I suppose.'

Beth nodded, and began to ride on, thinking back to someone else who had said they would like to come *home* to her.

It was all lies. Now, with winter coming and still no sight of any letter from John Dewar, she was truly beginning to believe it *had* all been lies: all nothing more than a summer fling. A sailor's brief interlude with a stupid island girl from Mull who didn't have the sense or experience to know any better.

Lizzie McLeod had been right all along.

'And what about you, Beth?' Lachlan tugged at his horse's reins to make him walk slower. 'Have you any wish in the new year to find yourself a husband?'

'No!' Beth looked at him with annoyance. 'No!'

'No?' Lachlan smiled. 'A wise girl. After all, you do not *need* a husband, do you? You have everything you need at home, and I will always be here to take care of you.'

Beth looked at him. 'Is that what you want? For me to stay living at Jarvisfield for ever?'

'I think you would be happier in the long run. There's not many men on this island who could provide you with the comfortable life I do.'

'As a brother?'

'As a loving brother,' Lachlan clarified.

'I don't want any of that love nonsense. I don't want anything at all to do with *men.*'

Lachlan smiled again. 'That's my girl. Have nothing to do with them, Beth, just stay at home as always, and all will be well.'

*

The first snowflake fell, just three days before Christmas.

On Christmas Eve, Beth drove the trap up to Tobermory to collect the last of the provisions Mrs Keillor needed for Christmas Day and for *Hogmanay* after it.

The land was covered in snow, and snowflakes were still

falling ... falling on her dark hair and wetting it. She pulled the hood of her cloak over her head but did not feel cold, the air always milder in the snow.

In Tobermory she collected the provisions, took them back to the trap, then remembered she had a letter from her mother to give to Lizzie McLeod.

As she turned back into Main Street, she suddenly stopped and stared at the scene in front of her ... and all around her. She had noticed a difference when she arrived in Tobermory, but gave it little attention, thinking it was because she had not been up to town for months.

But now she was looking at it ... Tobermory ... in a darkening December afternoon, so different to the quiet countryside. The streets and hills were covered in snow. Chimneys everywhere were puffing up smoke from the warm fires burning within: every window glowing with warm light. Clumps of red-berried holly were pinned on every door. Children were standing outside brightly-lit shop windows and peering in, jigging with excitement, and then merry laughter as they skipped by her ... and only then did she feel the enchantment of Christmas in the air, everywhere, in every smiling child's face that she saw.

And it was all ... so beautiful. The winter town covered in white, the lights, the laughter ...

And then she looked at the sea, and saw the snow was falling again, the snowflakes dissolving as soon as they touched the water.

Snowflakes were falling softly on her face, but her eyes were staring at the sea, staring far out to the horizon, and then her tears began to fall, slipping down her face with the snowflakes.

She turned and went into the Tobermory Inn. As soon as Lizzie saw her face she knew something was wrong.

'Still no letter?'

Beth shook her head.

'Then come.' Lizzie said quickly. 'Into my kitchen by the fire and I'll make ye some tea.'

Beth kept her cloak on as Lizzie sat her down in a chair by the fire.

'This has to end,' Lizzie said worriedly 'Beth, ye will have to accept that he is never coming back, that he has no intentions of coming back, and he has proved that now – so long a time has passed, and still not a word in a letter from him.'

Beth was staring into the fire, her tears still falling. 'I can't forget him, Lizzie. I've tried, but I can't. Every time I see something beautiful, I think of him.'

'Then ye must try *harder* to forget him, my pet.' Lizzie looked at the girl's face, and felt sad for her, so sad.

'Oh, hen,' she said in distress, 'I'm no' meaning to hurt ye. I just want ye to stop picking at the scab all the time and allow the wound to finally heal. It's over, hen, and he's long gone.'

When Beth kept crying, Lizzie knew she had to be cruel now, if only to be kind in the long run.

'Listen now ... he *has* sent ye a message, Beth. Canna ye see that? He's sent ye the usual sailor's farewell; silence from a faraway place. In the end all lasses get the message. And so must ye, Beth, so must ye.'

Beth nodded, and drew on her breath painfully. 'I shared so much with him. I put all my dreams into his hand, and then he just threw them all into the sea.'

Lizzie put an arm around her and kissed the top of her head.

'Listen to me now, Beth ... ye will have other dreams, bigger and betterer dreams, and one day ye will meet a fine man, who *will* love ye truly, and will no' leave ye to go away on any ship. A *land* lover is what he'll be, aye, just like ye, Beth, just like ye.'

Beth nodded in silent agreement to everything Lizzie said from then on, and it pleased Lizzie, made her smile with some relief.

At the door of the inn, as they parted, Lizzie gave Beth one last reminder.

'He was not the man for ye, Beth, that's all. But it will serve ye good to remember that from time to time. He was not the man for ye.'

'No, not for me,' Beth agreed, pulling the hood of her cloak over her head.

And then she suddenly looked at Lizzie with her sensitive dark eyes. 'But I'll never stop loving him, only him. And when I die, I'll go to my grave unwed.'

'Beth!' Lizzie gasped in frustration, back at the beginning again.

'That's the truth, and that's all,' Beth said, and then she went out into the snow and left Lizzie staring after her.

'Oh, I don't know ...' Lizzie said to Angus later. 'I feel bad for her, but I'm at a loss now to try and know how to help her. She's beyond help.'

'Cock's life, Lizzie! She's only a *young* lass of twenty,' Angus said with irritable dismissal. 'And she's *young* in her knowledge and her thinking. What she's thinking and feeling now will have changed by next week. I don't know why ye women have to carry on so.'

'Aye, Angus, ye are right,' Lizzie said thoughtfully. 'She's much younger in her ways and thinking than any of the Tobermory lasses. Too sheltered a life, ye see, down there in that Jarvisfield. Too much protection. Not only from Mary, but the laird also.'

'Aye,' Angus replied. 'And see now what all their protection has done for her – the first man who comes along and kisses her and she thinks he must be the love of her life – now how young and foolish is that?'

'Aye,' Lizzie agreed again, 'and he a *sailor,* for heaven's sake!'

'An officer, Lizzie, an officer. Let's be fair now, he was no common sailor.'

'*All* sailors are common,' Lizzie argued. 'And *all* Tobermory lasses know not to take them seriously, not for one minute. But Beth ... poor Beth ...'

'There's nothing poor about Beth,' Angus said with increasing irritation. 'She may be young and inexperienced about life, but she's no fool.'

'Ye just said she was young and foolish!'

'Aye, in matters of the heart and the ways of romance and all that, but she's no fool in her mind. She's clever enough to learn a lesson from this in time, and a *good* lesson she will learn from it too.'

How d'y'know?'

Angus sighed. 'What ye have to remember, Lizzie, is that she's the daughter of George Jarvis. Now ye *do* remember George, don't ye?'

'Oh, aye, I do, ' Lizzie replied. 'I certainly do.'

'And was he stupid or foolish?'

'Not a bit stupid or foolish. George Jarvis was ... what's the word now ... oh, aye – gorgeous!'

'There ye go then,' Angus said. 'Like father like daughter. She has his good looks, and in time ye'll see that she also has, at least, *some* of his intelligence. So don't ye be worrying so much about her, Lizzie. It would serve ye better if ye spent more time worrying about *me,* and went now and made me some tea, like a *good* wife would.'

Lizzie laughed, and slapped his arm. 'I look after ye good and plenty!' she insisted, and then went like a good wife to fill up the kettle.

THE WAYWARD SON

Gretta Curran Browne

88
Eighty-Eight Publications

Author's Note

In the time period of this book, the Island of Mull enjoyed almost sub-tropical weather in summer, with the Caledonia Tree Forest sheltering the island from easterly winds. Progress led to the destruction of the Caledonian Tree Forest at a later date.

Chapter One

'The first thing I did wrong,' said Lachlan, 'was to marry Isabella Campbell. That was a major misjudgement on my part. Although all fault for that cannot be laid at *my* door, because *she* was the one who lied to me.'

'Lied?'

'Yes, she *misled* me. All the way to the church door.'

Mr Baden Finlay, Notary and Commissioner of Oaths in Edinburgh, was not sure if he should be hearing this. The domestic lives of his clients were not really his concern.

He looked at the fair-haired young gentleman with some puzzlement. He was dressed in the finest of clothes and had obviously sought some merriment with plenty of wine during his luncheon, and the flushed effect of his intoxication served only to heighten his good looks. Although now, at twenty-nine, he was losing the clear eyes and fresh complexion of his earlier fine-looking youth.

'Mr Macquarie –'

'No, the *first* thing I did wrong was to join the Army. My marriage to Isabella Campbell was my *second* mistake.'

'Mr Macquarie, you do realise that my fees are charged by the hour?'

Lachlan Macquarie brushed an invisible spot of dust from his buff-coloured cashmere waistcoat. 'Of course I do, Mr Finlay.'

He looked at the lawyer. 'And, if I may say so, the extortionate amounts you charge in legal fees should be made illegal. Where is the law when it's needed for *real* criminals?'

Mr Baden Finlay was a small thin man wearing steel spectacles, and if it were not for the fact that this young gentleman was the son of the late General Lachlan Macquarie, former Viceroy of New South Wales, and now the laird of his father's rather large estate on the Isle of Mull, he would have called his assistant to eject him.

Instead he held on to his patience and said, 'It would help if you *paid* some of my fees, Mr Macquarie. I have sent you many invoices.'

'Have you?' Lachlan frowned. 'Then my apologies, sir, but you will have to blame all non-payment on the postal service. I have received no invoices.'

'No?'

'But then you have to remember that the postal service over to the western isles is very unreliable. In fact, it's my personal belief that much of the time those lazy postmen cannot be bothered to get the ferry over to Craignure or Tobermory and so throw the mailbags into the sea instead. I mean, who's to know? If a person is not expecting a letter, how can he know when he does not get one?'

'Mr Macquarie, if you wish me to continue to administer your affairs then –'

'If you have copies of the invoices to hand, then give them to me now and I will be very happy to pay them.'

'You will?' Mr Finlay's expression of astonishment quickly changed to a gleam of pleasure behind his spectacles.

'Oh, that would be *such* a relief, Mr Macquarie, a great relief indeed. Excuse me while I ask my clerk to bring all your outstanding bills.'

'Oh, before you go ...' Lachlan said, causing Mr Finlay to halt at the door. 'Am I not to be offered some refreshment? I seem to remember that I have always been offered some in the past.'

'Oh yes, how remiss of me!' Mr Finlay exclaimed, his mood jolly now that he knew his invoices were about to be paid. 'But I'm afraid all I can offer you is port. The last client finished off the last of my whisky.'

'Port will be fine,' Lachlan assured him.

'In fact, I think I will have a drop myself.'

Mr Finlay happily carried a small silver tray with two glasses and a crystal decanter of port and set it down on top of his desk.

He poured a small measure into a glass, and was about to hand it to his client when his client said, 'If you don't mind, I'll pour my own.'

Mr Finlay stood watching as Lachlan lifted the decanter and slowly poured the port into the second glass until it was three-quarters full.

'Mr Macquarie,' he said hesitantly, 'you do know that is a rather a large *wine* glass and not a small port glass?'

'And made of good Edinburgh crystal,' Lachlan observed, looking at the glass, and then taking a drink. 'And a very good port also. Well done, Mr Finlay, you have excellent taste.'

*

In his clerk's office, Mr Finlay lost his business-like air and eagerly ordered – 'Mr Coates, please bring in all of the Macquarie invoices.'

The burly young clerk at the desk looked up in surprise. 'All of them? Is he ready to pay?'

Mr Finlay nodded. 'The invoices – as soon as possible if you please, otherwise my decanter of fine Lisbon Port may well become a decanter of nothing at all and quite empty.'

'Aye, they do say Mr Macquarie is as hard and as fast a drinker as Lord Strathallan's son is.'

Mr Finlay frowned at how quickly rumours spread around the city of Edinburgh. 'That is mere speculation and also none of your business, Mr Coates.'

Although, as he made his way back to his own office, Mr Finlay knew the rumours were in fact truth. Lord Stratallan's son and Lachlan Macquarie Junior had been at school together, joined the Army together, and now had a reputation for livening up many an Edinburgh tavern together, not to mention all the rumours of their womanising. Shocking, quite shocking ... but, of course, none of that was any of his business.

*

Entering his office and returning to his seat behind the desk, Mr Finlay's eyes immediately went to the port decanter and saw that another large measure had disappeared and Mr Macquarie's glass had been refilled. By God, he thought, he must have drunk that first glass as easily as drinking water.

'Port is a very heady drink,' he said sternly. 'It is not wise to drink too much of it too quickly or it goes straight to the head and leads to mind-boggling. At least, that has been my

257

own experience.'

Lachlan was sitting with his legs crossed and his head bowed in thought as he played with the gold chain to which his watch was secured in his waistcoat pocket.

'Do you not find it so, Mr Macquarie? Port? Very heady?'

Lachlan stopped fiddling with the gold chain and looked across the desk at Mr Finlay with a curious frown.

'May I beg to ask ... who are you?'

After an astounded silence, Mr Finlay exclaimed, 'I, sir? I am your solicitor of course! My dear fellow, I know you must have been imbibing some good wine over luncheon before you ever came near my Lisbon port but – '

'But now we must attend to business,' Lachlan said with utter clarity. 'Forgive me, sir I am a dreamer and a philosopher and for a time there my mind was lost in a philosophical dream.'

'Hmm. Mr Macquarie, I must say ... there have been rumours ... reaching even as far as to here in Edinburgh.'

'About what?'

'About you, sir.'

'Then you must deal with those rumours, Mr Finlay, and make it your business to instruct a barrister to charge the perpetrators of such lies in a court of law.'

'But *are* they lies, Mr Macquarie?'

Lachlan looked back at him with eyes of pure innocence.

'They must be, whatever they are. I am a respectable gentleman, the soul of discretion in all things, and a devout Christian.'

'But on your Jarvisfield estate, over on the Isle of Mull, it is rumoured that you recently instructed all your male tenants and farm workers to grow moustaches, and any man who did not grow a moustache would be sacked and removed from your employment.'

Lachlan laughed. 'Oh that was just a jest, Mr Finlay!' He laughed again, still finding it amusing. 'I simply wanted to find out how *sheepish* they all were. Sheep are very important on a farming estate, y'know.'

Mr Finlay was not amused. He looked at his client's clean-shaven face and upper lip. 'Well it hardly seems the way – '

'No, I'm still jesting. Forgive me, Mr Finlay. The *real* reason I instructed such nonsense on my farmhands, was due to their constant admiration and bleatings about our new Queen's consort, Prince Albert. Now *he* wears a pretty little moustache, does he not? So I thought, well, if they admire him so much, then let them emulate him and grow a moustache in an attempt to *look* like him.'

Lachlan was still smiling.

'I mean, that *is* what people do, isn't it? People who have too much of the *sheep* mentality in their brains? Follow and copy the looks and dress of the famous people they admire? Already my wife is having all her new frocks made in the latest style that Queen Victoria is wearing.' He sighed, 'Now I ask you, *where* is her shame?'

Mr Finlay blinked, and replied indignantly. 'Many ladies are following the style of Queen Victoria, my own wife included.'

'Then shame on her also. Are you all forgetting that the last time we had a female monarch on the throne, Elizabeth of England, she ordered the murder of our own Mary Queen of Scots? And are *we* not all Scots?'

'Well, hmm ...' Well that was a subject Mr Finlay decided not to indulge in any further. Instead he asked:

'Your farm workers, Mr Macquarie, are they all still wearing their compulsory moustaches?'

Lachlan laughed again. 'No, as soon as they had learned their lesson they were free to shave them off. Although some of the lads were so taken by the dignity and distinction which their noble and royal moustaches gave to their appearance, they decided to keep wearing them. And now some look more like longhaired Highland goats than sheep.'

'And not one of them was sacked from his employment?'

'Of course not.'

The clerk arrived with the invoices, placed them on the desk in front of Lachlan and, after a nod from his employer, hurried out again.

'Now, Mr Macquarie, ' said Mr Finlay, 'in what way may I be of service to you? Or was your visit here solely for the purpose of paying your outstanding bills?'

'Oh yes, I came because ...' Lachlan tried to remember why he had come here but, search as he may, his mind remained blank ... other than it was something to do with Beth Jarvis, something about protecting his darling Beth ... now what was it?'

Finally he shrugged. 'You are right about the port, Mr Finlay, it appears to have done some boggling on my mind.'

He stood up, lifted the invoices from the desk, and placed them inside the pocket of his jacket. 'Never mind, it will keep for another time.'

Mr Finlay stared at him in alarm. 'Mr Macquarie, I know that you appear to have had one or two blank spells while you have been here, due no doubt to the amount of wi – '

'Lost in thought, Mr Finlay, lost in thought, that's all.'

'Indeed, but would you now give a small amount of thought to the outstanding invoices ... and pay them?'

'Of course I will pay them, but I cannot do it today.' Lachlan took out his watch and looked at it. 'It's almost five. The banks close at three.'

'But do you not have –'

'They will be paid tomorrow, on that you can rely.'

Mr Finlay was not prepared to rely. 'How can you pay them tomorrow when you are journeying back to Mull this evening?'

'No, my departure is not until tomorrow morning. I am staying overnight in Edinburgh.'

'Where?' Mr Finlay asked suspiciously. 'Where are you staying in Edinburgh?'

'Where I always stay, at The Blue Lion.'

When he had left the office Mr Finlay looked at the second glass of port, which had remained untouched.

'God's breeches!' he muttered, lifting the glass and taking a long gulp of the port. 'These rich young gentlemen are the worst payers of all.' He took another gulp. 'The very worst.'

His lips were still wet with port when his clerk knocked on the door and entered, asking eagerly: 'Did he pay the bills, Mr Finlay, all three hundred guineas of them?'

'No he did not. He says he will pay tomorrow after the banks are open.'

'But is he not –'

'No!' snapped Mr Finlay. 'He says he is staying overnight at The Blue Lion.' He drained the last of his port. 'But I don't believe him.'

'No?'

'These young gentlemen think that because they are never in need of money themselves, that no one else needs it in a hurry to pay their own wages and bills – but *we* do, Mr Coates, we do need it!'

*

And so certain was Mr Finlay that Lachlan had lied to him; upon leaving his office and before returning home for his evening meal, he made his way to The Blue Lion Hotel.

As it was the dining hour he looked into the dining room by opening the door just a fraction. As curious as he was, Mr Finlay knew it was imperative that he should not be seen *spying* on his clients.

Well, no sign of him in there.

He crossed over the lobby to the taproom and opened that door just a fraction. It was quite crowded but, a moment later, there at the back of the room he saw him – Mr Macquarie, standing in a corner with his hands around the waist of a pretty and plump-bosomed young servant girl with long brown hair who was smiling up at him adoringly. Moments later they kissed each other like old lovers reunited again, and Mr Finlay blushed at the shame of it.

But then, he reasoned, if the young man's wife insisted on dressing like Queen Victoria then who could blame him? Personally he thought his own wife looked hideous in the new style, but he did not have the courage nor the brawn to tell her that.

Happy to know that he had not been lied to, Mr Finlay walked out the door of The Blue Lion and continued his journey home, happily swinging his stick as he thought of the three hundred guineas he would receive in the morning.

A colossal sum, racked up over almost three years of legal work for the Jarvisfield Estate, and long overdue it was too.

*

At ten minutes to three the following afternoon, Mr Finlay lost all patience and ordered his clerk to go over to The Blue Lion to enquire if Mr Macquarie was still there.

The clerk said, 'Yes, sir,' and then went downstairs to send the postboy to carry out such a menial task.

When the postboy returned he gave the hotel manager's response to the clerk, who then took it up to Mr Finlay.

'He left this morning, sir.'

'Damnation!' Mr Finlay's fist smashed down on the desk in fury.

'Well that is it, Mr Coates. Now heed me and heed well – the next time Mr Macquarie comes here wishing to employ our legal services, do not allow him up the stairs until he has paid his outstanding bills. Furthermore, he is *not* to be granted any more consultations with me unless he pays for my service with a substantial deposit beforehand. No more *credit*, understand?'

'Yes, sir.'

*

Seven days later, Mr Finlay had almost recovered from his annoyance when his clerk knocked and popped his head inside the door, a thrilled smile on his face.

'Mr Finlay – Mr Macquarie has paid all his outstanding bills in full!'

'What!'

The clerk walked in carrying the Bank Draft and placed it into Mr Finlay's eager hands. 'The full three hundred guineas it is. Every penny of it.'

'By God ...' Mr Finlay looked lustfully over the Bank Draft in the same way young Mr Macquarie had looked at the serving girl in The Blue Lion. But then ... as he looked at the accompanying document he saw something that stopped his breath.

'This Bank Draft has not been instructed for payment by Mr Macquarie.'

'No?'

'No – did you not notice? Or were you too shocked and excited to see ... this payment has been made by Mr William

Drummond, the son of Lord Strathallan, on *behalf* of Mr Lachlan Macquarie.'

The clerk's eyes rounded. 'Viscount Strathallan's son? By! It must be nice to have good friends who'll just pay out money on your behalf like that. And three hundred guineas of it! That's more than I would earn in ten years!' He scratched his head. 'So Mr Macquarie and Lord Strathallan's son must be *very* good friends then.'

'Yes they are, very close, ever since boyhood. This is probably no more than a small and short loan between the two of them.'

Mr Finlay sat back with a serene expression on his face.

'You see, Mr Coates, this is the reason why I always say we should never ask *gentlemen* for money up front. We must take them on trust and at their word and in due time they will always pay. They know as well as we do that they are being charged a much higher fee than an ordinary citizen, so credit where credit is due.'

'Credit?'

'Of course credit – like any other respectable establishment. We are not petty tradesmen who cannot exist unless they are paid immediately. We are *gentlemen* who are not only willing, but *able* to wait on the convenience of other gentlemen, even if that means allowing their accounts to run for two or even three years in the knowledge and certainty that our high bills *will* eventually be paid. No sensible businessman settles for a little now instead of a lot later.'

The clerk looked perplexed. 'So when Mr Macquarie comes here again...?'

'Show him up to my office immediately and make sure my port decanter is full.'

Chapter Two

Having disembarked from the ferry at Craignure, Lachlan used a carrier's trap to take him home to Gruline.

During the three-mile journey the driver made several attempts at polite conversation, finally giving up and returning to silence when Lachlan made no reply – sitting back with his arms folded and his hat down over his face, trying to grab a bit more sleep.

Reaching the entrance of the leafy lane that led up to the Macquarie house, the driver pulled the horse to a halt. 'Here we are, Mr Macquarie.'

Lachlan pushed his hat back up onto his head and sat up, looking around at the lush green scenery.

'God,' he said, 'Edinburgh is such a cesspit in comparison to Mull.' He smiled amiably at the driver. 'Don't you think so?'

'I wouldna know, sir, I've never been so far abroad as Edinburgh.'

'Good for you,' Lachlan said, jumping down from the trap and paying him.

When he entered his house it appeared empty of everyone except for a voice singing softly upstairs.

He stood and listened for a moment and then realised the voice belonged to Mary ... singing an old Aboriginal song that took his mind back to Australia, the land of his birth and early childhood.

'Mary?'

The singing stopped and moments later Mary appeared at the top of the stairs, holding a duster in her hand.

'Now *why* are you doing the cleaning? Is that not what I pay Maggie and Lorna for?'

Mary smiled as she came down the stairs. 'What else am I to do? I'm not so old and decrepit yet that I can sit and do nothing all day. How was Edinburgh?'

Lachlan couldn't remember, other than he had spent some very nice time with a very nice girl there.'

'Oh, the same old dreary business discussions about the estate,' he said dismissively. 'You've got dust on your face.'

He lifted his hand and wiped the dust from her cheek and then kissed it.

'Oh, now – don't let Isabella see you doing that!' Mary smiled. 'You know how shocked she gets when you are too familiar with the *servants*.'

'And I've told her again and again that I have been kissing your cheek since I was a child in Sydney. The fact that she has now reduced you to the role of a servant changes nothing. I still love you, Mary, you know that, don't you?'

'Yes, I know it,' Mary smiled.

Lachlan was looking at her thoughtfully. 'Where did you learn that Aboriginal song? I've heard you singing it before and I've often wondered.'

'From George,' Mary said. 'As soon as he learned what the words meant in English, he taught the song to me, in its Aboriginal form, so we could say secret messages to each other when other people were around. It's a love song.'

'And who taught the English words to George?'

'King Bungaree.'

'King Bungaree ...' Lachlan smiled. 'I remember King Bungaree coming down with his people to Sydney Harbour to say farewell to us when we were leaving.'

He paused. 'You know, Mary, sometimes, I wish we had never left Australia.'

'Well we did, so no point in dwelling on the past.'

'Australia might well be the *future,* who knows? I still own my father's two thousand acres of land in Parramatta. Maybe one day I will go back there in some grand escape from it all.'

Mary frowned. 'Escape from all what?'

'Oh, the customs, the conventions, the snobbery of Britain in all its forms. England is bad enough, but Scotland is even worse.'

'My George is buried here and so *here* is where *I* will be staying,' Mary said, moving on towards the kitchen. 'Right here on Jarvisfield, until the end of my days.'

'Would you never consider marrying again?'

Mary turned her head and looked back at him as if

thinking he must be mad. 'Who could ever compare to George?'

Although he did not answer, Lachlan knew what she meant. George Jarvis had been the most wonderful of men; the kindest, the most intelligent, and so incredibly beautiful in his looks he made heads turn. Although Lachlan did realise that some of the time those heads had turned was because George was an Arabic Indian, quite exotic for this part of the world, and to some of the older community here on Mull, his brown skin, light as it was, was still a mark against him.

Yet Lachlan had never cared what others thought or said about George, because to him George was like an older brother, always there, always to be trusted, and as a boy he had simply adored him. And when George had died at the age of thirty-four, Lachlan had been so heartbroken, his mother had sent him away to school in England.

Entering the kitchen Lachlan looked around him. 'Where is Mrs Keillor?'

'She must be out the back.' Mary moved to the kitchen window, looked out, and then nodded. 'She's out in the vegetable garden with Maggie and Lorna.'

'She needs to come in then, because I need some breakfast.'

Stepping out into the sunshine of the back yard where Hector was busily brushing down the mare, Lachlan saw Maggie and Lorna – two local girls who came very day to the house as servants – bent over in the vegetable garden digging with their trowels while Mrs Keillor bawled out instructions like an Army drill-sergeant.

As he strolled towards the group he heard Maggie say, 'But *why* do we have to dig 'em all up again, Mrs Keillor, what for?'

'Not *all* of them, ye dolt,' Mrs Keillor replied impatiently, 'just *some* of them. Turnips have to be thinned out if we want to see a good showing in the summer. *Thinned out,* I say – not *all* of them dug up! And then those ye lift up now we can replant along that edge over there, and then we'll get *two* good crops growing 'stead of one.'

'Mrs Keillor.'

'Aye ...' The cook turned around and looked at him. 'Ah, so ye're back. Have ye had any breakfast?'

'No.'

'Then I'll be along in a minute to take care of ye. I've a need to sort out these two dolts first.'

Mrs Keillor had known Lachlan too long since his boyhood to have any notion of immediately jumping to his attendance. He was the easiest master in the world. Well, most of the time he was.

As Lachlan turned away he saw two female figures strolling across the bluebell field and paused to watch them.

One was his wife, Isabella, her hair curled into two bunches of brown ringlets at each side of her face, in imitation of the way the new English queen wore her hair. And her dress of blue velvet must have had at least a hundred starched petticoats underneath it, so wide was her skirt. It was not a dress for country living

Walking beside her was Beth Jarvis, George's daughter, her slender young body clothed in a simple blue cotton dress, her hair long and straight down her back.

Although Beth's skin was much paler than George's had been, almost white, but not quite; her hair was as black in colour, and a glance from her soft dark eyes often sent shivers down his spine. She was the *real* lady of the two, and very beautiful.

Seeing Beth now just made him feel depressed, filling him with regrets for the past.

He had married Isabella Campbell for her class, her money, and with the approval of all his friends. And now he was living long years in repentance for such a damnable mistake.

And even worse, the ten thousand pounds that Isabella had boasted would be given to him as her dowry turned out to be a mere *two* thousand and not ten. God, he had sold his life cheap to that lying slut.

'*Lachlan! Oh, oh, Lachlan!*' Minutes later Isabella was running and then she was upon him, her arms trying to reach him in a hug over the ridiculous width of her starched petticoats and skirt.

'Oh, I *missed* you!' she said fervently. 'Did you miss me?'

'Every minute of every day, my sweetness,' he replied dryly.

And then he was looking over her shoulder at Beth, who was following close behind her.

The lovely smile that Beth gave him served only to hurt him, knowing that of all the women in the world she was the one he could never have.

And married as he was now, he could not even try to seduce her, if only due to his respect for her father. George would have expected better of him. And also because Beth had never given him any sign that she would be willing to be seduced by him, if only due to the fact that he was now a married man.

Still, he knew he would never stop loving Beth, never stop hating his wife, and never stop despising himself.

Chapter Three

Beth continued on into the kitchen, leaving the reunited married pair alone outside. She stood for a moment watching her mother frying a pan of lamb chops.

'Are they for Lachlan?'

Mary nodded. 'He's had no breakfast and Mrs Keillor is busy.'

'Did Lachlan say if any post came on the Craignure ferry for us?'

'He didn't say, but he was not carrying any post when he came in, so I would think not.'

Beth strolled outside again towards the stables where Hector was still brushing down the mare.

'She will end up bald if you keep brushing her for such a long time, Hector.'

'Och nay, she loves it!' Hector replied 'It relaxes all her muscles.'

The mare raised her head and looked at Beth as if to say, 'Aye, it does.'

Beth patted her nose and laughed. 'Hector is spoiling you, girl!'

'Nay, she's no' a girl, no more,' Hector observed. 'Reckon now she be as old as Mrs Keillor.'

Beth turned her eyes from the mare and looked at Hector in a very serious way. 'Have you been up to Tobermory in the past few days, Hector?'

'I have, aye.'

'Was there any post waiting for us there ... from one of the ferries?'

Hector straightened up and looked at her with a cynical grin. He was the same age as the master, nine and twenty going on thirty, and he had known Miss Beth since they were all children.

'No post, nay, but I can tell ye what I *did* hear in Tobermory that might interest ye.'

'What?'

'A sailor alus has a girl in every port that he goes ashore on.'

Beth stared at him as if he had hit her across the face. Her dark eyes blinked. 'That's not true.'

'Aye, it is.'

Beth folded her arms into her waist as if protecting herself from bad news. 'Who told you that?'

'Sailors from one o' the ships.'

'John is not a sailor, he's an officer.'

'Ahh! So it's *him* ye're looking for a letter from – the young gentleman in Navy blue!'

Hector resumed his brushing of the mare. 'He won't be back, Miss Bethey, not if ye were so loose that ye let him kiss ye – and ye did! I saw the two of ye, down at the end of the lane – *kissing!*'

'That was none of your business,' Beth said quietly, and turned and walked away, furious at herself for revealing to Hector just *who* she was waiting for a letter from.

And now that Hector *knew*, he would continue to make his jibes unsparingly.

She went up to her bedroom and sat on her bed, painfully *longing* for a letter from John Dewar, if only to know that he was well and alive and had not succumbed to any of the fevers and tropical diseases that others had warned her about.

He was the greatest love of her life, and if she did not hear from him soon she would truly *die*. At least that's how she was beginning to feel – the waiting for his return was so hard, so very hard. Two years he had said, and two years had almost passed, and before that he had spent almost a year in the West Indies.

Surely she would receive a letter soon to say he was on his way back – or maybe he would do what he had done twice in the past – just appeared out of the blue from nowhere, smiling at her in that wonderful way of his.

She stood and walked over to the window, looking out over Loch Ba, which led out to the sea ...

Chapter Four

Lieutenant John Dewar was standing on the quarterdeck of *HMS Hydra* peering through his spyglass at a brigantine in the distance.

He lowered the spyglass, his blue eyes still fixed on the white sails of the brigantine, certain that she was a slaver. 'She's seen us and is changing course, sir, so she must have something to hide.'

Captain Young nodded. 'Then we will soon find out if that is so, Mr Dewar.' He called down to the ship's Master, '*All hands on deck.*'

Orders were shouted out by all petty officers and the *Hydra* erupted with activity as every sailor sprang into action, a welcome break from days of monotonous patrolling under the burning sun.

The first lieutenant ran up the steps to the quarterdeck. 'Will I board her, sir?'

Captain Young did not reply immediately. He moved to look down to the deck below where his second lieutenant was now standing, giving instructions to a very young ensign who kept nodding his head and no doubt saying the usual 'Aye, aye, sir.'

John Dewar was now twenty-six years old and he had worked his way up as an officer from ensign to third midshipman, second and first midshipman, to third lieutenant and now second lieutenant. Captain Young had a very high regard for his abilities, unlike his first lieutenant who had secured his high place in the Navy through patronage and recommendations from an uncle in the Admiralty. A nice enough fellow, and easy to get along with, but for this particular mission, Dewar would be his choice.

'No, Mr Storebridge, I think Mr Dewar should lead the boarding party this time. Unlike you and I, who are simply doing our duty to our Queen, our government and the Royal Navy, Mr Dewar appears to have made this business of slavery a personal issue, so if there are hidden slaves to be found, he will not give up until he finds them.'

Storebridge looked offended, but knew he could not argue against the captain's word. And also because he knew that of the last two slave ships that the *Hydra* had searched and captured, Dewar had led the boarding party.

The *Hydra* was making fast headway towards the fleeing brigantine but then it had the advantage. The Royal Navy's *HMS Hydra* was one of the new screw propeller steam paddle ships, so it did not have to rely solely on her sails and the wind to make progress.

Captain Young called down. 'Mr Dewar, you will board her.'

'Aye, aye, sir,' John Dewar replied, moving to prepare for his task.

'Mr Dewar!'

John halted in his steps and looked up at the captain, his white shirt hanging open.

'Your *coat*, Mr Dewar. You will be boarding in the Queen's name. Do not let her down by boarding an enemy vessel half naked.'

'Aye, aye, sir,' John grinned, and then looked around the ship to see that almost every sailor was stripped down to his waist, so fierce was the African heat. Even their Lordships at the Admiralty were not so heartless as to expect their officers to wear their coats and neck-cloths in a climate like this, and only a sadistic captain would insist upon it.

He glanced back to the captain who had also removed his coat and was commanding in the coolness of his shirt.

'All officers - uniforms!' Lieutenant Storebridge gave the order to a midshipman, for always when approaching a port or in sight of another ship, the wearing of the full Royal Navy uniform was mandatory, no matter how tropical the climate.

As he left the deck John passed the captain's steward who was rushing up holding the captains coat and accoutrements.

When John had disappeared down below, Lieutenant Storebridge felt bound to say, 'She may *not* be an enemy vessel, sir. We have no proof yet that she is a slave ship, no proof at all.'

'Actually, yes, we do,' Captain Young replied. 'On sight of

us she bent her sails to change her course, and that is proof enough that she deserves a routine search if nothing else.'

Storebridge peered through his spyglass again at the suspicious sloop.

'He's got all his sails spread, sir, looks like he's going to try and outrun us!'

Captain Young sighed at the folly of it. The British Royal Navy had a blockade all down the coast of West Africa and beyond Cape Town to prevent the kidnap and transportation of slaves to countries where slavery was still allowed.

'Need I say, Mr Storebridge, that he will *not* outrun us.'

Storebridge did not look so sure. The master of the suspect ship was commanding her superbly, all sails to the wind.

Lieutenant John Dewar had reappeared on the main deck, dressed now in a fresh white shirt and black neckcloth under the navy and gold-buttoned coat of his uniform. A line of armed red-coated marines also stood on the deck in readiness to support the boarding party.

John stared towards the fleeing ship thinking: *Why is she running?* There could be only one answer to that question – *Bastard!*

He shaded his eyes to look up at the yards and the push of the topgallant sails where a sailor was keeping watch on the masthead. A minute later the sailor shouted down, 'Deck there! She's showing the flag! *British!*'

'British?'

Captain Young did not believe it. Why would a British ship flee on sight of another British ship flying the flag of the British Royal Navy?

His decision was immediate. He called down to the master's mate – 'Tell the gunner I want her stopped!'

Minutes later John Dewar watched keenly as the gunner and his men moved quickly to the thirty-two pounder cannon at its open port on the forecastle.

'Ready, sir!'

'Fire!'

The explosion in the water erupted only yards in front of the bow of the suspect ship – enough to stop her and damage one of her sails which would take a few hours to repair.

'That will show him we mean business,' said Captain Young, and then he walked to the rail of the quarterdeck and called down:

'Ready, Mr Dewar?'

'Aye, aye, sir.'

*

The jollyboat was lowered. Dewar himself had handpicked the boarding crew; selecting only men he knew to be good fighting seamen. A small detachment of armed marines was also on board as a safeguard.

As commanding officer of the boat, John remained standing at the stern, his hand resting on the shoulder of one of the sailors for support as the boat lifted and fell in the water.

He looked back to the *Hydra* and saw it was following close behind, yet keeping its distance until Captain Young knew the result.

John also knew the result could be a hail of fire on the jollyboat killing all of its crew, but he doubted it. If that happened, any slaver or pirate ship knew it would be blown to smithereens within minutes by the Royal Navy's *Hydra*.

'He's given permission to board,' sir, said the master's mate, seeing the signal at the same time as John. 'Maybe he don't have anything to hide after all. They're throwing down the ladder.'

'Boat your oars!' John commanded, and watched as the bowman boated his oar and changed it for a boathook.

Minutes later he had pulled himself aboard the *Amelia* – a strange name for a British ship – followed by the rest of the boarding party and the armed marines.

Yet to his surprise the captain *was* British – an old seafarer if ever there was one. But not so his crew who were beginning to gather at either side of him. John noticed instantly that all appeared to be either Spaniards or Portuguese.

'By what right do you fire on my ship!' the captain demanded, greatly aggrieved. 'And by what right do you compel me to allow you to board my ship?'

John's response to the captain was unemotional and polite, as instructed by orders from the Admiralty.

'In the name of Her Majesty, Queen Victoria, and in accordance with the conventions and treaties agreed and signed between Great Britain and ...' He continued his mandatory speech about the Royal Navy's right to stop and search.

'*Slaves?*' You won't find any slaves aboard *my* ship,' the captain responded, outraged. 'You can search all you like, every bit of the hold, but you won't find any slaves.'

'So what is your cargo?'

'We have no cargo. We are returning from India and we last docked at Cape Town to bring up fresh supplies and water and now we are on our way back to Plymouth.'

John's blue eyes moved over the crew, their faces dark and tense. All appeared to have been willing enough to get involved with the trade, but now, with their eyes on the armed marines, none seemed willing to risk their lives for the trade by putting up a fight.

'A British ship?' John addressed the captain. 'And yet you do not have a British crew.'

'Many of my former crew proved either too inefficient or got sick and I had to unload them at Portugal on the outward journey and take on a new crew there. There are no rules in the treaties that say a British captain must only employ a *British* crew for his ship!'

The captain was becoming purple with fury as he continued. 'The *Amelia* is an honest and harmless merchant ship that has no business to do with smuggling or any unlawful trading and must be allowed to continue her journey up the Atlantic to Plymouth. So go on, search the hold and anywhere else you like and get done with it!'

'Post guards!' John ordered, and the Marines took up their positions, rifles aimed, while the boat crew began their search below deck and into the hold.'

John was still standing and looking at the captain as if appearing to believe every word he had said. 'My apologies for the inconvenience to your ship, sir. However, as a matter of formality, I must request to see your papers.'

'My papers are down in my chart room.'

'Then please proceed.'

The captain look surprised when John moved to follow him below.

Inside the chart room the captain fussed through his papers while John's eyes covertly moved over the chart on his desk ... and saw that the route charted was *not to* Plymouth, but St Salvadore in Brazil.

His heart jumped with shock – *St Salvadore* – the seaport were *Beth* had been born. The thought of Beth now filled him with adrenaline and he could no longer pretend to be unemotional, because now he was *determined* – Beth's father, George Jarvis, had been a child slave, snatched at the age of seven before being rescued by General Macquarie some months later.

He moved his gaze from the chart only seconds before the captain found the correct papers and turned to hand them to him. 'As you will see, all is in order.'

And the papers *were* in order, as good as any fake papers could be.'

'Thank you, sir.' John handed the papers back.

'Now, if we can return to my crew on deck,' said the captain in a more relaxed tone, 'I'm sure your men will have completed their search and we can all get on our way.'

John stepped aside to allow him to lead the way and followed him back to the main deck where the boat crew were returning. Two emerged from the hatch leading down to the hold and called out.

'Empty, sir.'

'Nothing down in the hold and all supplies are in the orlop, sir.'

Others returned with the same report and John could not believe he had been so wrong.

But why did she run at the sight of us? And why is he using fake papers? And why say Plymouth when the true destination is Brazil?'

He looked back at the *Hydra,* which was closer now – closer and waiting.

He stood irresolute for some seconds, not sure what to do

next. Normally he would just leave an innocent ship, but not this one. He was certain this bastard was a slaver – but *where* were the slaves?

'Did you search the wardroom?' he asked the master's mate.

'We searched everywhere, sir.'

Except ... the thought flashed into John's mind like a beam ... except the two places where no sailor would even *dream* of searching, or dare to, so contrary was it to the ways and discipline of life on a ship.

He looked again at the *Hydra* and knew Captain Young and Storebridge both had their spyglasses fixed on the deck of the *Amelia* waiting for a signal.

Dare he give it? He would be demoted down to first midshipman and possibly even thrown out of the Navy if he was wrong.

But it was worth the risk, the gamble on his instincts.

He turned to look at the officer in command of the marines and said, 'Post two men each side of the captain *now!*'

Then he signalled to the *Hydra* to make a full board.

Moments later, while the captain was protesting furiously at the indignity of his armed guard, and his Portuguese crew were looking terrified by the sight of the British Navy ship looming closer to them – John ran down the ladderway and then, ducking his head beneath the low beams, rushed aft through the narrow passage leading to the stern and the captain's cabin.

It was locked.

He took out the pistol he always wore in his waist belt during a stop and search and fired at the lock.

Seconds later, he had got the door open only a fraction when he knew he had been right – because he could *smell* the slaves even before he saw them.

The stench was horrendous. And the reason why no captain, unless he knew his situation to be desperate, would ever allow his official cabin to be used for the storage of slaves.

Or his sleeping cabin.

He pushed hard on the door but something was behind it.

It was only when he had finally managed to push it open further that he saw he had been pushing a small African child of five or six years old up against the wall. She was naked so he could see she was a girl and her eyes were filled with tears from the pain she was feeling in her head now jammed against the cabin wall.

Before even trying to help her he stood and stared at the sight before him – men and women hastily thrown one on top of the other in a heap, almost to the ceiling and filling every corner – all naked and all with feet and hands manacled, and all African.

'Jesus God!'

He had seen it many times before but it never failed to shock him, the *inhumanity* of it.

Many of the slaves were now craning their necks to look at him, unable to speak because of the gags tied into their mouths and around their necks.

'Molo, molo ...' he said quickly. *'Hoe gaan dit?'*

He spoke to them in basic Afrikaan, unsure if they understood English, but his language to them did not matter, because their eyes were staring at his blue and cream coat, his *Royal Navy* coat, and now their eyes were beginning to spill with tears because they knew they had been saved and would soon be freed.

He reached down to the small girl behind the door and slowly manoeuvred her body so he could lift her out to the companionway and sit her down while he carefully removed the gag in her mouth.

Some of the *Hydra's* crew joined him astern a few minutes later. Storebridge and his crew had now boarded the deck of the *Amelia*.

'Search the captain's *sleeping* cabin!' John commanded, while he and two others began to lift down the slaves one by one, and remove the gags.

'We will have to wait until we get up on deck to either get the keys or break these manacles off,' John said. 'So take them up one at a time, and remember – *slowly.*'

'I think I'll have to carry this one,' a sailor said, holding up a young African boy. 'He's fainted.'

John made his way back up to the main deck and faced the captain of the *Amelia* who was biting his lips nervously.

'It seems your hold is empty but your cabin is full, captain.'

The captain stared out to sea, refusing to answer.

'You are in breach of international marine law and therefore I am placing you and your vessel under arrest.'

'You cannot arrest me!' the captain roared furiously. 'You cannot take *my ship!*'

'And you cannot take human beings against their will and sell them like pieces of meat!' John snapped. 'And now it is *you* who will be wearing manacles on your hands and feet – courtesy of the Royal Navy.'

Returning astern John discovered that the captain's sleeping cabin was also packed to the rafters with African men and women. All just thrown on top of each other, unable to move or make a sound.

'He must have known this was the only place to hide the slaves when he saw the *Hydra* coming,' John said. 'He knew we'd search the hold and everywhere else but *never* his day cabin or sleeping berth.'

'And we didn't, sir,' a sailor said. '*You* were the one who thought to do that! But we'll know better in the future, eh? Live an' learn!'

*

The British Admiralty's orders for the treatment of freed slaves aboard a captured ship was that they be immediately brought up on deck for fresh air, given enough food and drink to restore them, and all officers and seamen to ensure "a kind and cheerful manner" at all times in the event that the freed slaves may not speak or understand English.

The crew from the *Hydra* that had boarded the *Amelia* were all cheerful enough as they went about their tasks, because the capture of a slave ship meant the Navy would eventually sell the ship and they would be paid a reward upon their return home.

The Portuguese crew of the *Amelia* were now tied up and held below in the hold, taking the places of the kidnapped slaves, while their captain had been taken on the jollyboat over to the *Hydra* where he would be held a prisoner until he could be tried before a naval court in Sierra Leone – where they *all* would be tried before a naval court in Sierra Leone.

Lieutenant Storebridge was smiling at Lieutenant Dewar in a manner of good grace as he said, 'John, as you captured the ship, Captain Young has ordered that *you* should be the one to command it back to Freetown.'

John smiled sympathetically, knowing that Storebridge had probably asked the captain if *he* could be the one to command the *Amelia* to Freetown – master and commander of his own ship – if only for a short time.

He heard a call and saw the jollyboat returning with extra supplies for the *Amelia*. 'I see your transport back has arrived.'

Storebridge nodded. 'And remember, the *Hydra* will always be in sight of you, and you of it, if you encounter any difficulty.'

It took a further two hours for the *Amelia* to be ready to set sail and John was happy to see he had all his favourite crew members from the *Hydra* with him.

The crew in turn were happy to serve him and obey all his commands, because of all the officers Dewar was their favourite. And hadn't he proved himself again today?

'One of the few "young gentlemen" officers in the Navy who possessed an intelligent mind as well as a fancy blue and cream coat,' they laughed amongst themselves, because they knew that *they* were the true seamen.

Although as Dewar had worked his way up the ranks from third midshipman, unlike Storebridge and Smithson, they knew Dewar had climbed up the masts and repaired sails and had come down from the tarred ropes with black stains on his white shirt and hands, just as they regularly did.

Half an hour before sunset the damaged sail was repaired and the *Amelia* was on its way.

John leaned his forearms on the rail of the quarterdeck and looked over the seventy freed slaves, a valuable cargo that would have fetched a high price for the captain and crew of the *Amelia* in Brazil.

All were all now lying down on either side of the deck.

They had supped their water and eaten ravenously and now they were happy to sleep in the cool evening air and stretch their aching legs and arms after being manacled for at least two weeks.

Every so often they stared up at him in his navy and gold-buttoned coat ... some continually raising their hands to him in a gesture of gratitude.

He turned away and stared out across the sea, glad the day was over and wondering where he himself would sleep – the captain's cabin was not a place he wanted to see again, nor the sleeping quarter.

As darkness fell over the ship, John thought, '*Now* they will sleep and stop staring at me.'

And he was half right in his presumption, because although the freed slaves no longer stared at him, they did not sleep – they started singing – one by one the voices joined together in an African song and although he did not understand the words, he knew from the tone of their voices they were happy.

Some of the crew had started to be affected by the singing, banging on the sides and wooden floor of the deck to make accompanying drumming sounds that encouraged the freed slaves to sing louder and happier.

John leaned his back against the rail, gazing up at the bright star fields across the dark sky, thinking about his own happiness, which seemed so far away now ... and as the singing continued he lost himself in his thoughts ... thinking about Beth.

Chapter Five

In Sierra Leone, at Freetown, when the *Amelia*'s boarding party had been relieved by an armed marine guard who began the process of removing the Portuguese prisoners from the ship, followed by the seventy Africans who would be taken to one of the new settlements to start a new life – the British naval officer in charge of the marines looked at John and shook his head despairingly.

'The ones who are truly culpable in all this are the African tribal chiefs who do business with the slavers and pirates and sell off their own people. The tribal chiefs are every bit as callous and greedy as the slavers.'

John watched the Africans being escorted away in a number of horse-drawn carts. 'At least they'll be safe from sale now in Freetown.'

'Are you going ashore?'

'No, back to my ship.'

The *Hydra* had already dropped her anchor and John could see Captain Young going ashore to make his usual reports to the commodore of the base.

An hour later John was back on the *Hydra,* lying in his berth in the cool shade, wondering how much longer they would have to stay on the African coast. They had been away at sea for much longer than had been predicted, and all he longed for now was to get back home.

Surely *this* time, when the captain was on base with the commodore, the new orders waiting for him from the Admiralty would be to return the *Hydra* back to her mooring at Portsmouth, if only for an overhaul to find any faults in the ship that might be in need of some repair.

Later that evening, the captain joined the officers for dinner in the wardroom, happy to accept their invitation to dine with them, but making no mention of any new orders from the Admiralty.

John bit back his disappointment, certain by now that he had lost Beth and the longer he was away the less chance he would have of finding her again. A girl as beautiful as Beth would not remain single for long.

Perhaps by now, due to his own long absence, she had given up and finally married the Laird of Jarvisfield? Although she had sounded very honest when she had told him that her affection for Lachlan Macquarie was similar to that of a sister for a brother.

Or if not the laird, then perhaps by now she had met someone else and was betrothed or married to a dashing army officer friend of the laird? Almost three years was a long time to wait, and even longer now.

What troubled him most, and it hurt him whenever he thought of it, as it must also have hurt her, is that she might have concluded that he had seduced her and then left her with no real intention of return.

Storebridge raised his wineglass in a toast to the captain.

John put the glass to his lips wondering, as he so often wondered, why she had not answered any of his letters. He had written her seven letters in the past eighteen months but she had not answered even one of them.

The captain answered Lieutenant Storebridge's toast, thanking everyone for a job well done.

'Of the six ships in the squadron,' Captain Young said proudly, 'the *Hydra* is now officially the most successful ship of all for catching the slavers.'

John barely heard him, deep in thought. Even allowing for the difficulty in receiving letters out here, with post bags being handed on carelessly from ship to ship – apart from naval despatches brought directly to the commodore from the Admiralty by a naval courier – at least one or two of her letters in reply should have reached him by now.

Impossible though, if she had not written any.

He suddenly realised that the captain was looking at him questioningly, and he snapped out of his thoughts.

'A final toast, Mr Dewar?' said the captain holding a refilled wineglass. 'Before we all retire for the night to our berths.'

John lifted his glass and waited for the captain to make the usual toast at the end of the night.

Captain Young raised his glass and smiled at every man around the table.

'The final toast tonight is to my new orders from the Admiralty. The *Hydra*'s service here in West Africa has come to an end, at least for a short time, while she is being examined for repairs. Gentlemen, we are all going home.'

Amidst the cheers John could think of only one astonishing fact – *less than a month.*

Assuming all the food and water supplies were brought aboard within the next few days, and with the *Hydra's* speed helped by fair winds, in less than a month, he calculated, they would be back in Portsmouth.

Chapter Six

The clerk knocked and then popped his head inside the door.

'Mr Finlay ... Mr Macquarie is downstairs, waiting to see you and not in a mood to be left waiting. Shall I bring him up?'

'Dear me, yes, yes, Mr Coates ... although he really *should* have arranged an appointment beforehand.'

The lawyer quickly bustled around his office, checking that his port decanter was full and beside it two gleaming glasses on the silver tray.

When Lachlan entered, Mr Finlay could see he was dressed as elegant as always in a dark grey suit and red waistcoat.

'Oh, Mr Macquarie, this *is* a pleasant surprise ...' the lawyer greeted Lachlan obsequiously, 'but any time I can be of service to you, only too pleased.'

'My father's Last Will and Testament,' Lachlan said without any preamble. 'Do you have it?'

'We do. I believe we have the original and two copies.'

'May I take one of those copies away with me? There's a copy at home, but no matter how much I have searched through his papers I cannot find it.'

'And that is *why* a man's Last Will and Testament should always be lodged safely with his solicitor, for occasions such as this. Are you familiar with the details of the Will?'

'I've read it, some years ago, but now there are a few details I want to read again.'

'Then excuse me, will you? I'll get my clerk to bring me a copy so that we can look at it.'

As he reached the door, Mr Finlay remembered. 'Oh, would you care for a drop of port, Mr Macquarie?'

'No, I would not care for a drop at all. A *glass* of port maybe, if that's what you're offering.'

'Of course, of course, "a drop" is just an expression you know,' said Mr Finlay, still smiling obsequiously as he carried over the tray. 'Here, help yourself to as much as you wish.'

'Thank you.'

Having instructed his clerk, Mr Finlay returned to his office to find that Lachlan had not touched the port decanter.

'Shall I pour?' Mr Finlay asked.

'For yourself if you wish. I've decided I don't want any?'

'No?

'No.'

The solicitor could see his client was not in a very good mood today, and wondered what he should say next, while they waited for the clerk.

'And how is your friend, the son of Lord Strathallan?'

Lachlan looked at him coolly 'How the devil should I know? Why don't you ask *him* how he is?'

'But I asked ... only because I thought you and he were very good friends.'

'Of course we are, the very best of friends. Doesn't mean I want to talk about him while you charge me your exorbitant fees by the hour.'

Mr Finlay was spared a response by the arrival of his clerk with a copy of the Will.

'Now, there are quite a lot of important clauses in your father's Will ... do you wish me to go through them with you?'

'No, thank you. If that's a copy I'll take it away with me now and study it in my own time.'

'Very well.'

Lachlan stood up and walked towards the door.

'And as I said Mr Macquarie ... any time I can be of service to you – '

'It will cost me a fortune, yes I know.' And with that he was gone.

Mr Finlay listened to his footsteps running down the stairs, and then sat back and sighed. These rich young gentlemen – one always had to be prepared to graciously take their moods as well as their money – or *they* might well take their business elsewhere.

He poured himself a glass of port and sipped it, wondering how much he should charge Mr Macquarie for providing him with a copy of his father's will?'

*

286

In the coach back to the west, Lachlan sat reading his father's Will, large parchment page after large parchment page, written exquisitely in black ink by a fine-tipped quill held by Mr Finlay's own steady hand, or more likely by one of his clerks.

There were no other passengers in the coach, so he had it all to himself and was able to open the sewn pages wide and carefully read each one.

His father had settled all his money, land and estates, including his estate in Australia, on his son. Lachlan flicked through those pages – he knew all that.

Turning the pages he came to the part entitled *The Macquarie Trust* which ensured that George Jarvis, his wife and their *descendants* be granted a home on Jarvisfield for ever.

So that was all right – Mary would always be protected with a home at Jarvisfield and so would Beth, and even Beth's children, if she were to have any. He had no problem with this part of the Will; it was not the section he was interested in.

There was an oddity included in it somewhere, but which part, which page?

When he eventually found the page, and read it carefully, he felt a deep sadness for his father, despite the oddness of his instructions.

And later, sitting back in the coach and thinking about it, Lachlan felt such a dark resentment sweep over him, infuriating him so much that he decided to break his journey halfway and go to Strathallan Castle, the place he had always regarded as his second home.

*

It was almost dark by the time he reached there, but William Drummond was still up, and very glad of the company too.

'Have you dined?'

'No.'

'Then I will instruct the staff to bring you something light. Some cold roast beef perhaps?'

'Roast beef will be fine.'

Lachlan stood watching as William Drummond, tall and strong and elegant, gave a few instructions to a footman, then turned back to Lachlan. 'You will stay the night?'

'It's too late to journey on to Mull now.'

'Lachlan, I cannot tell you just how *tedious* life has been here of late,' Drummond said as they walked to the library. 'My dear wife has fallen head over heels for a new love and her constant talk of Him – although I respect it – is beginning to grate on my nerves.'

'A new love? Your *wife*? Who?'

'God,' Drummond said wearily. 'Almighty God Himself. He has captivated her heart and mind and soul so devoutly that a mere mortal like myself would be foolish to try and compete.'

'I do believe,' said Lachlan seriously, 'that some women were born just to torment us ... if not in one way, then another.'

Inside the library Drummond immediately headed for the wine and filled two glasses.

'My wife now prefers praying to loving, only God knows why – but the annoying rub is, she keeps saying she is praying for *me.*'

He handed a glass of wine to Lachlan and asked in genuine curiosity, 'Now why should my dear deluded wife believe that she needs to constantly keep praying for *me*?'

'Because she knows you're a rascal, William.'

'A rascal?' William huffed. 'Only *children* are regarded as rascals.'

'A scoundrel then.'

'A very *respectable* scoundrel if I may say so. And for goodness sake – what man *isn't* a scoundrel now and then?'

'My father was never a scoundrel,' Lachlan said. 'He was made of a much stronger fabric than you or I. Although, I have discovered that he could be a little odd.'

'Odd? Well thank goodness for that! I've had enough of holy and perfect saints. In what way was he *odd*?

'In his Will. But it's not his oddity that infuriates me – it's the consequence.'

'How? I will need you to explain if I'm going to have a clue what you are talking about.'

'Look, I will show you.' Lachlan moved to the corner of the library where he had dropped his bag behind the door, opened it and took out his father's Will.

'Come over to the desk, William, and I will show you.'

William stood up from his chair and carried his glass and the wine decanter over to the desk as Lachlan opened the Will at the relevant page and spread it flat. 'There – read that section there.'

William glanced at the page and turned up his eyes. 'Lord save us: all that copperplate writing with its loops and curls. I've drank far too much wine tonight to be able to read that.'

He sat down in the leather chair on the opposite side of the desk and said: 'Perhaps you could read it to me? I will close my eyes as I listen.'

'No, if you close your eyes how will I know you are not having a short nap?'

William opened his eyes again and took a drink of his wine. 'Ah, yes, there is that danger I suppose.'

'Now, what my father says here ... is that everything goes to me and my descendants ... *but* he also stipulates that should any man marry a female heir of mine and lives on Jarvisfield, he is to assume the surname of Macquarie and to bear no other name.'

'Oh, that *is* odd.' William sipped at his wine. 'I wonder why he made such a strange stipulation?'

'It's obvious, isn't it?'

William drank more wine and crossed his legs with an impatient sigh. 'It's not obvious to me, old chum, apart from being obviously ridiculous.'

'Yes, but the motive behind it – my dear father's *intentions* are plain to see.'

'Are they?' William uncrossed his legs again. 'Not to me.'

'Why did my father buy so much land on Mull? Why did he build the town of Salen?'

'I have no idea.'

'The reason, my dear William, is that my father hoped to establish a *Macquarie* dynasty on Mull.'

'Ah,' said William.

'So that one day the name of the Isle of Mull and the name

of Macquarie would become synonymous to each other, identical, one and the same.'

'Ah, yes, I see ...' William reached to pour more wine. 'Buy why would he have wanted that?'

'It's obvious, isn't it?'

William sighed and crossed his legs again. 'Is it?'

'Yes! At least to *me* it is. His name is *everywhere* in Sydney – and one day his name will be in the history books of that land – Australia. But not *here* in Scotland. The land of his birth. The land of his death. Even Jarvisfield is named after his beloved first wife Jane Jarvis – *not* Macquarie – and I now believe he realised his mistake in that after I was born.'

'So ...'

'So knowing he wished that, even to going to the extent of stipulating that any male who marries one of my female heirs and so on down the line must take the name of Macquarie – it is now the *consequence* of that request that upsets me so.'

'Ah, yes.' William took a gulp of wine. 'And which consequence would that be?'

'The children.'

William took another gulp of wine. 'Whose children?'

'*My* children!' Lachlan stared at his friend. 'Where are they?'

'My dear fellow I have absolutely no idea! I was not aware you *had* any children.'

'Exactly! I don't have any. Married now almost *four* years and no sign of that wife of mine producing a child to carry on the Macquarie name.'

'Ah, yes, now I see. ... And have you – '

'Of course I have! I've done my marital duty by that woman many times. Not as much as she would wish me to, but more than enough to produce a few children.'

'Well, short of impregnating her myself, I don't see how I can help you.'

'The fault is not with *me!* And you should *know* that, William. Remember that girl of mine in Lancashire, when we were in the Army ... and then she lost the child halfway through the pregnancy.'

'Oh, yes, sweet girl ... Well, what a predicament, eh? My

wife has produced *three* children since our marriage less than five years ago ... D'y'know that *may* in fact be the reason why she now prefers her own praying to my loving.'

Lachlan poured himself a glass of wine. 'So what am I going to do?'

Drummond stood up and carried his wineglass over to the window, looking out at the dark night, now feeling genuine sympathy for Lachlan – now that he finally understood the problem. Every man expected his lineage to continue through a marriage.

'Well, my friend,' he said, 'apart from you carrying on doing your best, there's not much else you *can* do.'

Chapter Seven

'Husband?'

Lachlan looked up from his thoughts. 'What?'

'Would you like some more tea,' Isabella asked, holding the china teapot in readiness to pour.

'No, keep your tea! In fact I don't want any breakfast at all,' he added, even though he had already eaten a plate of fried bacon and two poached eggs.'

When he had walked out of the room, Isabella sat with a shaking hand stroking her own cheek to comfort herself, her blue eyes watery.

She did so *hate* it when he got into his bad moods, and at times she almost hated *him* too, but she knew he did not mean most of the awful things he said to her, and was quite certain that all blame lay at the feet of that William Drummond – that rakeshame son of Lord Strathallan. God knows how his wife put up with *him*? His reputation for being a womaniser was well known, but at least Lachlan would *never* do anything like that – betray her with another woman – and surely that proved his unassailable love for her.

Oh yes, she knew that deep down Lachlan loved her as much as she loved him, he just had a poor way of showing it, that's all.

And he was plagued so by the turbulence of his moods ... his erratic dark moods. Although she was sure his moods would be less erratic if he drank less at night. More and more he was drinking at least one full decanter of wine before he visited her in her bedroom at night, and during the last few weeks he had not visited her at all.

William Drummond and drink – they were the two culprits responsible for leading Lachlan astray from his otherwise happy marriage. They were the enemy. All this nonsense about her dowry was just a pretence on Lachlan's part because he could not bear to hear her say a word against that rakeshame friend of his.

But she *would* continue to speak out against Lord

Strathallan's rakeshame son, and more. She would tell Lachlan that if he did not abandon William Drummond and also abandon drinking too much, she would leave him and return to her family home at Craignish.

*

Lachlan's black resentment against his wife continued all the way during his walk through the back yard, the vegetable garden, the bluebell field and down to the banks of the Loch, thinking of how she had wilfully defrauded him in so many ways. The *injustice* of it all consumed him. If only he had married someone else, *anyone* else, and not a woman he had no interest in, no fascination, no quickening of the blood.

He stood at the water's edge feeling very sorry for himself as he gazed up at the green hills and the mountainous Ben More in the distance.

A moment later he turned his head and saw Beth strolling along the Loch's bank some good length away, her eyes also turned to the hills. She had not yet seen him and he studied her. She wore a pair of breeches tucked into riding boots and a white shirt rolled up at the elbows.

In the past, when they were younger, he had always disliked her wearing breeches which he thought made her look boyish and took away from her lovely femininity in a dress; but now as he watched her, fully grown and developed, his carnal eyes could see the length of her slim legs and perfectly shaped thighs in the breeches, not to mention the push of her pert young breasts under the shirt.

She saw him, and waved, and was still smiling as she approached him. 'You are up and out early.'

'So are you.'

Beth smiled again. 'I'm always up and out early, you should know that.'

'Where have you been?'

'Up on the hills with Robbie.' She frowned as she looked down at the water. 'I'm becoming concerned about him.'

'Why?'

'He's getting on in years now and I think we need to mate him with a female collie to make sure we don't lose Robbie's

293

magic eye.'

He looked at her. 'What has his eye got to do with it?'

'Well at least *one* of the litter would surely inherit Robbie's mesmerising eye for controlling the sheep. And we will need another sheepdog to take over when Robbie gets too old to do it, and he's nearing that time now.'

'The sheep ...' Lachlan said, thinking again with resentment of how everyone at Jarvisfield *worked* in some way or another: Mary, Mrs Keillor, Hector, the farm boys and so many others – even Beth worked all the time, either up on the hills with Robbie and the sheep or down here digging in the vegetable garden – yet that lazy wife of his did *nothing* for the estate except preen herself and lay around complaining about her weak and delicate constitution. And despite all that relaxing and laying around of hers – the lazy besom could not even get pregnant and help him to carry on the Macquarie name, if only for the sake of his dear father.

Beth must have noticed the change of expression on his face, because she asked, 'Lachlan, what's wrong.'

'Nothing.'

'No? Yet you seemed to be thinking some angry thoughts.'

'I was thinking about justice, Beth, and *injustice,* something I have suffered a lot from these past few years.'

'Which? Justice or injustice?'

'Both.' He looked at her. 'It's not something I can discuss with you, Beth.'

'As you wish.'

She moved to walk on and he turned and fell into step beside her.

'Are those *my* breeches you're wearing?'

'Heavens, no!' Beth laughed. 'Hector makes all claim on your old breeches these days. These were made for me a few weeks ago by the tailor in Salen.'

'And that's why they fit you so well,' he said quietly.

'Lachlan, about justice ...' she said hesitantly.

'No, Beth,' he cut her short, 'I cannot speak about that, not with you.'

'Then allow *me* to speak about justice,' Beth pleaded. 'I know you are unhappy and I know you have all the worry about the finances of the estate, but perhaps the exercise of justice will distract you, and then all the other things may not seem as bad as you think they are.'

He stopped and looked at her. 'Beth, what the pox are you talking about?'

Beth stooped down to pick up a few bluebells which she then twirled in her fingers when she straightened up again.

'A number of times, while you have been away,' she said, 'Mr Robert Dewar has had requests for you to fulfil your duty as the owner of Jarvisfield and take your turn on the bench as a Justice of the Peace. I think it would do you a lot of good. When you were in the Army your mother told us how much you enjoyed command, so now you could command for the greater good as a Justice of the Peace.'

After a long thoughtful silence, Lachlan said, 'It's my duty, is it?'

'Yes, as one of the few landed gentry here.'

A slow smile moved on Lachlan's face. 'You know, I might enjoy that – being the one to dish out some justice for a change.'

*

From the window of the dining room, Isabella watched the two of them as they came nearer to the house and her breath exhaled when she saw that Lachlan was smiling.

Oh good, Beth must have been talking some sense into him. Such a sweet-natured girl, and in all other ways many men would consider her to be extremely beautiful if it were not for her mongrel ancestry of mixed blood. An Arab and an Englishwoman ... appalling just to think of it. No wonder she was still unmarried at the age of one and twenty.

She turned away from the window with a feeling of satisfaction. All the farm boys on Jarvisfield may swoon at the sight of Elizabeth Jarvis – but none would ever dare to marry her. What man would want his fair children tainted by dark eastern blood?

Still, a sweet girl for all that.

Chapter Eight

Beth was beginning to wish she had never encouraged Lachlan to take up his position as a Justice of the Peace, because in the space of only one month acting as a magistrate, every offender who came before him left the courtroom shocked and dazed.

A minor offender who had expected the usual sentence of one day in the cells had been sentenced to a full *week* – on a diet of bread and water – for the sole reason that Lachlan considered him to '*look too fat and needs to slim down.*'

Another offender who expected a small fine, was sentenced to be ducked in the sea three times at Tobermory, and only after a good soaking was he to be allowed back on dry land, because he '*looks like he needs a good wash.*'

By the end of his first week the entire island was talking about him, but the case that caused the most shock and gossip was that of a young fisherman in Tobermory who stood accused of attempting to molest a girl of twelve – to which the fisherman pleaded his innocence on the grounds that he was just being friendly because she was "such a pretty young thing".

Lachlan sentenced him to a week standing on the waterfront of Tobermory – dressed from head to toe in the feminine clothes of a girl – and the two guards in attendance during that time must allow any foreign sailors coming in off the ships to molest him in any way they wished because they also thought him to be – "*a pretty young thing.*"

Inside the Tobermory Inn, Lizzie McLeod was shaking her head in puzzlement as she spoke to Beth.

'The people don't know what to make of him, Beth. Diets and duckings and a man being made to stand like a sailor's whore on the waterfront and allow himself to be molested ... Although,' she added with a gleeful smile, 'we all approve of that last one, because that will have taught *him* to no' put his hands on any young lasses in the future – if only for the fear of ending up before Mr Macquarie again.'

Beth had to admit that she was surprised at Lachlan's commitment to his role as Justice of the Peace, and his strange and harsh sentences to offenders.

'It's got so that people are now feared of doing the smallest wrong thing,' Lizzie said, 'because they don't know what to expect from him. He's thrown the rule book out the window and sentences them to whatever he thinks fit in his mood on the day – and whatever he thinks fit can be *anything!*'

Beth said finally, 'I know Lachlan can be wild and wilful and a prey to his impulses, but I don't think he would ever be *unjust* in his rulings.'

'Aye, well ...' Lizzie shook her head again, 'some people staunchly approve of him, and others think he's as mad as the vexed sea – but *me* – I just don't know *what* to think of him anymore.'

'Nor I,' Beth said quietly, as confused as Lizzie.

*

When Beth reached home and relayed Lizzie's gossip to her mother, Mary also looked troubled, and sad, very sad.

'I can't help thinking of his mother and father, and how they both adored him, and wanted only the best for him. I know it would break Elizabeth's heart to see him now, so unhappy in himself and taking it out on other people.'

'No,' Beth said quickly, always ready to defend Lachlan, 'he doesn't take his unhappiness out on other people at all ... or do you mean in his harsh sentencing?'

'Oh, that is nothing in comparison to the holy war he is now waging against all the *clerics* on the island.' Mary answered. 'No matter if they be of the Free Church or the Church of Scotland he is constantly challenging all their practices and beliefs – even going so far as to question the existence of God.'

'But he has always insisted that he is a devout Christian.'

'Well,' Mary shrugged, 'some days he is, and some days he is not. It all depends on what mood he's in.'

Beth sat silently, seeing no solution to it at all. If only Isabella would get pregnant and give Lachlan a child and a greater purpose in life, it might change things for the better.

'But I *will* say this for him,' Mary went on. 'He has got this estate back up and running again and has sorted out all his debts now. So this house and Jarvisfield is safe and secure, and for that alone his parents *would* be very proud of him. As I am also, very proud of him in that respect.'

Beth smiled at her mother. 'You still love him then?'

'Of course I do. I was his nursemaid even before you were born, and that's a maternal bond of affection that's hard to break. Oh, I know he can be opinionated and excitable and gets angry, but deep down I know he still has a *good* heart inside him, even though at times it doesn't seem that he has. And don't forget he is the child of two very *good* people, so he can't be as bad as he often pretends to be.'

Beth nodded, certain her mother was right.

PART TWO

Chapter Nine

On a sun-slanted evening in early July, Her Majesty's Packet Ship, *Windsor* docked at Leith Harbour, Edinburgh's main port.

Of the three passengers who disembarked, one was a young man wearing a Royal Navy uniform. He was being watched carefully by another young man named Jefferson, who was standing outside the *Leith Inn* enjoying the breeze and sea air.

Jefferson watched as a member of the packet crew handed down a bag to the young officer and then smiled and touched the side of his hat in a brief salute – as sailors always did as a sign of respect to the officers of Britain's superior sea service – the one that sailed the oceans in ships of the line and fought under sail.

When the young officer turned away from the ship in his direction, Jefferson could see that his face was very tanned from the sun, accentuating the vivid blue of his eyes. But it was his navy blue coat with the cream lapels and cuffs and gold buttons and the white waistcoat of his *uniform* that excited Jefferson. He would give away ten years of his life just to be able to wear a respected uniform like that.

*

Tired out after two and half days without much sleep on the cramped packet boat from London to Edinburgh, which was still preferable to being confined for six days in an overland coach, Lieutenant John Dewar walked to the nearest inn and had to bow his head to enter through its small door. It was an ancient and shabby little inn and once inside, John saw that the taproom was empty.

Ten minutes or so in here, John decided, then he would gladly catch a cab home to his father's house in the city.

He rang the bell and waited for someone to come and attend to him.

While he stood waiting he looked around the room

and saw a large wooden sign with red painted lettering nailed to the wall.

No Jews, Negroes, Gypsies or ANYONE FROM ENGLAND

A moment later a tall and slender young black man, aged somewhere in his early twenties, appeared from behind the counter. His face was cheerful and smiling.

'Yes, sor, how can we help you?'

John knew he was very tired, but wondered if he was now so tired that he had begun to hallucinate?

He again looked up at the sign that said 'No Negroes' and then lowered his eyes to the young black tapman who spoke with an Irish accent.

'Ah that? Don't mind that soyn at all now,' said the young black man. 'It's been up there since the seventeen hundreds. Least, so the owner says. Tis an antique he does say.'

No wonder the place was empty, John thought. That sign was enough to keep all but the locals away.

'So what can I get you?'

'A warm drink.'

'Is it tay ye mane? A pot of tay?'

The voice just did not go with the face, and John found himself grinning. 'No, a warm brandy.'

'Brandy it is, sor? Comin' right up – but I'll have to warm it in me hands so I will.'

He came back a few minutes later with a brandy glass cupped inside his hands. 'Here ye go, as warm as a slapped backside.'

A sudden thought struck John, a stupid thought, but nevertheless he had to ask, 'You're not a slave are you?'

'Jaysus, no! That's against the *law* in this country! I'm as free as them birds that fly in the air.'

John took a sip of his brandy.

'Though, it *does* get very lonely in here,' said the young tapman, looking bleakly around the empty room.

'Not surprising, is it?' John said. 'With that sign up there.'

'How d'you mean?'

'Well, think of it – ships from all over Europe come in at

Leith to unload, so many of the sailors would probably be Jewish or Negro or Spanish or any other nationality, so why the hell would they want to drink in a place that has a sign like that up on it's wall.'

'He won't take it down. Said it's an antique.'

'It's not an antique,' John argued. 'It's a disgrace.'

'But the sailors from the ships *do* come in here when a ship is in. That sign saying no Jews or Englishmen doesn't seem to trouble them at all, and I reckon it's because most of them never learned how to *read.*'

John looked at him thoughtfully for some seconds. 'Can *you* read?'

'Sure I can.'

'So what does that sign up there say?'

The young tapman looked up at the offending sign and then picked up a cloth and began to busily polish the surface of the counter.

'I *can* read,' he said finally. 'I can read the wind and the weather and the mood of the sky and I can even read the *time* on a clock!'

'Good for you,' John smiled. 'I didn't mean any offence. Not to you.'

The tapman looked at John's smile, liked it, and smiled back. 'You just come back from a voyage?'

John nodded.

'Where from?'

'Africa.'

The young black man pursed his lips and narrowed his eyes. 'I think I heard of that place. What was you doing there?'

John briefly told him about the work of the West Africa Squadron.

'Well, for *cryinoutloud* ... you really do that? Free black slaves?'

'No, not just me, the Royal Navy and everyone else in the squadron ... and why has your accent suddenly changed to American?'

'Irish, American, all the same. Can I ask your name, sor?'

'John Dewar.'

'And you free black slaves?' The young black man's face took on an elated expression as he looked at John and said with a sudden inspired passion, 'I *love* you, John Dewar, with my whole heart and soul I *love* you. Honest to God, I do!'

John almost choked on his brandy, swallowing it quickly. He *had* hoped to hear those words said to him on his return to Scotland, but *not* from a black Irishman

'So what is *your* name?' he asked curiously.

'Thomas Jefferson.'

'No!' John grinned. 'You were named after an American president?'

'I was, sor.'

'In Ireland?'

'Oh, them Irish *love* Americans!'

Now his accent sounded more American than Irish.

'I was named Thomas Jefferson after that great American president, God rest his soul now he's been dead twenty years, but most folks just calls me Jefferson. Although – them Irish – they sometimes call me *O'Jefferson.*'

John was getting confused by it all. 'So how come?' he asked. 'Black and Irish and named after an American president and yet – now you are here in *Scotland*?'

Jefferson leaned his elbows on the counter and said thoughtfully, 'Well now, ye see, it all happened like this ...

'Although – ' Jefferson added quickly in a low voice, 'I tell only you because *you* been freeing slaves out in Africa.'

And so he continued telling his story, although in the telling of it his accent changed back and forth from Irish to American and, eventually, John began to understand why.

His name truly *was* Thomas Jefferson and he had been born in the slave state of Virginia, on a tobacco plantation, the son of a slave named Sally-Gone.

'Sally-Gone? Was Gone her surname?'

'No, she was called that because one day she was just *gone!* No one knew where she gone, just that she *gone* somewhere and never seen again.'

'Did she escape? Run away?'

Jefferson shrugged. 'I was only a few months born, so too young to figure it out.'

And as Jefferson continued, John learned that because there were five other slaves on the plantation named Sally, the other women always referred to Jefferson as 'the son of Sally-Gone.'

'Till I was 'bout ten then *I* was *gone* – ran away hard and fast – so I s'pose after that the women called me Thomas-Gone, saying I was no better than my mama.'

The door of the taproom opened. An old man who looked like a local walked in. Instantly Jefferson jumped to attention and his accent became pure Irish again.

'Yes, sor, how can we help you?'

The old man grunted. 'I just need a light to get my pipe burning. Can ye help me with that?'

*

As the old man moved to saunter out again, smoking his pipe, Jefferson called after him. 'Do ye not want a drink, sor, to go with your smoke?'

'No thanks,' replied the old man sarcastically, opening the door. 'I'm a Jew.'

John looked around the empty taproom and then curiously at Jefferson.

'If your wages are based on your takings from this place, then the money you get paid must be a very small amount.'

'Jayz! I don't get paid *money*,' Jefferson replied. 'I get my food and a bed in return for my work and that's all I need *for now*.'

'For now?'

Jefferson nodded. 'While I'm waiting for my ship.'

'What ship?'

'Any ship that will give me work. I'm a natural born sailor.' His eyes moved over John's Royal Navy uniform. 'Like yourself.'

'I thought you said you were born on a tobacco plantation in Virginia?'

'I was.' Jefferson turned up his eyes. 'Honest to God and the holy Saint Patrick I was.'

John eyed him warily, unsure if Jefferson was in truth a former slave from Virginia, or just a great actor and an even better liar.

'I think it's time I was on my way home,' he said, moving to lift his bag. 'I hear enough made-up tales from sailors on ships.'

'Ah no, don't go!' Jefferson pleaded. 'Stay a while and I'll give you another warm brandy – on the house!'

'No, I have to go.' John met his eyes and said sardonically: 'And why should I stay here talking with you when I'm no longer sure if I can believe a word you say.'

Jefferson's eyes were wide with innocence. 'Every *wurrd* I said was the truth!'

'That you're a natural-born sailor?'

'I am.'

'Very well.' John put down his bag. 'Prove it by answering me this ...'

He then asked Jefferson a number of questions about a sailors work on a ship. Foremast? Topmast? Mizzenmast? How do you repair a sail?

'And if I say, "bring her up to the wind" what do you do then?'

Jefferson knew exactly what to do.

John followed with at least ten more questions to which Jefferson answered all correctly, smiling and enjoying it all as if it was a game.

'And if there is a raging storm throughout the night and every man must do what he can to keep the ship steady for as long as it takes?'

'I go on the sick list and stay in my hammock.'

John eyed him charily. 'You would allow a ship to go short-handed in a storm?'

Jefferson grinned. 'Just jesting.'

'So, you *are* a prime seaman, that's true,' John observed. 'Was the part about the tobacco plantation in Virginia true?'

'*All* of it was true!'

'So between being born in Virginia, and later becoming a seaman and ending up in a taproom in Scotland – what happened in the middle bit? How did you get that semi-Irish accent?'

Jefferson leaned his elbows on the counter and said, 'Well,

you see, it happened like this ...'

'No, wait, I think I *will* have that second brandy,' John said, 'but I'll pay for it. I don't want your employer ripping the sheets off your bed in recompense for you giving away free drinks.'

'Sheets? There's no sheets on *my* bed,' Jefferson declared. 'He gave me two blankets that's all. Two blankets and my bed and board – bread and cheese, that's all.'

After a pause, John asked, 'Will you have a drink yourself?'

'Thank you, I will. But if you don't mind, I'll be charging you for a glass of water.'

'Water? And how much is that going to cost me?'

'Ten shilluns.'

'*Ten* shillings? You must be crazy, man.'

'We could make it five shilluns,' Jefferson suggested, 'and I'll drink only half a glass.'

'Even in Edinburgh, water is *free*.' John couldn't stop smiling at Jefferson's audacity. 'So it's not only that sign that is keeping customers away and leaving this place empty – *you* are. How many other people have bought you a glass of water for ten shillings or half a glass for five?'

Jefferson smiled. 'I was hoping you'd be the first.'

At this John erupted with laughter. 'You're worse than the Arabs in Casablanca. In the Casbah there one Arab tried to charge me the equivalent in dirhams of five pounds for an orange.'

'That's disgraceful.' Jefferson tutted. 'My water's much cheaper than that.'

How much cheaper?'

'Two shilluns.'

'That's twice the price of my brandy.' John was still grinning. At least Jefferson was being more honest in his own way than many tapmen who said, '*Thank you, sir, I'll have it later,*' and then pocketed the money, and usually double the amount the drink should cost.'

He said: 'Jefferson, as it's my first hour back in Scotland after three years away, I'm feeling inclined to be generous as well as stupid. Go fetch the brandy.'

'And the water?'

'And the water,' John agreed, knowing he was being exploited by a man who was being even more shamefully exploited by his employer

*

Two brandies later, John had learned that at the time Jefferson had decided to become Thomas-Gone and leave the Virginia plantation far behind him, his greatest asset when he was ten years old was that he was small and thin and could hide anywhere.

So when he saw his master's carriage being loaded up with luggage, and heard that he was travelling to Pennsylvania, Jefferson slid underneath the carriage between the wheels and rode along with him, because he was sure that's where Sally-Gone had gone – to Pennsylvania, where slavery had been outlawed years before – a Free State.

'*Yankee* country,' Jefferson grinned, because when he eventually reached the northern border of Pennsylvania and crossed it, he found out that he was in the State of New York, and he knew it didn't get more Yankee than that – New York.

'How long did it take you to get there? To the border of New York?' John asked. He now had his own personal reasons for wanting to know all about Jefferson, but those reasons could wait.

'A year, maybe two, living like a cat, running from one farm to another, stealing food and drinking all their milk. Few times I nearly gets caught, but when I run – I *run* – and *fast*! No white man alive could ever catch *me!*'

'When did you reach the sea?' John asked. The sea was the part he wanted to know about.

'Oh, not till a long, long time before I gets me down to the town of New York – lots of places to hide in that town. And man! All those high buildings – some eight, nine, even *ten* floors high! I kept knocking into things and tripping myself over because I was doing all my walking with my eyes looking *up!*

'Then about the tenth time I tripped, I didn't just stumble and fall over – I went flying and my face fell down bang onto somebody's hard boot. And when I saw daylight again, blood was coming out of my nose and two men were helping me up and one said, "Jaysus! Tis a little black *boy*! I thought it was a black dog attacking me boot!"

'And then,' said Jefferson, 'they took me back into the tavern they'd just come out of, washed the blood off my face, and when they learned I had no home to go to, the biggest of the two men said, "In that case, ye may as well come along with us and we'll find ye a hammock and maybe even a bit o' grub. But ye'll have to work for it! Jaysus, we *all* have to work for it.'

Jefferson gave a small laugh as he remembered. 'Sailors they were, Irish sailors, trading between New York and Ireland. And after they had housed me on their ship, they let me stay aboard even when the ship set sail, and before I knew it ten years had passed and I was a better sailor than all of them. They looked after me though, looked after me good, and made me laugh all the time. Most of the Irish are crazy, d'you know that?'

'So what are you now – twenty-two?'

''Bout that.'

'And you never found Sally-Gone? Your mother?'

'No.' Jefferson closed his eyes and said almost reverently, 'The sea is my mother now.'

John noticed the clock on a shelf behind Jefferson and realised he had been inside the inn for almost two hours.

'I've got to go.'

'What?' Jefferson looked crestfallen. 'Ah no, stay a while longer because I haven't told you the *all* of it. About how I come to Scotland.'

'I can't afford any more of your water. You've had five glasses so far.'

'I'll drink some more for free. Won't cost you another penny.'

John picked up his bag. Jefferson had a likeable and winning way about him that pulled you in and carried you along, but he knew that if he stayed any longer he and Jefferson would still be talking at midnight.

'It will have to wait until some other time,' he said.

'So you'll be coming back sometime?'

'I may well do, if …' John paused, because right now everything in his life depended on a number of very big IFs.

He shrugged. 'But for now, it has to be *totsiens.*'

'What does that mean?'

John grinned. 'In African it means – goodbye!'

Chapter Ten

Beth had been following the changes of spring, carefully watching it unfold day by day through three long months, but now the air was hotter, the sea calmer, the sky a clear light blue. Summer had been here for over a month, and it made her feel sad.

Summer was the season when she thought more often about John Dewar, although she was trying very hard to forget him and get on with her life. In summer they had met, and in summer they had parted. She had no winter memories of him, no autumn bleak days to think back on; just happy summer days full of sunshine.

She was walking along one of Mull's volcanic cliffs, looking out to the sea and watching a small boat slowly rocking and two fishermen sitting among the fishnets, unaware of her eyes watching them.

Finally she came to a large flat rock and sat on it, taking out of her dress pocket the letter she had received that morning from Mr Ewan McPherson, the young postmaster in Tobermory whom she had met many times but had spoken to him only twice.

A nice young man who read a lot of books, finally asking her if she had ever read Voltaire? When she replied that she had never heard of Voltaire, he told her he was halfway through reading *Candide* – a wonderful book by Voltaire that had taught him to challenge life and to always expect the best from everyone.

Now he had written her a letter expressing his long-held devotion and love for her, and begging her forgiveness for his temerity in sending to her his proposal of marriage, as his dearest wish was to make her his wife. If she accepted his proposal, then he requested that she send him a note in reply to that effect, and he would then make a formal approach to the Laird of Jarvisfield for her hand.

Beth lifted her eyes and looked out to sea again, a frown on her face. How could he say he loved her when they had spoken only twice? How did he know her temperament, or the things that pleased her? Surely these things were important to know before proposing a marriage?

And *his* temperament? And the things that pleased *him*? She knew almost nothing about him. So how could she agree to spend the rest of her life with him?

It was not to be considered, and writing the reply would be difficult if she was to avoid hurting Mr McPherson's feelings, but there was only one man who could persuade her to leave her mother and Lachlan and Mrs Keillor and Hector and her beloved home in Jarvisfield – and that man had lost interest in her a long time ago.

Her eyes smarting with the onset of tears as they always did when she thought of her lost love, she stood up and walked to the edge of the cliff and looked down ... it was a long, long fall. She tore the letter in two and let the pieces fall onto the rocks below, where the sea would later wash them away. And now all that remained for her to do was write the difficult letter of reply.

She returned to the flat rock and sat on it again, watching the fishing boat for a few minutes, and then faced the hard task of mentally composing her reply.

'Dear Mr McPherson, I am deeply honoured by your proposal of marriage, but ... but ... but ...'

*

Mary was in the kitchen writing a list of provisions she would need from Tobermory at the end of the week, and enjoying the quiet peace of the kitchen while Mrs Keillor was up in her bedroom having an afternoon nap, as was Isabella.

This practice of sleeping in daylight was beginning to annoy her because it was becoming a contagion, draining the energy from the house, and Mrs Keillor was becoming influenced by too many of Isabella's lazy habits.

Only when Lachlan and Beth were around did the house regain it's feeling of young energy. And now that the days were so much warmer, even Hector had taken to snoozing on the straw in the stables. What was acceptable for one was now becoming acceptable for all – but it was *not* acceptable to Lachlan who could make them all jump out of their beds at the first sounds of his returning.

Some minutes later Mary lifted her head, sure she had heard a knock on the front door, but if so, where were Maggie or Lorna to answer it?

When the brass knocker rapped again, she got to her feet thinking; 'Those two madams are probably propped up against a tree down by the loch, chattering away as usual.'

She opened the front door, her eyes widening with disbelief and her hand going to her heart because she was not prepared – oh no, she was not prepared – for the sight of John Dewar standing there.

'Mr Dewar!'

'Good afternoon, Mrs Jarvis.'

'Oh my goodness ... come in, come in. Oh I *am* happy to see you, but I just need to get my breath back.'

His answering smile was very attractive, Mary thought. 'You look well.'

'I'm sorry if I have disturbed you.'

'Oh no, no, it's just ... well, a shock. We thought never to see you again.'

And now she was seeing him again, and he was everything Mary remembered, this young man whom she had always liked so much. The same dark brown hair with a lock falling over his brow which he pushed back, the same warm eyes of a vivid blue, and just as handsome as before, if not even moreso now.

'You've caught the sun,' she observed, also noting that he was not wearing his uniform, but a fawn riding jacket over a cream shirt and black twill trousers.

'Did you ride here?'

'Yes, from Tobermory.'

'Are you staying at the inn?'

'Yes.'

She led him into the drawing-room, thinking how shocked Beth would be to see him, and that thought made her stop suddenly and turn to look at him. 'Beth is not at home.'

'No?' He looked disconcerted. 'But she does still live here?'

'Oh yes.'

'She's not – '

'No,' Mary cut in sagely. 'Although you really have no right to ask,' she added in a mother's reproving tone, 'because you *did* release her from the understanding the two of you once had, and it *has* been three years.'

John nodded. 'Yes, I know, I'm sorry about that.'

'You could have written.'

'I did write – and here's the proof.'

Only then did Mary notice the packet he was holding which he placed on the small table near the door. 'All my letters to her, and all her letters to me – all still sealed and unopened.'

Mary was baffled. 'But how?'

John shrugged. 'Portsmouth is one of the busiest shipping ports in the world and post is often put on the wrong ship and travels all over the globe before making its way back undelivered. This packet was waiting for me in the Navy's mail office when I arrived back in Portsmouth.'

'Oh, my … ' Mary felt sad that so many wrong conclusions and so much unhappiness could be caused to two young people due to the negligent mistakes made by others.

She looked at the packet. 'And you say … you have not opened her letters to you? Have you not read them?'

'No. They all remain sealed.'

'Why?'

'Because …' How to explain …? 'Because once I saw these letters unopened, I realised that Beth had not heard from me in a very long time, and as I don't know what she has been thinking, or what her thoughts and feelings are now, I really don't want to read her letters.'

'Until you *do* know?' Mary guessed.

'Until I do know,' John confirmed.

Mary looked at the packet on the table. 'But why give the letters back to her, even her own letters, why not keep them until she has read yours, and then – '

'Mrs Jarvis, please, just give her my sealed and stamped letters, which she will see were sent but not delivered to her. And when she has read them, if she still wants to see me then she can send a note to me at the Tobermory Inn. If I don't hear from her in three days I will take that as her answer and return to Edinburgh.'

'How long is your leave this time?'

'I don't know yet.'

'And will it be to Africa again you ...' Mary had stopped speaking because she was staring at the open door of the drawing-room.

John turned his head to look and saw Beth standing there. She was wearing a simple dress of deep red cotton, a colour that accentuated her stunning exotic beauty. Her dark eyes were looking at him as if she was seeing a mirage – like some sailors who spend a long time staring at the horizon.

'Beth ...' he said, feeling the cold dread in his heart now beginning to erase all hope, because she was looking at him distantly as if he was a stranger, or someone she must have known in the past but could not quite remember who he was.

'Beth ... did you come through the kitchen?' Mary asked.

Beth did not answer, because she was slowly walking towards John and a moment later they were locked in each other's arms, hugging each other tightly without any words being spoken, no letters or explanations needed.

Mary looked on, realising that this long-awaited moment was theirs, and theirs alone, so she left them to share it in private.

Chapter Eleven

Beth packed some clothes and toiletries into a bag, changed into a riding habit, saddled her horse and returned with him to Tobermory. After three years apart and so many wrong conclusions during those years, they needed time and space to be alone, and talk alone, and Mary understood that.

Not that she could have stopped Beth, even if she had wanted to. She was one and twenty now, the legal age of an adult, and mistress of her own life.

'It's the *laird* that worries me,' Mary said to Mrs Keillor. 'If he knows that Beth has gone off with a man he has never met, he will go wild.'

'So tell him he's a Dewar, related to his farm manager, a respectable and responsible family, that should ease him.'

'Are you sure he's gone to Strathallan Castle?'

'Aye.' Mrs Keillor nodded with certainty. 'And from there he's going on to Edinburgh. That's what he told me. And tomorrow Mrs Isabella is going home to Craignish to spend a few weeks of the summer with her family while he's away.'

'Yes,' Mary nodded, 'that's what he told me. But you never know with him – sometimes he says he's going away for a few weeks and comes back in a few days – and other times he says he's going away for a few days and stays away for a month.'

'But what if Mrs Isabella comes looking for Beth later tonight?'

Mary shrugged. 'Just say she is over at the Dewars house with Kirsty. We don't want no talk or upset about this until we see how things work out with Beth and John Dewar. He may be gone again in a week or so, tied as he is to the Navy.'

'Beth must be mad in her head,' Mrs Keillor said. 'What good is there in having a man who is always away at sea?'

'All I can say to that, and all I know for certain,' Mary replied, 'is that once they had met there was no other man in the world for her, and I've a suspicion he felt the same about Beth. So I'm hoping they do some good talking together now about what's going to happen in the future.'

*

They did not talk at all during the long ride to Tobermory, but every so often they exchanged glances, looks, the occasional smile, and then turned their eyes back to the road ahead.

It was not a straight road, it was full of mounds and dips and narrow lanes, so riding was an attentive undertaking.

They eventually arrived in the town in a blue twilight and under a sky of early stars. At the far end of the waterfront they could see fishing boats and their lanterns bobbing up and down as they began their evening journey out to sea.

'I would like ... a short walk?' Beth said, as they dismounted in the stables.

John nodded, and deposited her bag inside the inn where he reserved a second room, leaving her waiting outside for only a few minutes until he returned, and they walked along the quay as if drawn by the lights of the boats.

At the end of the quay John spent some time talking to the fishermen who were preparing to go out, showing great interest in all they had to say, and not speaking to her at all, knowing her request for a walk was because she needed more time to adjust, to think, to examine her feelings because he had come upon her without warning and so unexpectedly.

They stayed watching until the last of the boats went out, and the moon was drawing nearer, a faint light on the sea.

Finally he looked at her and she smiled at him, more relaxed and at peace with herself.

'You can change your mind and we can go back to Jarvisfield,' he said. 'If you now feel your decision was rash.'

'No,' she said, slipping her hand into his, 'I want to stay with you.'

*

Inside the Tobermory Inn the dining room was quite full save for a small square table near the back window.

When they had taken their seats Beth looked around at all the candles alight on every table and the numerous lanterns glittering around the walls, giving the darkened room a

317

magical atmosphere.

'Everywhere I look tonight I seem to see lights, lights and more lights,' she said. 'Even the stars look brighter.'

'Because it's summer and the sky is clearer,' he said.

'Oh, so it's not just my imagination?'

'No.'

He was looking at her face, seeing her afresh and thinking again that she was simply the most beautiful girl he had ever seen. Her delicate femininity and shy manner had entranced him from the first evening he had met her. And now he was recognising again all her little mannerisms and facial expressions ... the way she turned her eyes up and pretended to look around her when she did not know what to say next.

Her hands were clasped together on the table and he reached to open them, taking one hand in both of his own and turning it palm up as if interested in the lines on it.

He said: 'Beth, I want you to know that since I met you, I have had no eyes, no thoughts, no desire for any other girl, and I always intended to come back, and I'm sorry you did not receive any of my letters from Africa telling you that.'

Beth's dark eyes blinked as emotion pushed at her throat. 'But they say a sailor has a girl in every port he goes ashore on. Do you?'

'Not since you, and before that, none like you.'

She sat silent with her head bowed for some moments, and when she looked at him again tears were glistening in her eyes as she said with a quiet honesty:

'I have missed you *so* much. And there were times when I thought I would *die* if you did not come back.'

He could feel his heart hammering in his chest as he looked into her dark eyes, filmed with moisture.

He looked away, around the crowded room, not wanting to eat anything and hating all the noise from other voices. They should not have come in here to this crowded room, not now, not tonight.

He looked at her. 'Are you hungry?'

She shook her head. 'I don't believe I could eat a thing.'

'Is there anything you want?'

'No, just lots of lights, candle lights, like bright stars.'

He released her hand. 'Shall we leave?'

'Yes.'

Outside the door of the dining room they met Angus who was coming in to take their order.

'Oh yes, Angus, good evening,' John said. 'We are not dining after all, but can you arrange a plate of something to be left outside my door before you go to bed?'

'I've got some nice grouse pie,' Angus offered.

'Anything.'

''Course, if ye were to dine inside, 'Angus said, 'there's some very tasty fresh lobster.'

'Yes, put that on the plate too.'

Angus looked at Beth. 'And ye, Miss Jarvis, do ye want a plate of something left outside your door too?'

'No, no, I will wait until breakfast.'

'Right ye are then,' said Angus, eager to get back inside the dining room and take more orders.

As they mounted the stairs John said. 'You can have whatever food he leaves under a lid outside my door.'

Beth was wide-eyed as she looked around. She had never been upstairs or seen any of the guest rooms in the Tobermory Inn, so this was a new experience.

'You're in room 2,' John said, 'so this must be your room.'

He opened the door into a dark room, but as soon as he had found a candle and lit it, Beth saw a large square room that was furnished very nicely, and had a front window overlooking the sea.

Above the small black iron fireplace there were three more candles in three holders and John lit them also while Beth moved to the window, gazing out over the harbour. The orange moon was in bright glow now over the water although one of its sides was missing ... a half moon, just like that night in Calgary Bay.

Remembering that night, she turned and looked at him, her hands clasped in front of her, watching him standing with head bent as he fiddled with the tinderbox and thinking he was surely the most good-looking young man she had ever seen, but there was more to his attraction than that, so much more.

Like a moth to a bright flame she moved towards the three candles on the mantelpiece and it was then he put the tinderbox on the shelf and looked at her, both listening in silence to the noise that was coming from the taproom downstairs, as if a party was going on.

He put his hands on her shoulders and bent his head and put his lips against hers hesitantly, as if he had not kissed a girl for a very long time. His lips were dry and cool but as they moved closer together and the kiss changed from hesitant to loving even the room began to feel very warm.

She drew back and looked at him with her sensitive dark eyes. 'I think ... I think I would like to read your letters now.'

'Do they matter anymore?'

'Yes, I think we *need* to read them now, both of us.'

'Why?'

'Because those letters are the only bridge we have across three long years of separation ... we can't just pretend those years did not exist.'

John thought about it, and then sighed his agreement. 'If nothing else, I suppose in the days ahead, it will save us hours of explanations.'

He moved to lift the tinderbox from the shelf and she quickly touched his arm. 'I still love you.'

'I know you do, my love.' He gave her a brief kiss on the cheek and then went to his own room to get the packet of unopened letters.

When he returned he had already sorted the letters and handed her his seven letters. 'These are mine to you.'

She took the letters and sat down on the bed. 'I think we should read them separately ... each in our own rooms.'

'If you wish.' He was not prepared to disagree with her about anything, not now, not tonight, not after three years of separation.

For a time each remained in their own rooms reading their letters to each other, written from so far away, and now seeming so long ago.

Beth was holding a letter and reading with tears in her eyes, surprised by the honesty of his language, the honesty of his feelings for her. He held nothing back, except any reference to the work he was doing in Africa.

In his own room John was also reading her letters with some surprise, standing by the window, candles aglow on the dresser beside him, his hand moving to press against his face as he read ...

'... *After our love in Calgary Bay, and the promises we made to each other that night, I would have been happy in my waiting for you to come back, no matter how long or how many the years –if you had not broken my heart by sending that letter setting me free – free to love any other man I met, as if love came so easily. So instead I have given my love to other things, such as the beautiful sunrises in the morning, the songs of the birds, the ewes birthing their lambs, the lowing of the cows, and the sweet smells of spring.*

The only thing I cannot love anymore, cannot look at anymore, no matter how beautiful, is the splendour of the sunsets, because they remind me too much of you and all the love of our last night together – '

A knock on the door, someone entered. John looked round.

'Ho, Lieutenant Dewar, I'm sorry to disturb ye,' said Angus McLeod, 'but I've come to ask ye if half past seven would be a good time to bring up yer hot water for washing in the morning?'

John nodded. 'But in future, Angus, don't enter my room unless I call for you to do so.'

'Aye, sir, my apologies, sir.'

Angus quietly closed the door and moved along the landing, about to knock on Beth's door, and then decided there was no point. His time would be her time too, no doubt.

*

Down in the kitchen, Angus reported to Lizzie: 'He's in his room, reading. And she's in her room, probably in bed by now. I could hear no sound or movement.'

'Are ye sure?'

'Aye, as sure as what my own eyes saw I'm sure. I had a quick glance around his room before I left and aye, he was in it on his own, standing by the window – reading.'

'What was he reading?'

'Papers. How in the Holy should I know *what* he was reading?'

'No matter,' said Lizzie, a frown on her face. 'I feel bad now for doubting him, and he an officer and a gentlemen.'

'And he did book *two* rooms,' Angus added. 'Not like some sailors who book only one and then slip a girl upstairs when our backs are turned.'

'It's my duty, though,' Lizzie said, 'my duty to Mary. Ye know how protective of Beth she is, so I must be the same in her absence.'

''Tis going to get known though,' Angus said worriedly. 'People saw them together in the dining room. 'Tis going to get known that Beth came here with a man and did not go home afterwards. Her *horse* is still out there in the stables. Everyone knows tis Beth who rides that brown gelding.'

'So? What's yer worry, Angus, what?'

'*Ewan!* said Angus. 'Are ye forgetting Ewan MacPherson and how sorely he's in love with Beth?'

*

He was still reading her letters when another knock came on his door. She had written so many more letters than he had, and this last one was dated less than six months ago.

Thinking it was Angus again, he chose to ignore the knock and continued reading, his heart moved and his eyes slightly blurring as he read: '... *They say no one ever died for love, but at times I feel so heartsick and desolate without you I could die ...*'

The knock came again. This time he walked to the door and irritably opened it, his expression changing and the letter slipping from his hand as the girl who had written the letter slowly walked into the room, the glow from the candles reflecting brightly in her dark eyes as she nervously smiled at him.

And then he knew he was lost, totally lost, or maybe he was found, finally found, he didn't know which, and he didn't care.

He put his hand on her arm for a second before he kissed her, and now they were in each others arms and the tightening and sway of those first few loving minutes allowed the night to catch them in its tight dark grip.

There was nothing more to say or to read or do but surrender to their emotions and forget all the uncertainty and unhappiness of those three lost years of separation.

Chapter Twelve

The following morning, when they had finished their late breakfast in the empty dining room, Lizzie McLeod ambled over to their table. They were sitting at a table for four, so she pulled out a chair and plonked her stout body down on it.

'Now then, Miss Beth,' she said sternly, 'I need to know what's going on and why you have left home and come to live here at my inn?'

Beth smiled. 'I haven't left home, Lizzie. John is on leave and I'm on holiday.'

'For how long?'

Beth looked at John. 'How long?'

'A few days. As Beth said, we're giving ourselves a holiday.'

'On holiday, *here*, in Tobermory?'

'It's the first holiday break I've had in three years,' John said. 'So where better than *here,* in Tobermory ... with Beth.'

Lizzie looked from one to the other. 'So it's all on again with ye two is it?'

'It was never off,' said John.

'Aye, it *was* off,' Lizzie argued. 'What else were we to think when no one had seen sight of you and heard nothing from you for years?'

'I was *working,* on duty, with the Navy,' John replied indignantly. 'And with all due respect, Mrs McLeod – '

'I know, I know, it's no' my business, and I apologise,' Lizzie said quickly, and then gave a great sorrowful sigh and rubbed a hand worryingly over her mouth.

'So what is wrong?' John asked.

Lizzie sighed again. 'I'm happy for ye both, I truly am, but I just needed to know for sure.'

'Why?'

'Because ... ' Lizzie said worriedly, 'if ye two are going to be spending your days here on holiday in Tobermory, walking along hand in hand like ye did last evening coming back from the fishermen's quay – then I'm going to have a very unhappy and broken-hearted young man to deal with. And I don't want him to start drinking too much again, or none of us will get any post for weeks.'

John looked at Beth, who only now was beginning to understand whom Lizzie was talking about.

'Ye haven't told our fine young lieutenant then?' Lizzie said. 'About Ewan McPherson's proposal of marriage to you?'

Beth was not only flummoxed but also hotly embarrassed as she said: 'Lizzie, it was only yesterday that I received his letter of proposal and I forgot all about it because I don't even *know* that young man, apart from speaking with him briefly no more than *twice.*'

'He's been in love with you for more than a year gone now,' Lizzie said accusingly. 'And I'm sure I did tell ye a few times now and ye never made any complaint or showed any dislike.'

'Probably because I was not *listening* to you,' Beth replied. 'You've been trying for so long to match and marry me off to every man *you* consider suitable whether I like him or not.'

'Only because your mother and I knew ye were still lovelorn about this one.' Lizzie's accusing glance now flashed at John, who was listening silently with interest.

'And in my opinion,' Lizzie continued, 'the best way to make a woman forget all about a man is to settle her down comfortably with another man.'

Beth was now feeling mortified, but she was not the type to stand up and flounce out on Lizzie. She looked at John with an expression of pure pleading in her dark eyes. 'Shall we ... go now?'

'Go where?' asked Lizzie in alarm. 'Out on those streets where poor Ewan McPherson might see ye walking hand in hand together and he anxiously waiting for a reply to his marriage proposal to ye? It could send him running to the nearest cliff and jumping off!'

Lizzie shook her head impatiently and folded her arms across her wide bosom. 'Och no, Beth, the first thing *ye* must do is to write a nice letter of refusal to Ewan McPherson, and if ye give it to me, I will prepare him – let him down gently so to speak – and then I'll give him your letter of reply.'

Angus, who must have been listening at the door in readiness, came rushing in carrying an inkpot and quill and a few sheets of the Inn's paper.

'It's the kindest thing to do now,' Angus said to Beth.

'It's the *only* thing to do now,' Lizzie said, clearing a space on the table and laying down a sheet of the paper and placing the quill into Beth's hand.

Beth was about to object to this intrusion and dominance of her time and will, but Lizzie was already dictating:

'My dearest Mr McPherson ...'

'No!' Beth objected. 'He is *not* my dearest because I don't even *know* him beyond a passing acquaintance.'

Beth wrote: '*Dear Mr McPherson*

'It gives me sad grief – '

'No!' Beth objected again. 'How can I feel grief about refusing him when I don't even *know* him.'

'Well then put it in your own words.' Lizzie shrugged.

'I will,' Beth said, and wrote: *I am deeply honoured by your proposal of marriage, but –*

Beth frowned, remembering this was the part where she had got stuck yesterday. She looked at Lizzie. 'I don't know what else to say.'

Lizzie leaned closer to read over what Beth had written, and then continued: 'But I am ... I am ...'

Lizzie wasn't sure what so say next either, or how to say it. She looked up at Angus for help and received a shrug. Angus looked questioningly at John who was trying very hard to hide his amusement.

'But I am ... I am ...' Lizzie said again, and then looked curiously at Beth. 'What are ye?'

'Bespoken,' John suggested. 'I think that is the correct word.'

'But I am *bespoken,*' Lizzie continued, watching keenly as Beth wrote it down, and then frowned and asked John, 'Bespoken how?'

'To another gentleman.'

'To another gentleman,' Lizzie dictated, 'but I thank ye kindly ...' Lizzie watched Beth's hand as she wrote so finely, and then her eyes opened wider and she looked at John. 'What other gentleman?'

John shrugged. 'Does it matter? It's only for the purpose of the letter.'

Beth signed her name, put down the pen and emitted a great sigh as she looked at Lizzie. 'Last night John asked me to marry *him,* and I agreed to do so. So the letter is not a lie.'

'But Ewan proposed first,' Angus said, as if that made any difference.

'Oh shut up, ye big lug!' Lizzie said, slapping his arm while her face beamed at John. 'And there was me feeling so disappointed in ye my lad. But ye came true in the end, just like I alus said ye would.'

Beth stared indignantly at Lizzie, who had constantly predicted that John would *never* come back.

And what Lizzie always said was – *'A man born and schooled in the city of Edinburgh and an officer in the Navy too – nay, tis no' an island girl from Mull he'll be choosing for a wife, twill be the daughter or sister of some other officer or a city-bred lady is what he'll be choosing.'*

And over time everyone had started to believe Lizzie, and now John had proved her wrong.

A feeling of triumph and happiness surged through Beth as she made her request to Lizzie. 'Now, Mrs McLeod, can we *please* go?'

'Aye,' Lizzie said, lifting up the letter, 'because I'll have to sort out poor Ewan McPherson in less time than I thought I'd have.'

She looked at John. 'But hark – a proposal is one thing, easy enough made by a sailor with a ship to jump back on. And it's not legally-binding if it's not put on paper, so *when* is the marriage to take place?'

'As soon as the arrangements can be made,' John answered. 'After our short holiday?'

'And the notice of the banns will have to be put up. And put up *here*, in Tobermory.'

'As they will in Edinburgh.'

'And when will that be done?'

'Lizzie!' Beth exclaimed indignantly. 'You have no right – you are *not* my mother!'

Lizzie looked at Beth, a new worry assailing her. 'If he's misleading ye up the coast road, Beth, ye'll have no proof for *a breach of promise* claim later. So aye, hen, I think ye should get him to put his proposal in writing. Here now –' she said quickly, 'while we have the paper and ink handy, get him to write it down now.'

She placed the paper and inkpot back on the table before John and plonked herself back down on the chair, lifting the quill from Beth's side of the table and handing it to him.

John took the pen she shoved into his hand and sat staring at her without writing a word.

Lizzie nodded for him to commence. 'What are ye waiting for?'

'For *you* to start dictating how I should word it.'

Lizzie tutted impatiently, 'Surely ye can do that without *my* help?'

'Surely I can,' John said, and began writing.

When he had finished he put down the pen, blew on the paper, gave it a few waves in the air to dry the ink, and then carefully folded the sheet into a square and handed it to Lizzie.

Lizzie blinked at him. 'It's Beth ye should be handing that to, no' to me.'

'Oh no,' John said, standing up, '*you* are the one who wanted something written down about my intentions.'

He gestured to Beth and she also rose from her seat. When they had quickly left the dining room, Lizzie opened the square of paper and read:

Dear Mrs McLeod,

Beth and I shall now be taking our holiday in some place other than Tobermory, and will be vacating our rooms immediately.

Sincerely
Lt. John Dewar

Chapter Thirteen

..... She was drawing him back to the ways of the land, he realised.

Innocently, and in her own natural way, she was showing him again all the wonders of the land and the wildlife of nature all around them, things most people would not even notice, but Beth saw it all.

In the lane where they stood there had been a hatching of new butterflies and their colours and fluttering wings were everywhere.

'Aren't they beautiful,' she said, looking up. 'All starting a new life and so excited about it.'

Later, as they strolled past a white cottage with a window-box full of flowers she paused and smiled despairingly at a large bee staggering slowly away from the windowsill.

'Look at him, he's completely intoxicated, drunk from all the pollen he has sipped from the flowers.'

John looked closer at the bee and he did indeed seem to be fat and staggering, his stomach too full.

'Will he recover?' he asked curiously.

'Oh yes. Once he gets back to the hive and starts to work on the honey he will recover nicely and be back at this box of flowers tomorrow, filling up again – that's if he hasn't greedily drunk them dry.'

John looked down at the bee again, a frown on his face as he thought ... 'If I saw that fat bee staggering along a windowsill in Edinburgh, I would think it was half dead and then probably kill it to spare it some agony.'

He looked at Beth ... but *she* saw everything in nature in a different way. And when the bee suddenly buzzed off on a slow flight, he was sure that undoubtedly *she* was right.

They stopped at a small country shop to buy some provisions to add to their saddlebags, and then returned to their horses and continued their journey to Calgary Bay.

The sky was a clear unbroken blue when they approached the bay, as was the sea beneath it. The soft sand looked as white as it did the last time they were here, and the green rugged hills all around the bay were empty of all dwellings. A beautiful, isolated place, where they could be completely alone.

John checked his horse and sat looking at the view before him ... A few days he had asked for. Just a few peaceful days of not making any plans or talking about anything serious and just taking one day at a time; and she had agreed without asking him why.

But if she had asked him, he would not have told her the true reason – that he needed to put some time and distance between him and the horrors he had seen in Africa to mentally recuperate and start living life normally again.

Yet she seemed to sense that he needed some peace and mental relaxation, so in tune was she with the rise and falls of the natural life, as he was with the ebbs and flow of the sea. A city girl asking him incessant questions about foreign countries and using the social coquetry of society in her speech would have driven him crazy now. Just as the fiasco with Lizzie McLeod this morning had made him wish they could just take off to Gretna Green and get married there without any fuss or noise or questions asked.

But no, he had realised, Beth deserved better than a hasty secret marriage in Gretna Green which might not even be legal, and then there was Beth's mother to consider. Mrs Jarvis would want to be present at the ceremony, as would his father. To wilfully hurt either parent was not to be thought of.

'Are you dismounting?' Beth asked, having dismounted herself and beginning to lead her horse down the track through the dunes.

He sat for while watching her, listening to her talking to her horse as she led him carefully down the steep slope, making sure he didn't slip or graze his legs on one of the rocks. The horse gave a few short snorts and to John it sounded like the horse was answering her.

He smiled and dismounted and followed her down to the white beach. They led the horses to a freshwater pool beneath the rocks where both animals lapped gratefully, drinking their fill.

It was a shadowless afternoon and the sun was high and hot.

Beth pointed to two big rocks on one of the dunes. 'That's where we made our camp the last time.'

John looked at the two rocks, and then at her. 'Did you like it there?'

Beth smiled. 'I *loved* it there.'

And although she had not meant it in a sexual way, they both looked at each other remembering the events of that night ... and the lapping of the horses began to sound very far away.

He glanced up at the sun, and then back up to the rocks, and then gave her a quick smile.

Their communication to each other was wordless.

He grabbed her hand and pulled her up over the dunes to the shade between the two rocks where they stood for some seconds before he took her face in his hands and kissed her with as much passion as he had the night before.

She leaned back against the rock with her eyes closed as he kissed her hair, her eyelids, her cheeks; his right hand fumbling to undo the buttons of her blouse.

The touch and pressure of his hand sent a hot colour into her face and her breath exhaled in a rush when he peeled the blouse back, pulled at the string bow of her petticoat and his lips moved down to the cleft between her breasts.

Then the space between the two rocks became all dark and secret and wonderful as he drew her down onto the soft grass and made love to her with even more tenderness than he had in the soft warmth of his bed the night before.

Only once was Beth aware of any light in that shaded and secret space between the rocks that afternoon; a light like a slow moving sunrise coming towards her, closer and closer and warmer and hotter until the fiery sun burst above her head and blinded her, making her cry out in stunned trembling, until he hushed her, kissing her mouth and stroking her face until she finally opened her eyes and saw that she was still in the shade between the two rocks, and the sun was still high in the blue sky.

*

Later, after they had returned to the beach to unsaddle and unbridle the horses to allow them to relax also, John carried the bags up to the rocks, while Beth carried the two horse blankets which were clean and smelled only faintly of horse.

Searching through the bag she found the large tea towel they had bought in the shop and set out a lunch of bread and ham, some cheese and some apples.

A yellow stillness lay over the bay. Nothing moved in the silence apart from the birds in the air and the waves of the blue sea gliding over the soft sand, bubbling with fringes of white froth and then leaving tongues of water behind as it receded back out again.

Walking along the water's edge, John found a piece of rope about two feet in length that must have come from a fishing boat.

He held it in his hands and stood staring at it for so long that Beth stopped swishing her bare feet in the water and asked him why the piece of rope was so interesting.

'Gretna Green,' he said. 'Earlier today I was thinking we might be better off going to Gretna Green to get married without any fuss.'

'Gretna Green, where is that?'

'Near the Scottish border. It's a place where many couples go to get married quickly without any parental consent.'

'So what has that got to do with a piece of rope?'

John smiled. 'Come here and I'll show you.'

She waded back to him and he took her hand and began to tie her left wrist to his left wrist finishing it off with a sailor's knot.

'It's called handfasting,' he said. 'In Gretna Green any couple that go there are married by a blacksmith who ties their hands together in the Celtic tradition of *Handfasting*.'

'Not a Minister?'

'No it has to be the blacksmith, that's the tradition, God knows why. And when the blacksmith has "tied the knot" in front of two witnesses the couple are then wed and the blacksmith enters the marriage in his register.'

He began to undo the knot with experienced fingers.

'How do you know all that?' Beth asked.

'From my mother. She spoke about it often, because that's how her and my father were married, an elopement to Gretna Green, and she never regretted it up to the day she died.'

'Why did they elope?'

'Because she was from a wealthy gentry family and he was an apprentice tailor.'

'It was a love match?'

'It was.'

She looked down at his hand. 'Why are you untying the knot?'

'Because in the Celtic tradition both of us would have to agree to it first.'

'I agree,' she said quickly.

He smiled. 'It wouldn't be a real marriage, just a pledge between ourselves, and for that we don't need a blacksmith or even two witnesses. The sea can be my witness and the land can be yours.'

'I agree,' she said again, almost skipping up and down with excitement.

He unwound the rope and held it in front of her. 'The symbol of a *binding* pledge,' he said.

She nodded.

He wound the rope around both of their wrists, binding them together, and then he looked at her. 'Do you want me to tie the knot?'

'I do.'

Again he used a sailor's knot that only another sailor would be able to untie.

'Done, that's it, you truly are bespoken now.'

'Now *you* say I do.'

'I do,' he said and kissed her. 'Although,' he added, realising – 'one thing my mother did not tell me is how long we are supposed to keep our hands bound together.'

'*Forever!*' Beth laughed, 'Then you won't be able to go back to the Navy unless you take me with you.'

'If I took *you* back to the Navy we would not be able to control the sailors.'

He untied the knot and unwound the rope; about to throw

it back into the sea when Beth said, 'Can I keep it ... as a keepsake?'

He hesitated. 'I think it should go back into the sea.'

'Why?

'Because then it will be floating in the sea forever, and will probably still be floating out there long after we are dead. The sea is eternal.'

After a moment's thought, Beth said: 'And the sea has been one of our witnesses. You found the rope, so let me throw it back.'

Once she had thrown the rope as far as she could, she stood watching it floating slowly away.

Standing behind her he closed his hands about her waist and they stood for a time staring out to the sea. He bent his lips to her ear and whispered his love for her.

Beth did not move nor answer, because she felt she was now living within a floating spell of some kind of extreme magic, brought on by her years of desperate longing for him, and she might wake up in her bedroom soon and find that none of this was truly real.

Chapter Fourteen

Inside the back parlour of her family home at Craignish, Isabella Macquarie was complaining sulkily to her parents about her husband.

'And not only has he started drinking too much, he goes away for weeks at a time to stay with his friend at Strathallan Castle.'

'Isabella, you are a married woman now,' her father said irritably, 'and have been for nigh on four years. You cannot keep running home to us every time your husband takes too much drink or loses his temper.'

'And now all of Mull is talking about the ridiculous sentences he gives to offenders of any small crime.'

'A ducking in the sea, is what I heard. And in that he has my approval. A sentence like that will serve the offender much better than a small fine.'

'And he neglects me. Neglects me terribly.'

'Perhaps you neglect him? Four years and no sign of a child?'

'That is *not* my fault! I cannot order my eggs to hatch into ducklings, can I?'

Her father put down his book and stared at her. 'What the pox have *ducklings* got to do with it?'

'Papa! Now you are using *his* curse word!' Isabella ran out of the room.

Mrs Campbell looked disapprovingly at her husband.

'Speaking to her like that won't help. You know she has a weak and delicate constitution.'

'She's no weaker and no more delicate than Mary, and Mary doesn't flop around complaining like Isabella does. I wonder sometimes how Macquarie copes with her at all!'

'You don't understand. You have never understood. But as Mary is so strong and perfect in your estimation, then perhaps we should send Mary back to Mull with her.'

'For what bally reason may I ask?'

'To look after Isabella, be a companion to her as well as a

sister and bring her out of herself. Isabella does not like the servants at Macquarie house at all, and one of them has a half-caste daughter, which tells me a lot about *her.*'

'Who – Mrs Jarvis? When I visited there I thought Mrs Jarvis was a lovely lady.'

'I don't believe *lady* is the right description for a woman like that.'

'Aye, well, she's nice enough. And that daughter of hers is a true beauty, half-caste or not.'

'What Isabella needs is someone of her own *class* to talk to; and with Mary there she would have that. I do think, my dear, that we should give it a trial, if only to find out if everything Isabella says about Mr Macquarie is true.'

'A trial? For how long?'

'I was thinking ... a month or two perhaps? And if it should turn out that Isabella is telling the truth about Mr Macquarie's behaviour and tempers, then I do believe that you should demand her dowry back in full – every penny of it.'

'Don't be stupid, woman. If I did that I would have Lord Strathallan and his son Drummond coming down on my head. Whatever you and Isabella may think of Macquarie, they seem to admire him and appear to find no fault in him whatsoever.'

And neither did Isabella's younger sister, Mary Campbell, who was standing outside the parlour door listening, a smile on her face.

Chapter Fifteen

The July warm weather had now turned into a heat wave. *'Almost as hot as the summers in Australia,'* Mary thought.

Having collected her provisions in Tobermory, she decided to pop inside the Tobermory Inn in the hope of seeing Beth and John Dewar who may at this time be having their lunch in the dining room. She would not stay long, she decided, only for a minute or two to say hello, and not to intrude upon their time together.

Consequently she was shocked when Lizzie McLeod told her that they had both left the inn after only one night.

Lizzie, still grumpy about losing the business, complained to Mary: 'First he books one room, and then he books two rooms, and when Angus asked him for how long would he would want the rooms, he says *"Indefinite"* as he didna know how long or short a time he would be staying in Mull.'

'That's because he didn't know how Beth would receive him,' Mary explained. 'Or even if she was betrothed or married to someone else.'

'Then he says, when he comes in and booked the second room, he says that aye, they would be coming into the dining room for dinner later,' Lizzie went on. 'But then later he says they didna want dinner at all, and asked Angus to prepare a plate to put outside the door of his room. And a handsome plate I prepared for him, with a whole fresh lobster all for himself, but when Angus went up to that floor the next day, the tray and plate left beside his door was still sitting there, and when Angus lifted the lid – the food had no' been touched.'

'Did they sleep in the same room?'

'Nay, that I can testify, because Angus went up to ask the time of the washing water, and he was in his room alone, reading. And there was no' a sound coming from Beth's room so Angus felt assured that she had retired to her bed – probably worn out after the long horseride.'

Seeing the uncertain look on Mary's face, Lizzie shook her

head and chuckled. 'Nay! We're talking about *Beth* hen, and she's a good girl.'

Mary was not quite as sure about that as Lizzie seemed to be. 'And what day was that, when they left here,' she asked anxiously.

'Five days ago. Just took off because he was asked to put his marriage proposal in writing.'

Mary's eyes widened. 'He asked Beth to marry him?'

Lizzie leaned closer and narrowed her eyes. 'I don't believe he intends to marry her at all, else why refuse to write it down? How many times have I told ye, Mary – ye canna trust a *sailor!*'

'Did *Beth* ask him to do that – write it down?'

'Nay, it was me who did that. After they had finished their breakfast.'

Taken aback, Mary looked at Lizzie. 'Well, no wonder!'

'No wonder what?'

'Lizzie listen, John Dewar is a very polite and agreeable young man, but he has been making his living out in the world for years, and he is not the sort to allow anyone to tell him what to do. Especially not by a woman he barely knows.'

'Of course he knows *me*,' Lizzie declared indignantly. 'Didna he stay here three years ago? And didna I meet his father at the same time when he come over to look at a house here?'

'Even *I* would not order him to write his proposal down,' Mary said. 'And *I'm* Beth's mother!'

Lizzie chewed her lip thoughtfully. 'So I did it all wrong?'

'You did. Do you know where they went after leaving here?'

Lizzie shook her head. 'Nay. And I didna ask neither, because I guessed he wouldna tell me.'

Lizzie leaned closer again. 'But if ye want my opinion – I reckon he's taken her to Edinburgh.'

'That far?' Mary looked concerned. 'Well, if he has done that then I *will* be annoyed with him, because he promised me that he would not take Beth away from the island.'

'Well that's sailors for ye,' Lizzie said triumphantly, feeling vindicated at last. 'Ye canna believe a word they say.'

Chapter Sixteen

Less than twelve miles away, the sun was high above the horizon and Beth and John were racing their two horses through the shallow white surf at the sea's edge – Beth glancing over her shoulder and sending up a shout of victorious delight as the gelding easily left John's hired horse far behind, pounding on and on knowing the gelding was ecstatic at being able to stretch his legs and race again.

'Well done, MacDuff,' she said when she finally drew the horse to a halt at the end of the beach and gave him a few pats of congratulations.

Turning the horse around and trotting back down the beach she saw John had given up and was sitting on his horse waiting for her.

'It was hardly a fair race,' he said, as she drew alongside. 'Pitting these two horses against each other is like making a fishing boat and the Navy's *Hydra* have a race.'

Beth laughed. 'Excuses, excuses.'

She was wearing only her white petticoat because of the hot sun and she was drenched from all the splashing.

John regarded her steadily. 'Why don't you let *me* ride the gelding, and you ride this one, and race again?'

Beth agreed to the challenge. 'Very well, but don't rein him too tight, give him his head and let him go – and I will *still* beat you!'

Returning to the far end of the beach they exchanged horses.

John was as scantily clothed as Beth, wearing only white linen trousers rolled up to the knee, accentuating the bronze African tan of his body.

'You can still give the call,' he said, mounting the gelding.

Beth could feel the energy of the hired horse beneath her, also having fun at the excitement of the exercise and the splashing of the water.

She leaned forward on her mount and glanced sideways at John. 'One, two, three – *go!*'

At the half way point the two horses were pace for pace but then John and the gelding raced on at terrific speed until they were gone from sight – completely *gone* from Beth's sight.

John turned the gelding around, smiling with victory and exhilarated by the speed of the gelding, until he saw Beth's horse snorting and shaking his mane at the water's edge and Beth nowhere to be seen.

Moments later she rose up from the waves, coughing and spluttering and wiping the wet hair out of her eyes, exclaiming with disbelief: 'He *threw* me!'

John trotted up to her. 'Excuses, excuses ... you knew you were beaten so you jumped in.'

'No!' Beth insisted indignantly. 'Half way through he decided he had raced enough – and *threw* me off his back!'

It was the first time it had ever happened to her and she could not believe a horse could be capable of such bad behaviour.

John dismounted and joined her in the water, walking further out and diving in, swimming strongly and going farther and farther out towards the horizon until she began to frown with worry.

From childhood she had swam in the waters of Loch Ba at the back of the house, but always slowly and keeping near to the bank.

When she saw him turn and begin to swim back she relaxed and began to swim, not too far out and keeping to the course of the horserace, down the length of the beach.

By the time she had slowly swam her way back, John was brushing the horses down at one of the freshwater rock-pools to get the sea's salt off their legs and bodies.

She stayed in the water watching him, feeling a sudden tiredness sweeping over her, making her blink her eyes hazily.

They had gone to sleep very late, after sitting on a dune watching a bonfire of stars in the sky, stars everywhere; talking together and learning more and more about each other; and then they had been awakened early by the blue light of dawn, so much earlier in the summertime.

John had strolled along the beach, collecting a number of

mackerel that had come in on a wave with the morning tide, while she collected twigs from the dunes and trees to build anew their small beach fire.

Even then she had felt tired, but after John had cut and cleaned three of the fish and cooked them at the side of the fire for their breakfast, her energy had come back in a happy rush, but now she was beginning to feel exhausted. John may be used to only four hours sleep at a time while doing his watches on ship, but she was not.

She left the sea, walking slowly, and threw her wet self down on the sand under the sun; her arms stretched wide each side of her saying, 'Oh, I can't keep my eyes open!'

She was beginning to doze when John slowly and gently laid his body on top of hers and the kissing began again.

She put her arms around his shoulders and closed her legs around his calves and said softly, 'Do you think we will still love each other in winter?'

'Why winter?'

'Because we have only ever been together in summer, never in autumn or winter or even in early spring. And this is the longest time we have been alone together, the longest and the loveliest.'

'And you think our love might fade in winter?'

'Not *my* love, but maybe yours.'

'Oh, I doubt that.'

A whinny from one of the horses caught his attention. He looked at the two animals and saw that both were showing signs of extreme thirst.

He eased himself off her body, drawing back away from her, and she touched his arm to make him stay.

'Later,' he said smiling. 'You're very tired now, so sleep.'

'Where are you going?'

'To the waterfall, to get more water.' Again he looked over at the horses. 'Their tongues are hanging out, they're parched, and this heat is drying up most of the rock pools. How far away is it?'

'Less than half a mile.' She pointed in the direction of the small waterfall she had found up behind the northern section of Calgary the day before.

'I'll go now, or *we* will have no water to drink either. Both flasks are empty.' He gave her a quick kiss on the lips. 'You sleep now.'

She turned on her side and watched him collect the two leather water bags and sling their straps across his shoulder; watching him, loving him, adoring him, until her eyes slowly closed and she drifted into a long sleep that lasted until late in the afternoon.

There were a few white clouds floating in the sky when she awoke, and the sun was lower. Her white petticoat was completely dry now and she stood for some time brushing the sand off it. Then she looked around but he was nowhere to be seen.

She walked over to the horses and saw that the rock pool near to where they stood was half full of water now, and both horses were looking content, no longer thirsty.

She looked at the two leather water bags lying near to the rock pool and lifted each one; both were full. So he must have made two journeys to the waterfall, one to supply the horses and the second to fill the bags again for them to drink. They were living on a sparse diet, but she did not care, and neither did he. Her eyes moved searchingly around her ... so where was he now?

*

He was down where the otters played, but there were no otters around. He had been sitting on a rock for a long time, looking out to sea, thinking his thoughts, and making his decisions. He felt completely refreshed and rejuvenated, all stress gone, and able to think very clearly.

Thoughts had randomly come into his mind over the last days and he had toyed with them, especially late at night when she was asleep. But now he was sure, very sure.

He saw her walking along the sand in his direction and he watched her thoughtfully.

These last days had been like living on a desert island, not another human in sight. They had brought nothing from the world to help them enjoy themselves. No wine, because the shop did not sell it. No books to read. Even their food had

342

come from the sea. They had brought only enough basic provisions for two or three days, and they had been here for five days now.

And now it was time to leave.

When he had been forced to leave her behind in the past, it had been difficult, hard on his heart. This time, he knew, he would find it impossible.

She sat down beside him; her hands flat on the rock each side of her as she looked at him closely. 'Have you been sitting here for a long time?'

He nodded, and looked out to sea. 'It's time to leave here, Beth.'

'Is it?' She looked away. 'Is your leave time nearly over?'

'No, not for another four weeks ... but I've decided not to go back. I'm resigning my commission in the Navy.'

After a long silence, Beth said, 'Don't do it because of me. There's no need. If we were married I would not mind staying at home and waiting for you to return from your voyages.'

'No, I've seen the marriages of too many naval officers founder that way. If I'm to be your husband then I must also be your protector. And how can I be that if I am away at sea for years?'

'Do you *want* to leave the Navy?'

'If it's a choice between you and the Navy – yes.'

'But I've told you, it doesn't *have* to be a choice between me and the Navy.'

'For me, it does. And it's not only because of you,' John added, 'but also my father. It's time I also gave some better consideration to my father.'

Beth was still perplexed, her brows puckered, still unable to believe it.

A swirl of birds flew overhead, breaking the silence.

'This is not a quick or rash decision, Beth. It's something I gave a lot of thought to when was I stuck out there in Sierra Leone. You get a lot of time to think about things when you're patrolling the West African coastline day after monotonous day.'

'You're serious?'

'Very serious.'

'You'll not be going away for years again?'

'No, and that's why we must leave in the morning. I have a lot of things to arrange, and the most important is that I have to tell my captain that I won't be going back with him in four weeks time to Sierra Leone.'

He stood up. 'Come on, let's get the fire burning and cook those fish and then have an early night before a dawn start in the morning. We'll have to leave that early because I need to get down to Edinburgh as soon as possible.'

As they walked back along the beach, and it all began to sink in, Beth's thoughts veered between disbelief and excitement.

'It's like a dream, all these changes to my life, all this lovely *magic* floating around me! And it has all happened so quickly!'

She ran in front of him, turning to face him and walking backwards. 'It *is* a dream, isn't it? Just a wonderful dream! Slap my face and wake me up!'

Smiling, he smacked his hands together in front of her face without touching her.

But she stopped dead and blinked rapidly, swaying into him.

'Beth, what is it? I didn't touch you. *Did* I touch you?'

'No,' she said, tears spilling down her face.

He put his arms around her to steady her. 'The loud clap – it gave you a shock?'

'No, I was already in shock – the clap ... brought me out of it.'

'So why are you crying?'

'I don't know. I think ... I think it's because I'm so happy.'

*

Later, after the last pink trails of the dimming Hebridean evening were moving down towards night, they went to bed between the blankets but did not lie down, both sitting to gaze at the sea and watch the fishing boats in the far distance, the small lights of their lanterns bobbing up and down.

All around the hills were getting darker and the seagulls had stopped calling. He looked up as a furry little bat flew above his head on its way to the trees above.

Of a sudden he felt like walking one last time along the beach. She shook her head and he went down alone, while she watched him walking slowly as if in deep thought, a solitary figure in his white trousers rolled up to the knee and a cambric shirt hanging open.

He looked up to the sky and saw the Northern moon on its slow course upwards, cooling the darkening sugar-soft sand beneath his feet. He had made a decision that would change his life, but no, he had no regrets.

In truth, he knew he had made the decision two years ago, upon his return from Jamaica, and discovering he would not be able to get up to Mull to see her before going to West Africa. Empty days on an empty sea wondering if she would wait for him. At times, at night, on watch on deck aboard ship, he had wished he had never met her. The first time he had looked at her and she had looked at him, it had been like looking straight into the sun, blinding him, changing his view of the world, his own personal world.

During that first summer with Beth he had known the difference, because he had been in love before, twice, but both times the infatuation had faded as soon as he had returned to the sea. Strange, he could barely remember them now.

He looked around him again, at the dark hills and the rugged basalt cliffs that he been here since the ice age. This was a timeless place.

He returned to the dune and the rocks where she was still sitting with her hands around her knees, lost in her thoughts as she gazed out to sea, her white petticoat bright in the darkening light, her long dark hair hanging down her back.

He walked around her and sat down on his side of the blanket. He saw the fishing boats were still busy at work with their lights twinkling here and there on a calm sea.

He glanced at her and saw that she was not happy, a frown on her face.

'What's wrong?'

'I'm still worried.'

'About what?'

'My back,' she said. 'After all these nights lying on only a blanket on the grass I feel it should be very stiff and sore by now.'

'And is it?'

'When I first wake up my lower back is a little stiff, but as soon as I stand up and look around at the sea and the sand and the silent hills, it's as if some soothing angel balm has been rubbed over my entire back and within minutes I don't feel sore or stiff at all.'

'Angel balm ...' he smiled. 'So why are you worried?'

She looked at him earnestly. 'Is all this, everything that's happened here ... is it all true?'

'Heaven knows ... I'm not so sure myself anymore.' He gazed down at the white fringes of the waves gently lapping over the dark sand and then slowly swishing back in the opposite direction.

'This is a timeless place,' he said again.

'It's not timeless, because we have to leave here at an early time tomorrow morning.'

'Yes, alas, tomorrow we have to go back to the real world.'

'The real world?' Again she looked at him earnestly. 'So is all this *not* true?'

He smiled and brushed the back of his fingers over her cheek. 'It's true, my angel, it's *true.*'

'So if all this *is* true then I want the *trueness* to last as long as possible ... push tomorrow away as far as we can.'

'And how do we do that?'

'We don't go to sleep. We stay awake all through these last precious hours of this last night, before we go back to the real world.'

'No, if you don't sleep you will be too tired to ride your horse in the morning. You could fall off, and if you do, I will leave you behind and keep going.'

She laughed, and then with a sudden idea she pointed to the slowly rising moon.

'We stay awake and don't lie down until the moon rises to its highest point above the bay, yes?'

He looked at her silently for some seconds, and then answered her by bending closer to kiss her mouth once, and

346

then kiss her again. A soft breeze blew a strand of her long hair across her face. He lifted his hand to remove it.

A longer and deeper kiss laid her back on the blanket and her hands went around his shoulders. The rising Northern moon eventually reached its highest point over the bay, and moved on unnoticed.

Chapter Seventeen

Lachlan had decided to leave Edinburgh for another time. He caught the ferry and then used a hired trap to take him back to Jarvisfield, arriving home in the late afternoon.

As soon as he entered the house he felt its emptiness and silence. He walked through to the kitchen and found Mary alone, sitting at the table drinking a cup of tea.

She looked at him with surprise. 'Lachlan ... we were not expecting you back so soon.'

'Where's Isabella?'

'She's gone to Craignish.'

'Oh yes, I forgot. How long for?'

'She didn't say.'

'I need some food. Where's Mrs Keillor?'

'She's ... well, she wasn't feeling too good,' Mary said quickly, 'so she's gone to her room to have a short rest.'

He looked concerned. 'She's that ill, is she, needing to take to her bed in daytime?'

'No, no, it was just ... her legs were giving her grief. I told her to put them up for a while and take the strain off them.'

'Will you cook something for me? Something light. Anything will do. Perhaps an omelette?'

'Of course I will.'

When Mary moved to the shelf of saucepans, Lachlan stepped through to the yard and looked around for Beth ... no sign of her in the vegetable garden, and no sign of her in any of the rooms he had passed, so where was she?

He wandered over to the stables. The first thing he saw was Hector, sprawled fast asleep on the hay, his mouth open. The second thing he saw was that the gelding's stall was empty.

He walked back into the yard, filled a bucket of water from the pump, then carried it back and emptied the bucket over Hector's open mouth.

Hector awoke in a terrified spluttering panic, thinking he was drowning. He clawed his way to his feet and looked around him in daze ... and then he saw the master pumping water into a bucket in the yard.

'Sir?'

'Is that what I pay you for – to sleep throughout the day?'

Hector wiped his wet hair from his eyes. 'Nay, sir.'

'Where's the gelding?'

'Miss Beth took him.'

'And Miss Beth took him where?'

'I dinna know, sir.'

Lachlan strode back into the kitchen and asked Mary: 'Where's Beth?'

Mary paled. 'She's ... over at the Dewar house.'

'When will she be back?'

Mary answered truthfully. 'I don't know.'

Lachlan looked around him. 'Where's Maggie and Lorna? Usually I can hear their voices from the end of the lane.'

'I think they took a wander down to the loch.'

'When they should be here working?'

'Oh, it's all done – well, most of it.'

Lachlan strode back out to the yard and lifted the second bucket of water and carried it down to the loch where he could see Maggie and Lorna propped up against a tree chattering.

They saw him only seconds before he reached them and too late – screaming in fright when the water drenched them.

'Is that what I pay for you for – to sit here idling all day?'

He threw the bucket down and said to Maggie. 'You can carry that back to the pump.'

He walked back to the yard where Hector was at the stable doors, cowering in fright.

'Did I not tell you that Beth could only take the gelding when I gave her permission to do so?'

'Aye, sir?'

'And I could not have given her permission if I was not here, could I?

'Nay, sir.'

'So why the pox did you let her ride off on it? What kind of a stupid stable guard are you?'

Hector was still cowering. This was the fourth or fifth time that the master had found fault with him of late and he was beginning to seriously worry about losing his employment.

Hector could think of only one thing to say to get him back into the master's favour. He lowered his voice.

'It's no' my fault, sir. Mrs Mary has been lying to ye, and Mrs Keillor knows all about it.'

'About what?'

'Miss Bethey's no' gone to the Dewar house. She went riding off with a man.'

'A man?' Lachlan gripped both of Hector's arms and pulled him inside the stable doors.

'Tell me about it, Hector, tell *me*.'

'Them in there, Mrs Mary and Mrs Keillor, they keep telling *me* that she's gone to the Dewar house, but I know tis a lie cos I saw them, I saw them riding away together, Miss Bethey and a young man.'

'What young man? Do you know him?'

'Nay.'

'Have you ever seen him before?'

'Aye, a few years ago, before ye were wed to Mrs Isabella. I saw him with Miss Bethey many o' times then, always together o'er the fields and hills they were. And then, sir, and then ...'

Hector lowered his voice so low that Lachlan had to bend his head to hear him:

'One day, I saw them *kissing* – at the end of the lane. It looked like he was saying goodbye to her.'

Lachlan's head shot up. 'Kissing? *Beth* – kissing a man?'

'Aye, sir, and then he vanished from my sight for years and I didna see him again until about five or six days ago when he came here and took Miss Bethey riding away with him – and it was *she* who took the gelding – with no' asking of *me*.'

'Wait a minute, wait a minute – are you saying that Beth has been away from here for five or six *days* – in the company of a strange *man?*'

'Oh, he's no' a stranger, sir. Yer mother knew him and even dined with him. He's an officer from the Royal Navy. His name is John Dewar.'

'John Dewar ... John Dewar ... Royal Navy ... Is he a relative of *Robert* Dewar?'

'Aye.'

Lachlan began to pace the floor. 'I remember now ... at the Dewar house one Christmas ... the guilty look on her face when someone mentioned him ... John ... and then she said something about him being a friend ... a *friend!*'

Lachlan stared furiously at Hector. 'And you've known all this for a few years – even saw the two of them *kissing* – and have never told *me!*' He slapped Hector across the face. 'Pack your things and get out!'

Chapter Eighteen

In her bedroom above the kitchen, Mrs Keillor awoke to hear the shouting between Lachlan and Mary and quivered with nervousness. 'Oh, Lord, he's found out I'm in my bed in daylight!'

Minutes later, as she reached the kitchen door, she saw Mary with an arm outstretched towards the front of the house, her hand pointing and saying, 'Out there, in that front garden, my husband is buried in the same tomb as your own father and mother – so no, I will *not* get out! As the wife of George Jarvis I have a legal *right* to be here, a right stipulated by your own father!'

The mention of his father and George had a sudden calming effect on Lachlan. He turned as Mrs Keillor entered.

'Did you know about it – Beth and a man?'

'Beth and a man,' said Mrs Keillor, her eyes full of surprise, 'oh, surely yer jesting?'

'No, *you* are jesting – thinking you can fool me!'

'Now listen,' Mary said to him crossly, 'what is wrong with Beth having a male admirer? She's of legal age. She admires him. And he's a good and respectable man.'

'But are they *lovers*? That's what I want to know!'

'That is none of *your* business,' Mary declared. 'That is *their* business. You are the laird of this estate – not of my daughter!'

'So they *are* lovers. And you know it. And you've allowed it. You should be ashamed of yourself.'

'I know nothing,' Mary said furiously, 'other than that they went to the Tobermory Inn for a few days to talk things out.'

A second later Mary realised her mistake as Lachlan said, 'The Tobermory Inn?'

'No, they're not there, not anymore. They left after the first day.'

Lachlan did not believe her, but he had heard enough. He looked at Mrs Keillor. 'How are your legs now?'

'My legs? My legs are grand, thank ye.'

'Good, then *you* can cook me something to eat, and quick! Because I don't want any food cooked by that former convict – no wonder her daughter has turned into a whore.'

When he had strode out of the kitchen Mary and Mrs Keillor looked at each other. 'What did he mean? Calling you a former convict?'

'I have no idea,' Mary said with an impatient shrug. 'He grew up surrounded by convicts for the first eight years of his life, and now he's calling *me* a convict because he's sick jealous about Beth and John Dewar, and because of that he's annoyed with me too.'

Tears of anger were spilling down Mary's face. 'And what he said about Beth – how *dare* he?'

Mrs Keillor walked across the room and put her arms around Mary to comfort her. 'Ah, hen, pay no heed to him. I'm sure he didn't mean it when he called Beth a whore.'

'I'll not forgive him,' Mary exclaimed, wiping her eyes. 'I'll not.'

But she did, partly, later that night when he became intoxicated and wandered into the kitchen looking for her and begging for her forgiveness.

Mrs Keillor made a quick exit, knowing Mary would tell her all about it tomorrow.

'I'll make you a cup of coffee,' Mary said, but he caught her hand. 'I didn't mean it, Mary, anything I said. You know I love you, and I love Beth too.'

'But you've got to *stop* loving Beth and acting as if you own her. You're a married man now. You made your choice four years ago. And it's not fair to Isabella.'

'Isabella, yes.' He nodded. 'I loved her too ... for about ten minutes ... once upon a long time ago.'

Mary sat down at the table opposite him, her blue eyes looking directly into his, in the way she had so often done when he was a child.

'Could you not *try* to get on with Isabella and like her a bit more than you seem to. I know it was not a love match on your side, but if you don't *try* and make life better between the two of you, it will be her life that you'll be ruining too, as well as your own.'

Lachlan thought about it, and then finally shrugged. 'I'll try a bit harder then. It's not going to be easy, getting on with her, but I'll do my best.'

'That's my boy,' Mary said, rubbing his hand in the same way she did when he was a child.

'Where's Hector?' Lachlan suddenly asked. 'Will you ask him to come in. There's something I need him to do.'

Before Mary could even turn round, Hector came bounding in like an eager puppy. 'Aye, sir?'

'Do you *never* stop listening at doors?' Mary demanded impatiently. 'One of these days, Hector, you're going to hear something that will make you drop dead in shock and that will teach you!'

'What do ye need, sir, because whatever it is, Hector's yer man!'

'Just the support of your arm to help me up the stairs. I'm feeling a slight dizzy.'

'Aye, sir, and am I still employed?'

'Of course you're still employed.' Lachlan looked at him quizzically. 'Why would you not be?'

'Och, no reason, sir, no reason.'

*

Later that night, when everyone was in bed, Mary lay wide awake, still trying to understand how Lachlan had come to know so much about her past.

That she had once been a convict had always been kept a secret, even by Elizabeth ... although Lachlan *may* have suspected – seeing as nearly *all* the servants in Government House in Sydney were convicts.

But even if Lachlan had suspected down through the years, and wondered, it had never seemed to trouble him before. And *never* before had he spoken to her, or about her, with such disrespect and scorn.

It hurt her that he should do so, and also worried her, because it was not in his true nature to be so heartless, so vicious to others. Except ... she suddenly remembered how vicious he had been to Isabella when he discovered her dowry was two thousand and not ten.

Something had gone wrong with Lachlan, something very wrong, as if his discontent with his life was making him bitter in his attitude to everybody else.

But then, it had been so long since Lachlan had a strong man to guide him, to advise him, to keep him on track and remind him of the rights and wrongs in life, the rules of respect towards other people. Not since George, who had showed him great love as a boy, guiding him with kind gentleness and understanding, but also firm discipline.

Then there was William Drummond, his bosom chum from his schooldays, but that was a case of two rakes together; although William Drummond possessed an appealing charm and likeability that would get him out of the gates of Hell if he wished it. He also possessed his own personal fortune, which Lachlan did not.

And there was the rub.

She could think no more about it. She turned over and tried to sleep, until a thought came into her mind that sent her out of her bed and down to the study, pulling on a robe as she went.

And there, still open on the desk, she saw that her sudden thought had been correct.

Lachlan had been reading through all his father's papers, and even his private journals – but then of course, they were *his* property now.

She began to search through the journals, looking for the one that was about New South Wales detailing her arrival at Government House and her elevation to the position of Elizabeth's personal maid. And yes – there it was – '*Mary Neely, transported for seven years for borrowing (charged with stealing) a small mirror from her mistress's bedroom. Elizabeth is quite certain that she is a good and decent girl, wrongly accused, and would be a suitable maid for our household.*'

Mary quickly tore out the page, tore it into four pieces, and shoved them into the pocket of her robe. An hour later, with four more torn pages in her pocket, she placed the journals back in the pile and arranged them into the haphazard way she had found them.

Not that Lachlan would notice, she told herself. He had probably forgotten most of what he had already read, so bad was his memory these days from all his drinking.

Inside the dark kitchen she lifted the poker and stirred the smoored embers of Mrs Keillor fire, and placed the torn pages on the fire, pushing the small pieces deep down under the embers until they flared into small flames and then extinguished into ash.

Ashes of the past, Mary thought, and then laid down the poker, feeling enormous relief as she walked back upstairs to her room.

It was not that she cared about the rest of the world and its people, she thought as she lay in her bed again, but it would destroy her if Beth ever found out that she had once been a convict.

And not because Beth would feel ashamed of her, or anything like that, because she knew that once she had explained the circumstances and the injustice of her sentence and transportation, Beth would understand.

No, it was not that. It was because she knew that Beth, with all her sensitivity of feelings and inclination to spend time in silent thought, would be unable to stop herself from *imagining* what it must have been like for her mother suffering on that filthy prison ship, and it would *hurt* Beth, and cause her so much silent pain. So, no, she was determined that her daughter would *never* find out.

Not even if she had to brand Lachlan as a liar to prove it. And how could *he* prove otherwise? She had destroyed all the written proof. There was not a page left intact in General Macquarie's journals that referred to her as a convict, only as *'George's wife'*.

Chapter Nineteen

The following morning, with no food left, John and Beth split and shared their last apple and then packed their bags, saddled the horses and left Calgary Bay.

Just after sunrise they had taken a quick swim in the sea. And now, dressed in her brown riding habit and her hair tied back, Beth looked prim and neat and nothing at all like the carefree and scantily-dressed girl of the day before, or the passionate young woman she had been in the night.

They rode through the lanes in silence, both lost in their own thoughts, until Beth suddenly said: 'John ... you don't *have* to leave the Navy on my account, you don't.'

'I know that.'

'I don't want you to start hating me one day because of it.'

'I could never hate you.' He smiled. 'Beth, you're my once in a lifetime.'

'I couldn't bear to lose you again ... ever. And I told you I would be happy to wait at home for you. Isn't that what all Navy wives do?'

'Yes, but few are as vulnerable as you.'

Beth turned her head and stared at him. 'I am not vulnerable. And I *don't* need to be protected.'

John was not too certain about that, not after what his father had told him upon his return to Edinburgh.

His father was Lachlan Macquarie's personal tailor at Mortimers, and on his first night back, during all the catching up of news from each other, his father had said: 'The Laird Of Jarvisfield – that place where young Beth lives – have you ever met him?'

'No,' John had said. 'He was away in the Army on the two occasions I visited there.'

'You know he's married now – to the daughter of the Laird of Craignish?'

John remembered feeling only relief.

'Macquarie's father was such a fine man, a true gentleman in every respect, but the son – I don't know what to make of

357

the son at all.'

'In what way?'

'He's so ... so erratic! I dread him coming in to Mortimers and having to deal with him. One day he's determined on wanting his jacket cut one way, and then the next day he's changed his mind and wants it cut some other way. I tell you, son, I'll be glad to retire.'

After a sip of brandy his father had continued: 'But that's not the worst of it. He's earning himself a reputation for drinking and revelling with women in a way that a married man should not do, and often doing his drinking and womanising with some of the worst dregs of Edinburgh. He's beginning to give Mortimers a bad name, because as you know, we only cater to the most *elite* of gentlemen. And *elite* gentlemen of true refinement do not let others – especially loose women – spend all their money for them. I often wonder about young Beth living up there in the same house as him.'

'The same house where his *wife* lives,' John had said. 'Men like that are usually perfectly behaved in their own home.'

'Men like that, yes, but he's ... he's a law unto himself. I think all his drinking is affecting his brain.'

John came out of his thoughts and looked at Beth, who had allowed him his silence, riding along in her own world, looking up at the trees and along the hedges, watching all the wild life of nature around her.

Beth remained silent for some moments and then asked, 'Do you still have it in your mind to leave the Navy?'

'No, that left my mind yesterday, after I had made the firm and final decision to leave.'

Chapter Twenty

They arrived back in Tobermory before noon. Beth tethered her horse outside the Inn while John rode on to return his hired horse to the blacksmith.

The days of the Tobermory blacksmith hiring out old or poor horses to customers were now long gone, ever since he had hired out a half-blind nag to Lachlan Macquarie, who had later threatened to shoot him if he did it again and ordered him to take better care of his horses.

And now that the same young man was the Laird of Jarvisfield *and* a Justice of the Peace, the blacksmith trembled in his shoes at the thought of what Macquarie might do if he did not adhere to his command. A ducking in the sea would be the least of it.

'By! He's looking fit and healthy!' said the blacksmith when John returned the horse. 'Did ye give him much riding?'

'A few hours exercise every day,' John replied. 'Other than that he has had a good rest.'

'Now then, ye hired him for *three* days,' said the blacksmith, 'but ye've had him for *five* days, so will ye pay the extra now? Or will I add it up and send the bill to ye at the Tobermory Inn?'

'I'll pay it now.'

The blacksmith talked a few pleasantries while John paid him the money, but John was more interested in a sign he had seen in the window of a house on Main Street as he rode past.

'There's a house vacant,' he said to the blacksmith, 'on Main Street, about six or seven doors down from the Tobermory Inn. Do you know who the agent is?'

'Aye, tis Angus Macintyre the Bank Manager who is handling that. If ye go up to the Bank and go in and ask to see him, he'll be able to tell ye about it quick enough.'

*

Beth was in the empty dining room talking with Lizzie

McLeod when John found her.

'Nay, ye're wrong, Beth, ye're wrong!' Lizzie was saying emphatically. 'It takes longer than that to get to Edinburgh, a lot longer.'

As soon as she saw John, Lizzie jumped alert. 'Now tell me, yer lordship, how long did it take ye to get from Edinburgh to Oban by stage coach?'

'I didn't come by coach. I caught the steam train from Edinburgh to Glasgow, and *then* I caught the stage coach.'

'*Steam* train? Ye mean – they've got trains of coaches running on steam now as well as ships?'

'Yes, a train of carriages pulled by a steam engine. It cuts the journey time in half. The world out there is changing, Mrs McLeod, and changing fast. Soon there will even be a steam train from Edinburgh all the way to London.'

'By! I don't like the sound of that!' Lizzie turned her horrified eyes to Beth. 'Give me four strong horses and a stagecoach every time. Ye won't get me journeying abroad on nothing but steam from a kettle.'

'Beth, I want you to see something,' John said hurriedly. 'Outside, come now.'

Lizzie got to her feet in exasperation. 'Don't tell me ye willna be taking lunch after all? Beth has just said ye will.'

'We will, Mrs McLeod, we will,' John assured her. 'In about half an hour.'

'You're certain about that now, are ye?'

John nodded. 'Certain.'

Out on the street Beth was perplexed by John's excitement. 'What is it?'

'A house for my father, right here on Main Street. Remember he said he would like to live on Main Street?'

'Yes, to avoid the hills.'

Seven doors down from the inn, Beth stood looking up at the three-storey Townhouse. It was a wide house, with two large windows on each floor and a narrower window in the centre: the smaller windows were obviously on the landings.

'There's no front garden,' Beth said. 'Would your father like that, no garden?'

'He has no front garden in Edinburgh.'

John opened the door with the keys that Mr Macintire had given to him.

Beth followed him into the hall. The ground floor had four high-ceilinged, spacious square rooms one of which was a kitchen. At the side of the kitchen was a small passage that led to a small square bathroom; the white bath stood in the middle of the room. The small yard outside the bathroom had a big-handled water pump, and beyond that a small garden.

'It's a nice house,' Beth said.

'Mr Macintyre gave me a copy of the floor plan.' John took some folded papers from the pocket inside his jacket and looked at them. 'Let's see what it is like upstairs.'

The first floor had another four high-ceilinged square rooms and appeared exactly the same to Beth, apart from no passage to a bathroom.

John was looking at something on the floor plan and smiling. 'Come with me,' he said, leading her into a large room at the back of the house. 'This must be the drawing room, and look – '

Beth stared at the glass doors that opened onto a small balcony and had a flight of solid black iron steps leading down to the garden, which she could now see was bigger and greener than she had first thought.

'Oh, John, oh ... it's lovely! Your father will love it.'

He found the key to open the glass doors and stood aside as Beth walked down to the garden filled with mature plants, shrubs and trees, and *'perfect for the birds and bees to find a home here too!'* she called back excitedly.

There were also a number of natural rocks from the hillside here and there at the back of the garden.

She turned and looked up at the back of the house and saw another black iron staircase leading up to the second floor. 'Look, you can come down to the garden from up there too!'

'I can't find the key,' said John, searching through the bunch of keys and reading their labels. 'We'll have to go up there from the inside.'

On the second floor they found the same four spacious square rooms, with one of the back bedrooms having a door that opened onto a small balcony with the steps down to the garden.

'Oh, this is lovely!' Beth exclaimed. 'You would not guess from the outside that the house had this lovely garden at the back. And the garden is so quiet and *private!*'

John had opened the door of the room opposite on this second floor and saw it contained a white bath and a number of white ceramic washing bowls with water jugs.

Beth was still standing and staring down into the garden.

John joined her saying, 'All the rooms at the front have a clear view of the harbour and the sea.'

'And all the rooms and bedrooms at the back are just as bright and have a lovely view of the garden and trees and the wide blue sky,' Beth answered.

'Do you think my father would like it when he retires here to Mull?'

Beth was not sure. 'After all the fuss your father made about the last house you found him – that lovely white house, remember?'

'Yes, but that was up two steep hills and as he has spent his life sitting down tailoring, it was not the house he disliked, it was the climb up the steep hills.'

'So if he did not like climbing the hills, how will he feel about these stairs?'

'Beth, he's not decrepit, he's only fifty-five, and he climbs the stairs every night to his bedroom in the house in Edinburgh.'

'Oh, I see ... well, in that case I am sure he will *love* it.' Beth smiled. 'Anyone would love this house.'

'What I think he will like *most* about this house when he sees it,' John said, 'is that it's only a short walk to the end of the harbour, has a clear view of the sea from all the front windows, and it's just a minute's stroll to the Tobermory Inn for his nightly brandy and some socialising.'

'And he already knows Angus and Lizzie McLeod from his last visit,' Beth put in. 'He got on so well with them when he came here three years ago, remember?'

John smiled. 'I do.'

'Which leaves only one problem that I can think of.'

John lifted an eyebrow. 'Which is?'

'It's too big. Even with a housekeeper this house is much too big for one man on his own. And would a house this size not *cost* too much?

'Not if he and I were to buy it between us. Would *you* like to live here? Or must you have the countryside?'

'Me?' Beth was so startled she had to look for a chair to sit down on, but there was no furniture at all.

'When we marry, am I not supposed to provide you with a home to live in? Or do you intend to remain living at Jarvisfield?'

'I hadn't thought ... so much has happened so quickly.'

'Because I certainly will not be asking your laird to accommodate *me*.'

Beth now needed not only a chair to sit on, but also a small dram of whisky or a big cup of tea.

'It would be wonderful,' she said quietly, 'living here with you, by the harbour in Tobermory ... And the town is surrounded by hills and countryside only a few minutes walk away.'

'So?'

'And I did like your father when we met ... especially when he told me he had met my papa all those years ago. But ... how would *he* feel about you and I sharing a home with him?'

'He would love it. The more the merrier. He has been dying of loneliness in Edinburgh since my mother's death. That's why he wants to come back to Mull where he has relatives. And that's why he has been so desperate for me to leave the Navy.'

'Your father wants you to leave the Navy?'

'He just wants to be able to *see* me sometimes, that's all. And for the last two years he has been terrified that I might die of some deadly disease out in Africa.'

Beth smiled with understanding. 'He loves you.'

'He does, and I love him. And this way, with the three of us living in this house, I would not only be able to go to sleep hearing the sound of the sea at night, but also be able to take care of both of you without having to travel too far.'

'No, just up and down these stairs,' Beth said, and started to laugh, putting her hands to her eyes.

John looked at her curiously. 'You're not crying again?'

'I can't help it.' Tears were bubbling in her eyes until she was laughing and crying at the same time.

'John, can you please take me back to the inn and buy me a glass of something strong, something *very* strong. My head is dizzy with all these lovely surprises.'

Chapter Twenty-One

Knowing that John wanted to get back to Edinburgh, Beth left the Tobermory Inn straight after lunch, eager to return home herself and tell her mother all her good news.

Before she left, she walked back down Main Street and took one more look at the outside of the house and felt her excitement bubbling again.

She tried to restrain it, knowing nothing was yet definite, because as John had said, 'No decision can be made until my father has seen the house and also given it his approval.'

She had been gone from the inn less than half an hour when Lachlan entered and walked up to Angus McLeod; looking at Angus as if he would like to hit him.

'Miss Elizabeth Jarvis – where is she?'

'Beth? She's gone. Left only a short while ago.'

'And the man she was with, Mr John Dewar. Has he left also?'

'Oh no, he's still here. He wanted to change into his travelling clothes before he left for Edinburgh, so I gave him a room to use.'

'And Mr Dewar –'

'It's *Lieutenant* Dewar,' Angus said proudly; always keen to show that he had many fine visitors to his establishment.

'And which room did you give him?'

'Room One'

'Thank you.'

As Lachlan walked on down the passage to the door that led to the dining room and the stairs up to the guest rooms, Angus suddenly got a hint of trouble brewing, and hurried after him, catching him at the open door.

'Is it to the dining room you're going, Mr Macquarie?'

'Mind your own business.'

'But this *is* my business,' Angus declared, 'and I canna be having my paying guests disturbed unannounced. Is it Lieutenant Dewar ye want to see?'

'It is.'

'Then let me go up and knock on the door and ask him if he is free to see ye. I will need to announce ye and tell him who ye are.'

'He will soon know who I am.'

And knowing Lachlan Macquarie as he did, Angus knew there could be no arguing with him. He rushed to the kitchen to find Lizzie.

'Stay here and don't get involved,' Lizzie advised wisely. 'They're both gentlemen and I'm sure all Lachlan wants to do is confirm that Lieutenant Dewar's intentions towards Beth are honourable – just like I wanted to do. Nay, don't worry, Angus.'

Lizzie gave a decorous sniff. 'And I think our fine lieutenant will learn that he won't be able to act so clever with Lachlan Macquarie as he did with me. And if he tries it, Lachlan will kill him stone dead.'

Angus nodded. 'That's what I'm worried about, Macquarie's temper – and I *like* Lieutenant Dewar a lot more than I do Macquarie.'

'So do I,' Lizzie agreed, 'but he shouldna have been so smart with me, giving me that note about leaving here, when all I wanted was a declaration of marriage.'

*

John was inserting a pair of plain cuff links into the cuff of his clean shirt when the door banged open and Lachlan walked into the room.

John turned his head and looked at him while continuing with his task. 'It's polite to knock before entering.'

'It is, but I could not be troubled to do so.' Lachlan closed the door behind him.

'And who are you?'

'Lachlan Macquarie, the Laird of Jarvisfield.'

'So how may I be of service to you?'

'Service? Oh, I like that word. Well, Lieutenant Dewar, you would be doing me a great *service* if you left Tobermory and returned to the Navy and never came back.'

John gave a small smile and lifted the second pair of cuff links and began to insert them. 'I'm in a hurry, Mr

Macquarie, so you would be doing *me* a great service if you came down off your high horse and left my room.'

'You do know that Beth lives in *my* house. And both she and her mother are in *my* service?'

John eyed him cynically. 'And you believe that makes both of them your property?'

'No, but, they *are* part of my family ... can I take a glass?'

Lachlan walked over to the low dresser where John was standing and pointed to the bottle of brandy and two clean glasses. 'May I?'

'If you must.'

The only sign of John's inner tension was the difficulty he was having inserting the second cuff link.

Lachlan poured himself half a glass of brandy, took a drink, and then looked at John insolently over the rim.

'Well, well, our virginal Beth has found herself a handsome lover. Tell me, Lieutenant, did she like it?'

'Like what?'

'Having a man between her legs.'

John's fist shot out and struck Lachlan across the face, knocking him back into a sitting position on the windowsill and sending the brandy glass smashing onto the floor. 'Speak about her in that way again and I will murder you right now.'

Lachlan stared at him, touching his throbbing cheekbone, which was colouring a deep red from the force of being struck.

'Well, I must say ... this is not the refined behaviour one expects from an officer and a gentleman,' Lachlan said slowly, and then gave a crooked smile. 'But spoken like a true Scotsman! I think I like you, sir.'

'I think you should leave.'

'This is poor hospitality you are offering me. I think I should be consoled by a fresh glass of brandy.' Lachlan straightened up and reached for the second clean glass, filling it up while John finally succeeded in inserting the cuff link.

Lachlan took a long drink and then shoved away the pieces of broken glass with his boot, watching John as he moved to the bed and lifted his jacket.

'It may disappoint you to know,' Lachlan said

informatively, 'that as light as Beth's skin is, she is in fact a half caste of low blood.'

John shrugged on his jacket. 'I know all I need to know about Beth.'

'And did you also know,' Lachlan continued with a hint of slight mockery, 'that her mother is a former convict?'

John looked at him. Clearly he did not know that.

Lachlan smiled. 'Oh yes, sentenced to seven years in Botany Bay for stealing a mirror. Manacled and chained on a prison ship with all the filthy criminal scum of the earth. So if you intend to marry Beth, I think you should know what a fine family you will be marrying into.'

'I thought you said they were part of *your* family.'

'Yes, but not by blood.'

'No, but it *will* be by blood!'

'What will?

'My response if you are determined to ruin Mrs Jarvis's reputation on this island by revealing that fact to anyone else.'

John lifted his bag in his left hand and walked towards the door, then suddenly veered over to Lachlan and swung a fist into his face again, sending the laird staggering back against the window.

'And that's my second warning,' John said. 'First you insult Beth, and now her mother. And both of those women are soon going to become a part of *my* family.'

He turned and walked out of the room, with Lachlan's brandy glass rolling across the rug on the floor behind him.

When he descended the stairs down to the ground floor, Angus and Lizzie were standing behind the reception counter, both looking up from the sign-in ledger as he approached.

'Have I paid you for everything?' John asked Angus.

'Ye have paid, and thank ye. So when will we be seeing ye again?'

John smiled. 'I can't say for sure, but I'll be back as soon as I can.'

'And the proclamation of the banns?' Lizzie said importunately. 'You know they have to be up and public at least three weeks before the wedding. So *when* are they going up?'

'As soon as possible.'

'Would that be before this Christmas or *next* Christmas?' Lizzie asked dryly.

'I would say ... *this* Christmas,' John replied. 'And now I must go – *totsiens,*' he grinned, and then he was gone.

Angus looked at Lizzie. 'Well now, that must have all gone off well and peacefully. He looked his same pleasant self.'

'Aye, Lizzie agreed, surprised. ' I feared Lachlan was going to give it to him hard. You know how he hates any man even *looking* at Beth.'

She lowered her voice and leaned closer. 'Mebbe, Angus ... mebbe the lieutenant lied, and denied that he'd just spent five days alone with her somewhere.'

Angus thought about it, and then nodded. 'Aye, that must be it. But cock's life, Lizzie, I canna see what business it is of his. They had two separate rooms, and she had her mother's consent, and Macquarie is no' her lord and master.'

'Oh, he is, Angus, he's her *laird.* And if John Dewar intends to marry her – which I truly *doubt*, him being a sailor an' all – then he will have to ask for Lachlan's permission first.'

A few minutes later they both looked around as Lachlan came walking down the passage towards them. His face was badly swollen and looked a dark red colour on one side. There was also some dried blood around his nose.

'Mr Macquarie,' Angus gasped, 'what happened to ye?'

Lachlan glared at him. 'What do you think bloody happened to me – one of your rotten old *doors* slammed into me! You'd better get those door hinges fixed, Angus, or I'll have you up before the Bench.'

And on that he walked out of the Tobermory Inn, leaving Angus and Lizzie staring open-mouthed after him.

'Doors,' said Angus at last. 'All our doors are good and fine and I oil the creaky hinges and tighten the loose ones every week.'

''Course ye do,' Lizzie agreed, beginning to smile. 'Nay ... I think ye will find it was no door that done that to him. I think that someone we know went to the trouble of taking the laird down a peg or two from his high shelf. And it's about time *someone* did it!'

Angus looked at her. 'Ye mean … ?'

'I do, Angus,' Lizzie nodded. 'I certainly do.'

Chapter Twenty-Two

Mary was torn between two emotions that day. First, her delight at Beth's arrival home and all her good news; all told with a face radiant with happiness.

And second, her dismay at the sudden change of mood in the house when Lachlan arrived home a few hours later, one side of his face swollen and bruised, his mood dark.

'What happened to your face?' Mary asked with concern.

'I can't remember. Oh yes, now I do – I fell off my horse.'

'Oh, dear ... are you hurt anywhere else?'

'No.'

'Have you been drinking too much?'

'Mind your own business.'

'*Lachlan!*' Beth came into the hall still aglow with happiness and excitement. 'We thought you would be away for weeks.'

'I know you did,' Lachlan replied curtly, and then pushed past her without another word.

Throughout the following two days his mood remained dark, speaking only when spoken to, and not at all to Beth, not even when she spoke to him. He ignored her entirely, as if she did not exist.

Beth could not understand it, totally perplexed by his attitude towards her.

'I don't understand it,' she said to Mary. 'He was happy enough when he left here two weeks ago, but now he's come back and he's not speaking to any of us. Do you know why?'

Mary felt too tired to tell her. 'I'm sure he will tell us himself, soon enough.'

And that's what Mary now dreaded – the day when Lachlan found his voice again – and so she was conserving her emotional energy in preparation for that battle.

'I don't like to see him this way,' Beth said anxiously, 'in this long doldrum. He's so dull and quiet, and that's not in Lachlan's nature, as you know.'

'Yes, I know,' Mary agreed. During the past few years

Lachlan was either very cheerful and amusing, pleasant to all – or angry, angry. No dull quiet periods in-between.

Later that morning, after having been brushed aside by Lachlan again, Beth decided she could wait no more and decided to confront him.

She found him sitting down on the bank of the loch, staring towards the hills, staring into space.

She sat down beside him, saying quietly, 'What is it, Lachlan? What has you like this?'

He continued staring into space without answering her.

'Are we not friends anymore?'

He stopped staring and slowly turned his head to look at her, his eyes like dark pools, his voice quiet. 'I know about you and Dewar.'

'Oh ... do you? John? He came back from Africa while you were away, and I was going to tell you about him as soon as you returned, but you kept *refusing* to speak to me.'

'I'm surprised at you, Beth. With me, in the past, even when all I did was hold your hand or kiss your cheek, you were always as timid as a partridge with me. Yet now, with him ...' He shook his head.

'I'm older now, and I *love* him.'

'But not me ... not even back then?'

'Of course I love *you*. I did then, and I do now, and I always will.'

'Like a brother?'

'Yes,' she said emphatically, 'yes, like a very dear brother. You and I have *always* been like a brother and sister, have we not? We were small children together, brought up in the same house, by the same people, a part of the same happy family, so how could we *not* love each other after all that?

A long silence fell between them.

Lachlan said: 'I can't give you permission to marry him?'

'Why not?'

'Because this *love* of yours is nothing more than a girlish infatuation for the first man who has properly courted you. You are not familiar with men. You don't know what men are really like. And this John Dewar may be your handsome gallant now, but *marry* him, Beth – and he'll knock you black and blue the first time you cross him.'

Beth almost laughed at the absurdity of such a statement, but then her indignation came quite close to anger.

'How can you *say* such a thing? You have never met John! But anyone who *has* met him and gets to *know* him, soon discovers that he is a man with the kindest heart, the refined manners of a true gentleman, as well as having very real *goodness* in his soul.'

'Oh, stop! Or I'll end up kneeling in prayer at the feet of such a paragon.'

'And I also know that he is the type of man who would prefer to be struck down himself rather than strike a woman – any woman – and least of all his *wife*. In truth, one of the reasons he wants to marry me is because he says he wants to *protect* me.'

Lachlan looked at her. 'Protect you from who?'

'I don't know. I believe he means in a general sense.'

'But the whole of Mull knows that *I* am your laird and protector,' he said desperately. 'It has always been so – you're a Jarvis – a *Macquarie* – and so it should stay, Beth, so it should stay.'

After another long silence, Beth said very quietly:

'Is that what you want, Lachlan? For me to stay living here like your spinster sister for all of my days, growing old with you and Isabella, and never to have a life or love of my own?'

Lachlan did not answer, because tears were slowly running down his face.

'Lachlan ...'

'It could all have been so different ...' he said, 'because back then *I* was different ... Years ago, I smashed Drummond in the face for calling you a half-caste of low blood, and two days ago he smashed me in the face for doing the same.'

'Who – William Drummond?'

'No, Dewar. And he was right to do it, Beth. My father would have been sadly ashamed of me. And George Jarvis ... my dear George ... You know George *died* because of me, because he went out in that winter night and the falling snow to get me some medicine because I was sick.'

'No, no, he went out to get medicine for *both* of us. We

were *both* sick. You mustn't blame yourself. Is that what has been tormenting you all these years? Is that why you drink so much?'

'No, but I did hope to make it up to George by marrying you and taking care of you.'

'And yet you married Isabella?'

'Yes, because I had *changed* by then. Don't you understand? The Army and the indolent superficial social life we officers led then, all the gambling and drinking and women, *changed* me, until I was no longer my father's son, not the son he would have approved of anyway. Or maybe it wasn't the Army's fault, maybe I was just *born* wayward, I don't know. But I never stopped loving you, Beth, never.'

'As a sister?'

'No ... not exactly ... yes, as a sister in a way, but more than that ... enough to make me realise I could never be happy with Isabella, not with you around. Apart from that, she drives me crazy because she displays so little intelligence at times, well, *all* of the time.'

'Do you not love her, not even a little bit?'

'Beth, she gives me *no* happiness at all, and now my life gives me *no* happiness at all. The only place I can forget it all and feel more cheerful is when I'm with Drummond, because we've been friends for so long and William never judges me, always supports me, and to me he truly *is* like a brother.'

Beth lifted one of his hands in both of hers and clasped it tightly, and then gently rested the side of her head against his for a long silent time as both their tears ran together.

*

Mary – coming worriedly down through the bluebell field to see what was going on, because Beth had been gone for so long – stopped dead in her tracks and stared in astonishment at the sight of the two of them by the loch ... sitting silently with their heads together.

It was the strangest, most unexpected sight, because she had not seen them sitting like that since they were children, since they were so much younger, since the days before he had joined the Army ... when they had often sat that way ... one comforting the other.

She turned and walked slowly back to the house, her mind whirling, hoping for God's sake that he had not talked Beth out of marrying John Dewar.

Chapter Twenty-Three

The Dewar House in Edinburgh was a two-storey nicely furnished townhouse down a Mews of terraces off Charlotte Square.

Inside the drawing-room John Dewar Senior was staring at his son with incredulity. 'I don't believe it! No, I *don't* believe it!'

'You will have to believe it sometime.'

'But this girl, young Beth – she's beginning to *concern* me!'

'Why?'

'Because she's turned your head, son, *dazzled* you in some strange way until it appears that you're now willing to do just about *anything* for her.'

'I'm not doing it for her alone, I'm doing it for me, and *you*.'

'Leaving the Navy?'

John nodded. 'Leaving the Navy.'

John's father had to sit down in a chair. 'And getting married as well?'

'Yes, the two go together. Look,' John said, 'how many times have you said to me that you wished I would leave the Navy?'

'But you still wouldn't give it up, would you? Not for *me*. Not for your father.'

'I was younger then.'

'By! That's a poor excuse. You're only twenty-six now.'

'Old enough to know my own mind and make my own decisions.'

John's father decided to light his pipe, a rare thing to do, only at times of extreme gloom.

'So now you are leaving the Navy, but not to come home to live with *me*, no. But to take off and get married, and once she has you in her clutches I will never see you *at all* then. You'll be in your own home with her, and I'll be left on my own and out in the cold for good and all.'

'I thought you wanted to retire to Tobermory and resume

your relations with the Dewars of Mull.'

'Aye, I do. It's something I've wanted to do for a while now, you know that.'

'So?'

'So I suppose you would like to leave me plonked up there, wouldn't you? While you and she come to live here in Edinburgh.'

John gave a small laugh. 'Beth could never be happy living in a city like Edinburgh. She's an Island girl. She needs the fresh air and the green hills in the same way I need to be near the sea.'

'So where then?'

'I think I may have found the right house in Tobermory – a house big enough for the *three* of us to live in.'

John's father took the pipe out of his mouth. 'The *three* of us? Living together? Even after ye two are married?'

'Yes.'

'You mean ... *you* would be willing to live out there too?'

'Why not, it's an island surrounded by sea, not much different to a ship, just bigger. I could never give up the sight of the sea.'

'Oh, well now ... you should have spoken earlier, because that's an entirely different story.'

He stared at John, his smile of relief and delight spreading wider. 'A proper home again? Not stuck here on my own. This has been a sad house without your mother and not a soul to talk to at night. But look, would *she* agree to that, young Beth?'

'Agree to what – having you in her clutches? She says not.'

'You've both discussed it?'

'We've seen the house. All that remains now is for *you* to see it and give your opinion?'

'It's not up a pile of steep hills, is it?'

'No, it's on Main Street, directly opposite the harbour.'

'Oh, grand – and so near to the McLeods as well!'

John watched his father puffing away on his pipe, his excitement growing. 'I had a gleg old time up there with Angus and Lizzie McLeod last time. When you were up there did they ask after me?'

'They did. Both of them asked.'

'What did you say?'

'I said you were well.'

'Oh, that's not true – did you not tell them about the trouble I'm having with my knee?'

John turned up his eyes, and then reached into the pocket of his jacket and took out a folded page of paper he had taken from the Tobermory Inn and opened it. He had spent the entire train journey from Glasgow to Edinburgh jotting down notes with a pencil.

'What's that?' his father asked curiously.

'A sheet of paper.''

'I can see that. So why are you looking at it?'

'Oh ... just looking at my options for work in the future.' He folded the paper and put it away again. 'But first I have to get down to Portsmouth.'

'When are you going?'

'Tomorrow.'

'On the morning coach?

'Maybe.' John frowned at the thought of making that long journey by coach, confined in such a small space for such a long time, and often with people who never bathed.

'Or I could go down to the Leith docks and see if there is a packet boat leaving for London tomorrow. And if there is, then I would prefer to go by sea and take the coach from London to Portsmouth.'

His father's gaze turned to the window and the sky outside. 'The weather is fair, so it should be a smooth passage.'

He looked at his son curiously as John stood up, patted his pockets, and prepared to leave.

'Are you sure this is not just a whim you may later regret?' he asked.

John nodded. 'Very sure.'

'Sakes alive ... I still can't believe it. That girl of yours must have something very special about her, seeing as you're now willing to give up the sea for her.'

'Oh, no!' John stared at him. 'I said I was leaving the *Navy*. I never said I was giving up the sea.'

Chapter Twenty-Four

Two hours,' Mary said from the window to Mrs Keillor. 'The two of them have been down there now for over two hours ... *what* are they talking about?'

'They used to spend a lot o' time talking together in their young days.'

Mary turned her head and looked at Mrs Keillor. 'They are *still* young, both of them.'

'Aye, but I tell ye this, *he* wouldna be allowed to spend so long sitting out there talking with Beth if Isabella was here.'

'No, it would only lead to yet another jealous fight between those two, so it's a good thing Isabella is *not* here.'

Mrs Keillor licked her lower lip, confused. 'So why then, hen, are ye so worried? All they are doing down there is *talking*. Nothing wrong with that.'

'Oh, there is, Mrs Keillor, a lot wrong with it. Especially if he's trying to persuade Beth to change her mind and end the betrothal.'

'Mary, listen now, do ye not think ye worry *too* much about Beth? She's not so simply led. She's a lass that knows her own mind, and when she knows it, she's not so easily swayed.'

Mary moved away from the window, a small frown on her face.

'Do you think I do that? Worry too much about her?'

Mrs Keillor chuckled wryly. 'Let me put it this way, hen. If ye were a mother *cat* with her kitten ye'd be spending all your time licking her.'

Mary half smiled. 'I'm that bad, am I?'

'Aye, ye are, that bad. But then, I suppose ... with her having no father all these years.'

'And that's why I want her to have a good *husband* in the years ahead.' Mary exclaimed. 'And my choice for that is John Dewar. Because I *know* he will look after her.'

'How d'y'know?'

'I just do.'

'Even so, she's of age now, fully grown to womanhood. So

ye should let her make up her own mind from now on, and cut down a bit on all the licking and purring. Here, let me make ye a cup of tea, and ye can purr over that instead.'

*

She was still holding his hand, but their heads were no longer together. They had talked honestly, and shared some long silences, and now they felt closer to each other than they had done for years.

Lachlan turned his eyes from the hills and looked at her.

'Are you sure it's not just some fancy or an infatuation?'

'Lachlan, I have loved him for more than *four years*. If it was infatuation it would have faded long ago.' She shook her head. 'In these past three years, when you have seen me so disinterested in other men, it was because I was waiting for *him*.'

'And if he had not come back?'

She hesitated. 'I could never be confident that he would come back ... to Mull, or to me. He had set me free, and so had set himself free, that's ... that's what I thought. But if he had not come back when he did, I would still have waited. I would still have kept hoping and praying ... because I do *love* him, and I have loved him since I was seventeen.'

Lachlan sighed, and looked once more at the green hills.

'Then marry him,' he said. 'I'll put up no protest or objection. I will not stand in your way.'

Beth smiled.

'But I won't be *paying* him to marry you. There will be no dowry. He takes you without one or he doesn't take you at all.'

'He has made no mention of any dowry.'

'Good.' He looked at her. 'If he's willing to wed you without a sizeable dowry, or indeed, no dowry at all, then that will prove something.'

'Prove what?'

'That he's not marrying you because your name is Jarvis, and you live on the Jarvisfield estate.'

Beth frowned.

'Or, to put it in a more simple term ... that he's not

marrying you for money.'

'As you did with Isabella?'

Lachlan nodded. 'As I did with Isabella.'

'He will still want to marry me, even with no dowry, I know it.'

She clasped his hand tighter. 'And when he does, Lachlan, will you not then at least *try* to be happy for us?'

'I'm not very good at trying. I fail every time,' he said, smiling. 'But for you, Beth, I will – as they used to say in Australia – give it a "fair go".'

*

Together they walked slowly back towards the house, much slower than usual, because Beth had her head down, in thought.

'Two days ago … where did you meet John?'

'At the Tobermory Inn.'

'You went there to see him?'

'Yes'

'And he hit you … for calling me a half-caste?'

'He nearly broke my jaw!' Lachlan looked at her. 'I'm still worried about you marrying him, Beth.'

'And some years ago, *you* hit William Drummond for the same reason?'

'Yes, but *he* deserved it – well, at that particular time he did.'

Beth stopped walking and turned to him, bewilderment on her face. 'But *why* do you men think it so necessary to hit each other because of that? I *am* of two races – I *am* a half-caste, as you call it – but I am *not* ashamed of that. I am very *proud* of who I am.'

Lachlan met her eyes, beautiful dark eyes that held no lie.

'I am the daughter of the most wonderful man, George Jarvis, and I am proud to carry in my veins some of his eastern blood. My mother is English and I am as proud to carry in my veins some of her English blood. Together they made me, together they loved me, and I will never lower my eyes in shame because of them – because of *either* of them. So when you responded with violence when William

381

Drummond called me a half-caste, then you *insulted* not only me, but also my parents, because we have never seen anything to defend. We see no shame in who we are, and I certainly *feel* no shame, none at all.'

Lachlan was so taken aback, he was unable to answer for some seconds.

'And John *knows* that,' Beth continued. 'The fact that I am of two races and have mixed blood has never mattered to him, never, not since the first day we met. So why would he hit you for calling me a half-caste?'

Lachlan sighed, trying to remember. 'Well, maybe it was something else I said ... oh yes ... a question I asked about you and him ... a very *simple* question from one man to another.'

'Which was?'

Lachlan gave a slight shrug of indignation, 'Nothing that warranted a smash in the face. A simple yes or no would have sufficed.'

PART THREE

Chapter Twenty-five

'Yes, sor, and how may I help ... Well, for cryinoutloud ...'

Jefferson stared in disbelief when John entered the taproom of the Leith Inn, took a stool at the counter and smiled. 'Still no sign of your ship coming in?'

'Where's your Navy uniform?' Jefferson demanded.

'I don't wear it ashore. We are not at war, so I'm not forced to wear it on land.'

Jefferson looked disappointed. 'Oh, that's a shame, that's a *big* shame.'

'Why?'

Jefferson leaned his arms on the counter and said, 'Well, ye see, it's like this ... I was dreaming ... hoping ... wondering ... praying ...'

John sighed. 'I'll have a brandy.'

'... if I saw you again ... if you would let me try on the blue coat of your Royal Navy uniform – just for a minute! Ten seconds!'

John glanced down at his civilian clothes. 'Even if it was *not* against the rules, which it is, as you can see, I can't oblige you.'

'But if you *was* wearing it now, would ye let me?'

'No.'

Jefferson sucked his teeth. 'That's mean.'

'That's the rules.' John looked around the almost empty taproom. 'Man, this is a bad graveyard you're in.'

Two old women sat on a settle against the far wall; two old fishwives with empty glasses on the table in front of them, both slumped in drunken sleep.

He looked at Jefferson. 'What happened to your Irish sailor friends? What happened to their *ship?*'

'Some of the wood on the hull was badly rotting, and there was a crack in the mainmast. They took it back to Ireland to try and fix it.'

'But *you* got off at Scotland?'

'I thought it might sink before getting to Ireland.'

'So you jumped ship?'

'No. No!' Jefferson looked offended at such a suggestion. 'They left me ashore here till they came back for me.'

'And when will that be?'

'If the ship sank ... never.'

'So when was that – when they left you here?'

''Bout five ... six weeks ago. But them Irish, when they get to Ireland they never want to leave again. I could be stranded here till I die.'

John sighed, shook his head, still wondering if Jefferson had jumped a damaged ship.

'Will I get you a glass of water to go with your brandy?' Jefferson asked.

'Only if it's free.'

Jefferson sucked his teeth again, and then went to fetch the brandy, returning with a glass and looking at John bleakly. 'All my shilluns are gone.'

'So why do you stay here?' John asked in puzzlement. 'Wasting your life? Working for nothing?'

'It's this or the streets,' Jefferson admitted. 'Least here I get a bed and a roof over my head. The owner don't care 'bout no customers, because he's put the inn up for sale now, cheap too.'

John was still puzzled. 'Why did you not go back to Ireland with the ship and crew?'

'I told you – rot on the hull and the cracked mainmast – I thought the ship might sink.'

'I don't believe that. No true seaman would jump ship and leave his crewmates to it.'

John grinned, a very wicked grin. 'Had they had enough of you? Did they throw you ashore and sail off?'

'No. No!' Jefferson looked offended again. 'Them Irish were my *friends,* my *good* friends. Ten years! They'd never do a bad thing like that. Not to Jefferson.'

'So why did you not go over to Ireland with them?'

Jefferson sighed forlornly and rubbed a hand over the back of his neck. 'You never been to Ireland?'

'No.'

'Then let me tell ye ... it's not a country for a man like me ...

a few weeks in dock is tough enough, but *months* – while the ship is being repaired. I knew if I went and had to stay there that long I would end up running away – just be *gone* – like my mama.'

'Why?'

'Ireland is ... prim ... prim ...'

'Primitive?'

Jefferson nodded. 'That's it. No black people in Ireland. No black men. So the women and children scream and run away when they see one – when they see *me*. They've all been taught that the Devil is a black man and when they see me they run ... screaming in fright.'

John wished he had not asked. After a short silence he said, 'I think I will have that glass of water.'

'For two shilluns?'

'Bare-faced robbery,' he replied in a tone of disgust, and Jefferson grinned.

John turned on his stool as one of the two old women woke up and began talking in a slurred voice to no one in particular, and then slumped into sleep again.

'Those two have had too much gin,' Jefferson said, and went off to get his glass of water.

John watched the two sleeping women, but did not see them, his mind reflecting on what Jefferson had said. Of course, here in Britain ... the term 'black' referred to anyone who was not white European, and that included Indians and Asians and Arabs and even Greeks and Spanish.

It seemed as if Ireland must be living in a very old world if the people where still reacting in such a way, when here there were thousands of black men and women living in Britain, and not all of them were former slaves: fourteen thousand in London alone at the last census.

Jefferson's lineage, he reckoned, was more Caribbean than African, more the dark brown of the West Indies than the deep black of Sierra Leone or Cape Town.

'Your Royal Navy ship,' Jefferson asked, coming back holding his glass of water and looking a lot happier. 'How many guns does it have?'

'The *Hydra*? Four. Two thirty-two pounders, and-'

'*Thirty-two* pounders! Man, them's *bigggg* guns! But why only four? I thought all Navy ships carried 'bout twenty guns.'

'The line-of-battle ships carry treble that, some carry as many as a hundred guns, in times of war, but the *Hydra* is a vessel built for speed and capture.'

'Capturing slave ships?'

'When we can, and our aim is not to blow the ship apart, else we would kill any slaves that might be locked down in the hold.'

'Man, *you're* lucky! Me – I'd give ten years of my life to be in the Royal Navy, working on a ship like that. Better than transporting merchant cargo back and forth.'

Jefferson smiled boyishly. 'At sea, all these years, whenever I'd see one of them Royal Navy vessels, maybe a thousand tons, with their flags flying, I'd always stop what I was doing and put my hand on my heart and say, '*Oh Mother!*'

John sat looking at him, puzzled. 'If you're that obsessed with the Royal Navy, then why don't you *join* it?'

'Me? The Royal Navy? Have *you* not yet noticed that I ain't a *white* man!'

'So? What difference does that make? There are plenty of black sailors in the Royal Navy. And black sailors are treated the same as white ones and given equal status and equal pay.'

'You're jesting!' Jefferson was staring at him. 'You mean *I* could join the Royal Navy? Me? Thomas Jefferson?'

'As a member of the crew. And you appear to know all the ropes and everything else needed on a ship. With your experience you may well be taken on as an *Able* Seaman, not a common seaman.'

Jefferson was still staring at him, his mouth half open.

'In fact.' John said, 'I know there is a ship leaving for Sierra Leone in less than four weeks time. There's always a shortage of crew below deck up until the last day.'

Jefferson gulped down his water feverishly. '*Oh, Mother!*'

John realised he had not touched his brandy. He lifted the glass, swirled it slowly, took a drink, and then looked at Jefferson.

'I'm heading down to London tomorrow morning and then

on to Portsmouth, leaving Leith at seven. If you are truly serious about wanting to join the Navy, you could come with me, and I could speak to the ship's captain on your behalf.'

'You know him? The captain?'

'Of course I know him. I've just served under him on the *Hydra*. That's who I'm going down there to see.'

Jefferson dropped his water glass on the floor. Miraculously it did not break. He bent and picked it up with trembling hands. 'You'd do that, for me?'

'I'd do it for any prime seaman who needed a job. It's not as if I have to go out of my way to do it.'

John stood up. 'I have to get back. If you want to go to Portsmouth, then tomorrow morning be outside at six sharp.'

Jefferson's mind was still spinning. 'But ... but why six – if the packet boat doesn't leave till seven? It's a small walk.'

John paused at the taproom door. 'Jefferson, six sharp – or I go to Portsmouth on my own.'

*

When John arrived at the Leith Inn at six the following morning, Jefferson was waiting outside. His hair was still wet and his face was gleaming from the scrubbing he had given it. He had attempted to spruce up his clothes but they were still as shabby as any worn by the unemployed who wandered the streets of Edinburgh's old town.

John, in contrast, was wearing his Royal Navy uniform. Jefferson eyed it admiringly. 'You going back to your ship now?'

'No, but I am going on Navy business.'

When they had boarded the packet boat, John gazed around at the crew, all busy at their tasks in preparation for the voyage.

He looked at Jefferson. 'If I'm going to recommend you to the captain, on my word and my name, you understand that I have to be sure that everything you have told me is true.'

'In what way?'

'See the crew working all around us? If I point to each man in turn, then you tell me exactly what he is doing, in nautical terms.'

'Is that why we've come on board so early?'

John nodded. 'It is.'

'Then start pointing.' Jefferson rubbed his hands together, his face resuming its usual boyish cheerfulness as if this was going to be a game he would enjoy playing again.

John spent the next half an hour pointing, and Jefferson answering with all the knowledge of a true sailor, becoming so cocky in one instant that he actually moved forward to tell one of the crew what he was doing wrong.

'Bugger off,' the Scotsman told him, and then looked at John, his eyes moving up and down his uniform. 'Is he with ye, sir?'

'About ten minutes before we sail?' John asked.

'Aye, about that, ten or fifteen minutes.'

John turned to Jefferson who was waiting with head cocked and eyes wide in readiness for the next question.

'I think we have enough time left to take some hot coffee.'

'Did I pass the test?'

John shrugged, unwilling to make Jefferson even more cocky. 'Well enough.'

And later, as the ship got under way with a cool breeze off the sea, John stood by the rail and watched two of the passengers sitting on the deck bench, their faces white with fear and their hands clutching the sides of the bench for dear life as the ship began to rise and fall in the long swells.

He was too used to standing on a deck to sit down, and standing beside him, he noticed that Jefferson had taken up the same stance, easily balanced, like a man who could move quickly and steadily over a tilting deck when necessary.

Jefferson was inhaling deep breaths of the sea air, his face beaming with the pleasure of being on a ship again.

'After being at sea for a long time,' Jefferson said suddenly, 'I always find it hard getting used to standing on land again. Do ye?'

John nodded. 'Sometimes. Usually only for a day or two, trying to adjust to sitting or sleeping in a room where the walls are not slowly swaying up and down.'

Jefferson laughed. 'That's why sailors *sleep* so well. All that rocking.'

An hour later, when the two passengers had staggered down below, John finally moved over to the bench and sat down, folded his arms in a relaxed way and stretched his legs, crossing them at the ankles.

Jefferson joined him on the bench and arranged his body in the same way.

John looked at him. 'Do you know who you remind me of?'

'Who?'

'William Brown.'

'Who's he?'

'The first black man to join the Royal Navy. Every sailor in the Navy knows about William Brown.'

'Because he was black?'

'No, not exactly ...' A seagull flew past their faces across the deck then zoomed upwards again and John continued:

'William Brown joined the British Navy in Grenada in about 1804 and signed on as a landsman – a volunteer, willing to learn the ropes and everything else.'

'I don't need to *learn* any more?' Jefferson said indignantly.

'No, but William Brown knew nothing about life on a ship. He was only about sixteen at the time, and Britain's engrossment in the war with France meant that any extra new hand on deck was grabbed. Those were the days of the press gangs when men were badly needed to serve on Britain's warships.'

Jefferson nodded. 'My Irish friends told me all about that – said it was bad, like slavery.'

John thought about it. 'I suppose it was like slavery, but slavery was legal then, and those that didn't get killed in the war were set completely free afterwards, paid off by the captains and allowed to go home.'

Jefferson tutted sarcastically. 'That was kind of the captains – we've almost killed you, sailor, but as you ain't *dead* yet, and you've still got one arm and one leg left – you can go home now.'

John laughed. 'Fortunately we are young, and that was all before our time.'

'Is that why they took William Brown into the British Navy,

because of the war?'

'No, William Brown *volunteered* to join the service when the *Queen Charlotte,* a warship carrying one hundred guns, went into port at Grenada. And within a year or two he had proved himself to be one of the best Able Seamen the *Queen Charlotte* ever had. Skilled and athletic and full of stamina, he was eventually promoted to be Captain of the Foretop, put in charge of the other sailors in that part of the ship, and William Brown eventually became one of the lower-deck aristocracy. He served for eleven years on the *Queen Charlotte* until he was paid off in 1815 when the war ended.'

Jefferson squared his shoulders proudly. 'And he a black man like me! But the *white* crew – how did *they* like him?'

'According to all the reports, Brown grogged as boisterously and messed as happily with the white crew as anyone else. And it's because of William Brown that so many black sailors were welcomed into the service.'

'Into the Royal Navy?'

John nodded. 'Into the Royal Navy.'

'And that's what you want *me* to be – if your captain takes me on – as good as him?'

'I'm hoping you will do as *well* as him, but – '

'I'll be *better* than him,' Jefferson said determinedly. 'After a few years I'll be so great that the name of Thomas Jefferson will be even more famous than the name of William Brown.'

John laughed. 'I think it already is.'

'How?'

'Thomas Jefferson ... the late American President?'

'Oh, yeah ...' Jefferson took a deep, disappointed breath, and then pursed his lips thoughtfully. 'Maybe I should do like the Irish did, and change my name to O'Jefferson?'

After a silence he resumed his determination and said cheerfully, 'If the Navy signs me on, I'll be *so* great, *so* skilled, so *fast* up the maintop, I'll have the white sailors saying that Thomas O'Jefferson is like William Brown all over again.'

John stopped smiling. 'Oh God, I hope not.'

'Why not?'

'Because I have not told you the *end* of William Brown's story. In 1815, when he was paid off by the *Queen Charlotte* and was being examined in port to make sure he was bringing no infectious diseases ashore, William Brown turned out to be a young woman of twenty-six – and not a man at all.'

'Jaysus!' Jefferson jumped up from his seat in shock and stood staring at John. 'You're jesting? A *woman!*'

'A woman in disguise ... all those years, pretending to be a man.'

Jefferson slowly sat down again.

'Seems she had run away from her husband in Grenada who enjoyed battering her brutally every night, so she ran away to sea, the safest place she could find, and never went back to Grenada.'

Jefferson was pursing his lips.

'Of course, by then, the *Queen Charlotte* had captured so many enemy ships as prizes, he – she had become quite rich with her share of the prize money and went to live in style somewhere in London.'

'So why ... *why* did you say that *I* reminded you of William Brown?'

'Only because you're black, and I think you will make an excellent sailor.'

'Not because you suspect I'm a *woman* under my clothes? Because I can prove to you that I'm all man, nothing womanly about me.'

John erupted with laughter as Jefferson jumped up again and began to undo his coat and unbutton his shirt and then pulled the shirt back to display a brown chest as flat as any other man's chest.

'Button yourself up, man – half the crew are looking at you.'

Jefferson looked around and saw at least three of the crew staring at him.

'*Oh, Mother!*' he quickly buttoned his shirt and jacket and sat down again with his arms folded, sulking.

'I wish you hadn't told me 'bout William Brown. I was proud of him – then he turns out to be a *woman.*' Jefferson tutted with disgust.

John looked at him. 'Do you not *like* women?'

'I *lovvve* women!' Jefferson exclaimed. 'But not women

that pretend to be men!'

A few seconds later, Jefferson decided to add to what he had said, putting a hand up to his mouth and saying secretively, 'But I don't like *white* women. They all look like ghosts to me.'

'Ghosts?'

Jefferson nodded. 'Skinny *white* women, looking like all the blood has been drained out of them. If I found one in my bed I would jump out the window in fright.'

John was laughing again. 'Well, luckily for you, a lot of white women don't like black men.'

Jefferson nodded. 'I'm lucky in that. I don't want any of them ghosts hanging around me when my beautiful dark brown dream woman comes along.'

He looked curiously at John. 'Have you got a dream woman?'

'No, mine is real.'

'So yours has come along?'

John nodded. 'Mine has come along.'

'Does she mind when you are away at sea for a long time?'

John's glance travelled along the deck and then aloft to the sails and then returned to look at Jefferson.

'When *you* are at sea, Jefferson, grogging and messing with the crew, don't tell anyone that you were once a slave.'

'No? Why not?'

'It's wiser not to. If you tell them you were once a slave, some of the men may try and treat you like a slave. Human nature.'

'So where will I say I come from?'

'America, that's enough.'

Jefferson nodded. 'That's all I'll say ... I'll say I was born in New York ... and I went to sea with the Irish merchants when I was twelve. Can I say that?'

'Oh yes. At sea since you were twelve – they'll respect you straight away if you tell them that.'

'And it's true – apart from being born in New York.'

John uncrossed his ankles but kept his arms folded, his glance constantly moving over the ship, watching what was going on aloft.

'If you do get signed on, and it's the same crew going out on the *Hydra* as the last time, there will be four more black sailors messing on the lower deck with you.'

'*Four* black sailors?' Jefferson almost jumped out of his seat with joy. 'So I'll have *four* new friends from the first day!'

John looked at him sideways. 'They may not like you.'

Jefferson laughed. '*Sure* they'll like me!' Everyone likes Jefferson – even *you!*'

'I know I'll save a fortune when I get rid of you onto a ship. No more buying you expensive free water.'

Jefferson laughed again, his spirits elated and his mood fizzing with excitement. 'Those shilluns bought me some nice dinners – some big tasty meat pies ... and now I'm going to have *four* new black friends!'

He rubbed his hands together in anticipation. 'Oh, I *love* you, John Dewar! Honest to God and the holy Saint Patrick I do!'

Before John could respond – Jefferson, his excitement now too great now to be contained – caught him in an affectionate clasp and placed a big kiss on his cheek.

'Get off!' John pushed him away and sprang out of his seat, walking a few paces across the deck wiping a hand over his face.

Jefferson laughed even louder and John swung round to face him. 'That reminds me – if you get to Sierra Leone, do *not* go ashore at night.'

'Why?'

'Because the damned mosquitoes will suck the face off you.'

Chapter Twenty-Six

'Lord save us – now there's *two* of them!' Lachlan exclaimed wearily, coming in from the garden to the kitchen and hearing Isabella and her sister clamouring excitedly in the hall.

He caught Mary's arm and quickly pulled her outside, bending close to her and speaking in low urgency. 'Mary, if Beth does get married sometime soon, *you* won't leave me, will you ... living alone here – with those two?'

Mary laughed. 'No, of course I won't leave you, *or* Jarvisfield. And why would I? When Beth gets married she will want to live her own life. But now, what did you promise me only a few weeks ago? That you would *try* to get on better and be more considerate to Isabella.'

'Yes, but that was before I knew ... Mary, that *sister* ... there's something *strange* about that sister of hers. She hates me, and I can't understand why.'

'What makes you think she hates you?'

'Whenever I've been at Craignish, she always stares at me, watching me with those big condemning eyes of hers, staring at me as if she would like to devour me for my sins, and then kill me dead.'

'Nonsense, she's only a young girl of eighteen. Maybe she's short-sighted and that's why she stares at you – have you thought of that?'

'But you won't leave me, will you? You won't ever leave Jarvisfield?'

'I've told you I won't.'

'I couldn't cope with Isabella *and* her sister on my own.'

'You won't have to. I'm here, and so also is Mrs Keillor and Hector and Maggie and Lorna and all the farm hands. We'll protect you from a staring eighteen-year-old girl.' She tutted and laughed. 'Now get inside and welcome your wife back home.'

*

In the days that followed Mary could see nothing *strange* about Isabella's sister at all, coming to the conclusion that anything odd about her must be put down to a misjudgement or a fault in Lachlan's imagination.

Mary Campbell of Craignish appeared to be a very warm girl, full of laughter and unrestrained chatter. She was much fairer than her sister and, unlike Isabella, she exhibited a mind of sharper intelligence. Her eyes were as blue as Isabella's but her hair, more flaxen in colour and thicker in texture, was always worn drawn through a gold ring at the back of her head and fell in curls onto her neck.

And her eyes didn't seem to stare, not as Mary noticed. Although she did appear to be constantly watching and taking in everything around her, as if all was new and captured her interest, asking Mary question after question about the normal run of life at Jarvisfield, and in particular – how well Lachlan and Isabella got on together when there were no visitors?

'Oh, well enough,' Mary had answered, thinking it an odd and rather impertinent question.

The girl also seemed very alert in her interest in Beth, until she was told that Beth was betrothed to a Naval officer and was hoping to marry him sometime in the near future; and on that she seemed to relax and all her interest in Beth vanished.

Lachlan was also noticing a difference in his wife's young sister. The way she dressed, with lower necklines that left the upper part of her bosom exposed, as if she was eager to show off her developing figure.

Even her staring eyes had changed in the year or so since he had last seen her. Now she no longer stared at him, but instead she gave him secret little smiles across the table, especially when he had disagreed with his wife, showing him that she was on *his* side in the difference of opinion, and not Isabella's.

'Those two seem to be getting along quite well now,' Mary said to Mrs Keillor, noticing that for two days running Lachlan and Mary Campbell had taken a talkative stroll together down to the loch, while Isabella was having her afternoon nap ... Or was it that *he* was taking a stroll, and

Mary Campbell had quickly followed him?

Mrs Keillor chuckled. 'Nothing gets past ye, does it, Mary?'

'Now what does *that* mean?'

'Nothing, hen, just that of late ye've become the eyes and ears of this house.'

'I know, I know ...' Mary sat down. 'And I don't know why ... other than I've got a bad feeling in my bones. And I don't know if that bad feeling is to do with Beth and John Dewar, something going wrong with their betrothal ... or if its to do with Lachlan and Isabella.'

Mrs Keillor bit on her lip. 'Isabella doesn't seem to mind him being more friendly with her sister now.'

'No,' Mary agreed. 'She's most likely very relieved that the two of them are less frosty with each other than in the past at Craignish, making *her* life a whole lot easier.'

Hector came running up to the open door of the kitchen, his face shocked. 'Something bad's happened! The master has just pushed his wife's sister into the loch!'

'What?' Mary stared at Hector. 'And is he helping her out again?'

'Nay.'

'Then *you* go and help her, Hector. We don't even know if she can swim!'

Hector went tearing off across the yard, and minutes later Lachlan came walking back into it, heading across to the tables, still smiling.

'What's going on?' Mary asked.

'I'm going on MacDuff,' Lachlan replied, unlooping the gelding's reins and leading him out.

Mary stuttered – 'B-but Hector said ... *where* are you going?'

'Over to the Dewars' house to see my farm manager. I'll be back for dinner.'

'You're going to Salen?'

'That's where he lives.'

He mounted, looked at Mary, and smiled again. '*Adieu!*'

He was just turning the horse around when Hector appeared holding the arm of Mary Campbell who was soaking wet from head to foot with water dripping down her face from her tangled hair.

Lachlan looked back at the girl, laughed his amusement, and rode off.

'Oh, my dear ...' Mary said as the girl drew nearer. 'Come inside and I'll get you a clean towel to dry your hair.'

The girl stepped into the kitchen and took the towel to dry her face, and then looked at Mary and Mrs Keillor with laughing blue eyes that were beaming.

'Isn't he *dashing*? Isn't he *different*? Isn't he *fun!*'

When she had tripped off out of the kitchen to go upstairs and change her clothes, Mary looked askance at Mrs Keillor and Hector, and then all three looked askance at each other.

'By!' said Mrs Keillor. 'She must be living a very lonely life with no visitors over there in that Craignish! If she thinks *that's* fun – being pushed into a loch!'

Mary was lost for words. Only Hector finally came up with a conclusion. 'I think she's as mad as all the rest of ye! I'm going back to my horses.'

*

When Lachlan arrived at the Dewars' place he could see many of the farm hands sitting around in groups in a field, eating their mid-day bread and cheese while their tankards were being filled by some of the wives who had brought the food and drink to them.

He walked through the open door of the house and looked inside the rooms but the house was empty.

Peering through a window he saw Robert Dewar sitting in the sun with a second group of farmhands, laughing and enjoying his mid-day break as much as the rest of them.

He decided not to disturb him until his meal break was over and wandered into the kitchen to pour himself a glass of water while he waited.

He had just lifted the jug when he heard Beth's voice outside the window at the side of the house, but what she was saying he did not hear because Kirsty Dewar was speaking over her:

'No! No! Ye canna get married in *red*, Beth. Ye know what the tradition says – "*Marry in red, and you'll soon wish ye were dead".'*

'I suppose ...' Beth replied, 'I could wear a nice primrose yellow?'

'No! *"Marry in yellow, you'll be ashamed of your fellow".'*

Beth laughed. *'Me* – ashamed of John? I could never be that.'

'How d'y'know? Ye don't know the future. He could do something very bad later on that would make ye ashamed of him – and all because *ye* wore yellow at the wedding.'

'Blue?'

'"Marry in blue – your lover will be true".'

'I'll wear *blue* then!'

'Or ye *could* marry in white – *"Marry in white, all will be right".*

'No ...' Beth decided, 'I would prefer my lover to be true, than for the marriage just to be *right*.'

'Or, because my cousin John is a sailor, you could get married in grey.'

'Grey – because he's a sailor – why?'

'"Marry in grey – you'll live far away".'

'But I don't *want* to live far away, Kirsty, I want to live here in Mull.'

Lachlan poured his glass of water, thinking it was the most idiotic conversation he had ever heard.

*

A few days later, at home, he found himself subjected to the same idiotic female nonsense when he heard Maggie and Lorna giving more wedding advice to Beth in the garden outside the dining room window.

'Saturday is a verra bad day to get married on,' Maggie Kennedy said authoritatively. 'Saturday is *verra* unlucky for weddings.'

'So when do ye think the wedding will be?' Lorna asked.

'I don't know ...' Beth replied uncertainly. 'Maybe, the end of September.'

'Och, no! Ye canna marry then!' Lorna cried. 'If ye marry in *harvest* time, then ye will spend all yer life *gathering* – working hard!'

'Aye, that be true,' Maggie agreed. 'September brings with it the autumn – the start of the *dark* half of the year.'

'Aye,' Lorna added. 'The best time is in spring or summer – in the *light* half of the year.'

'But it's August now,' Beth protested, 'and John has to arrange so many things ... and the only thing *I* have done is to decide that my dress will be *blue.*'

'Then ye'll have to put the wedding off until at least spring,' Maggie commanded. 'That is if ye want to be a happy wife all your days.'

'But not in May,' Lorna warned forbiddingly. '"*Marry in May – rue the day!*"'

'And even when you *do* get married in the luckier light half of the year,' said Maggie Kennedy with a look of caution, 'it would be a *verra* good plan to lock the groom in the church the night before – in case he changes his mind overnight.'

Lachlan had heard enough: his increasing irritation finally forced him to walk over and yank the window down, slamming it shut.

Under normal circumstances, he would not have allowed Beth to be dragged this way and that way by all their stupid Celtic superstition, but for the moment he was content to intervene no more than slamming the window shut, a small part of him enjoying her confusion.

If the wedding *never* took place he would not grieve over it.

But still, it was unfair ... those females were tormenting Beth with all their stupid beliefs and superstitions – tormenting his beloved Beth!'

He marched outside and the three girls turned around to look at him – and seeing him at the pump and filling the water bucket – Maggie and Lorna jumped and sprinted into a fast gallop towards the fields.

Beth stood staring after them, and then turned her surprised eyes to Lachlan. 'Why did they run away like that?'

'Because they knew it was their *wash* time,' he said with a wry grin, and immediately turned away from her as Isabella stepped into the yard.

'Oh, my cherub ...' he said. 'The afternoon sun is still

401

shining and yet you are *awake*? What happened? Did the bed collapse?'

Beth began walking quickly in the direction of the fields, and as soon as she was out of the sight of the yard she grabbed at her dress to lift the hem of her skirt and then started running as fast as a ten-year-old after Maggie and Lorna, collapsing down beside them when she found them hiding under a tree.

'Why did *ye* run as well, Beth?' Lorna asked curiously.

Beth sat back and exhaled her breath in relief, but she did not answer or tell them that running *anywhere* was preferable to standing as a witness to yet another marital quarrel.

'He's getting worse,' Lorna complained. 'I don't ken how his wife puts up with him.'

'Me neither,' Maggie agreed.

'I ken we be only servants,' Lorna said, 'but that doesna excuse him dowsing us wi' buckets o' water whenever he gets himself in a bad mood.'

'It's not his fault,' Beth defended. 'It's just that his life has gone all wrong ... and now he doesn't know what to do about it.'

'My life has never gone right,' Maggie Kennedy gruffed, 'but I no' take it out on others.'

Beth looked at the glum faces of her friends, and then said, in an attempt to resume where they had happily left off – 'So, you were both advising me ... if Saturday is an unlucky day to get wed, then what day *is* lucky?'

'Sunday would be a good day,' Maggie advised.

'Nay!' Lorna argued. '*Thursday is* the luckiest day of all.'

Chapter Twenty-Seven

A week later John Dewar arrived back in Edinburgh after disembarking from the evening packet boat. When he reached the Leith Inn he dropped Jefferson's keys through the letterbox of the locked door.

A '*For Sale*' notice was now stuck on the window, but the two old women who loved their gin were sitting on the pavement outside, evidently unable to read, and still waiting for the taproom to open.

He stepped around them and walked on.

Reaching home and entering the house, the housekeeper greeted him cheerfully. 'Ah, ye've arrived home in nice time, Mr John. I've just prepared a nice dinner of lamb and mint with asparagus.'

His father was already seated in the dining room and looked up at him, questioningly, 'Well, is it done?'

'More or less.' John sat down on the seat opposite him.

'Now what does that mean – "more or less"? Is it done or is it not done?'

John looked at him. 'It's done.'

'Ah.' Mr Dewar smiled as the housekeeper carried in the platter of lamb which she had already sliced, followed by tureens of steaming vegetables.

'When I retire to Mull,' Mr Dewar said to the housekeeper, ' I'll be lost without you and your fine cooking, Mrs Edin. Will you not reconsider coming out there with me?'

'Out there to the western isles?' She shook her head. 'I'd sooner go up to the moon.'

'Why?' John asked. 'It's beautiful out there.'

'To ye mebbe, but to me it's all wild and lonely and too few people – only seven hundred people in Tobermory they say – and only the same number again throughout the rest of the island. Nay, who would leave Edinburgh for a lonely place like that?'

'Oh, who indeed?' John said wryly. 'Who would wish to have only fourteen hundred neighbours?'

His father chuckled. 'Sounds more than enough to me.'

'And then there's my husband to consider,' Mrs Edin added. 'Now he would *never* agree to leave Edinburgh, not even for a sack of gold bullion. His family have been here all the way back to the beginning of Edinburgh itself.'

She spooned some mint onto Mr Dewar's plate. 'Of course, in the auld days, his ancestors were called Edinburgh, as were all the people who settled here in those ancient times, but over time and to avoid confusion, our family name got shortened to Edin.'

John was looking at the amount of roasted lamb she had forked onto his plate, thinking about Jefferson. At least now, in the Navy, Jefferson would get regular meals every day, and would also get *paid* for his work.

And somehow ... he smiled to himself ... he had a very definite feeling that he and Jefferson would meet up again in the future – especially if one of his own new dreams eventually became a reality.

'Are ye not eating, Mr John?'

'Oh, yes ... thank you.' John lifted his knife and fork.

'She'll be a sore loss,' said Mr Dewar when Mrs Edin had left the room. 'Does Beth know how to cook?'

'I've no idea.'

'What? You asked her to marry you without also asking her if she could *cook*?'

'A small detail I overlooked.'

'And a big problem if she cannot,' said Mr Dewar, chewing his mouthful of delicious lamb with a worried frown on his face.

'Did Mother know how to cook when you married her?'

'No ... they had servants ... but she knew how to boil eggs and cut bread and cheese and make plum pudding with honey syrup and ... that's all. But we got by well enough.'

'As will we.'

'Though your mother was a fast learner. Within a year she was serving up veal with rosemary sauce and apple pie with nutmeg and all of it learned from a book. A wonderful cook she turned out to be, as well you d'know.'

John allowed his father to ramble on about his mother's

varied and special cooking recipes while he let his mind dwell on Beth, his thoughts loving and lustful: her ability to cook was the last thing on his mind.'

'So now – the wedding? When?'

'Oh ... ' John looked vaguely at his father. 'As soon as you approve the house.'

*

In the Macquarie house at Jarvisfield, dinner was also in progress, and turning out to be a very silent affair.

Lachlan sat at the top of the table with the two sisters on either side, his glance moving over the empty chairs at the far end where he knew Beth and Mary should rightly be sitting, and where they had always sat in the past, before *she* banned them off to the kitchen.

He glanced at Isabella who seemed to be lost away somewhere in one of her daydreams, no doubt due to all those trashy penny novelettes she read in her bed at night. And now she was reading them during her afternoon rest periods too.

Rest periods? All she ever did was lounge about and *rest*. And all because of her so-called weak and delicate constitution.

Her sweet and delicate fragility had appealed to his masculinity in the early days, until he had wed her and discovered it was all a mask for her utter *dullness*. Dullness of mind, dullness of body – Lord save us!

He thought of his mother, of her energy and her pioneering spirit, eager to change the world and make it a better place.

No, he decided, Elizabeth Macquarie would have been unable to comprehend the lazy ways of Isabella ... his own dear mother, Elizabeth Macquarie, who had always refused to lie in her bed in daylight, even when she was sick.

He glanced at Mary Campbell, and his glance lingered. Now what would his mother make of Isabella's sister? The neckline of her dress was so low tonight, the top of her breasts were exposed above it like two half moons ... that dress was outrageous enough to make even a whore blush.

But there she sat, innocent-faced and blue-eyed, chewing her food as delicately as a bird.

She noticed him looking at her and met his eyes, giving him one of her secret little smiles, and then she lowered her eyes and decorously forked a slice of carrot into her mouth.

A sly and canny little temptress if ever he saw one. In comparison to her younger sister, Isabella was as guileless and naive as a child.'

Finally, Mary Campbell spoke. 'Are you still feeling sickly, Isabella?'

Isabella glanced at her, and nodded. 'Yes, yes, just a little, in my stomach.'

'Then you were right, dear, and you *have* now started your menses,' Mary said with a sigh. 'No wonder you feel unwell.'

'Mary!' Isabella replied in shock, her face reddening hotly at such a thing being mentioned in front of a man.

Mary waved a hand dismissively. 'He's a husband. He must know about these female things by now.'

Lachlan pushed back his chair, stood up and immediately left the room; a despairing frown on his face when he walked into the hall. Now – thanks to her naughty little sister – he had learned that Isabella was not pregnant, yet again!

He wandered into his study and concentrated his mind on the accounts books for almost an hour, a task that depressed him and made him idly wonder if he should go over to Strathallan Castle in the morning ...

A few days in Drummond's cheerful company always elevated his spirits, not to mention the copious amounts of Canary wine and Madeira they usually drank.

Someone knocked on the study door. Mary Campbell opened it and stepped inside without being asked to enter.

He lifted his eyes from the books and looked at her questioningly. 'Yes?'

Her eyes flickered around the room. 'I was ... looking for something.'

'Looking for what, pray?'

'She stood awkwardly for a moment, and then cleared her throat. 'A pencil,' she said. 'I thought I would do some sketches. Do you have one spare?'

Lachlan looked around the desk, and then picked up a pencil. 'Is *this* what you are looking for?'

She hesitated, and then nodded.

'Are you sure?' His eyes were challenging her, watching every small reaction on her naughty young face

'Yes, I – ' Her face flushed a deep pink, as if suddenly feeling intimidated by the amused look in his eyes.

'This sketching of yours,' he said. 'Is it something new? A new hobby?'

'No,' she said haughtily, 'I have been sketching pictures since I was twelve years old.'

'Oh, so you've been doing it for two or three years then?'

'Yes ...' her eyes flickered again. '*No!* I'm not fourteen or fifteen – I'm *eighteen!*'

'Are you really? Eighteen?' His eyes moved over her low neckline and her half-exposed plump breasts. 'I never would have guessed.'

He held up the pencil and smiled at her. 'And you came in here looking for *this?*'

'Yes – thank you!' She grabbed the pencil from his hand and rushed out of the room.

*

Later that evening, as the sun was slanting down behind the hills, Mary Campbell sat sulkily in the garden drawing doodle after doodle and sketching not a line of anything in particular.

Mrs Jarvis came out of the kitchen and walked towards her. She quickly closed her sketching pad.

'Are you all right, Mary? You seem to be sitting here in a state of gloomy despond.'

Mary Campbell shook her head of flaxen curls haughtily. 'I *am* an artist, you know. And we artists often sit in deep creative thought.'

'An artist? Well, I didn't know that. Have you painted many pictures?'

'A few ... but mostly pencil sketches of Craignish and the lands around Jura.'

'I'm sure your sketches are very good,' Mary said kindly.

'Oh, they are. My father says they are excellent, quite excellent.'

Lachlan came into the yard. 'Mary?'

The two Marys looked round and answered together. 'Yes?'

Lachlan addressed all his words to Mary Jarvis. 'Just to let you know, I'll be heading off to Strathallan in the morning.'

'For how long?'

'A few days.' He nodded and raised his hand in farewell. 'Don't worry yourself about breakfast. I'll be gone before you get up.'

When he had gone back inside Mary looked at the girl and shrugged. 'He always says that, and more often he is gone for weeks on end.'

'Weeks?' The girl seemed to gulp on her breath. 'But ... is that a proper thing to do, when there are *visitors* in the house?'

'What visitors?' Mary Jarvis asked innocently.

'Me.'

'You ... oh *you*.' Mary smiled. 'Oh, I'm sure Lachlan regards you as more than a mere visitor – more a member of the resident family. And he does have business matters needing his attention.'

The girl bit her lip sulkily. 'Isabella is so *lucky*, having a husband like him.'

'Who, Lachlan?' Mary was taken aback. 'Are you forgetting that he cruelly pushed you into the loch?'

The girl smiled. 'Oh, that wasn't cruel – that was all in good *fun*. And he *knew* I could swim. Only minutes before I had been telling him how *well* I could swim. I'm an excellent swimmer, quite excellent, and he said to me "So prove it" and pushed me into the loch.'

She chuckled at the memory. 'I don't intend to be mean ... but Isabella doesn't *deserve* a man like him. She complains about him all the time at Craignish, and says not a word about his good points and all the other fine things about him.'

'Which are?'

'Well, he's very good-looking – tall and fair and extremely handsome on a horse, and he can be very funny and enjoyable company when he's in a good mood ... and

408

compared to so many other men I have seen, I think he's perfectly *divine.*'

Mary was frowning. 'Well, you seem to have it all totalled up ... but are you not forgetting one other important thing about him?'

The girl came out of her trance of admiration and turned her blue eyes to Mary. 'What other thing?'

'He's your *brother*-in-law.'

Chapter Twenty-Eight

The table had been long cleared of all plates and dishes and now that Mrs Edin had said her farewells and gone home, Mr Dewar carried a decanter of brandy over to the table where John was still sitting, reading a page from a newspaper.'

'What's that?' his father asked curiously.

'A page I tore out of a newspaper.'

'I can see that. So why did you tear the page out?'

John stopped reading and looked at him. 'You know, I can rejoin the Navy at any time, as long as there's a voyage and a need for an experienced officer. Once an RN man always a RN man. And in the West Africa Squadron – a posting that all officers hate – there will *always* be a need.'

'Aye, and after eight years you must have a good service record.'

'I do. And that's why Captain Young has insisted I take more time to think about it.'

'What?' His father stopped pouring the brandy. 'You said it was done!'

'It *is* done. But ... as of three days ago, after three years non-stop service in the slave prevention squadrons, Jamaica and Africa, I have a number of months paid leave due to me. And after that ... I will be relieved of all active duty and on indeterminate leave of absence without pay.'

'But still on the Navy's books?'

John nodded. 'Still "on the books". So if Britain ever goes to war again, I will have to go back immediately, like it or not.'

'War?' His father shrugged. 'The chances of that are very slim. According to the *Edinburgh News* France is now declaring itself our ally against all others. And talking of *France*, it seems ...'

John waited while his father took a drink from his glass.

'... it seems that now, *in France,* all the young gentlemen are insisting that their clothes be cut in the *English* style. British designs are all the rage over there.'

'That's probably because of Prince Albert.'

'Yes, now he's a very *pretty* young fellow, isn't he? And quite a fashion plate in his dress. Most likely that's why the French like him so much.'

John showed his lack of interest in French fashion by returning his gaze to the newspaper.

'But if you *don't* go back to the Navy –'

'I have no plans to go back.'

'But you'll stay on the books and on the Reserve List?'

'In the event of war, yes. The Admiralty is not so certain about France as the *Edinburgh News* seems to be.'

'So what other work would you do? Of course, years ago, in the evenings, I did give you some very good training as a tailor.'

John turned up his eyes irritably. 'And that's why I ran away to sea, remember?'

'Aye, and you would still be out there now, if I had not made you do it properly and join the Navy. You were always such a *wayward* lad. Stubborn and wayward, just like your mother. She defied her entire family to marry me. And Lord Donaldson is not going to be too pleased with *you* now ...' He took another drink ... 'Although, when I tell him you'll be settling down and getting wed to a woman, he'll understand.'

John smiled. 'What else could I get wed to? Apart from a woman?'

His father chuckled. 'Well, son, there was a time when I thought you would spend your entire life wedded to the Royal Navy ... and I still can't believe you've walked away from it.'

John looked down at the newspaper page and said: 'Now, work-wise, I have a number of options.'

'Such as?'

'A few years ago, Samuel Cunard, the shipping magnate, with the backing of the Admiralty and the Royal Navy, has been running the first Royal Mail Atlantic Packet Service between here and Halifax in Canada. Steamships. Very fast. And the voyage there and back takes only twenty-eight days. That means if I were to apply – '

'Cunard would snap you up in flash – you being Royal Navy.'

'That means ...' John continued, 'I would only be away at sea for a month at a time.'

'And is all that in the newspaper?'

'No.'

'So why do you keep looking at it?'

'Another option,' John went on, 'is to transfer to the Navy's own packet service. They carry dispatches and occasionally naval passengers and dignitaries to Portugal, Corfu and Gibraltar, just about everywhere in the Mediterranean. That means I would only be away at sea for a couple of months at a time.'

'And would you go in as an officer?'

'Of course I would. It's still administered by the Admiralty.'

And Cunard? What are their uniforms like?

'Semi-naval. Blue coat, the usual.'

'My choice would be Cunard's Atlantic service to Canada and then you would be away for only a month.'

Again John looked down at the newspaper. 'And then there is our own packet service between Scotland and England and Ireland, the same as the European one, but more local, closer to home.'

'That sounds the best of all.'

John's thoughts moved on, contemplative: a flashing of images coming into his mind from a possible future ... *a tilting ship, high and deep swells, sails spread, winds strong, the rigging groaning and taking the strain ... Jefferson standing on the deck, looking up and carefully watching ... knowing exactly what to do ...*

'Do you agree?' his father asked. 'Our own packet service?'

John shrugged out of his thoughts. 'If a parcel was sent on tomorrow evening's packet boat,' he asked, 'would it reach Portsmouth within the next fifteen days?'

'Portsmouth? It should do, easily.'

'So if I leave out some of my clothes tonight, the ones I rarely wear, shirts and trousers, will you fold and parcel them for me? You know how to fold clothes without too much creasing.'

'Aye, I can do that for you. Who are you sending them to?'

John told him about Jefferson; and his father, an ardent

abolitionist in his younger days against slavery of all kinds, readily agreed.

'Appearance is everything,' he said. 'If he arrives on the ship before the captain in decent clothes, then the first impression he gives will be a good one.'

'Will you see to it for me?'

'I will.' His father nodded. 'I'll take them into Mortimers in the morning and pack them into one of their boxes, and get it sent.'

John grinned as he imagined Jefferson's face when a large fancy Mortimers box was delivered to him ... *'For cryinoutloud ...'*

'Will your clothes fit him?'

'They should do, we are roughly the same size. The address of the hostel he's in is – '

'Wait till I get some paper and my pen.'

'Although – and this is important – he is very insistent now that his name be Thomas O'Jefferson, so don't leave out the "O".'

When the details had been written down, Mr Dewar looked at his son and resumed their earlier conversation.

'So you agree? That's the best option – our own packet service?'

John thought back to all the options he had spoken about earlier.

'And then ...' he said, 'there is *this* option.'

He handed the page of newspaper in his hand to his father. 'And this would be *my* choice.'

'This, what's *this?* I thought you were reading from that newspaper about our packet service.'

John smiled as he watched his father reach into his breast pocket for his spectacles, put them on, and began to studiously read the item he had marked on the torn-out page from *The Times* ... waiting and waiting for his father to explode – and then it came:

'WHAT? You must be *mad!* Completely and stupidly *mad!*' His father stared at him. 'That girl has turned your mind insane! To come up with something like this! *Deranged!*'

John remained calm. 'I don't see any real difficulty. I'm

sure the same accusation was thrown at Samuel Cunard when he was younger. And my ambitions are *minuscule* in comparison to his.'

'Your own ship?'

'Just one. That's all I need.'

'Now listen ... I may be just a tailor and a designer of men's clothes, but I'm not so simple as you think. I know what's going on in the world, I hear it all in the fitting rooms from the gentlemen who are obsessed with business – and I read my newspaper every night.'

'So?

'So I know something about Samuel Cunard that *you* obviously don't know! I know he owns a pile of coalmines over there in Nova Scotia. That's how he got the contract from our government for the Atlantic mail service, because he's got the *coal* to fuel his steamships. So I know he's *rich!*'

'In his world, yes, he's rich. And in my world I am not so poor. Neither are you.'

'So how will you pay for this ship?

'With the trust money Mother left me.'

'That? The same money her family left *her*? You can't use *that*! You were supposed to be saving that for the long future to keep you comfortable in your old age.'

'And the world could stop spinning tomorrow. So I thought I would use it to keep *you* comfortable in *your* old age.'

'By buying me a *ship?*' His father stood up in agitation and walked to the fireplace, shaking his head in bewilderment. 'What use to me is a blasted ship? I'm a *tailor,* for God's sakes, not a *sailor!*'

'I will master the ship. You can stay at home with Beth while I go out and earn our living on *my* ship. And my Navy pay has been stacking up month after month for years while I've been away at sea.'

'But why, son, why do something as mad as that when you could have a good job with Cunard or the Navy's packet service?'

'Or why work for the packet service when I could make ten times as much sailing the same route and doing the same job working for myself? And as well as that – there's the freedom and the *adventure* of it all!'

'Adventure? Sakes alive – you're not a boy any more?'

'Oh, I am at heart,' John grinned.

His father turned away, and then quickly turned back and stared at John. 'That grin ... that *wicked* grin of yours ... you're *jesting* me!'

'I am.' John was still grinning as he lifted his brandy.

'Ye bugger!'

'But seriously,' John said, 'it *is* my dream to have my own ship one day.'

'But not now, not *this* one?'

'Alas, no, not that one.' John sighed regretfully. 'That full-rigged three-masted ship of one hundred and sixty tons is moored at Bristol and going under the hammer at an auction tomorrow. I'd never get down there in time. I saw the notice of the auction only yesterday, in a newspaper I found on the packet boat coming back here. So even then it was too late. But there will be other ships, and I can still dream, I can still plan – '

'Now lookit, son ...' His father sat down again. 'Dreaming, planning ... are you not running ahead of yourself? You've got your dream girl, and now you're supposed to be planning a wedding to her and securing a house to live in after you're both wed. Can you not be content with that for now?'

'I can be *very* content with that – for now.' John said seriously. 'But just like leaving active duty in the Navy, you'd better start to believe it because come hell or high tide, I *am* going to own my own ship one day.'

'One day ...' said his father, knocking back the last of his brandy and heaving a sigh. 'Let's leave it at that, son ... one day.'

Chapter Twenty-Nine

Darkness had fallen, an intense darkness that was very relaxing after the bright glare of the day. Everyone had gone tiredly to their beds in anticipation of a good night's sleep.

In his bedroom, Lachlan was placing some folded clothes into his travelling bag, glancing at the clock on the dresser which showed it to be almost half past eleven.

When the knock came on the door he assumed it was Mary again, asking him last minute questions about things he might need for his trip to Strathallan.

'Yes.'

The door opened very slowly, and Mary Campbell's face appeared, only half visible in the lamplight, the rest half in shadow. Lachlan was so surprised he dropped the shaving box in his hand.

He picked up the shaving box and threw it into his bag. 'Well? What is it?'

She spoke in a very small and low voice. 'Can you help me?'

He flicked the flap of the bag down and looked at her with concern. 'Is something wrong?'

She stepped quickly into the room and turned to close the door quietly behind her. He was even more surprised when he saw she was wearing only her nightgown, a long white nightgown with long puffy sleeves.

She stood looking at him with her big blue eyes and said quietly, 'Do you have a nail scissors I can borrow?'

'What?'

'I've just finished my bath,' she said in almost a whisper, 'and I need to cut my toenails but I have no nail scissors.'

'What?'

'They've grown so long they scratch my legs when I'm in bed.'

'So why didn't you ask Isabella for hers?'

'She's asleep,' she whispered, 'fast asleep. I am certain she takes laudanum.'

'Laudanum?' This was news to him. No wonder the woman

couldn't get pregnant, and even if she did, the conception would be destroyed within days.

He turned irritably to the dresser, opened one of the drawers and took out a nail file and then rummaged through the various items in the drawer, searching for a pair of nail scissors. 'In future,' he said, 'if Isabella is asleep, ask Mrs Jarvis. She has all kinds of scissors in that sewing box of hers.'

'Mrs Jarvis is asleep too. My poor leg ... the scratches look quite angry and feel very sore and stinging, possibly because of the rose water I put in my bath.'

He turned with the scissors in his hand, stopping dead in his tracks and staring at her. She was bent over, her nightgown pulled up to her knee, looking at her bare leg where one or two red scratches were scarcely visible.

'Can you see?'

He could see. Her leg to her knee was long and slender and perfectly shaped, the skin very pale and smooth. His eyes moved down to her foot and he saw that she had good regular toenails that did not need cutting at all.

He held out the scissors to her and asked her quietly, 'Was *this* what you came for?'

She dropped the hem of her nightgown and looked at the scissors, yet did not reach to take them.

'Yes ...'

'Are you sure?'

'Yes ...'

He threw the file and scissors on the bed beside the bag and moved closer to her, his hand tugging open the ribbon at the neck of her nightgown. 'Or was it *this*?'

His sudden action startled her. She took a step back, her eyes wide. 'No ...'

'No? Are you *quite* sure?' His hand was moving over the cotton of her nightgown, his palm beginning to caress one of breasts. A tremor ran through her body.

'Oh ...' she emitted a shaky breath, 'you should not do that.'

'No? Not touch the fruit that has been on display for weeks?'

'All I wanted was for you to *kiss* me ... just once.'

'Oh, my sweet,' he said wryly, 'I am not one of your Craignish farmboys that you can brazenly tantalise all the livelong day ... and you *know* I am not.'

Her arms slid around his shoulders, her body pressing closer, her mouth reaching up to his. 'I know I love you.'

'You also know that I am married ... or are you forgetting that we are related?'

She lifted her eager gaze from his mouth and looked into his eyes. 'I know you are married to a wife you don't even *like.*'

He smiled casually. 'Poor me.'

Chapter Thirty

Mrs Keillor, Mary, Beth and Hector had finished their breakfast and were drinking their tea and discussing the coming harvest.

'They d'reckon tis going to be a good one,' said Hector, slurping his tea happily.

'Aye, because we've had such a warm and lovely summer,' said Mrs Keillor.

'A *lovely* summer,' Beth agreed with a smile.

Mrs Keillor nodded. 'Even my turnips have done better than I expected.'

'Good morning, good morning ...'

The conversation stopped as all looked at Mary Campbell standing in the doorway, looking as bright and cheerful as the summer sun itself, dressed in a blue and white striped dimity dress that was buttoned up to the neck.

'Oh, Miss Campbell ...' Mrs Keillor pulled herself to her feet. 'I havna started the family breakfast yet.' She frowned for a moment. 'Do ye want me to do yours now?'

'Yes please.'

'The usual two boiled eggs?'

'No, I want everything, a full plate – bacon and eggs and fried liver and all the rest.' She looked at Hector and giggled. 'I could eat a *horse!*'

'No need for that kind o' talk,' Hector replied sourly, standing up to leave the kitchen. 'No need for that at all.'

She followed Hector out to the stables, skipping after him lightly. 'I'll need the mare saddled this morning, Hector, in about an hour or so.'

Hector turned and stared at her. 'The mare? Why – I've never seen ye even *sit* on a horse.' His brows shot up suspiciously. 'I hope ye're no' thinking of *learning* on the mare – nay, she doesna like beginners.'

She folded her arms daintily. 'Don't be silly. Unlike my sister, I am an excellent horsewoman, quite excellent.'

'Nay,' Hector shook his head in refusal, 'I canna let ye do

that without the master's permission, and he's no' here now to give it.'

A moment later Hector's head shot round as he heard Lachlan's voice in the kitchen, talking to Mrs Mary. 'Is that he? Is he still here? He told me he was going to Strathallan.'

Mary Campbell smiled. 'I believe he has changed his mind.'

Later that morning Hector was still sulking as Lachlan mounted the gelding. 'If I'd known ye wanted to ride MacDuff and ye were no' going to Strathallan I'd have got him ready all nice and shiny, but I would've liked some warning.'

Lachlan looked down at Hector. 'We *all* would like some warning, Hector, but sometimes things unexpectedly overtake us.'

He grinned and then kneed the gelding forward, following Mary Campbell who was already riding the mare down the lane.

Beth came out and stood with Hector to watch them.

'She sits well,' Beth observed, watching Mary's straight back on the mare. 'She's balanced well and looks in full control.'

She patted his arm. 'Don't worry, Hector, the mare will be fine.'

'Which one? My mare or the one riding her?' Hector snapped, and walked off huffily back into his stables.

Beth sighed and returned to the kitchen. 'Poor Hector is still upset about Mary saying she could eat a horse. He will hate her for days now.'

She picked a small piece of cake off Mrs Keillor's teaplate and chewed it. 'It's such a pity that Isabella does not like horses, because if she did like them, then she and Lachlan would have been able to share a common interest and ride around the estate together, just as he is doing now with her sister.'

'What's got me in a quandary,' said Mrs Keillor, 'is why he changed his mind about going to Strathallan Castle?'

Beth looked at her mother. 'Did he tell you?'

'Yes,' Mary answered, carrying two pots over to the sink and looking in no way troubled. 'He said Miss Campbell had expressed a wish to see all of the Jarvisfield estate, and as she was a visitor here, and also his wife's sister, he felt he should submit to her request.'

She looked around for a clean dishcloth. 'And in my opinion, that's a far more worthwhile thing for him to do – riding around his own estate where all the tenants and hands will see their laird showing an interest – instead of him going off to the mainland for weeks on end when we all *know* he drinks much too much while he is there.'

'He drinks much too much when he is *here*,' Beth said. 'At least one decanter of wine every evening.'

Mrs Keillor tutted and moved over to the sink. 'Here, Mary, let *me* wash them pots. You go and see to the dining room.'

Mary nodded, and then looked at her daughter. 'Beth, would you be so kind as to go into the drawing-room and speak to Isabella. She's got her head stuck into one of those books again. She needs to get out and take some fresh air, so will *you* suggest accompanying her on a short walk?'

'She'll say no, but I'll suggest it,' Beth agreed, and then strolled down the hall towards the drawing-room.

*

In the week that followed, it seemed that Lachlan and Mary Campbell were always riding off together, and eventually Isabella agreed to join Beth for a walk along the banks of the loch.

Beth had always found conversation with Isabella difficult, often finding herself at a loss for what to say next.

'You must feel a lot happier having your sister here for company now?'

Isabella shrugged. 'I feel a lot happier now that Lachlan is taking her out and about around the estate and out of my hair. That girl is so *tiring*. And my goodness, all her non-stop questions! No wonder I hide away in my books.'

They had reached the bank and Beth paused for a moment to stare across the water at the green hills.

'Do you read many books, Beth?'

'No, not many, and none at all of late.'

'None at all?' Isabella frowned. 'Why is that?'

'Well, I have my work on the farm to do ... and in the evenings I prefer to spend my quiet time writing in my diary.'

'Writing in your diary? Isn't that a bit like talking to yourself?'

Beth smiled. 'I suppose it is. I do it because I like to *remember* things.'

'What kind of things?'

'Special things ... words, voices, the *way* something happened, or the *way* something was said. Sometimes, I just write down my own thoughts and read them again at a later time.'

'I'm reading the most wonderful book at the moment,' Isabella said smiling, and her face seemed to come alive at the thought of it.

'It's all about this handsome young viscount who absolutely *detests* his father and so he leaves home and takes a voyage to China where he meets this beautiful Chinese girl, but because he cannot marry her and bring her home to his father's estate, not with her being a foreign Oriental, he stays in China and takes her to live with him as his *concubine.*'

She clutched Beth's arm and looked at her with a grin of absolute delight. 'Isn't that *shocking?*'

Beth looked at her. 'Did he never come back?'

'Well, that's where it all gets very *dramatic,* when his father arrives in Shanghai and starts looking for him ...'

The story went on and on and was hard to follow because Isabella kept skipping back to the bits she had forgotten to tell, and then raced on again ...

Beth's mind began to wander as she gazed vaguely at the scenery all around her ... a smile of pleasure coming on her face, but it was not because of anything Isabella had said, it was because she was thinking of the sheepdog puppy that was birthed two days ago by the collie that Robbie had been mated with ...

The most adorable little black and white puppy, all sleepy-eyed and cuddly, but Beth had known instinctively, when he kept opening one eye to look at her, that *he* was the *one* to be chosen from the litter to eventually replace Robbie's work with the sheep. *He* was the one that would one day have the *mesmerising eye* that would hypnotise the sheep and keep them under his control.

They had turned back towards the house, strolling across the bluebell field ... and Isabella was still telling her story, engrossed in the telling of it, the reliving of it, until Beth realised that Isabella had not left her novelette books behind her at all.

Isabella had not seen a bird fly, nor looked up at the sun slanting down the green hills, nor looked at the clearness of the pale blue sky, nor heard the tweets of the lovely birdsong all around her.

Beth sighed, and then consoled herself with the thought: 'Oh, well, at least her body has had some exercise and her lungs have had a good dose of cleansing fresh air.'

But other than that ... other than that she felt very sorry for Isabella, and wished that Lachlan would pay more attention to her.

Chapter Thirty-One

On Saturday morning Mr Dewar arrived in Tobermory to take a look at the house on Main Street.

At one o'clock Mr Macintyre, the bank manager who was acting as agent for the property, rushed into the Tobermory Inn full of apologies for his delay.

'The bank, ye see,' he said to John, 'it's our busiest time on a Saturday morning, and we close at twelve, but this morning we had a fisherman who did not appear to know his shillings from his sixpences or his crowns from his half crowns and the amount of recounting delayed our clerk for some considerable time before I could close up and come to ye.'

'That's all right,' John responded. 'We are in no hurry.'

'Now look here,' said John's father. 'You look to me like a man who has been badly pushed this morning, so will you not take a breather and have a wee dram before we go to look at the inside of the house?'

Mr Macintyre hesitated. 'Well, perhaps a wee one would restore me.'

He sat down wearily. 'But I canna delay too long. My daughter and husband are coming to visit this afternoon and I promised my wife that I would not be late home.'

'I'll see to it,' John said to his father, glad of the delay, because Beth had still not arrived.

After placing the drink on the table for Mr Macintyre he walked to the door of the inn and stepped outside, looking towards the road that led from Gruline ... but no sight of her.

Strange. She was usually so punctual and reliable, and although his letter had said to meet at the inn at eleven, he had half expected her to turn up at half ten or thereabouts.

'So you've seen the outside of the house then?' Mr Macintyre was saying as he returned to the table.

'Yes, and I like the look of it,' his father replied. 'It's a fair size and the windows have a good view of the sea and the harbour.'

An hour later, after Mr Macintyre had enjoyed three wee

drams, he decided it was time that they *must* now view the house, but he was cheerful: 'I'll tell the wife I had people up from Edinburgh to view it and they took a long time, so when we go inside – will ye no' take *too* long about it.'

'One look up and down will tell me if it's right,' Mr Dewar assured him. 'But it's the young couple that need to be satisfied with it, more than me.'

'The young couple?' Mr Macintyre looked at John.

'She must have been delayed,' John explained, 'but we'll hold you up no longer, let's get it done.'

As they left the inn, John took another look back in the direction of Gruline but all he saw was an old man driving a cart down the road.

*

At Jarvisfield, Beth had changed from her riding habit into a white dimity summer dress with a red sash around the waist, and then she exchanged her ankle-high riding boots for walking shoes. Her planned ride to Tobermory would now have to be a long walk.

'Are you still going?' Mary asked when Beth came back down to the kitchen.

'Yes, I'm still going. How would it look if I did not arrive, after Mr Dewar has travelled all the way from Edinburgh to see the house.'

'You have already seen the house, so why is it so important that *you* be there today when he views it.'

'I wanted to see his face when he looked around the rooms and *see* for myself if he would be happy there, never mind his words. He might *pretend* he likes it just to make John happy, but that would not bode well for the future.'

'It's quite bad of Lachlan and Mary Campbell to take the horses again.' Mary said. 'That's almost every day this week.'

'Aye and that Mary Campbell is a bare-faced liar,' Mrs Keillor put in. 'I watched her standing there – right there,' she pointed, 'assuring Beth that she would have the mare back in less than an hour, but I could see from her cheeky face that she had no intention of doing so.'

'Did you?' Beth looked at Mrs Keillor. 'I did not see that. I believed her.'

'Ah, well ...' Mrs Keillor winked an eye. 'That's because ye are no' as old nor as wise as me, Beth, no' by half.'

'And she *knew* that I had an important appointment in Tobermory today,' Beth said indignantly. 'So why would she lie to me?'

'Because she's a born liar,' said Mrs Keillor. 'And God knows what lies she has told the master to get him wrapped around her little finger the way she has.'

'Oh don't be fooled,' Mary said. 'There's not a female alive that could wrap *him* around her finger, not anymore.'

'Well she's making a fair job of it to me.' Mrs Keillor observed, folding her arms across her wide bosom. 'Still, I suppose the *good* thing is that all this riding around the estate gets her out of *our* way for a few hours every day.'

Beth said: It's over three hours since they left. I cannot wait any longer.'

As she walked to the door, Mary said anxiously, 'But, darling, it's a *nine* mile walk to Tobermory.'

'And I have not seen John for over *two* weeks!' Beth returned with emotion in her voice. 'Mama, can you not understand how *hard* it has been – not being able to see him or speak to him for so long?'

After a pause, Mary relented. 'I do understand, sweetheart, I do.'

And she did understand, remembering when she was young herself and the tormented bouts of love and longing she suffered when George was away on a tour with General Macquarie in Van Diemen's Land, or up country in the Blue Mountains. And even sometimes when he was away for only a few days, yet to her it had felt like a century had passed before his return.

'Could she not have gone to Tobermory in the trap?' Mrs Keillor asked when Beth had gone.

'Hector is out in the trap, gone to see his father in Salen.'

Mary sat down at the table, clasping her hands together on its wooden surface.

Mrs Keillor leaned forward, her eyes shrewd. 'Tell me, hen, why did you try to stop her from going today?'

Mary shrugged. 'Nine miles is a long walk for anyone.'

'Is it no' because ye are a wee bit jealous that his father will be living in the house with them?'

Mary smiled weakly. 'I am a bit.'

'Only natural when ye have cared for her from the day she was born.'

'It's more than that,' Mary admitted. 'I may as well tell you … my constant anxiety and *worry* about Beth started on the first day we arrived in Scotland. I knew that as she grew up the Scottish people would see her as being different to them, more foreign than the English … and my God, when we first arrived here they treated *me* like I was the daughter of some hated foreign enemy, just because I was *English.*'

'Aye, well, we still have a bone or two to pick with the English,' Mrs Keillor responded darkly. 'They've no' been fair to the Scottish people nor to Scotland. Treating us like we were a people no' as good as them.'

'And that's exactly how I did *not* want Beth to be treated by the Scottish people, as not as good as them.'

'And she hasna been!' Mrs Keillor defended. 'Everyone on Jarvisfield loves Beth, and how much more proof do ye need of that?'

'Yes, but I did not know that back then. How could I know? And so from back then my worrying about her became a habit … a habit I have never been able to lose.'

'Well it's time ye did lose it. Ye have to try and let go of the strings now, hen, because if she sees ye are jealous, even a wee bit, of his father living with them, it could lead to resentment against the father later on.'

'No! No.' Mary was quite certain. 'Beth would never feel like that, it's not in her nature.'

'Her nature is to love her mother first, so don't make it hard for her. Don't make her feel in the future that she is favouring one over the other.'

'I know Beth better than you. She will love John's father because she loves John. And even if, in time, she grows to love his father for himself, irrespective of John, I know that love will never come close to her love for me.'

'So why are you crying?'

'Am I?' Mary had not felt the tears slipping down her face. She wiped a hand over her eyes. 'No, you have it all wrong. I'm happy she will have someone in the house for company when John is away at work. And I could never, ever, leave Jarvisfield, because this is my home, and George is here, Elizabeth too.'

'And me?'

'And you. And Hector – even though he drives me mad at times: and Maggie and Lorna and all the farmboys. But most of all, I could never leave my other child, the one who worries me the most.'

'Who?'

'Lachlan ... at the end Elizabeth entrusted him to my care, made me promise that I would always look after him. And I have been doing that, and I will keep on doing it. He's still my golden boy, as bad as he is at times.'

Mrs Keillor sat back and frowned. 'Well, I have to tell ye, Mary, something I feel ye should know. He's no' a child, and he's no' a boy, golden or otherwise – he was *thirty* in April gone.'

Chapter Thirty-Two

'Now, you do understand,' said Mr Macintyre, 'that it is only the *lease* of the house you will be purchasing. The land on which the house has been built will still be owned by the Duke of Argyll.'

'How long is the lease?' John asked.

'Ninety-nine years.'

Mr Dewar looked at his son. 'Ninety-nine years? Well that's long enough for me. What about you?'

John smiled. 'I reckon ninety-nine years will be long enough for us too.'

'Of course,' Mr Macintyre added, 'when the term of the lease comes to an end, a renewal for another ninety-nine years would most likely be possible.'

'In the case of any children or descendants living here,' John said.

'Aye, that's correct. Some leases go back for centuries and are renewed time and time again. Now, I have the papers here, do you want to sign them and pay a deposit to secure the property?'

'Aye we do,' said Mr Dewar. 'And the property will be in both names, my son's and mine. It's my only security against young Beth throwing me out with the rubbish when she gets fed up with me.'

Mr Macintyre was eager to rush off. He shook both men's hand and said to each in turn. 'A pleasure doing business with you, a pleasure.'

When he had gone, Mr Dewar said to John. 'I hope you don't intend to put me in one of those bedrooms on the top floor. It would be cruel to my knees.'

John was surprised. 'I thought you would prefer the four rooms on the top floor. The windows are bigger, the rooms are brighter, and it has its own bathroom up there.'

'Up all those stairs to the third floor? You must be jesting with me again.'

'It's the *second* floor. This is the ground floor and the one above it is the first floor. There's no *third* floor, no three flights of stairs only two, so don't exaggerate the difficulty.'

'Oh, I'm not exaggerating. I'm merely saying that I would prefer my bedroom not to be so close to the clouds.'

'You've never had an aversion to high rooms before.'

'No, but to be honest with you, son, when the three of us *do* move in here, well ... I don't want to be left stuck up there feeling like the old man in the attic.'

'Then choose whatever bedroom you want. Beth and I will have the rooms on the top floor – the *second* floor.'

'Easier for you two than for me.'

John couldn't help smiling. 'At times you talk as if you are seventy-five, not fifty-five.'

'Son, at times I *feel* seventy-five. I've been working almost every day since I was fifteen, and now I've had enough of it.' He walked to one of the front windows and looked out. 'But I have a feeling now that this place is going to rejuvenate me and bring me back to life. I might even get myself a fishing boat. What do you think about that?'

John was looking at his fob watch ... almost three ... and still no sign of Beth.

At half past three, inside the inn, while his father was busily talking to Angus and Lizzie McLeod, he looked at his watch again, and decided to take another look outside.

Still no sign of her. A slight frown crossed his eyes, wondering if the Laird of Jarvisfield had deliberately detained her.

He decided to take a walk in the direction of the lane that he knew she would ride her horse along into Tobermory.

At the top of the lane he continued walking down, past the Pine trees and then past an old cottage that had a large brown dog stretched in sleep across its doorstep.

He paused and gave a short whistle to the dog. The dog opened his eyes for a moment, lifted his head and looked at him, then flopped his head back down and closed his eyes again, not interested.

He shrugged and turned to walk on, but then he saw her slim figure in the distance, coming round from another belt of trees, wearing a white summer dress with a slash of red around her waist.

Her head was lowered, as if in deep thought. He moved to sit on the low garden wall of the cottage and wait for her, watching her.

And as he did he realised, yet again, that it was only *her* he wanted, Elizabeth Jarvis, not some pink-cheeked pretty miss from behind the red velvet curtains of Edinburgh, nor the most seductive houri that Casablanca could provide, and not even – as some sad sailors still believed and hoped for – the most voluptuous mermaid with golden hair that might arise out of a large seashell floating on the water.

No, only *her,* Elizabeth Jarvis.

He smiled as he thought of the sailors looking for the illusory mermaids, something that was obviously encouraged by the Admiralty and owners of all ships – because most ships had a large sculpture on their bowsprit of half a woman with long flowing hair and her naked breasts thrust out to the wind. And as she had no lower half, most sailors believed that she *must* be a replica of the mermaids floating around in large seashells somewhere – if *only* they could find one.

At least *he* wasn't that stupid. And when it came to city girls or houris or mermaids, Beth could outdo them all. She had the most beautiful golden breasts with very dark nipples, and now he couldn't wait to get hold of her.

And now she had lifted her head and seen him. He smiled and moved off the wall to go and meet her as she began to quicken her steps and run towards him, rushing breathlessly into his arms, smiling her delight. '*Nineteen days,*' she said, 'but it has felt like *forever!*'

'And ever and ever,' he replied, swinging her round into the enclosure of some trees where he took the opportunity to kiss her in private, knowing there would be little chance back at the inn with his father and the McLeods around.

She moved to lean back against the trunk of the tree, pulling him with her, but missed her footing and fell back against it, causing all the branches to shake as he steadied her.

She looked up. 'What was that?'

'What?'

'Something fell past your arm ... don't move.'

Her eyes searched the ground around them, and then widened as she gave a little cry and pointed to the ground beside him. 'Look ... oh the poor little thing!'

She crouched to the ground and then rose slowly, holding in her cupped hands a small motionless bird.

'My fall against the tree ... it must have knocked her out of the nest and now she's stunned. But she's alive, her heart is still beating because I can see and feel her body pumping.'

'Is it a baby bird?'

'No, it's just a *small* bird. It's a female chaffinch.'

He looked closer at the bird. 'How do you know it's a female?'

'Because I can *see* it's a female – greenish brown. The breast of the male chaffinch is a brickish red colour.'

She ran her finger gently down the bird's pulsing body as if to comfort it, and John had to smile as he watched her. This was the tender girl his father feared might one day throw him out with the rubbish.

'What are you going to do with it?'

She looked up to the nest, halfway up the tree, nestling inside a fork of branches.

'The nest is up there. We really should try and put her back.'

He stared at her. 'You want to put her back in the nest?'

'It's the best thing to do. If we leave her here unconscious she could be eaten alive by stray cats. And it would be *my* fault.'

He looked at the small bird again. 'Are you sure she will recover if she is put back in the nest?'

'I can't be sure, but if she comes round in her own environment, her own nest ... and her mate must be flying around somewhere.'

'Maybe it was not *you* who made her fall. Maybe it was her mate who kicked her out of the nest.'

'No!' she laughed. 'Birds are very loyal to each other. They mate only once and they stay with each other for life. And when one dies the other dies soon after.'

'Oh, well, in that case ...' he said, carefully taking the bird into his own hands and placing it in the pocket of his jacket.

Beth had an immediate change of heart – 'No, John, it's very high... maybe we can make a little nest for her in the bushes ... '

But he was gone, climbing the tree easily and lightly, using the jutting branches as steps. At the nest she watched him holding with one hand as he carefully lifted the bird out of his pocket and placed her back inside the shell of grass and green leaves; and then began the climb down again.

When he jumped back onto the ground he looked at her wryly and said, 'The things I do for you, Miss Jarvis!'

Beth held a hand over her mouth, smiling. 'I did not expect you to go up so fast, and it's so *high!*'

He looked up to where the nest was clearly visible. 'Beth, do you know how high the topmast on a ship is?

'No.'

'Fifty foot high on most ships, and I spent years regularly climbing up and down the rigging as a midshipman, and still occasionally have to do it now when necessary. But I did *not* expect to have to do any climbing today.'

She stood looking at him, smiling, her eyes flirting with him.

'That's a dangerous thing to do,' he warned her, bending down to wipe his hands clean on the grass. And then he suddenly realised – 'Where's your horse? Why did you not ride here?'

She had stopped smiling, stopped flirting.

'I decided to walk.'

'He rose and looked at her, questioningly. 'You walked all the way from Jarvisfield – why?'

'All the horses were out ... and I wanted to come today.'

'A nine or ten mile walk – just to see the house again?'

'No, to see *you,* just you.' She looked at him with serious dark eyes. 'I don't care about the house, any house. I would be happy to live in a shack, if you lived in it too.'

He looked at her silently, and then smiled. 'Then come ...' he said quietly, taking her hand. 'Let's go and see our shack.'

Bewildered, she walked with him. 'Is the agent still there?'

'No, he's gone.'

'So how will we get inside the house?'

'Very easily,' John grinned, taking some keys from his pocket and jingling them in front of her.

'Would you believe ... when I put that stunned little bird in my pocket, I felt some keys that I didn't know were still there.'

'The keys to the house?'

'Yes. Mr Macintyre was in such a rush to get home he forgot to ask for the keys back, and I did not realise I still had them until a few minutes ago.'

'Honestly?'

'Honestly. I'm not devious.'

She smiled. 'So the little chaffinch has already repaid the favour?'

'The favour of you knocking her out of the tree?'

'No, the favour of *you* putting her back.'

He stopped walking and looked at her candidly. 'Beth ... my love, my angel, my *beautiful* ... I will not know if she has returned any favour at all, until if and when we get inside the house, and if and when you allow me to ravish you.'

She was smiling, her eyes flirting with him again. 'That would be nice,' she answered, 'because I would very much like to ravish you. And we are *half* married.'

'Which half?'

'Remember – Calgary Bay – our *handfasting,* the way they marry in Gretna Green?'

'Oh yes ... oh well then, say no more and lets get on our way.'

They had walked only a few steps when she stopped again, her eyes raised upwards, her ears listening. 'Did you hear that?'

'Hear what?'

'Listen.'

He listened ... and heard a *'pink... pink'* sound, like the fall of raindrops ... *'pink ... pink ...'*

Beth turned back to look at the tree, a huge smile on her face. 'She's awake – she's conscious again.'

A small *squeak* followed another *'pink ... pink'* sound, followed by a long *trilll.*

'She's calling for help.'

Seconds later a red flash flew above them as her mate returned twirping frantically – '*twooo-eee twooo-eee.*'

John was amazed. He had been sure the bird was on her way to dead, not just stunned, and he had agreed to put the bird back in the nest simply to indulge Beth and make her feel less guilty.

'Do you understand *all* the sounds that birds make?' he asked as they walked on.

'Yes, most of them. For instance, the "*pink ... pink*" sound is the female chaffinch's natural call. The *squeak* sound is the chaffinch's injury call, and the *trillll* is the call for assistance.'

He pretended to listen in a serious way as she explained and trilled all the different bird calls while they walked on towards Tobermory's Main Street.

'When the female chaffinch wants to call the others in the flock to prepare for flight, she makes a "*tupe-tupe*" sound. And then the *male* chaffinch's alarm call to warn other chaffinches of a predator, such as a hawk or an owl is – "*huip! ... huip!*" '

All the twirps and trills sounded exactly the same to him, and when they reached Main Street he was glad to see that neither his father nor the McLeods were anywhere near the entrance or windows of the Tobermory Inn.

Less than a minute later, when they had reached the house, Beth didn't seem to notice, her mind still up in the air.

'All small birds really speak the same language and understand each other,' she explained.

He inserted the key into the lock and opened the door of the house, standing back for her to enter.

'So when a robin sees a cat on the prowl,' she said, walking into the hall, 'the robin gives a loud "*tic-tic*" call to warn all the other small birds.'

He shut the door and stood with his back leaning against it, twirling the keys in his hand.

'Beth, tell me,' he said, 'that bird you nearly killed and I saved ...'

She turned and looked at him. 'The female chaffinch?'

'Yes ... what sound does she make when she wants to let

her mate know that she is ready to copulate with him?'

She stared at him, a startled expression in her eyes, as if he had said something very wicked.

Oh, John ... ' she blinked. 'Surely you know that only animals and birds *copulate?*'

'I do know. That's why I used that word and why I am asking about the birds. You have me *captivated* with interest in all the little sounds they make.'

And then she saw his grin, a very wicked grin, and realised he was not being serious.

She tried not to smile, but he had changed her thoughts and changed her mood and she gave no resistance when he caught her to him and kissed her.

His hands moved over the length of her silky black hair falling down her back, almost to her waist, then closed around her body, holding her tighter and feeling her quiver. Her lips parted under his, welcoming his hunger, their tongues dancing, their hands clutching tighter.

She suddenly drew her mouth away, and he could plainly see the struggle that was going on in her mind, in her eyes.

'I want to,' she breathed shakily. 'I *desperately* want to, I love you so much, but not here, not in an empty house.'

There was silence.

'Not until this house is *our home.*'

He did not speak for some seconds, and then he smiled. 'So what sound does she make?'

'The chaffinch?'

'The female.'

She smiled with him, her lips moving close to his lips, saying softly, 'The sound she makes is "*seeeep*".'

'Oh I like that sound, it's very seductive, say it again.'

'No.'

'You are very cruel.'

She put her fingers lightly on his lips. 'If you want to hear it again you will have to book me a room in the Toberymory Inn, because I will be too tired to walk all the way back to Jarvisfield tonight.'

'I'll do that, of course I will ... but only if you promise that as soon as dinner is over, you will complain of a pain in your neck or your back and retire to your room early.'

'And then?'

'And then I'll plead a crushing headache and be reluctantly forced to retire also.' He grinned. 'And then we can "*seeeep*" together.'

'Will you father not be disappointed if we leave him early?'

'God, no! He is so wrapped up in his new friends the McLeods, he will not even notice we are gone.'

And John had not been exaggerating, because down the street in the Tobermory Inn, Mr Dewar had not even noticed that his son had been absent for almost an hour, until John and Beth entered a short time later and he looked with surprise at Beth.

'Oh, my dear ... ' he immediately rose to his feet. 'Here you are at last ...'

Beth greeted her future father-in-law with a smile and a small kiss on the cheek, which seemed to please him.

He stepped back and looked at her. 'By! You've changed, lass, all grown up now. You were only about seventeen when I last saw you.'

'Eighteen,' Beth said. 'I'm twenty-one now.'

'Older and even bonnier.' He turned to Lizzie and Angus. 'This bonnie girl is soon going to be my daughter-in-law.'

'Not until the banns are put up,' Lizzie said, flashing an impatient look at John. 'So when *are* they going to be put up?'

John rubbed his eye. 'They went up in our local church in Edinburgh a few days ago.'

'*Did* they?' Lizzie turned surprised eyes to Angus, but then shot a suspicious leer at John. 'So why are ye rubbing yer eye? People only do that when they're lying.'

'Oh, he's not lying,' Mr Dewar said. 'He gave me all the details and asked me to do it for him, which I did, three days ago.'

'So they *are* up?'

'Indeed they are,' replied Mr Dewar. 'At our end anyway.'

Lizzie turned back to John, who appeared offended. 'There was a speck of something in my eye.'

'Oh now, oh now ...' Lizzie said, eager to make amends and

moving towards him, 'Will I dab it with some water for ye? Here, let me look at it?'

'No, no.' John moved her hand away. 'It's fine now ... but Beth will need a room tonight. She has walked all the way from Jarvisfield.'

Lizzie turned to Beth. 'Walked! All that way?'

Beth shrugged, unable to understand John and Lizzie's concern about her walking here.

'It's not *too* long a walk,' she said. 'Not when you consider that some of our farm hands walk six miles to work every day, and six miles home again.'

'It makes me *shrivel* just to think of it!' Lizzie declared. 'And so what about *your* banns, Beth? Here in Tobermory? Are they done yet?'

'Tomorrow,' Beth smiled. 'Now that I know John has done his banns in Edinburgh, I will visit the Rector and do mine here tomorrow.'

'So she will need a room here for a few nights,' John put in quickly. 'And she's very tired.'

'Aye,' Lizzie nodded. 'And who could blame her feeling tired after a walk that long. I'll go and see to it now.'

'And myself?' Mr Dewar added. 'Do you have a nice room for me also, Mrs McLeod?'

'I do, Mr Dewar, I certainly do. And when will ye be returning to Edinburgh?'

'Monday, and the first thing I will have to do is inform Mortimer's of my retirement, and then sort out all the furniture in my house; which pieces will be shipped up here and which pieces will be left for whoever takes the house.' He sighed. 'But for now, and all day tomorrow, all I want to do is relax.'

'And this is the place to do it.' Lizzie smiled fondly at him. 'And lookit now – because ye are going to become a close neighbour, just a flit down the street – for the two nights ye are here, I'll be charging ye only *half* the price for the room.'

Angus looked at his wife sharply, and then followed her out to the passage.

'What's this, what's this – *half* the price? I've never known ye to do that before, Lizzie.' He narrowed his eyes suspiciously. 'Now ye're not getting a fancy for Mr Dewar, are ye, Lizzie, because I canna allow it.'

Lizzie laughed, surprised and elated by his jealousy.

'The only Dewar I have a fancy for,' she replied mischievously, 'is the *younger* one – I could *eat* him alive and smack my lips afterwards – but he's bespoken now to Beth so it's eyes-off. And Mr Dewar the father, well, he is still pining for his dear wife, so ...' she gave a huge and sad sigh, 'so I'll just have to keep making do with ye. Angus, won't I?'

'Ye will,' Angus replied, his eyes narrowing jealously again. 'Oh, I can see I'm going to have to keep my eye on ye, girl, ye were alus a flighty little piece.'

'*Little*, did ye say, Angus ... *little?*' Lizzie's fat body shook with such a big and happy laugh it could be heard all the way up to the top floor of the Tobermory Inn.

Chapter Thirty-Three

Five weeks later, Beth and John Dewar were married in the parish church of Tobermory.

Beth was dressed in a slender flowing gown of blue silk; the skirt and the facings on the bodice were covered in a fine net of white lace. The dress had been designed and made for her within a week by the groom's father. She wore her hair long and smooth as always, but on her head she wore an entwined wreath of white flowers, which she had made herself.

As John was still officially an officer of the Royal Navy, he followed protocol and wore his lieutenant's dress uniform.

Mary sat in the front row with tears in her eyes as she listened to John and Beth making their vows in front of Reverend McAulay, thinking how happy George would have been to see their daughter now. She was marrying a good man, of that Mary was certain.

'Oh, she looks so bonnie,' Mrs Keillor whispered, dabbing a handkerchief to her eye.

'Beautiful,' Mary answered.

Lizzie McLeod was beaming victoriously as she turned and whispered to the Dewar family of Salen sitting in the pew behind her: 'I alus knew he would marry her.'

Apart from the bride's mother and the groom's father, the only witnesses to the event were supposed to be Kirsty Dewar, who had insisted on being Beth's bridesmaid; Mrs Keillor; Angus and Lizzie McLeod; the Dewar family of Salen; and Maggie Kennedy and Lorna McLaughlin who had also insisted on being bridesmaids, much to Kirsty's annoyance.

A small, private ceremony was the intention, but on the day more than half of the residents of Gruline and Salen turned up at the church. The lands of Jarvisfield had been left deserted, all eager to be there at the wedding and wish their beloved Beth all the happiness in the world.

John had stubbornly refused to allow the wedding to take place at the house in Jarvisfield.

Lachlan had stubbornly refused to attend the wedding, because he insisted that on that day he had "important business in Edinburgh", although it was a Sunday.

Mary Campbell and Isabella were happy to attend and have a jolly day out, dressed in their best, until they reached the outside of the church and saw that all the locals from the lower class had turned up as well.

Isabella immediately ordered Hector to turn the trap around and go back home.

Hector was so furious he drove the trap back over the bumpiest ground he could find, making the two sisters jolt and jump in discomfort, and later told Mrs Keillor that he had wanted to dump the trap and the two sisters into the sea for making him miss the wedding and the party after it.

Four hours later John and Beth left the crowd in the Tobermory Inn behind and caught the evening ferry to the mainland to begin their honeymoon.

In the dining room, Lizzie McLeod curiously asked John's father: 'Where are they going? I asked the groom but he – as usual – wouldna tell me.'

Mr Dewar sat back with his brandy. 'Well what he told me, was that he wanted to take her on a slow boat to China, but she told him that she has always wanted to see Loch Lomond and would prefer to go there instead, so that is where he has taken her.'

'It's beautiful around Loch Lomond,' Mary said. 'Miles and miles of the most breathtaking scenery, and there are many nice inns along that route. Beth will love it.'

'And it's in our own bonny Scotland,' Mr Dewar smiled. 'So much nicer than China.'

This was the first day that John's father and Beth's mother had met each other. They were getting on well together, until Mr Dewar said to Mary, 'Did young Beth tell you that many years ago I met your husband, George Jarvis?'

Mary's blue eyes stared in shock. 'George? *You* met my George? But how can that be?'

'Did Beth not tell you?'

'No, it must be one of the many things Beth keeps to herself – or as she calls them – her secret little treasures.'

So Mr Dewar told her how and when and all the details, and then he told her all about John's mother, his beloved wife, and after that a bond of fond friendship was forged between them.

Out in the taproom, Mrs Keillor was dancing with Robert Dewar while his wife looked on laughing. Maggie Kennedy was dancing with Lorna.

Kirsty Dewar was dancing with Ewan MacPherson, the young postmaster of Tobermory who seemed entranced with her, and Kirsty with him, both of them blushing shyly.

But now that the newlyweds had left – the main topic of conversation between the locals was the puzzlement of – 'Why did the Laird of Jarvisfield not attend the wedding? Surely it was his duty? Why did he not give her away?'

It was a question that was still being asked between one local and another for many days later.

PART FOUR

Chapter Thirty-Four

A week after the marriage, while Lachlan was still away in Edinburgh or Strathallan or wherever he had taken himself to avoid Beth's wedding, Mary made an alarming discovery.

She came down from upstairs to the kitchen, her face pale as she looked at Mrs Keillor.

'Do you remember what you were said to me a few weeks ago ... that you thought Lachlan may have married the wrong sister?'

'Aye, but it was just in jest, all the horse riding they do together. Why, what's up?'

'I think he's been *sleeping* with the wrong sister.'

'What?' Mrs Keillor's eyes popped wide. 'No! That canna be! I know he's reckless but ...'

Mary opened her hand and showed Mrs Keillor the gold hair ring in her hand. 'I found this in his bed.'

Mrs Keillor stood up to take a peer at the ring. 'Aye, that's hers ... Mary Campbell's ... she alus wears that gold ring in her hair.'

Mary snapped her hand shut. 'It's not *real* gold, it's a cheap imitation. She has six or seven of them on the dresser in her room.'

'But ... but he's been away for over a week.'

'And I change his bed linen *every* week. So this must have got there sometime in the days just before he went away.'

'By!' glared Mrs Keillor. 'The deceitful hussy! Slipping into bed with her sister's husband.'

'Now this is not proof, not definite proof ...' Mary warned, sitting down at the table, her hands trembling. 'So I'll say nothing to her, and I'll not judge him beforehand— not until I ask him for an explanation as soon as he gets back.'

'What other explanation can there be? *Her* hair adornment in *his* bed.'

'I don't *want* to believe it,' Mary answered. 'The two of them ... and Isabella just across the landing. But if they *have* been carrying on ... why have I not seen the signs? There *must* have been some signs, so why did I not see them?'

'Tis because all women are blind as bats to all but themselves,' said Hector, who had been sitting outside the kitchen door whittling away at a piece of wood with his knife.

Mary jumped to her feet. 'Hector! For God's sake! How long have you been out there? How much did you hear?'

'Nothing I didna know,' Hector shrugged. 'I could've told ye about those two more'n three weeks past.'

'How? Why?'

'Because *I'm* no' blind like ye. I've more time in ma day to look around. And I seen the two of 'em down by the loch, standing by one of the trees and they was kissing – but it was *she* that was doing all the kissing, putting her hands all over him, behaving like a female animal in heat she was.'

Hector looked at the gold ring Mary had earlier placed on the table. 'So she's been in his bed, has she? That's a sin ... a bigger sin than just kissing ... and a biggerer sin than that ... because he's already got one wife. He canna have two. Tis against the law.'

Mary grabbed Hector's free hand urgently in both of her own. 'Now listen to me, Hector, listen to me. Promise me you will not say a word about this to anyone – not *anyone,* do you understand? It could bring shame on our house, shame on the laird, shame on all of us.'

'No' shame on *me*. I've did nothing bad.'

'No, you're a good man, Hector and I want you to stay a good man – by keeping your mouth shut. This is something that must be kept private and sorted out amongst the family in private. And *you* are one of the family.'

'Aye, I am, and have been for nigh on twenty years.'

'So now you must protect the name of the family, and protect the laird. He has been good to you all these years. Feeding you and paying you and keeping you in a job you love, taking care of the horses.'

'Aye ...' Hector frowned. 'But what about the sin? Are ye no' going to talk to him about it and tell him to stop sinning?'

'Yes, I will speak to him, and it *will* stop, I promise you.'

'What about *her*? Are ye going to talk to her? She should be sent back to where she came from. She's a bad 'un.'

'I will speak to her ... but not yet, not until the laird returns. Until then, Hector, *no one* must hear a word about this – especially Isabella.'

Mrs Keillor stood up, eager to get rid of Hector. 'Now, me handsome,' she said cajolingly. 'How would it be if I cut you a thick piece of bread and spread some fresh yellow butter on it, and on top of the butter a few slices of cold pork. Would ye like that, eh?'

Hector's mouth was instantly watering. 'And a ring of onion?'

'*Two* rings of onion,' Mrs Keillor agreed indulgently. 'Now ye get back to yer work in the stables and I'll bring the plate out to ye.'

'I've done all me work.'

'Then do it again! I need space to cut the bread and prepare your plate and I canna do it with ye in the way.'

Hector looked around the large kitchen full of space, but now that his mind had been turned to food he could think of nothing else.

'The sooner ye go, the sooner I'll have it ready for ye,' Mrs Keillor said, knowing Hector so well. 'Go on, me handsome, off ye go.'

He was gone in a flash. Mrs Keillor quickly cut the bread and made him a nice plate to keep him occupied for a while, and took it out to the stables.

When she returned to the kitchen she shut the door and slammed over the bolts at the top and the bottom to make sure it stayed shut.

She turned and looked at Mary. 'Now what was *that* all about? Ye'll speak to him and ye'll speak to her and the laird *must* be protected? Are ye not going to give him some hard rebukes for his behaviour?'

Mary slowly shook her head, unable to believe that Mrs Keillor had forgotten so quickly.

'It was *you* who carried the news to me,' she said angrily. 'So are you now *forgetting* that Lachlan has been challenging and taking on all the clerics on the island and now even many of the *people* are annoyed with him. And rightly so, because he has been challenging the very foundation of their existence, their faith in *God*.'

'Oh, aye, the clerics ...' Mrs Keillor said slowly, now realising the danger.

'If a word of this gets out it will be like throwing bait to a shoal of sharks – the clerics will snap it up and use it to *destroy* him.'

'Aye,' Mrs Keillor nodded her head worriedly. 'They'll call him out from the pulpit as an adulterer. My God ... they will *slaughter* him.'

'Not if no one finds out.' Mary answered.

'What about Hector?'

'Hector has known about it for weeks and has said not a whisper to us. Hector can be trusted in some things.' Mary sighed. 'But you will have to keep feeding him treats and keeping him happy until all this blows over.'

'I will,' Mrs Keillor agreed determinedly. 'I'll cook Hector all his favourite dishes and give him more than enough on his plate, along with his apple pies and jam tarts and his favourite syllabubs. He'll be so content with so much good food in his belly that he'll start to wonder if he has died and gone to Paradise.'

With a wave of relief, Mary stood up and gave Mrs Keillor a small appreciative kiss on the cheek. 'You're a love,' she said. 'What would I do without you?'

Mrs Keillor flushed and gave an embarrassed little chuckle: such demonstrations of affection from Mary were usually reserved solely for Beth.

'I know what ye'd do, hen,' she replied, walking over to her oven. 'Ye'd starve!'

*

About a week later, when the laird had still not returned to Jarvisfield, Hector's joy and contentment with life, due to all the plentiful good food and pampering he was now receiving from Mrs Keillor, was suddenly brought to an end by a stinging shock.

As Hector's contentment had increased, Mary Campbell's had vanished altogether, her mood grumpy and irritable.

While Mary was dusting the drawing-room, Isabella's

sister began a litany of complaints to her about Isabella.

'Isabella has *always* been such a wet fish. Do you not find her so?'

Mary kept on dusting and gave no answer.

'I do believe that the people in her books are more real to her than even *I* am. Do you know, I went into her bedroom the other night and caught her in rivers of tears, and all because one of the silly women in the book she was reading had suffered some calamity of the heart.'

After another silence, the girl asked grumpily, 'Mrs Jarvis, can you *hear* me talking to you?'

'Yes, but I'm busy.'

'Do you know when Lachlan is coming back?'

'No.'

Another silence, then the girl gave a heavy sigh and flounced out of the room. Mary could hear her going up the stairs and across the landing to her bedroom.

Ten minutes later she came downstairs again dressed in her riding habit and carrying her crop.

'Mrs Jarvis, I'm going out for a short ride.'

Mary still gave no answer, finding it difficult to even look at the girl, never mind speak to her.

Out in the stables Hector was nowhere to be found, so Mary Campbell saddled the gelding herself, brought him out to the yard and began to mount him.

A shout came from the direction of the bluebell field and she turned to see Hector running towards her.

'Ye canna do that!' he said breathlessly as he approached her. 'Ye canna ride the gelding!'

'Why not?'

'Ye must have the master's permission first.'

Mary Campbell smiled, unconcerned. 'Oh, I'm sure he won't mind.'

She pulled herself up into the saddle and began to turn the horse around.

'Nay!' Hector caught hold of the bridle. 'The master'll drown me again if I let ye ride out on MacDuff. Ye can take the mare.'

Mary Campbell glared down at him. 'Who are *you* to tell

449

me what I can or cannot do?'

'Tis orders, from the laird, and I canna disobey him. Tis like I said – if I let ye ride him he'll drown me till I'm soaked for doing it.'

'If you don't take your hands off the bridle, *I* will flay you alive!' she snapped. 'Now get out of my way!'

'Nay, I canna – '

She raised her crop to give Hector a hard lash on the shoulder but the end of the whip slashed across his face and made him stumble back.

He stood staring after her in shock, a hand to his stinging face as she rode off. A moment later he brought down his hand and looked at the red line of blood on his palm.

His anger erupted. Even his own father had never raised a whip to him like that. He rushed into the stables and saddled the mare. 'I'll get her!' he said to the mare. 'I know how to get *her*! She'll no' be able to show her face anywhere in Mull by the time I'm done with her!'

Mrs Keillor came out to the yard as he was mounting. 'What's all the shouting for, Hector ... Oh dear God ...' Her eyes stared at the bloody rip down one side of his face. 'What – how did that happen?'

'*She* did it! The whore of Jarvisfield! Slashed me with her whip and took the gelding. But I know how to get her! She'll no' slash me and get away with it!'

He rode off and left Mrs Keillor standing open mouthed. 'Oh dear God, she muttered nervously, then turned and rushed into the house to find Mary.

'He was seething, Mary, *seething* with rage. In all my years I've never see Hector look like that.'

'And she did that to him?' Mary could scarcely believe it. 'Slashed him with her crop?'

Mrs Keillor nodded. 'The blood was running down his face ... poor Hector.'

'Yes, poor Hector ...' Mary agreed, and then flared up. 'She will have to go. That girl will have to go! She has caused nothing but trouble with the men since she arrived here – sleeping with one and slashing another. She'll have to go – even if I have to throw her out myself.'

450

*

In another part of Mull, in the Dewar's house in Tobermory, discontent was being voiced there also.

John and Beth had only been back from the mainland for four days, yet Mr Dewar decided he had suffered enough, and decided to speak to his son about it.

'Beth is a lovely lass, very easy to live with, and I know you think she is perfect – '

'She is.'

'To you, son, to you – but not to me.'

'Why?'

'Because, now let's be honest, when it comes to the food – the girl cannot *cook* to save her own life, never mind mine! Take this morning's breakfast, for example. Now you *must* have noticed – surely you did – that the porridge was watery, the eggs were as hard as bullets, and the toast was as pale and as limp as a dead man's hand.'

'It was not good, no,' John admitted. 'But she's doing her best. They have a resident cook at Jarvisfield and I don't think Beth had anything to do with the kitchen. The cook did it all.'

'So, as we have *no* adequate cook in residence here, what are we going to do about it?'

John looked thoughtfully at his father. 'Could you not try to be a bit more patient, for a little longer, while she learns?'

'And how long do you think that will take? For her to learn how to cook something eatable?'

'For as long as you patiently waited for Mother to learn how to cook from a book when *she* was first married.'

'Oh, your mother ...' He suddenly sat forward. 'Now here's an idea! Why don't you go and ask Lizzie McLeod to give Beth some lessons in cooking? A wonderful cook is Lizzie McLeod. And she's very fond of Beth, so I'm sure she will agree.'

John sighed. 'I'll ask, but I think you are being unfair. Expecting Beth to be an excellent cook after only four days.'

'Maybe ... yes, maybe, but now here's a solution. You try and keep her lying in the bed with you a little later in the mornings, and *I* will get up and cook the breakfast for us all in future?'

451

John looked dubious. 'Oh, I don't know about that. It's going to be very hard to try and keep her in bed with me a little longer in the mornings.'

'Is it?'

John grinned. 'Don't be dense, man.'

'So you're jesting again.'

'I am.'

'And you'll go and speak to Lizzie? Or do you expect me to cook the dinners as well?'

'I'll go and speak to Lizzie.'

'Today?'

'This *minute,*' John replied impatiently, and moved to leave the room, then suddenly swung around to face his father:

'But don't you let Beth hear or see even a hint of your dissatisfaction with her. She is *my* wife – not *our* servant.'

Chapter Thirty-Five

That same afternoon, at Jarvisfield, after the news of Hector's lashing, Mary had worked furiously to relieve her anger. The surface of every piece of furniture was dusted and polished, all the beds had been changed. The dining table set for the evening supper. Finally she returned to the kitchen and gratefully accepted a cup of tea from Mrs Keillor.

'I've been thinking about Beth and John,' Mary said tiredly. 'They seem to be the only two young people in this family who behave in a normal way. No tantrums. No petty bickering.'

'Aye.'

'And the only two who are happy.'

'Aye, well ...' said Mrs Keillor, 'that's because it was always a true love-match with them, no dowry money involved.'

'I wonder where Hector went? He's been gone a long time.'

Mrs Keillor glanced at the clock. 'No more than an hour or so. No' very long.'

'But I'm wondering *where* he has gone?'

'He's gone chasing after her to get the gelding back. Where else would he go?'

Mary sighed. 'I'd hate to think of him sitting somewhere out there alone, feeling upset and humiliated – being whipped with a crop like a horse. He may *love* his horses, but he would still detest being treated like one.

'Aye, that's true; he canna even bear to see the *horses* being whipped.'

Hector returned with the mare a short time later. He made no attempt to come into the kitchen.

Mrs Keillor stood at the kitchen door and called over to the stables – calling him to come in to her so she could have a look at his wounded face.

'Come on Hector, now ye do as I say.'

Hector was slow in his movements when he approached the kitchen door, his eyes down. Some attempt had been made to clean his face, but the blood was still slowly trickling.

'Oh, let me attend to that wound,' Mary said quickly. 'It needs cleaning and then I'll put some ointment and a strip of lint on to cover it.'

'Nay,' Hector said quietly.

'Yes,' Mary insisted, turning from the sink where she was wetting a flannel. 'If it's not cleaned and covered it will take longer to heal and could leave a deep scar. You don't want that, do you?'

'I'm no' caring about any scar.'

Mrs Keillor was observing Hector's face shrewdly; his eyes were still lowered, his shoulders hunched ... She had known Hector since a he was a small lad and she knew that lowered look, that hunch of the shoulders ... Hector was feeling badly guilty now about something.

'Hector,' she said slowly, 'Hector, what have ye gone and done?'

'I've been to ma father's house ... I told him about *her* ... the whore of Jarvisfield.'

Mrs Keillor frowned. 'Ye told him it was her who hit ye with her crop? Did ye tell him anything else?"

'Aye, I told – ' Hector gulped on his breath, 'I told him about *her* and the laird ... and the sinning they've been doing behind her sister's back.'

Mary dropped the small tin basin of water in her hands.

'Hector, I told you – I *told* you not to tell *anyone* about that.'

'Aye, but my head was all turned back to front with my anger at her *whipping* me.'

'And what did your father say when you told him?' Mary demanded.

'I told him to keep it a secret, aye a *secret!*' Hector insisted. 'And no' to shame this house by telling others. And Father told me no' to worry, that he wouldna tell anyone but the Rector.'

'The Rector at Gruline – one of the clerics that Lachlan has been disagreeing with? Oh dear God...' Mary had to sit down. 'Hector, do you have *any* idea what you have done? *Do you?*'

'Nay.' Hector could not understand why she was acting so. 'The Rector's a good man. He'll come and talk to the laird and put him on a righteous path again. That's what ma father said. A righteous path again.'

Mrs Keillor had picked up the tin basin and had filled it with more water. 'Let me clean your face, Hector,' she said with heavy sigh. 'And then I think ye should take a righteous path up to your room above the stables and have a lie-down. Ye've had a hurtful day. I'll bring the plate with your bread and cheese up to ye when I've done it.'

When Hector's wound had been tended to and he had gone, Mary was still sitting with her face in her hands.

Mrs Keillor stood looking at her anxiously for a long moment. 'I think ye are worrying too much, Mary. The Rector will probably come and give Lachlan a quiet word of advice about mending his ways, and that will be it.'

'And what about *her* mending her ways? You heard what Hector said – *she* was the one crawling all over him down by the loch like a bitch in heat. And *knowing* he is married – and to her own sister! So who will be having a quiet word with *her* about mending her ways?'

Mrs Keillor bit her lip, thinking. 'Well, it canna be Isabella, because she must no' find out.'

'No, never.'

'And if twas left to *me,* I'd put her over my lap and give her a good paddling on her cheeky backside.

She looked at Mary. 'So it *will* have to be you that speaks to her, Mary, because you know how to deal with these things in a sensible and *sedate* manner, just like Mrs Elizabeth knew how to do it in the old days.'

*

Mary was upstairs in Beth's bedroom, folding the last of Beth's clothes and packing them neatly inside a box in readiness to be taken up to Tobermory, when her attention was distracted by the sound of a horse clopping in the yard down below.

She moved to the window and looked down, seeing Mary Campbell dismount and then casually throw the reins over the post, leaving the gelding for Hector to deal with. Her manner seemed cheerful enough as she did her little skipping walk into the house.

Only a half an hour earlier, Mary had seen Isabella go down towards the loch with one of her books and knew she would stay down there for hours. She had found a favourite spot under a tree and that's where she always went now to lose herself in her fantasies.

Mary walked out to the landing and the top of the stairs where she paused, taking a deep breath, thinking about Elizabeth ... that great *lady*. And then in the manner of Elizabeth she began to walk sedately down the stairs.

Mary Campbell was in the drawing-room when Mary entered. She had lifted one of the 'Ladies' magazines from Isabella's pile on the small table, turning and walking towards the door when she saw Mary and stopped, her face smiling happily.

'Oh, Mrs Jarvis, I had a *wonderful* ride along the coast line, quite wonderful, and *so* refreshing.'

Mary closed the door and said quietly: 'Why did you use your whip to lash Hector?'

'Who?'

'Hector – our groom.'

'Oh, *him*?' Her face became haughty. 'He was insolent to me, quite *insolent*.'

'No, *you* are the *insolent* one!' Mary said, slapping the girl's face so hard she stumbled back halfway across the room.

'*Insolent* enough to slash one man and *insolent* enough to sneak into bed with another! *Insolent* enough to bring *shame* on this house!'

Mary Campbell reached a hand out to one of the armchairs behind her, a hand to her face, her eyes wide with shock.

'No, no, I don't know what you are talking about! I've slept in no man's bed!'

Mary took the gold ring from the pocket of her dress. 'So how did *this* get between the sheets of your *brother-in-law's* bed?'

Mary Campbell stared at the gold hair ring that was undeniably hers ... her mouth moved to speak, but no words came.

'Your own sister's husband! Did you not give even *one* thought to Isabella?'

'Did *he* not?' the girl countered defiantly.

Mary took a step back, breathing deeply. So now it was confirmed.

'Now you may have noticed, Miss Campbell,' she said more calmly. 'When you rode into the yard, that the mare is harnessed to the trap and both are ready and waiting. And out there in the hall you will find that all your possessions have been packed into your portmanteau. Keep your riding habit on, because now I am going to take you to Craignure in time to catch the evening ferry.'

'No, no, I'm not going anywhere. I'm not *leaving!* If Lachlan knew –'

'If Lachlan knew you used your *whip* to lash one *his* employees he would not hesitate to order you out! He would take you to Craignure and dump you on the ferry himself.'

'That's not true! I know he loves me because I gave him –'

'You gave him nothing more than any whore in Edinburgh would give him! Now grow up, get on your feet, and get out of this house before Isabella gets to learn about this – and if *she* gets to know about it, so will your father and mother in Craignish. So will the whole of Jura. Isabella will make sure of it.' You will be known as the girl who came as her sister's houseguest, and then shamelessly slept with her sister's husband. Do you understand?'

The girl's face showed that she did understand, and she gave no answer. Then she slumped down and began to cry, small blubbering sobs like a five-year-old child.

*

When Mary returned from Craignure she entered the kitchen looking worn out.

'Don't ask,' she said to Mrs Keillor, 'She's gone, so let's hope that's the end of it.'

Mrs Keillor quickly made her a cup of tea and gave it to her. 'I have your supper simmering on a pot here, do ye want it now or later?'

'Later, I need to catch my breath and relax for a while.

Goodness, what a day!'

'All I was *going* to say ...' Mrs Keillor added, 'is that I don't think ye handled it in quite the same sensible and sedate way that Mrs Elizabeth would have done – slapping the girl from here to Sunday.'

'I know, that was wrong, but I lost my temper when she showed no remorse for lashing Hector.'

'And that's unlike ye, Mary, to lose yer temper. But now that ye *have* resorted to violence, when the laird gets back will ye be giving *him* some of the same punishment as well?'

Mary sighed and sipped her tea. 'Did Isabella come in for her supper?'

'She did. And for a change she ate everything on her plate.'

'That's unusual. Did she ask where her sister was? Make any inquiry as to why she was not at the table? You remembered what I told you to say?'

'I remembered sharp enough, but she asked no questions. She just sat there reading one of her books while she was eating her food.'

Mary sighed again. 'One of these days she is going to start *eating* those books instead of the food, she loves them so much.'

'Still, tis good that she has the books to keep her company, because nobody else in this world seems to give a damn about her.'

'I do!' Mary exclaimed. 'And have I not just proved it – by getting rid of her sister?'

'Aye, in a way, I know ye feel as sorry for her as I do.'

'And, in a way,' Mary countered, 'Isabella has brought a lot of her problems on herself. She has not behaved like a fit wife, all her laziness and lack of interest in the household. And she has not even *tried* to show any interest in the estate or any of the workers. All she wants to do is lounge around like the Queen of Sheba and be waited upon hand and foot. Do you know, when she gets undressed at night for bed, she doesn't even trouble herself to hang up her day clothes – she just leaves them lying on the floor for me to pick up the next morning.'

'Aye, I know, I know ...' Mrs Keillor sat down, 'but don't ye be fooling yerself, Mary, because today the only one ye have proved that ye truly care about in all this – is the *laird*.'

Chapter Thirty-Six

Isabella did eventually notice her sister's absence, and asked the housekeeper where she had gone. Mary responded with a lie.

'I believe she received a letter from your mother asking her to come home. Something about being needed again at Craignish.'

'It will be father,' Isabella said knowingly. 'Mary has always been father's favourite. And she *has* been here for almost two *months*, which is long enough to give her the change they said she so desperately needed. Oh, well ...' Isabella sighed. 'Thank you, Mrs Jarvis, that will be all.'

*

When Lachlan returned three days later, Mary's response was very different. As soon as he left the yard and walked into the kitchen – Mary greeted him with the truth of it all – 'How *could* you, Lachlan? Your wife's sister!'

'Mary, I *did* warn you that she was strange and asked you not to leave me alone with either of them. And it was *her* who seduced *me*.'

'And you let her.'

'How could I not? She flaunted herself in front of me for weeks, all her secret smiles, and then she came into my bedroom very late at night wearing only her nightgown and *seduced* me.'

'And you let her,' Mary said again.

'No, I didn't *let* her, not at first – but I am a *man*. I'm not made of stone. And then I discovered she was a little harlot! I wasn't her first, or even her second. She boasted to me that she had lain with a few of the farm boys at Craignish and even seemed proud of it. She was no innocent. If I had not been here, and no other man present, I think she probably would have succeeded in seducing Hector in the end.'

'And speaking of Hector ...'

Lachlan's nonchalant manner completely vanished when

460

she told him that Mary Campbell had lashed Hector's face with her whip.

'How *dare* she?'

'Indeed, but she did dare to, and it hurt Hector badly, and not just his face.'

'And you sent her back to Craignish?'

'I did, on the evening ferry, the same day she did it.'

'You did right, and it now saves me the task of having to do it myself.'

He stood up. 'I'll go and see Hector now.'

Mary nodded. 'And if you have a half-crown or even a crown in your pocket, you should give it to him.'

'I've got a sovereign. I'll give him that.'

Mary's eyes widened. 'If you give him a *sovereign* he may think the lash was worth it.'

'No matter.'

*

In the weeks that followed, autumn came in bleak and brown, or so it seemed to Mary. Life at Jarvisfield had returned, more or less, to normal, other than the shocked gossip that was now running through Mull about the young Laird of Jarvisfield.

The Rector of the church at Gruline had given a long sermon decrying Lachlan from the pulpit as a "*sinful adulterer*". No name had actually been said, but all the hints and references left every member of the congregation in no doubt as to whom the Rector was speaking about.

Another cleric used the pulpit a week later to declare: "A man of our community, a man so wrongly considered to be a *gentleman,* a man of position and responsibility, who must now be regarded as being not only unconventional and *opinionated* in his wrong and reckless religious views; but, also, sadly – *morally* insane!"

Lachlan responded to all the fevered gossip in his usual careless and offhand way, shrugging away Mary's worries: 'Let the dogs yap.'

And when the letter came from the General Council, dismissing him from his "honoured" position as a Justice of

The Peace, Lachlan showed no care about that either, because he was now tired of playing that game.

He smiled as he showed the letter to Mary: 'It was fun while it lasted though,' he admitted. 'All those duckings of men who badly needed a good wash.'

Mary found it hard to deal with his nonchalance, suspecting that although he was showing no concern at the destruction of his reputation, deep down he was very hurt by it all.

A fact that seemed to be proved to her, when many a night he drank himself into a haze. Not in the old, amusing and sophisticated way, but as if a darkness came over him at night which he was desperate to blot out.

Isabella could take no more of the gossip that had reached her ears in the churchyard on Sundays, and decided to return to Craignish.

At Craignure, as she waited to board the ferry to the mainland, she said quietly to Mary: 'He has shamed me, and betrayed me, but I have always loved him. I know he does not dislike me as much he pretends to.'

She wiped the tears from her eyes. 'Sometimes ... he has been very tender with me, very caring. And I would rather have one night of tenderness from Lachlan, even just one night in every year, than a lifetime with anyone else.'

'But, Isabella, *now* is not the time to desert him,' Mary said. 'Not now when the whole island is against him.'

'No, but he has you. And I *will* return eventually, when all the gossip has quietened down, because I am sure ... yes, I am *very* sure that in the future, as the years pass and we both get older, Lachlan will turn back to me, if only for companionship, and that will be enough for me.'

'Oh, Isabella, I am *so* sorry ...' Mary put a hand on her arm. 'Don't leave it too long. Come back soon.'

Isabella wiped more tears from her eyes, and gave a small smile. 'Yet not *too* soon. According to my books – absence really *can* make the heart grow fonder.'

Driving back in the trap, Mary could feel the tears slipping down her own face, and kept wiping them away with her hand: tears for Isabella, tears for Lachlan, tears for them *both.*

Back at the house, in the kitchen, Mrs Keillor's eyes were questioning. 'Well?'

'Even though he has done wrong, she is prepared, at a later time, to forgive him.' Mary said quietly. 'She still loves him.'

And Mary left it at that, turning to go up to her bedroom and have a short lie down and say some prayers for them all.

*

Yet, when the gossip about Lachlan reached as far as Strathallan Castle, neither William Drummond, nor his father, Lord Strathallan, were prepared to be so forgiving.

They unleashed their own onslaught against the clerics of Mull, demanding to know in an open letter to Mull's newspapers – yes, *demanding* a public apology from all the clerics who had – without any admission or any definite proof – set out in their religious zeal to *crucify* the reputation of a man without question or inquiry, without trial or jury. Clerics who had acted, *not* with the philosophy or souls of Christianity as taught by Jesus, but like a savage pack of Pontius Pilate's slavering henchmen.

William Drummond was so incensed by all the attacks on his friend, he ventured over to Mull, accompanied by two of his lawyers, threatening legal action against every cleric who, without proof, had defamed the name of the Laird of Jarvisfield.

The girl had denied it, had *strenuously* denied it, even to her own parents. And although the laird had not lowered himself to respond to their scurrilous allegations, they had sought to publicly destroy him in any case.

In the weeks that followed, every Sunday, the locals of Mull were rendered more and more into a state of utter confusion; and then guilt-ridden with red faces as the clerics rebuked them from their pulpits, preaching that only God Himself should be the judge of men.

And surely it was only the *wickedest* members of their congregation who could deem a man to be guilty of *any* sin – solely on the word of a simple-minded ignorant groom – a stable boy with no sense nor education, who had carried the rumour against the laird to his father – and all because a young lady of the house had reprimanded him with a touch of her crop.

Now all the fury was turned against Hector. His father arrived at the stables and began to beat him mercilessly while Hector cowered under his fists.

Afterwards, Mary was certain that Hector's father would have beaten his son senseless if Lachlan had not rushed out and given the man such an angry and powerful fist in the face he fell down unconscious, and then was later sent off at running speed with Lachlan's injunction that he was *never* to return to Jarvisfield.

'I'm *never* going back there,' Hector declared, while Mrs Keillor was repairing his face again. 'I'm staying put here on ma own Jarvisfield. I've been here since General Macquarie was the king here. And I've alus been safe from hunger and harm here, aye I have, *safe*.'

'We *all* have,' Mrs Keillor muttered. 'And now we're all safe here together in my own kitchen and all the trouble is over, so what else matters, eh?'

Hector gave her a crooked and happy smile; unaware of the two missing front teeth his father had removed for him.

Chapter Thirty-Seven

Mary sat in dismal silence while Hector and Mrs Keillor chattered happily together.

The trouble was not over, She knew it was not, because Lachlan had paid and was *still* paying a heavy price for his sins, and already she could see that too much damage had been done to him. Whether it was due to all the gossip that he had pretended to ignore, or all the extra drinking he was doing at night, she did not know – but *damaged* he was.

His dizzy spells had returned, his periods of blankness were taking longer to clear. At times he could be very serious, or very amusing; but most of the time there was a quiet darkness in his eyes and in his manner. And now, of late, she had seen him too many times walking down to the loch, alone and solitary, not wanting any company.

It was not until he received a letter from William Drummond, inviting him to spend a week or two at Strathallan Castle – and Lachlan strangely showed no interest in going – that Mary finally sent for Beth.

Beth arrived in Lizzie McLeod's trap, pale of face and anxious, draped in a thick burgundy velvet cloak.

Mrs Keillor gasped at the luxury of such a cloak. 'By! Where did you buy that?'

'I didn't buy it. Mr Dewar made it for me.' Beth answered. 'He is very concerned that I should remain warm now that winter is almost upon us.'

'It's not *that* cold,' Mary said.

'Oh, it is getting cold now up in Tobermory, Mama. Don't forget we have the sea opposite our doorstep.'

'And John?' Mary asked.

Beth smiled. 'We're that happy, just the two of us, so truly happy; and even when his father is present too. Mr Dewar is a nice man, Mama, you should come up to see us more often.'

And as she had not once been up there at all, due to her preoccupation with Lachlan, Mary felt guilty and promised she would go up to Tobermory the following week.

'But now,' she said more urgently. 'Beth, please go out and speak to Lachlan. He spends too much time alone down by that loch, locked away in his own thoughts.'

'I wonder why?' Beth asked, and as soon as she had asked it, Mary realised that John Dewar and Lizzie and Angus had all kept the gossip about Lachlan and Mary Campbell from reaching Beth, because they all must have heard it – it had travelled even beyond Mull itself, never mind up to only nine miles away in Tobermory.

'Go on now,' Mary urged, 'go out to Lachlan. Try and persuade him to go to Strathallan for a few weeks. William Drummond always sends him back as cheerful as a cock robin at Christmas.'

Beth smiled. 'I will, I'll try. And will he tell me why he has been so despondent of late?'

Mary closed her eyes for a second. 'Perhaps he will.'

After an hour, a very long hour of waiting, Mary could not restrain herself from stepping out to the yard and walking slowly down towards the loch, her steps halting as she saw them ... Beth and Lachlan together, standing motionless, yet locked together in a tight hug like two lovers ... and she could see that it was Lachlan who was holding on to Beth, his arms tightly around her ... and as she moved quietly closer ... she could see that both of them were crying.

Stealthily she moved away, and returned to the kitchen, waiting and waiting for another long time, until Beth finally returned to the kitchen, a smile on her face, and showing no evidence of the emotion that had taken place down by the loch earlier.

'Well?' Mary asked, while Mrs Keillor also sat waiting.

Beth appeared reluctant to answer, but then she said quietly: 'I think ... I think Lachlan is a little unwell.'

Mrs Keillor stood up and moved closer. 'What makes ye think that, Beth? What did he say to you?'

Beth turned her serious dark eyes to Mrs Keillor. 'Whatever he said to me was in confidence.'

'Aye, but we *still* want to know.'

'No.' Beth replied firmly. 'It was a private conversation and private it will stay.' She turned more brightly to her mother.

'But he *has* agreed to go to Strathallan for a while. First thing in the morning.'

'Oh, good!' Mary was delighted at this. 'And where is he now?'

'Oh, he's coming along. He said he will be coming back in another few minutes.'

'Will you have something to eat now, my Bethey?' asked Mrs Keillor.

'No, thank you, I must get back. I'm having another cooking lesson with Lizzie this afternoon.'

Mary and Mrs Keillor stared at each other, and then both said Beth together: 'Can you not *cook?*'

'No!' Beth exclaimed. 'Because neither of you bothered to teach me.'

The two older women stared at each other. 'No, we never have,' said Mary.

Beth smiled. 'Not to worry, because I'm getting much better at it, and Mr Dewar and John have never made a single complaint about anything I have cooked so far.'

Lachlan entered the kitchen, a smile on his face as he looked at her, and Beth said, 'Well, I must get back.' She moved over and gave Lachlan one last kiss on the cheek, and then the same to Mrs Keillor and Mary.

Mary followed her out to the trap, an inquisitive expression in her eyes.

'Beth, I know it's the end of autumn, but it's really not *that* cold, so why are you wrapped up in such a thick cloak? It's unlike you to be so sensitive to any slight chill in the weather.'

Beth's face flushed a deep pink as she moved to climb onto the trap. Mary caught her by the arms and held her back from taking the step up.

'Beth?'

Beth was blushing even deeper now, her dark eyes flickering nervously. 'It's Mr Dewar ... he's very cosseting to me ... and so is John. Now that winter is almost here, the weather in Tobermory feels much colder to them than it did in Edinburgh.'

'Beth?' Mary slipped a hand inside the thick cloak and placed her palm on Beth's stomach, feeling the small rounded swell. 'You're carrying a child?'

Beth nodded, her eyes down.

'When is it due?'

Beth took a deep intake of breath, and answered truthfully. 'In five months.'

'Five months? But you have only been married for two.'

'It must have happened when ... when ...'

'The two of you went away somewhere for five days.' Mary was quickly adding it up. 'When he first came back ... in July. He made you pregnant then?'

'Yes, but he didn't *know* he had made me pregnant then, and neither did I. Not until about a month ago.'

'Did he know you were pregnant on your wedding day?'

'No! I've already *told* you. Neither of us knew until about a month ago.'

Mary smiled. 'So John's father is not as good at cosseting you as I am then? If you had been living here with me I would have seen it long before a month ago.'

Beth was close to tears. 'Mama, I know we shouldn't have ... before –'

Mary put her arms around her daughter and hushed her. 'I'm happy for you, darling, for both of you. Did you tell Lachlan?'

'No!'

'And that's why you are wearing the cloak? So people don't see that you are more pregnant than you should be after only two months wed?'

Beth nodded. 'Lizzie knows though – but I didn't tell her. It was *Lizzie* who told me that I was pregnant.'

'And you didn't think ... when you missed your menses?'

'No, I thought it was because of all the excitement of being in love and all our –' Beth clamped her mouth shut, her embarrassed eyes glancing around her, as if seeking some path to run away and escape.

'I must go now,' she said quietly.

Mary nodded, and helped her up onto the trap. When Beth lifted the reins and gave her mother one short, last smile, Mary smiled back and gave her one short, last piece of advice.

'Keep wearing the cloak, Beth,' she said tiredly, 'because,

God knows, we've had enough whispering and gossip around here already.'

*

She stood watching until Beth and the trap were out of sight: her own little girl, now on the road to being a mother herself.

She sighed; she should have been more congratulatory about the pregnancy. She had no right to question Beth any more.

Robbie came slowly lolloping down the lane, knowing Beth was near and looking for her.

Mary bent and gently scratched his ear. 'She's gone, Robbie.' She felt sad to see the dog so old and slow now.

She looked again towards the empty road, and then the sky above it. Dark clouds were showing in the west, and she wondered if Beth would get rained upon.

But more important now, and more urgent, was her need to help Lachlan get over this dark and difficult period he was going through.

She entered the house, wondering with faint dread how Lachlan would receive the news when he found out that Beth was expecting a child.

*

Lachlan never found out. He could not eat any dinner that evening, suffering from one of his dizzy spells, and decided to retire early to his room and bed.

Mary kissed him goodnight in the hall and walked back to the kitchen while he went up the stairs. Moments later the sudden banging sounds made her swiftly turn back into the hall, her heart jumping with fright as she watched Lachlan crashing backwards down the stairs.

'*Lachlan!*'

Mrs Keillor came rushing out from the kitchen. 'His dizzy spells!' Mary cried. 'He must have fainted on the top step and fallen backwards!'

'I'll send Hector for Dr McLean!'

Mary gave no answer as Mrs Keillor turned and rushed to the stables. She knelt down, staring at Lachlan's inert body,

469

and then dropped her head onto his chest, crying silently and painfully, because she knew that Lachlan was dead.

Dr McLean later confirmed it. In the twist and fall down the stairs, Lachlan's neck had broken.

Hector and Mrs Keillor began to sob loudly: Hector the loudest of all, unable to restrain his sorrow. '*Ma master, ma master...*'

Mary could only stare silently at her golden boy, thinking back to the beautiful and innocently happy child he had been in Australia, his hair as golden as the sun, his happy laughter always ringing through the corridors of Government House, loved by all.

The boy his parents Lachlan and Elizabeth Macquarie had adored so much, and had wanted only the best for; a good and happy life on the estate of Jarvisfield with his own growing family to care for, and to pass on the family name and the family estate.

Yet he had died childless, at the age of thirty. The pain was too great. Mary had to turn away and walk away ... leaving Dr McLean's questions unanswered.

Chapter Thirty-Eight

For Mary, the funeral was mostly a blur. Only now and again did she notice some of the people who had gathered in the small walled garden where Lachlan's coffin was placed inside the stone mausoleum with his parents and baby sister and her own beloved George Jarvis who had also died too young, at the age of thirty-four.

She looked towards George's daughter, her own beloved Beth, whose face was as frozen as ice, no tears, no emotion, just cold shock.

During the walk from the church, Mary had noticed that every now and then Beth's steps had faltered, but John Dewar was at her side, his arm supporting her all the way.

Isabella was beyond consolation; hopelessly devastated. And yet, as Mary gazed around at all the people gathered here today, the one who surprised her the most was William Drummond, who looked absolutely heartbroken and unable to control his tears as he stood silently beside his father, Viscount Strathallan, who kept putting a comforting hand on his son's shoulder.

Lizzie and Angus McLeod left to return to Tobermory as soon as the ceremony was over. Many of the people who had travelled here today would be later putting up at their inn, and so they had to return and ensure that all was prepared in readiness for their comfort.

Maggie, Lorna and Kirsty and many of the other locals had 'come in' to help with the serving of the food and drinks to the visitors. It was a cold lunch, of course, it had to be. Mrs Keillor was still too distraught to spend the day on her feet cooking.

'Tis the shock, ye see,' Mrs Keillor said to Mary, 'I still canna cope with the shock, or the sadness.' And then she had started sobbing again.

So Mary had done most of the cooking herself the day before: joints of ham and chickens had been roasted and then sliced: pies and tartlets and cream laid out in readiness that morning. She had been glad to be busy, glad to be doing something worthwhile, glad to be too tired to think.

Soon, one day in the future, she would be able to think about it all rationally, less emotionally, and then she and Mrs Keillor would return to their old ways, spending their days and evenings in the kitchen talking together and drinking tea, all problems discussed and sorted out before bedtime.

If she had managed to eventually deal with life and start coping again after George's death, the time would come when she would be able to do the same after Lachlan's.

Smoothing her fair hair back, and also smoothing down her black dress, she walked out of the kitchen ready to be the perfect hostess to all the mourners – and they *were* all mourners, very few cheerful faces. It was not an expected death: it was a tragic *young* death.

So Mary kept her head high and her shoulders brave and did what she had to do, as sedate in her manner as Lachlan's mother, Elizabeth Macquarie, would have been, ready to help and assist anyone who needed anything, and having no premonition whatsoever of another disaster still to come.

After about an hour of attending on various people, Mary suddenly realised that she had not seen Beth at all since they had all come into the house after Lachlan's body had been interred.

Searching through the crowded rooms she could not find Beth anywhere, nor outside in the cold garden, not anywhere – until she ventured upstairs to Beth's old bedroom, where the curtains had been drawn, and Beth was lying on the bed with her eyes closed, still draped in her warm velvet cloak, and John sitting on the side of the bed beside her, holding her hand.

Mary took a step into the silent room and, even in the dimness of the drawn curtains, she could now see the shining residue of tears on Beth's face.

She looked questioningly at John, who shook his head, silently advising her not to speak to Beth, to just let her be.

Returning downstairs she was immediately accosted by Lorna. 'Oh, Mrs Jarvis, ye are wanted in the study.'

'By whom?'

'A man named Mr Finlay. He asked for ye to be sent in.'

'Do you know why?'

Lorna nodded. 'There's another lawyer man in there with him. I think they want ye because they're going to do the reading of Lachlan's will.'

When Mary entered the study, one man who was obviously a lawyer, a thin man wearing spectacles, was sitting behind the desk. The second lawyer was sitting to the side of the desk. Both had documents in their hands.

Only two other people were present: Isabella and her father.

'Mrs Jarvis,' said the man behind the desk, 'I am Mr Baden Finlay, the late Mr Macquarie's solicitor.'

'Good afternoon,' Mary said.

'Please sit down.'

Mary sat on a chair beside Isabella.

'Now, if you don't mind, due to myself and Mr Langdon having to catch the evening ferry back to the mainland, I think we should go through the details of the will as speedily as possible. It's quite short, but two codicils were added by Mr Macquarie during the past two years, codicils that I must explain ... ' he looked at Isabella, 'to *you*, Mrs Macquarie.'

Isabella nodded.

'In his Last Will and Testament, Mr Lachlan Macquarie left to you, his wife, Isabella Macquarie, this house, all the furniture therein, and all the china and plate and silver, so that you will have a secure home to live in.'

'And the estate,' asked Isabella's father, 'the Jarvisfield estate? Surely that all passes to Isabella too?'

'No, I'm afraid not,' said Mr Finlay, adjusting his spectacles.

'In his will, and in the two later codicils added thereto ... Mr Macquarie has bequeathed his entire Jarvisfield estate to his "long and steadfast friend" William Drummond.'

'What?' Mary's eyes popped wide. 'But he cannot do that. This is *Macquarie* land. Jarvisfield cannot be bequeathed to the *Drummond* family.'

'Jarvisfield has *not* been bequeathed to the Drummond family,' Mr Finlay corrected her politely. 'It has been

473

bequeathed to Mr William Drummond personally, and no one else.'

'And where is he? William Drummond?' Mary looked at Isabella. 'Why is *he* not here to learn of this?'

Isabella shrugged vaguely, she did not know.

Mr Finlay turned to his colleague. 'I believe this is where I hand over to you, Mr Langdon.'

Mr Langdon nodded, and opened his own file of documents. 'Yes, now I am Mr Philip Langdon, solicitor-at-law, and the legal representative of Mr William Drummond.'

He paused for a moment to look at his papers. 'Mr Drummond, you may have noticed, left to return to Strathallan immediately after the interment. He was too distraught at the loss of his friend to become involved in any reading of the will, and so has left all such matters to me.'

'So he knows?' Isabella said. 'He *knows* that Lachlan left Jarvisfield to him.'

'I think it is only fair to say,' Mr Langdon continued, 'that Mr Macquarie did not know that he was going to die so young, and no doubt he hoped to have all these documents rendered out of date at some time in the future.'

'Yes, that was his intention,' Mr Finlay corroborated.

'And over the past eight years,' Mr Langdon went on, 'Mr Macquarie found it necessary, from time to time, to borrow very large sums of money from Mr Drummond ... ' He looked down at his papers again. 'The largest amount on one occasion being the sum of twenty thousand pounds.'

'Oh, dear God!' Mary exclaimed.

'Added to this were a number of other very large sums, and many small sums of no more than one or two thousand pounds, all of which Mr Macquarie signed documents pledging Jarvisfield as surety for these loans. The total does *not* amount to anything near the full value of the Jarvisfield estate.'

Mr Langdon looked at Mr Finlay, who coughed uncomfortably, and took over again:

'No, that is correct. The loans do not amount to the full value of the estate, but Mr Macquarie wanted to leave the rest of the Jarvisfield estate to Mr Drummond in any event, if only to repay the interest he would have had to pay, if he had borrowed the money from a bank.'

After a silence, Mr Finlay added: 'It was also Mr Macquarie's fervent wish that all of his father's papers and journals be entrusted to the care of William Drummond.'

Mary had heard enough. She stood up and walked to the door.

'Mrs Jarvis, one moment please ... we have sought your presence because there is a small bequest to *you*.'

'I don't want it!' Mary snapped. 'You have just removed the floor from under my feet and the roof from above my head and the *name* of *Macquarie* from the deeds to the Jarvisfield estate! So I will *not* accept any bequest to me – Lachlan should have given *that* to William Drummond also!'

She slammed the door behind her and marched to the kitchen where she suddenly stopped at the open door ... her eyes taking in Mrs Keillor busily preparing more food on a large silver tray, and Hector standing by the kitchen door chattering over to her in his usual way.

Would Isabella keep those two on? Keep them all on? Maggie and Lorna? Keep them all employed? Even Hector? Isabella did not ride horses!

She received the answer an hour later when Isabella and her father came out of the study, both moving hurriedly.

Mary approached them. 'Isabella, where are you going?'

'Home to Craignish. On the evening ferry. I cannot stay here, not now.'

'But Lachlan left this house and all its contents to *you*.'

'Yes ...' Isabella's tears were flowing again. 'But without Lachlan, why would I want to stay here now, in this house, or on this island of Mull?'

'Come on, m'lass.' Isabella's father arrived on the scene, handing Isabella her cloak, and then looking at Mary:

'It's a bally disgrace, Mrs Jarvis, bequeathing everything he owned to his friend. A bally disgrace, that's all I can say.'

'Yet ... the house ...'

'I'm selling the house' Isabella said. 'It is all that Lachlan left to me, and so I must sell it as soon as possible to provide me with enough money to live on as a widow.'

'Your putting the house up for sale?'

Her father butted in. 'Mrs Jarvis, I can see that you need to understand what's happening – and what's *going* to happen – so I'll tell ye all that *we* know from what has been said in there.' He gestured his head in the direction of the study.

'Please do,' Mary replied.

'It seems that William Drummond knew all about the contents of the will. His solicitor informed him about it after the death. Now, he intends to keep the estate running, and keep on all the workers. And his solicitor has told us that Mr Drummond will agree to buy the house from Isabella, if that should be her wish. And if it is, then ... I'm afraid his intention is to close the house down, and open it up again for a few weeks only once or twice a year, whenever he wants to bring people over for a shooting or fishing party.'

Mary was stunned. 'But what about those of us who have lived and worked in this house for decades? What are we to do?'

Isabella looked somewhat guilty as she placed a hand on Mary's arm.

'I'm sorry, Mrs Jarvis, but I *must* sell the house to Mr Drummond quite quickly. So I'm afraid that you and the rest of the staff will have to find other accommodation as soon as possible.'

As soon as Isabella had left, Mary marched to the study, her heart pounding.

She opened the door without knocking. The two solicitors were standing talking.

'Oh, Mrs Jarvis ...' said Mr Finlay. 'Have you come back to know about your bequest?'

'No. I have come to remind you two gentleman about the *Macquarie Trust*. If you will recall, in his own will, General Lachlan Macquarie set up a trust that stipulated that George Jarvis, his wife, and all his *descendants* would have a home on the Jarvisfield Estate *forever*. Even under conditions of sale, this stipulation could not be revoked, not by any of *his* descendants, and not by any new owner.'

Mary paused, her mind frantically trying to remember every word of that document and others relating to it, which she had read herself many times.

'That stipulation was confirmed and repeated again in the will of Mrs Elizabeth Macquarie.'

'Oh, yes,' said Mr Finlay, 'and indeed the late Mr Lachlan Macquarie has confirmed and upheld the stipulations of the *Macquarie Trust* in his will also.'

'So why has his wife just advised me to find other accommodation?'

'Because, Mrs Jarvis, the trust clearly states that the Jarvis family and all descendants must be allowed a home on the Jarvisfield *estate*. It does not clarify that this home should be within the Macquarie *house*.'

Mary was so shaken she had to sit down. 'But if not the Macquarie house – where, then – *where*?'

Mr Finlay looked questioningly at Mr Langdon, who took out his notes again.

'Mrs Jarvis, I must inform you, if you do not already know, Mr William Drummond is a very kind and generous man – '

'Is he though, *is* he?' Mary snapped. 'If he had not been so *generous* to Lachlan through the years, Lachlan would not have got himself into so much debt!'

She stood up again. Now her head was pounding as well as her heart.

'It seems to me, that all Mr Drummond has been doing over the past years, is slyly using his generosity to buy the Jarvisfield estate.'

'That is not true, I assure you,' said Mr Langdon curtly. 'Mr Drummond has his own personal fortune, and in time he will inherit Strathallan Castle and all the grounds and lands on that fine estate.'

'He who has much, always wants more. Isn't that what they say?'

Mr Langdon ignored the question. 'As to yourself, Mrs Jarvis, I can also assure you that Mr Drummond has no intention of breaking the *Macquarie Trust*. He has asked me to inform you that any vacant cottage you may find on the Jarvisfield estate is yours for the asking, for as long as you live, and without the payment of any rent.'

'And what about Mrs Keillor and Hector and others who

have depended upon *this* house for their bed and board or employment all these years?'

'I'm sorry, but the rest of the household staff are not Mr Drummond's concern. And as the house is now going to be closed throughout the year, apart from short periods in the summer – '

'And the *name* of the estate? Is it still going to retain the name of *Jarvisfield*?'

Mr Langdon was not sure about that, not sure at all.

'All I can say, Mrs Jarvis, is that when an estate receives a *new* owner, it always receives a *new* name.'

'So it's all gone! Everything General Macquarie and Elizabeth built and worked for – the house, the estate, their son – all gone now.'

She left the office blinded by tears and pain, stumbling her way up the stairs towards her room, wishing *she* was dead and gone also; mumbling incoherent words and almost falling forward until someone coming down the stairs managed to catch her and steady her.

'Mrs Jarvis … what is wrong … here, let me help you?'

The voice sounded very distant, like an echo, and the hand that took her arm belonged to someone she could not see, her eyes blurred to blindness, all the worry and traumas of the past week, weeks, months, shutting down her mind.'

'I must … *lie down,'* she said, 'I must … lie …'

'Which is your room?' the distant voice asked. 'Is it this one?'

A moment later as the darkness became even darker, she was aware of nothing more than being lifted up and carried and being placed down on a bed … a soft, soft bed beneath her … a warm, warm cover going over her, and then she fell into a sudden sleep.

'She's not asleep, she's unconscious,' John said to Kirsty Dewar, who had seen Mrs Jarvis stumbling on the stairs and being caught by John, and had now come running into the room.

'Send someone for the family doctor and then bring up a glass of water.'

'Dr McLean is downstairs,' Kirsty said.

'Then bring him up, and the water – bring both up, quickly.'

'But, John, this is not Mrs Jarvis's room, this is Lachlan's room – see – all his things are still there on the dresser.'

'*Kirsty!*'

'Aye, aye, I'm going.'

Chapter Thirty-Nine

John did not return to Tobermory until four days later, and without Beth.

His father studied his preoccupied expression as he removed his riding cloak and threw it over an armchair in the front parlour.

It was unlike John to do that, not hang his cloak up in the hall. Life aboard a ship had its own firm discipline – a place for everything, and everything in its place – Navy training.

'Beth is not with you – is she unwell?'

'No, no, she is fine ... apart from feeling desperately sad of course.'

'Yes, oh, yes, death is a sad business. Is that why she has stayed down there?'

'She has stayed to look after her mother for a week or so.' John then explained about Mrs Jarvis's near accident.

'It was quite possible, just for a moment, that she might have fallen down the stairs and broken her neck also.'

'So sad about that young man. He must have been drinking too much again. Is Mrs Jarvis all right now?'

John sighed. 'I don't think so. She's grieving, as they all are. Dr McLean said she has mentally worn herself out with worry. And now she has lost everything. All gone. She can't take it in.'

'Lost everything? What do you mean?'

John then explained to his father, in the same way that Mary had explained to him, the details of Lachlan's will, and the consequences.

'So the Drummonds of Strathallan now own Jarvisfield?'

'Every tree and brick of it – except the walled burial garden. They have promised to keep that sacred to the memory of the Macquaries and leave it there for all time.'

'So what have you been doing down there these past days? Just hanging around?'

'Hanging around?' John looked at his father with irritation. 'It's not in my nature to *hang around* anywhere.'

'No. So?'

'I have spent the last two days driving Mrs Jarvis around in that trap of hers, looking for a vacant cottage for her to live in. She may be ill, but she won't stay lying down. Not when she needs to find a place to live.'

'And did she find one? A cottage?'

'Yes. The only empty cottage that the farm manager knew about.'

'Robert Dewar – my cousin?'

'Yes. He was as helpful as he could be. But the only one he knew about, and had keys for, was a desolate little place on a hill containing only two rooms.'

'Two rooms? That's almost as bad as whole families crowded into two rooms in the tenements of the slums in Edinburgh's old town.'

'Mrs Jarvis has taken the cottage, because there is nowhere else. She insists she will be able to whitewash it and furnish it and make it reasonably nice to live in.'

Mr Dewar stood up and lit his pipe with a taper from the fire, and then sat down again, smoking it thoughtfully.

After a long preoccupied silence, John said: I have been thinking a lot about her.'

'Who?'

'Mrs Jarvis.'

'Indeed.'

'On the ride back here, I could think of little else.'

'Well, she is Beth's mother.'

'And I am her *son*-in-law.'

Mr Dewar sucked on his pipe. 'I have a lot of esteem for Mrs Jarvis. A nice lady. And very easy to talk with.'

'She's a better cook than Beth.'

'Any beggar out there on the street would be a better cook than Beth.'

Mr Dewar looked sharply at his son. 'I'm sure I must have lost stones in weight since I moved in here. And she *still* can't get the porridge right.'

John smiled. 'You have to make allowances.'

'Why?'

'Because she's carrying a child. *Your* grandchild.'

'Indeed. That could be a disadvantage to her cooking skills I suppose.'

'A disadvantage that is bound to get worse as she goes along,' John said.

'By! This is like those ruddy chess games we used to play when you were younger! And knowing *you* it will go on all night until we reach stalemate. Why don't you just come out with it and say it?'

'I could not say anything without your approval. You own half the house.'

'Then let's jump straight to checkmate and consider the game done. She comes to live *here*. She moves in with us – not some two-roomed desolate cottage on a hill. A woman who has kept the Macquarie house running in fine order for years. She would shrivel up and waste away in a place like that.'

'She would,' John agreed. 'But you will have to be the one to go down there and tell her.'

'Me? Why not you?'

'Because tomorrow morning I will be leaving here and sailing to Gibraltar.'

'Gibraltar?' 'Sakes alive – what's this now?'

*

Over dinner in the Tobermory Inn, Mr Dewar complained:

'I can't keep up with you, son. Oh, you spoke true when you said you did not hang around.'

He reached for the salt. 'And there was me thinking my life in retirement was going to be very peaceful, if perhaps a little dull at times. But by God – you'll keep my brain alert and me living to ninety at this rate.'

'Do you not *want* to live to be ninety?' John asked.

'A hundred would suit me better. But now then, what's all this about Gibraltar?'

'I meant to tell you last week,' John explained, 'but with the sudden death of Lachlan Macquarie, and the awful affect it had on Beth, and then ... well, with everything else, I forgot.'

'*Forgot* to tell us you would be disappearing again for

months on end?'

'Not months.'

'Years?'

'Twenty days, there and back, twenty days, that's all. Three weeks at sea, and three weeks at home. That will be my regular timetable from now on.'

'I thought you said Cunard's Atlantic service took twenty-*eight* days?'

'It does, but I'm not sailing across the Atlantic, I'm going to the Mediterranean.'

His father sat back, realisation dawning. 'So, in the end, you couldn't do it —leave the Navy.'

'No, not completely. And this way I can at least remain a part of it.'

'You first love ... the Royal Navy.'

'My *second* love.'

'Cunard pays a much higher wage than the Navy pays.'

John put down his knife and fork and looked at his father with irritation. 'It's done ... it's *done* ... now leave it at that.'

*

Mary was still busily packing up her things when Mr Dewar arrived in Jarvisfield a few days later. Her surprise at his visit was evident on her face.

'Oh, Mr Dewar ... please, come in. Have you been over at your cousin's house?'

'No, this is my first port of call, as John would say.'

She led him to the drawing-room where he stood and looked at her. 'My dear ... how are you?'

Mary smiled weakly. 'Oh, much better, but it's less than two weeks since ... And yesterday Isabella sent a servant from Craignish to collect all Lachlan's personal belongings and bring them back to her ... I found that rather hard, the *packing* of his things, I mean.'

'I understand.'

'Is it Beth you have come to see? She's gone off for one her solitary walks down by the loch, but I'm sure she won't be long.'

'May I sit down?'

'Oh, yes, of course ... I'm sorry. My mind ...'

'Is distracted, and the last thing you need right now is a visitor.'

'Would you like some tea?' Mary offered. 'You must need it if you have come straight here from Tobermory.'

Mr Dewar sat down. 'On my journey here I was thinking more about what *Beth* might need as she goes along in her pregnancy.'

'Oh?'

'You know John has gone to Gibraltar?'

Mary sat down herself. 'No, he did not mention anything about that.'

'Well, with his child on the way, he was eager to get back to work and start earning a wage for the three of them.'

'But in *Gibraltar* – and away for how long?'

'There and back – twenty days – so in less than a month he will be home again. He has not left the Navy after all, not completely. I knew he would find it hard.'

Mary said: 'But ...'

'But he *has* left all active duty in the slave prevention squadrons in the West Indies and Africa.'

Mary was confused. 'So what is he doing now?'

'On a Naval courier ship, carrying dispatches to the British Naval base in Gibraltar. He chose that option because it allows him to spend more time at home.'

Mary sat thinking about it.

'John said the ships are well armed and gunned, just like the regular Navy ships.'

Mary nodded. 'Yes, now I can understand why you are so concerned about Beth. If John is going to be away for three weeks at a time on a regular basis ...'

'She will need all the help she can get, especially when the birth of the child gets closer. And I'm not going to be much use to her, sadly no – not with my arthritic knee – and not with their rooms being all the way up on the *third* floor.'

He looked at her curiously. 'How are your knees, Mrs Jarvis?'

Mary swallowed. 'Very strong. I've been active all my life.'

'So would you consider coming to help us? If only ... for

Beth's sake?'

Mary stared at him, the constriction in her throat preventing her from answering.

'We have a number of spare rooms sitting unused,' Mr Dewar said. 'We could accommodate you very easily, if you could agree to come and help us.'

Mary clasped her hands together on her lap. 'Mr Dewar,' she said, her voice a croak. 'Are you asking me to move to Tobermory?'

'I know it is a great imposition on you – '

'No, it is not an imposition on me at all. In truth, there is nothing I would love more than to live in the same house as my daughter, and even moreso when she has her child, and to be a part of a family again ... but I'm afraid I cannot do so. I simply cannot.'

'No? Oh, dear ...' He looked at her. 'Whyever not?'

She did not speak for a time. 'Mrs Keillor ... Mrs Keillor and I have been such close friends for such a long time. She has ... no one else, no relatives. So we were going to share a small cottage together. I couldn't leave her ... to live there alone with no other soul for company.' Mary shook her head. 'I couldn't do it, Mr Dewar, I just couldn't ... after everything that has already happened, it would be too cruel.'

'Have I met Mrs Keillor?'

'Mary nodded. 'Yes, I think you have ... she was at the wedding.'

Mr Dewar thought back. 'Now which one was she?'

'A stout woman, wearing a purple velvet dress that was at least ten years out of date.'

'Oh, yes, now I remember ... and wearing a large purple feather in her hair?'

'Yes,' Mary confirmed with a smile. 'But although her clothes and style may be old fashioned, her recipes are some of the best ever to be created.'

'Recipes?'

'On the day of the wedding,' said Mary, 'it was Mrs Keillor who spent most of the morning and afternoon in the kitchen of the Tobermory Inn cooking all that delicious wedding food – not Lizzie McLeod. All Lizzie did was to occasionally help

Mrs Keillor and keep a close eye on her, so she could steal all her recipes.'

'So this Mrs Keillor is a *cook?*'

'Yes, she has been the resident cook for the Macquarie family for over twenty years.'

'The *resident* cook?'

'Indeed. When General Macquarie was here, Mrs Keillor served up food to Lord Strathallan and other gentlemen of the highest rank, and after such occasions General Macquarie or Elizabeth always came to the kitchen to give Mrs Keillor their thanks.'

Mr Dewar sat back in his chair, wishing he had his pipe to smoke, or even the hard stem of the pipe to chew on. This news about an excellent cook was *very* interesting ...

Chapter Forty

The winter days in the Scottish Highlands and Islands were very *short* days. The morning light did not come until after half past eight, and by half past three it was dark again. And today was the shortest day of all, the day of the Winter Solstice.

John pulled his heavy navy cloak around him as he walked past the Tobermory Inn; it's windows bright in the darkness, its doors firmly closed against the freezing cold winds coming off the sea.

The tide was in full flow, swishing and bubbling and sending waves of white foam crashing against the harbour wall.

A man was bending his way along the street towards him, the wind blowing the man onwards and unsteadying his steps. He held onto his hat and looked at John from under the brim as they drew close. '*Desperate weather,*' he said in greeting. '*Desperate!*'

John nodded and walked on, thinking these westerly winds were nothing in comparison to some of the storms he had experienced at sea.

Reaching the house he saw that all the front windows on the ground floor and first floor were aglow with lights; lamps brightly burning in every room.

He inserted his key into the lock and opened the front door, feeling the immediate warmth ... and the fresh outdoor fragrance of pine trees ... which was strange.

He removed his cloak and hung it up, and then slowly pushed open the door of the front parlour: it was empty, a huge black and golden fire burning within the fireplace ... and there, in the corner, was a huge evergreen tree of Scottish Pine, decorated here and there with leaves of red-berried holly and long strips of red and green tartan ribbons twirling through its branches.

It was the strangest sight he had ever seen in a Scottish home, and explained the smell of fresh pine trees ... *outdoor* trees.

He moved on down the hall and opened the kitchen door and was instantly greeted by steam and the enticing aroma of bubbling fruit and spices.

He walked further into the kitchen and behind the steam he found Mrs Keillor stirring a pot on the stove.

'Mrs Keillor? What are you doing here?'

She turned and looked at him. 'What does it look like I'm doing here – I'm *cooking*.'

She wiped the back of her arm over her hot brow. 'And there's such a lot still to do. Now *here,* ye see, I'm steaming the Christmas pudding. I've put in a fair drop of brandy, aye and I'll make some rum sauce for over it – I like to have the pudding done at least two weeks before Christmas, it helps with the fermenting and blending of the flavours.'

'And then over here –' she turned to the long wooden table behind her – 'is the Christmas cake all ready and done.'

The table was laden with trays of golden mince pies. He looked at the cake – a *huge* cake covered in white icing with a sprig of green holly and red berries sitting on the top.

'Course, I didna have as much time to prepare this year as I have other years, what with all the furniture-moving an' all – we both brought our own beds, but I'll tell ye all about that later.' She looked down at the cake. 'Now the cake, ye see – I like to make the cake itself at least six weeks before Christmas, and then the marzipan made and laid over it two weeks after that, and yesterday I was able to complete the icing. Look here now – look at the way I've piped these white garlands of icing around the sides ...'

He bent slightly to look at the icing around the sides and so did Mrs Keillor. Their heads were close together and she looked into his blue eyes. 'So, what d'ye think?'

He returned her look, and spoke in the same calm and quiet way he would speak to any member of the crew. 'Carry on, Mrs Keillor, carry on.'

Upstairs in the back drawing-room he found another bright fire burning, and Mrs Jarvis and his father sitting in armchairs on each side of the fireplace. Mrs Jarvis had her head bent, sewing; and his father had his spectacles on, reading a newspaper.

Due to the noise of the wind outside they had not heard his arrival into the house.

And then he saw another huge Scots Pine tree in the corner of *this* room also, decorated in a similar way to the one downstairs.

'What's that?' he asked. 'Since when did we bring outdoor trees *inside* a house?'

They both looked up. 'Oh, my goodness ...' said Mrs Jarvis, standing up to greet him.

He gave her a smile and a kiss on the cheek, and then glared accusingly at his father. 'Did *you* bring those trees in here?'

His father nodded. 'I did.'

'But why, for God's sake? Isn't it enough that they stand outside our back doors protecting us from the winds, so why chop them down in their prime?'

His father folded his newspaper. 'Ach, it's a new *German* tradition, brought in by Prince Albert. It seems we must all have a "Christmas" tree in our homes now, like they do in Germany. So, while you've been away, there's been a mad scramble up here by the English to chop down our Scottish pines, because what Queen Victoria and Prince Albert do, the whole of England wants to do.'

'And yet,' John said in mock amazement, looking at the Scots Pine tree in the corner 'the last time I was in Tobermory, only four *weeks* ago, I was certain I was *not* in England.'

'Now to be fair,' Mary said to John, in defence of his father, 'it was *Beth* who insisted on two of the trees being brought inside the house.'

His father nodded. 'Not my doing at all. Your apology is accepted.'

'After the trees had been cut down by the lumberjacks,' Mary explained, 'a few of the smaller trees were left strewn about on the hills, so Beth *made* your father carry two of them back – to *save* them. And that's why they are both stood in wooden tubs of earth, and she waters them every day.'

'And the tartan ribbons?'

Mary smiled. 'Oh that's just Beth's way of trying to cheer up the trees – she talks to them every day, telling them they may have been struck low, but they are still *Scottish* and so must stand tall and stay brave and grow new roots if they can.'

He smiled. There was no one in the world like her. 'Where is Beth?'

She went up to the bedroom a short while ago?'

'And is all well?' John asked.

'All is very well,' Mary replied.

At the door of the drawing-room, John paused and looked back at his father.

'And Mrs Keillor?'

'Oh!' his father exclaimed exultantly. 'Last evening she cooked us the most *wonderful* roasted venison, followed by a delicious bowl of Tipsy Laird.'

'Tipsy Laird?'

'It's similar to the English trifle,' Mary explained, 'made with fresh fruit and oats, but instead of adding sherry to the cream, Mrs Keillor likes to add a dram or two of Scottish whisky instead.'

'And I have asked her to cook us a nice roasted goose on Christmas Day, and maybe some nice Highland beef for Hogmanay,' his father said. 'Son, we are going to be grand here through the winters and summers, with Mrs Keillor in the kitchen doing the cooking and Mrs Jarvis taking care of the house. Yes, we're all going to be grand.'

He gave his son a significant look. '*All* of us.'

John nodded, and moved on, up the stairs to the bedroom he shared with Beth.

It seemed as if the whole house had been re-arranged in his absence. More furniture from the house in Edinburgh, and even some from Jarvisfield by the looks it.

But it felt *comfortable* – Mrs Jarvis had worked her wonders. As soon as you walked in the front door the house felt warm and bright and welcoming.

And now here, on the top floor, was his *favourite* room, the most comfortable of all. Beth had made a blue quilt for over the large bed, fresh white sheets always under the blankets On the windowsill and on his chest of drawers she always had vases filled with sheaves of whatever wild flowers were in season. A coloured rug on the floor, a yellow cushion on the easy chair, matching the green and yellow cotton curtains on the window, insisting they were the colours of summer. More feminine than masculine, but a restful and comfortable room: a welcoming haven.

Beth was sitting at her dressing table, engrossed in writing in her current diary when he entered. She glanced up, saw him through the mirror, and dropped her pen. Seconds later she was up on her feet and hugging him. 'Oh, my love ...' she said. 'You are *home!*'

*

The winter days continued on dark and short but not too cold. The restless sea was occasionally calm but always unquiet. Beth had become used to drifting off to sleep to the *swish ... swish* sounds of the waves, as had all the other occupants of the house.

The wind and rain came and went, and so did John, sailing back and forth to Gibraltar, where the gustiness of the prevailing winter winds in the Strait and around the peninsular often made the winds of Scotland feel like a soft breeze in comparison.

During his weeks at home, he and Beth spent every moment they could together, often walking for miles, hand in hand, in the winter sunshine.

By the beginning of March their walks became shorter, the stiles in the fields too difficult for Beth to climb over, and the more he lifted her, the heavier she felt, and he knew the time was near.

Beth's only worry was that John would be away in the Mediterranean when the time came. John worried about that also. His one consolation was that she would have her mother nearby, close at hand, living in the same house.

In mid-April, after a sunny and temperate spring day, it happened in the middle of the night, as labour pains often do, but Mary was prepared and ready. During the previous months she had learned everything there was to learn about delivering a child, as well as her own experience in giving birth to Beth.

When Mr Dewar appeared on the landing and stood at the bottom of the stairs leading up to the top floor, Mary waved a hand dismissively and told him there was no need to send for anyone.

Mrs Keillor pushed past him carrying a basin of steaming water and told him to make himself more useful.

'How?'

'By going back to bed!'

John was away at sea, but was due back any day now, and Beth tried to hold on and stop the birth by gripping the bed frame behind her head and gritting her teeth, until Mary had to reprimand her.

'Beth you are supposed to be *giving* birth, not stopping it. If the child is ready to come you *cannot* hold it back!'

'But I want John to be in the house when the baby comes!'

'Such romantic nonsense!' Mary declared.

'It's *his* child too.'

'Now come on, Beth, be a good girl.'

'No!'

Beth kept holding on, gasping in pain, her knuckles white, but the baby came quickly and easily, giving a confused bawl of annoyance.

Mrs Keillor was at Mary's side, holding a white towel in readiness to wrap up the baby, and while Mary was doing that, Mrs Keillor leaned over the bed and smiled at Beth.

'There now, ye did that nice and quick, didna ye?'

Beth's hands slowly relaxed on the bed frame, her breath still heaving as she blinked the mist out of her eyes.

'A boy,' said Mrs Keillor. 'A bonnie wee boy.'

*

John arrived in Tobermory Bay on the morning tide, having caught a Packet Ship from London.

On entering the house, the first sight he saw was Mrs Keillor coming out of the kitchen. She was wearing only her long night shift, a black shawl thrown around her shoulders, her hands carrying a tray with a teapot and cups and saucers towards the stairs.

She stopped dead when she saw him, fully clothed in his uniform, glancing down towards her night shift with embarrassment.

'I've been up all night,' she explained. 'Awoken from my sleep. Tending to that lass of yours.'

John's eyes widened. 'Has the child come?'

'Aye.' Mrs Keillor smiled. ''Tis a boy she's been carrying for ye. A fine and healthy wee boy.'

And on that she moved towards the stairs to carry up her tea tray, but John ducked in front of her and took the stairs up two at a time, disappearing from sight before she had put her foot on the first step.

Up in the bedroom, John peered down at the new little human in the crib; tiny and pink with a shock of black hair, his two little fists held tight under his chin.

'He's got your hair,' he said to Beth. who was lying in the bed, and then he carefully lifted the tiny boy who whimpered for a moment and then opened his eyes ... a startling and vivid blue ... under coal-dark lashes, and it was then John saw the resemblance to both of them.

He looked at Beth and grinned, one of his wicked grins. 'Made in Scotland, born in Scotland, so he should – '

'No,' Beth said quickly, 'no, I don't wish him to have a Scottish name.'

'No?'

She gave him a pale smile of apology. 'Please, John, if you would grant me this *one* wish ... this one very *special* wish '

He looked at her silently, knowing he would willingly grant her a hundred special wishes if it were in his power to do so.

*

Down in the kitchen, Mrs Keillor and Mary were back to their old ways, sitting at the table together drinking tea and discussing the night's events. Mrs Keillor was still in her night shift and shawl, but Mary had dressed for the day ahead.

'Mr Dewar is feeling very happy and emotional about it all,' said Mrs Keillor. 'I saw him drop another dram of whisky into the tea I brought him up.'

'Who – John?'

'Nay! His father.'

Mary glanced down at her black dress. 'It seems wrong, somehow, today … wearing a dress of mourning.'

Mrs Keillor nodded. 'Aye, we've had some verra sad days … and some *black* days – I'll ne'er forget that day I went with Hector to see that two-roomed cottage and a big rat wandered out from the back room to say hello to me. I turned and ran out screaming as loud as a vexed wind.'

Mary sipped her tea.

'And then when I comes back to the house that same afternoon, I couldna believe how my fortunes had swung back when Mr Dewar – of all people – comes into my kitchen and says, "Mrs Keillor," he says, "I'm afraid I am in great danger of dying before my time from starvation. We are desperately in need of a *good* cook."'

She looked accusingly at Mary. 'Beth did badly let us down there – a girl of one and twenty not knowing how to cook! Course the fault was more yours than mine. Porridge now! Seems she didna even know how to cook porridge. Mr Dewar said she alus put the water and milk in the pan before she added the oats – now that's the wrong way round! The water and milk should be added to the oats until ye get the *right* texture.'

'Porridge is not the only thing she got the wrong way round.' Mary gave a small chuckle. 'Imagine! Trying to *stop* the baby from coming until John arrived.'

'Aye, like Romeo and Juley they are. Weren't those two mad about each other also?'

'Yes.' Mary frowned. 'But those two died young at the end.'

'Ah, well …' Mrs Keillor's face straightened, her eyes darkening. 'Mebbe tis the wrong story I'm thinking of …'

After a silence, Mrs Keillor sniffed. 'Still, I'm verra glad that Mr Dewar offered me this position and saved me from the rats.'

She reached out to fondly pat Mary's hand. 'And I'm *verra* glad that he allowed ye to come along with me. I couldna have left ye behind and alone in that cottage, and I *told* Mr

494

Dewar that.'

Mary continued sipping her tea, saying nothing.

'And another thing I'm *verra* glad about,' Mrs Keillor went on, 'is the way the Dewars at Salen agreed to let Hector sleep in their barn and give him the job of taking care of the farm's horses. They'll feed him good an' all ... Aye, Hector has a lot of good reasons to give thanks to the Dewars.'

Mary put down her cup. 'We *all* have a lot of good reasons to give thanks to the Dewars.'

*

Later that afternoon, now that the evenings were beginning to get brighter, Mary stood by the drawing-room window looking down on the back garden, noticing how it was slowly returning to life.

The shrubs that had been dormant in the winter were now sprouting some new small green leaves, and Beth's seedlings from wild flowers were showing small buds of various colours.

And here too, within this house, new life and new happiness was also triumphant.

She turned and looked at John, holding his baby son, as delighted as a young boy with a new toy. And Mr Dewar also, looking younger and less tired, and happily pouring himself another celebratory brandy.

And Beth ... well Beth looked radiant, sitting gracefully in a long cream morning robe and laughing at something John had said.

Mary smoothed her hair back, thinking it must be so wonderful to be at the beginning again, at the start of it all, as Beth and John were now ... the joy, the love, the hopes and dreams, the long future ...

She thought back to those early days in Australia when she and George had been at the beginning of it all ... the love, the enduring love, and then their happiness at the birth of their child ...

So wrapped up was she in her thoughts, in all her memories, she did not realise that John had come over to the glass doors where she was standing alone.

He said something to her, but she did not quite hear him.

'Please?' she said.

'Would you like to hold him for a while?' John asked.

She looked at the child in his arms, fast asleep. 'Oh, yes, thank you, I would like that.'

'Come and sit down.'

She moved to an armchair and sat down, and then watched as her son-in-law crouched down and carefully placed the tiny child in her lap.

'Have you got him?'

'Oh yes, I've got him,' she said, putting her hands and arms around the small boy and feeling the warmth of his soft body through the white shawl.

'I don't know if you heard, when you were standing over there ...' John said.

'No, I heard nothing.'

'His name is George.'

She looked up at him, startled.

John smiled. 'George Jarvis Dewar ... in honour of Beth's long lost father.'

'Oh!' Mary put a hand to her mouth and looked over at Beth, and saw her smiling.

Mary then looked down at the child, *her* grandchild, and *George's* grandson too ... the tears slipping down her face as she looked at the boy's black hair, realising that she *was* at the beginning again, and *was* a part of it all, as was George – still here in their hearts, still remembered. They had just moved up a few rungs on the ladder of life: her beloved George a lot higher than herself of course.

'I propose a toast,' John said, holding up his glass of wine. 'My very first toast of the day.'

'I'll drink to that,' his father said.

John looked at him sardonically. 'I haven't *said* the toast yet.'

'No, but I'll drink to it anyway.'

'To George Jarvis Dewar,' John said quietly, holding the glass towards his sleeping child. 'My own bonnie son.'

'To George,' they answered and drank, and Mr Dewar turned to Mary. 'Will you not take a sip to salute the toast,

Mrs Jarvis?'

'Do you know, I think I will, but ...' she looked down at the child in her arms.

'I can hold your glass to your lips,' he suggested.

'Please do,' Mary smiled.

He held the glass to her lips and she took a small sip of the rich red wine.

'After all, George is *your* grandson too,' said Mr Dewar.

She accepted another sip. 'To George,' she smiled.

'Amen.'

Mary looked at the sleeping child, realising that through this boy, the arrival of this tiny boy, they had *all* now become a real flesh-and-blood family together. The Jarvis's and the Dewars. And so yes, she was *entitled* to celebrate and feel happy and wonder what amazing events the bright future would bring next – and with John and Beth – especially John, she knew the future could bring *anything*: no matter how surprising or out of the blue. Because John was a young man who always acted upon his thoughts, and always had his eyes and his mind fixed on the horizon.

She gently stroked her palm over the soft dark hair on her grandson's small head, wondering if this boy, also, would one day find himself standing by the wall of Tobermory harbour, his blue eyes gazing out to sea, staring at its far horizon, wondering what lay beyond.

Author's Note

Under the towering sweep of the mountain of Ben More, in the district of Gruline, in a place once known as 'Jarvisfield', the circular walled "burial" garden with the stone mausoleum standing in its centre, containing the remains of General Lachlan Macquarie, known to history as "The Father of Australia", and his wife Elizabeth, his son Lachlan, and his baby daughter Jane Jarvis Macquarie, still stands today within that garden; a place where many Australians from Sydney come to visit.

The upkeep and care of the garden is paid for by The National Trust of Australia, and is maintained by The National Trust of Scotland.

On the pink marble walls inscribed with black and gold lettering, placed there by William Drummond, 9th Viscount of Strathallan, there is no mention of the containment therein of George Jarvis, the father of Elizabeth Jarvis. However, all documents, as well as a document within the Mull Museum in Tobermory show that George Jarvis is buried there, beside his guardian, Lachlan Macquarie.

Records of the old Jarvisfield estate show that the *Macquarie Trust,* providing the entitlement of a home on that land for all or any descendants of George Jarvis, was still in force in 1950.

Also by Gretta Curran Browne

(The Macquarie Series)

By Eastern Windows
The Far Horizon
Jarvisfield
The Wayward Son

*

(The Liberty Trilogy)

Tread Softly On My Dreams

Fire On The Hill

A World Apart

*

Ghosts In Sunlight
(Part Thriller, Part Love Story)
*

Ordinary Decent Criminal
(Novel of Film starring Kevin Spacey)

Relative Strangers
(TV Drama Series Tie-In)
*

Short Stories

Dark Days, Dark Nights
First Class

www.grettacurranbrowne.com